*My love
for you is
fathomless…
a thing of
darkness…*

D0019516

Dear Reader:

With FOREVER AND THE NIGHT I've ventured into
an exciting new realm of romance where an ordinary
woman can ignite passion in an extraordinary man—
he's a vampire, a handsome, artistic young man turned
into a night stalker against his will. Aidan Tremayne is a
wonderful hero desperately looking for a way to have a
lasting, fulfilling relationship with Neely Wallace.
Theirs is a love as searing as any forbidden romance
you've ever read about, yet as beautiful in its dark form
as any new springtime romance.

My fascination with night stalkers began with Bram
Stoker's *Dracula* and Anne Rice's *Vampire Chronicles*,
and after absorbing those engrossing stories, I knew I
wanted to write about such dramatic creatures. They
are dark and mysterious, yet sensual, too. I've tried to
combine what I do best—spin a romantic, spirited,
sexy yarn—with the deliciously spooky elements of
the vampire world.

If you enjoy reading FOREVER AND THE NIGHT and
its successors as much as I enjoyed writing them, we'll
both be very happy indeed.

All best,

Linda Lael Miller

Turn the page for rave reviews of
Linda Lael Miller and her
thrilling new novel . . .

PRAISE FOR
FOREVER AND THE NIGHT . . .

"Move over, Anne Rice! *New York Times* bestselling author Linda Lael Miller has created a sensually luscious supernatural romance . . . a nonstop roller coaster . . . thrilling . . . chilling . . . This novel provides such a powerful empathetic link between readers and the unforgettable characters that the audience will feel their joy, rage, fear and hope . . . Ms. Miller's first supernatural romance is so good that readers will consider *Forever and the Night* an immortal classic."

— *Affaire de Coeur*

"*Forever and the Night* is one of the best books that Linda has ever written, if not the best. It has appeal for Anne Rice fans as well as romance readers. It's a great story. It's a strong story. It's captivating!"

— Janet Carroll,
The Book Emporium
Long Beach, CA

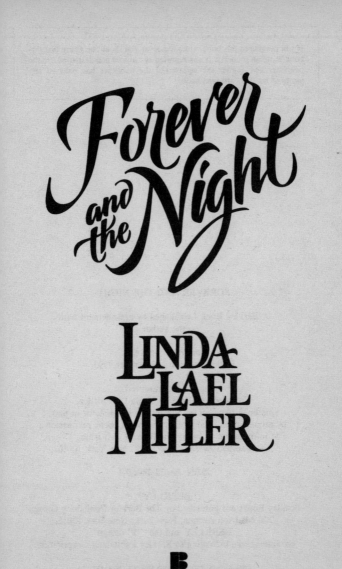

Forever and the Night

LINDA LAEL MILLER

B
BERKLEY BOOKS, NEW YORK

FOREVER AND THE NIGHT

A Berkley Book / published by arrangement with the author

PRINTING HISTORY
Berkley edition / November 1993

ISBN: 0-425-14060-1

BERKLEY®
Berkley Books are published by The Berkley Publishing Group, 200 Madison Avenue, New York, New York 10016.
BERKLEY and the "B" design
are trademarks belonging to Berkley Publishing Corporation.

PRINTED IN THE UNITED STATES OF AMERICA

10 9 8 7 6 5 4 3 2 1

I wrote this book for myself;
it was a gift from me, to me.
For that reason, and many others,
I dedicate it to the best of who
I am and to all that I hope to become.

Special acknowledgments are in order for Alex
Kamaroff, who saw the vision more clearly than I
did and helped me to bring it into focus; to
Irene Goodman, who was a light in the darkness when
things seemed hopeless; to Debbie Macomber, whose
confidence in me seemed unwavering; and to Pamela
Lael, who fearlessly marked errors of logic and
spelling and raved in all the right places. Last
but not least, I wish to thank my editor, Judith
Stern, for her tireless efforts to make the book
shine.

" 'Tis now the very witching time of night,
When churchyards yawn and hell itself breathes out
Contagion to the world: now could I drink hot blood,
And do such bitter business as the day
Would quake to look upon."

—*Hamlet*, **Act III, Scene ii**

Chapter 1

—••✕✕••—

That year, on the afternoon of Halloween, great glistening snowflakes began tumbling from a glowering sky, catching the maples and oaks by surprise in their gold and crimson housecoats, trimming fences and lampposts, roofs and windowsills, in shimmering, exquisite lace.

Aidan Tremayne awakened at sunset, as he'd done every day for more than two centuries, and felt a strange quickening in his spirit as he left the secret place in the woods. He allowed himself a wistful smile as he surveyed the snowy landscape, for he sensed the excitement of the town's children; it was like silent laughter, riding the wind.

All Hallow's Eve, he thought. How fitting.

He shook off the bittersweet sadness that had possessed him from the moment he'd opened his eyes and walked on toward the great stone house hidden in the stillness of its surroundings. There were birch trees among the others, gray-white sketches against the pristine snow, and a young deer watched him warily from the far side of a small mill pond.

Aidan paused, his eyes adjusting to the dusk, all his senses fluttering to life within him, and still the little doe returned his gaze, as though caught in the glow of head-lights on some dark and forgotten road. He had only to summon the creature, and she would come to him.

He was hungry, having gone three days without feeding, but he had no taste for the blood of innocents, be they animal or human. Besides, the life force of lesser creatures provided substandard nourishment. *Go,* he told the deer, in the silent language he had become so proficient at over the years. *This is no place for you, no time to be abroad in the night.*

The deer listened with that intentness so typical of wild creatures, white ears perked as fat flakes of snow continued to fall, as if to hide all traces of evil beneath a mantle of perfect white. Then the creature turned and scampered into the woods.

Aidan allowed himself another smile—it was Halloween, after all, and he supposed the occasion ought to have some celebratory meaning to a vampire—and walked on toward the house. Beyond, at the end of a long gravel driveway, lay Route 7, the first hint of civilization. The small Connecticut town of Bright River nestled four and a half miles to the north.

It was the kind of place where church bells rang on Sunday mornings. Local political issues were hotly debated, and freight trains came through late at night, the mournful cry of the engineer's whistle filling the valley. The children at the elementary school made decorations colored in crayon, pumpkins or Pilgrims or Santa Clauses, depending on the season, and taped them to the windows of their classrooms.

Aidan still smiled as he mounted the slippery steps at the back of the house and entered the mudroom. He stomped the snow from his booted feet just as a mortal man might have done, but he did not reach for the light switch as he entered the kitchen. His vision was keenest in the dark, and his ears were so sharp that neither cacophony nor silence could veil the essence of reality from him.

Usually.

He paused just over the threshold, focusing his awareness, and knew in the space of a moment that he was indeed alone in the gracious, shadowy house. This realization was both a relief—for he had powerful and very treacherous enemies—and a painful reminder that he was condemned to an eternity of seclusion. That was the worst part of being the monster he was, the wild, howling loneliness, the rootless wandering over the face of the earth, like a modern-day Cain.

Except for the brief, horrified comprehension of his victims, flaring in the moment before their final heartbeat, Aidan knew no human contact, for he consorted only with other vampires. He took little comfort from the company of his fellows—except for Maeve, his twin, whom he loved without reservation—for they were abominations, like himself. As a rule, vampires were amoral beings, untroubled by conscience or a need for the fellowship of others.

Aidan sighed as he passed silently through the house, shoving splayed fingers into dark, unruly hair. The yearning to live and love as an ordinary man had never left him, even though older and wiser vampires had promised it would. Some remnant of humanity lingered to give unrelenting torment.

He had not known peace of mind or spirit since the night *she*—Lisette—had changed him forever. Indeed, he supposed his unrest had begun even before that, when their gullible and superstitious mortal mother had taken him and

Maeve to a gypsy camp, as very small children, to have their fortunes told.

The old woman—even after more than two hundred years, Aidan still remembered the horror of looking into her wrinkled and shrewd face—had taken his hand and Maeve's into her own. She'd held them close together, palms upward, peering deep, as if she could see through the tender flesh and muscle to some great mystery beneath. Then, just as suddenly, she'd drawn back, as though seared.

"Cursed," she'd whispered. "Cursed for all of eternity, and beyond."

The crone had turned ageless eyes—how strange they'd seemed, in that wizened visage—on Aidan, though her words had been addressed to his now-tearful mother. "A woman will come to him—do not seek her out, for she is not yet born—and she will be his salvation or his damnation, according to the choices they make."

The ancient one had given each of the twins a golden pendant on a chain, supposedly to ward off evil, but it had been plain, even to a child, that she had little faith in talismans.

The chiming of the doorbell wrenched Aidan forward from that vanished time, and he found himself in mid-pace.

He became a shadow among shadows, there in the yawning parlor. Cold sickness clasped at his insides, even though they had long since turned to stone. *Someone had ventured within his range, and he had not sensed the person's approach.*

The bell sounded again. Aidan dragged one sleeve across his forehead. His skin was dry, but the sweat he'd imagined had seemed as real as that of a mortal man.

"Maybe nobody lives here," a woman's voice said.

Aidan had regained his composure somewhat, and he moved to the front window with no more effort than a thought. He might have come as easily from his hiding place to the house, except that he liked to pretend he had human limitations sometimes, and remember how it felt to have breath and a heartbeat.

He made no effort to hide himself behind the lace curtain, for the woman and child standing on the porch would not see him—not consciously, that is. Their deeper minds would register his presence and probably produce a few spooky dreams in an effort to assimilate him.

The child, a boy no older than six or seven, was wearing a flowing black cape and wax fangs, and he gripped a plastic pumpkin in one hand. His companion, clad in blue jeans, a sweater, and a worn-out cloth coat, was gamine-like, with short brown hair and large, dark eyes. Their conversation went on, ordinary and sweet as music, and Aidan took the words inside himself, to be played over and over again later, like a phonograph record.

Perhaps the other side of him, the beast, willed solidity and substance to his body and made him open the door.

"Trick or treat," the small vampire said, holding up the grinning pumpkin. In his other hand he held a flashlight.

The woman and child glowed like angels in the wintry darkness, beautiful in their bright innocence, but Aidan was aware of the heat and warmth pulsing through them, too. The need for blood made him sway slightly and lean against the doorjamb.

That was when the woman touched him, and parts of her past flashed through his mind like a movie. He saw that she liked to wear woolen socks to bed, that she was hiding from someone she both cared for and feared, that despite her close relationship with the child, she was as lonely as Aidan himself.

All in all, she was delightfully mortal, a tangle of good and not-so-good traits, someone who had known the full range of sadness and joy in her relatively brief existence.

Aidan felt a wicked wrench, in the darkest reaches of his accursed soul, a sensation he had not known before, in life or in death. It was both pain and pleasure, that feeling, and the possible significance of it dizzied him.

Why had he recalled the words of the gypsy, spoken so long ago, words tucked away in a child's mind and forgotten five minutes after they were offered, now, on this night?

A woman will come to him . . . she will be his salvation or his damnation . . .

No, he decided firmly. Even given all he knew of the world, and of creation, it was too fanciful a theory to accept. This was not the one who would save or damn him; such a creature probably did not even exist.

Still, the gypsy's prediction had been otherwise correct. He and Maeve had both been cursed, as surely as the rebellious angels had been, those banished from heaven so many eons before, following the legendary battle between Lucifer and the archangel, Michael.

"Are you all right?" the woman asked, pulling him sharply back from his musings. "You look a little pale."

Aidan might have laughed, so ludicrously accurate was her remark, but he didn't dare risk losing control. He was ravenous, and the woman and child standing before him could have no way of knowing what sort of monster they were facing all alone, there in those whispering woods.

Their blood would be the sweetest of nectars, made vital by its very purity, and to take it from them would be a bliss so profound as to sustain him for many, many nights. . . .

The soft concern in the visitor's manner was nearly Aidan's undoing, for he could not even recall the last time a woman had spoken to him with tenderness. He drew in a deep breath, even though he had no need for air, and let it out slowly, holding the inward demons in check with his last straining shreds of strength. "Yes," he said, somewhat tersely. "I've been—ill."

"If you don't have any candy, it's okay," the child put in with quick charity. "Aunt Neely won't let me eat anything I get from strangers anyhow."

Aidan was almost deafened by a rushing sound stemming from some wounded and heretofore abandoned place in his spirit. *Neely*. He made note of the woman's name—it was a detail that had seemed unimportant, in the face of the devastating affect she'd had upon him—and it played in his soul like music. His control was weakening with every passing moment; he had to flee the pair before he broke his own all-but-inviable rule and ravaged them both.

Still, he was so shaken, so captivated by this unexpected mortal woman, that movement was temporarily beyond his power.

"I have something better than candy," he heard himself say, after a desperate inner struggle. He made himself move, took a coin from the ancient cherry-wood box on the hall-way table and dropped it into the plastic pumpkin the little boy held out to him. "Happy Halloween."

Neely's brown eyes linked with Aidan's, and she smiled.

He watched the pulse throb at the base of her right ear, imagined the vitality he could draw from her, the sheer, glorious *life*. The mere thought of it made him want to weep.

He did not risk speaking again.

"Thank you," she said, turning to start down the porch steps.

The small vampire lingered on the doormat. "My name's Danny. We're practically your neighbors," he said. "We live at the Lakeview Trailer Court and Motel, on Route Seven. My dad is the caretaker there, and Aunt Neely cleans rooms and waits tables in the truck stop."

The blush that rose in the woman's cheeks only made Aidan's deadly hunger more intense. Just when he would have lunged at her, he thrust the door closed and willed himself away quickly—far away, to another time and another place, where he could stalk without compunction.

Aidan chose one of his favorite hunting grounds, a miserable section of nineteenth-century London known as Whitechapel. There, in the dark, narrow, stinking streets, he might select his prey not from the prostitutes, or the pickpockets and burglars, but from procurers, white slavers, and men who made their living in the opium trade. Occasionally he indulged a taste for a mean drunk, a wife-beater, or a rapist; circumstances determined whether his victims saw his face and read their fate there or simply perished between one breath and the next. He did not actually kill the majority of his victims, however, and he had never made vampires of his prey, even though he knew the trick of it only too well. It was all a matter of degree.

He kept a room over a back-alley tavern, and that was where he materialized on that particular night. Quickly he exchanged his plain clothes for an elegant evening suit and a beaver top hat. To this ensemble he added a black silk cape lined with red, as a private joke.

A cloying, yellow-white fog enveloped the city, swirling about the lampposts and softening the sounds of cartwheels jostling over cobblestones, of revelry in the taverns and whoring in the alleys. Somewhere a woman screamed, a high-pitched, keening sound, but Aidan paid no attention, and neither did any of the other shadowy creatures who haunted the night.

He'd walked only a short way when he came upon a fancy carriage stopped at the curb. A small man, clad in a bundle of rags and filthy beyond all bearing, was pressing a half-starved child toward the vehicle's open door.

Inside, Aidan glimpsed a younger man, outfitted in clothes even more finely tailored than his own, counting out coins into a white, uncalloused palm.

"I won't do it, do you 'ear me!" the little one cried, with unusual spirit for such a time and place. Although Aidan sensed that the small entity was female, there was nothing about her scrawny frame to indicate the fact. She couldn't have been older than eight or ten. "I won't let some *bastard* from Knightsbridge bugger me for a shilling!"

Aidan closed his eyes for a moment, filled with disgust, vividly recalling the human sensation of bile bubbling into the back of his throat in a scalding rush. After all the time that had passed since his making, it still came as a shock to him to realize that vampires and werewolves and warlocks weren't the only fiends abroad in the world.

"Get'n the carriage and tend to your business!" shouted the rag-man, cuffing the child hard between her thin shoulders. "I'll not stand 'ere and argue with the likes of you all night, Shallie Biffle!"

Aidan stepped forward, deliberately opening himself to their awareness. Closing one hand over the back of the rag-man's neck, instantly paralyzing the wretched little rodent, he spoke politely to the urchin still standing on the sidewalk.

"This man"—he nodded toward his bug-eyed, apoplectic captive—"is he your father?"

" 'ell, no," spat Shallie. " 'e's just a dirty flesh-peddler, that's all. I ain't got no father or mother—if I did, would I be 'ere?"

Aidan produced a five-pound note, using that special vampire sleight of hand too rapid for the human eye to catch. "There is a woman in the West End who'll look after you," he said. "Go to her now."

He put the street name and number into the child's mind without speaking again, and she scrambled off into the

shifting murk, clutching the note she'd snatched from his
fingers a second after its appearance.

The horses pulling the carriage grew restless, but the
dandy and his driver sat obediently, bemused, as helpless
in their own way as the rag-man.

Aidan lifted the scrap of filth by the scruff of his neck
and allowed him to see his fierce vampire teeth. It would
have been the purest pleasure to tear open that particular
jugular vein, to drain the blood and toss away the husk like a
handful of nutshells, but he had settled on even viler prey—
the wealthy pervert who had ventured into Whitechapel to
buy the virtue of a child.

He flung the procurer aside, heard the flesh-muffled sound
of a skeleton splintering against the soot-stained wall of a
brick building. *Fancy that*, Aidan thought to himself with
a regretful smile.

He climbed easily into the leather-upholstered interior
of the carriage, and there he settled himself across from
his intended victim. With a thought, he broke the wicked
enchantment that had held both the driver and his master
in stricken silence.

"Tell the man to take you home," Aidan said companionably enough, examining his gloves to make sure he hadn't
smudged them while handling the rag-man's dirty person.

The carriage was dark, but Aidan's vision was noonday
perfect, and he saw the young nobleman swallow con-
vulsively before he reached up with a shaking hand and
knocked three times on the vehicle's roof. The lad loosened
his ascot as he stared at Aidan in confounded fear, his pulse
plainly visible between the folds of silk.

Yes, Aidan thought with quiet lust, eyeing the man's
throat. Soon, very soon, the terrible hunger would be satisfied, at least for the time being.

"Wh-Who are you?" the nobleman finally managed to
stammer out.

Aidan smiled cordially and took off his hat, setting it carefully on the leather seat beside him. "No one, really. You might say that you're having a remarkably authentic nightmare—Bucky."

The young man paled at Aidan's easy use of his nickname, which, of course, he hadn't given. Bucky swallowed again, gulped really, and a fine sheen of perspiration broke out on his upper lip. "If it's about the child—well, I was only looking for a little harmless diversion, that's all—"

"You are a man of peculiar tastes," Aidan said without expression. "Does your family know how you amuse yourself of an evening?"

Bucky squirmed in the seat. On some level, Aidan supposed, the specimen's mind was developed enough to discern that the curtain was about to come down on the last act. "If this is about blackmail—"

Aidan interrupted with a *tsk-tsk* sound. "For shame. Not all of us are willing to stoop to such depths as you do, my friend. Blackmail is far beneath me."

A flush flowed into Bucky's pasty face, sharpening Aidan's desire to feed to something very like frenzy. He would wait, however, allowing the prospect to grow sweeter, in much the same way he had let fine wine breathe before indulging in it, back in those glorious days when the only blood he'd needed was that which coursed through his own veins.

"What do you want then, if not money?" Bucky sputtered.

Aidan smiled, revealing his fangs, and watched in quiet, merciless resolution as a silent scream moved up and down Bucky's neck but failed to escape his constricted throat. He looked frantically, helplessly, toward the carriage door.

"There is no escape," Aidan told him pleasantly.

Bucky's eyes were huge. "No more—no more children—I swear it—"

Aidan shrugged eloquently. "I quite believe you," he conceded. "You will never again have the chance, you see."

The carriage rattled on through the foggy London night, and the trip must have seemed endless to Bucky. Indeed, for him it was surely an eternity. Finally, when Aidan knew time was growing short, that dawn would come soon, he decided he'd savored the salty, vital wine long enough.

Slowly he put his hands on Bucky's velvet-clad shoulders, drew him close, even snarled a little, as a media vampire might, to give the moment a touch more drama. Then he sank his teeth into the tender flesh of Bucky's neck, and the blood flowed, liquid energy, not over Aidan's tongue but through his fangs.

As much as he hated everything he was, feeding brought the usual ecstasy. Aidan drank until his ferocious thirst had been quelled, then snapped Bucky's neck between his fingers and flung him to the floor of the carriage.

Aidan rarely fed in Bucky's circles, and he frowned as he imagined the furor the finding of a dandy's blood-drained hulk would arouse in the newspapers. He felt some regret, too, for the confusion that would reign among the diligent, well-meaning souls at Scotland Yard when they tried to make sense of the incident.

They would, of course, blame the Ripper.

Aidan stopped the carriage by freezing the driver's already addled mind, bent to straighten Bucky's stained ascot, then climbed out onto a virtually empty sidewalk.

His sister Maeve's grand house loomed before him, beyond an imposing wrought-iron fence, its chimneys and gables rimmed with the first gray-pink tatters of dawn.

The vampire met the carriage driver's blank stare, dismissed him with no memory of visiting Whitechapel or even encountering a stranger. The vehicle lumbered away through the slow, silent waltz of the fog.

Aidan let himself into the house via a special entrance next to the wine cellar and took refuge in a dark, tomb-like room where inhabitants had once hidden from Oliver Cromwell's men. He bolted the door, then removed his hat and the cloak and settled in a half-crouch against a cold stone wall.

He yawned as the fathomless sleep began to overtake him. He'd been careless, coming here, but after his dawdling with poor, misguided Bucky, there hadn't been time to return to his lair in twentieth-century Connecticut. Besides, satiation always dulled his wits for a while.

He would just have to hope—it was futile for a vampire to offer a prayer—that none of his enemies had been watching when he came to this only-too-obvious place to rest.

Aidan yawned again and closed his eyes. He didn't fear most vampires, for all but a few had to hide from the sun just as he did, but there were other arch-demons, other abominations of creation, who preyed upon his kind, terrible, beautiful things that flourished in the daylight.

Usually Aidan did not dream. All consciousness faded to dense blackness when he slumbered, leaving him vulnerable while his being assimilated the food that made him immortal.

Tonight, however, Aidan saw the woman, Neely, on the stage of his mind, and the little boy with wax vampire teeth, and even in his stupor he was wildly troubled. In two centuries no mortal female had captured his imagination. This one, this Neely, was different.

It wasn't just her looks—she was pretty enough, though by no means beautiful—but something far deeper, an ancient and cataclysmic affection of the soul, a bitter-sweet paradox. It was as if he'd been captured by a cunning and much-feared foe and at the same time found a vital part of himself that he hadn't known was lost.

Again, the long-dead gypsy witch's ominous words echoed, fragmented and sharp as splintered glass, in his mind. *Cursed—damnation or salvation . . .*

When he awakened, many hours later, he knew immediately that he was not alone in the dark chamber.

A match was struck; the light flared, searing Aidan's eyes. Before him stood Valerian, majestic in his vampirism, a giant, beautiful fiend with chestnut-brown hair, patrician features, and a dark violet gaze that could paralyze any lesser creature in a twinkling.

"You are a fool, Aidan!" Valerian spat, and the motion of his lips made the candlelight flicker. Like Aidan, Valerian had no breath. "What possessed you to come *here*?" He waved one elegant arm in barely bridled fury. "Have you forgotten that she searches for you? That she needs neither darkness nor sleep?"

Aidan yawned and raised himself to his feet, using the wall behind him for support. " 'She,' " he quoted mockingly. "Tell me, Valerian, are you so terrified of Lisette that you will not even say her name?"

The older vampire's eyes narrowed to slits; Aidan could feel his fury singing in the room like the discordant music of a thousand warped violins. "I have no reason to fear Lisette," he said after a moment woven of eternity. "It is you, Aidan, who have incurred her everlasting hatred!"

Aidan scratched the back of his neck, another habit held over from mortal days. The only itch that ever troubled him now came from far beneath his skin, driving him to take blood or die in the cruelest agony of thirst. He arched one eyebrow as he regarded his long-time acquaintance.

"No doubt, if Lisette is near, it's because she followed you," he said reasonably.

Again Valerian's lethal anger stirred. "I am nearly as powerful as she is—I can shroud my presence from her when I wish. You, on the other hand, might as well have laid down to sleep in the full light of the sun as to take refuge here! How long will you walk about with your thoughts naked to whatever demon might be listening? Do you *want* to perish, Aidan? Is that it?"

Against his will, Aidan thought of the woman, Neely, who lived and breathed back in the cold, fresh air of twentieth-century Connecticut. He felt the most torturous and inexplicable grief, coupled with a joy the likes of which no fiend could expect to entertain. "Perhaps I do," he confessed raggedly. Then he lifted his eyes to Valerian's magnificent, terrible face and asked, "Do you never yearn for peace? Don't you ever grow so weary of what you are that you'd risk the wrath of heaven and the fires of hell to escape it?"

"Fool," Valerian spat again, plainly exasperated. "Why do I bother myself with such an idiot? For us, the pure light of heaven would be as great a torment as the blazes of Hades! We would escape nothing by fleeing this life!"

"This is not life," Aidan replied with unexpected fury. "This is a living death. Hell itself could not possibly be worse!"

Valerian gentled, for he was an unpredictable creature, and laid his gracious hands on Aidan's shoulders. "Poor Aidan," he mocked. "When will you accept what you are and stop playing at being a man?"

Aidan turned away and snatched his cloak and top hat from the top of the wine crate where he'd left them that morning before giving himself up to a tempestuous sleep. Valerian's words had struck a chord of terror in his spirit.

Did the other vampire know about Neely and the little boy? Was that what he'd meant by "playing at being a man"? If Valerian had taken notice of their existence while Aidan's mind was unguarded in slumber, he might see it as his duty to destroy them.

In the next moment Aidan's worst fears were confirmed. "You are an even greater fool than I thought," Valerian said with rueful affection. "Imagine it, your being besotted with a fragile mortal!" He paused, sighed. "You do me injury," he murmured, before going on to say, in his usual imperious way, "Come with me, Aidan. I will show you worlds and dimensions you have never dreamed of. I will teach you to cherish what you are, to *relish* it!"

Aidan retreated a step, covered his ears with his hands, as though that could keep out the brutal truth of Valerian's words. "Never!" he gasped out. "And if you go near the woman or the child, I swear by all the unholy vows, whatever the cost may be, *I will destroy you!*"

Valerian looked stung, which was another of his many affectations, of course. Aidan knew the other vampire was not capable of anything so prosaic as getting his feelings hurt, and he certainly didn't fear a being of lesser powers.

The creature sighed theatrically. "Perhaps Maeve can reason with you," he said. "I am weary of the effort."

"Leave me," Aidan replied.

Miraculously Valerian conceded the point and disappeared.

Aidan tilted his head back as if to see through the thick ceiling. His senses told him that Maeve was not in residence but off hunting in some other place and century.

A small, aching coil of loneliness twisted inside Aidan's breast. Whatever their differences, he cherished his sister. Her companionship would have been comforting, a warm hearth in the dark bewilderment that tormented him now.

He closed his eyes and thought of Connecticut, and when he looked again, he was there, standing in the darkness of a bedroom he never used.

Aidan tossed the top hat and cloak onto a wing chair upholstered in rich leather and wrenched at the high collar that suddenly seemed to constrict his throat. Somehow, in those few treacherous minutes when Neely had stood on his doorstep, escorting a little beggar in a vampire suit, Aidan had made a truly terrible error. He had brought the woman into his mind, just to admire her effervescence for a few moments, and she had taken up stubborn residence there.

What in blazes was this fascination he'd acquired?

He looked toward the bed, remembering what it was like to lie with a daughter of Eve, to give and take physical pleasure, and was possessed of a yearning so fierce that it horrified him. He had merely *glimpsed* this troublesome woman, and yet he found himself wanting her, not as sustenance, but bucking beneath him in wild spasms of passion, clutching his bare shoulders in frantic fingers, crying out in the sweet fever of ecstacy . . .

He had to see her again, if only to convince himself that he had built her up into something more than she was, to end this reckless obsession that could so easily end in obliteration for them both.

When he had regained his composure somewhat, Aidan exchanged his gentleman's garb for well-worn jeans and a wheat-colored Irish cable-knit sweater. He brushed his dark, longish hair—a style suited to the current century and decade—and formed a clear picture of Neely in his mind.

In the space of a second he was standing in the parking lot of the truck stop on Route 7, a soft Connecticut snow falling around him, and she was just coming out through the front door, scrambling into her cheap coat as she walked.

She stopped when she sensed his presence, met his gaze, and sealed his doom forever simply by smiling.

"Hello," she said. Her gamine eyes were bright with some hidden mischief, and the snowflakes made a mantilla for her short hair.

Long-forgotten and deeply mourned emotions wrung Aidan as he stood there, powerless before her innocent enchantment. "Hello," he replied, while sweet despair settled over him like snow blanketing a new and raw grave.

Somewhere deep inside him a spark kindled into flame.

It was true, then, what the gypsy sorceress had said so long before. Here, before him, stood the reason for his creation, the personification of his fate.

Chapter 2

―•※※•―

It almost seemed that he'd been waiting for her.

Neely Wallace felt both an intense attraction and a rush of adrenaline as she stood in the parking lot of the Lakeview Café, gazing into that enigmatic pair of eyes. A spontaneous "hello" had tumbled over her lips before she'd given full consideration to the fact that this man was a virtual stranger.

Remembering that there were people in the world who wanted to silence Neely, or even kill her, she was surprised at her own reaction. Briefly, futilely, she wished she had never worked for Senator Dallas Hargrove, never found the evidence of his criminal acts, thus making herself a target.

He smiled, the snow drifting and floating softly between them, cosseting the land in a magical silence. Something about his gaze captivated her, made her want to stand there looking at him forever.

It was as though he had looked inside her, with those remarkable eyes of his, and awakened some vital part of her being, heretofore unknown and undreamed of.

Neely cleared her throat nervously but kept her smile in place. She should have taken the time to call her brother, Ben, when her shift was over, as he was always telling her to do, so he could come and walk her back to the trailer court. If she hadn't seen the man the night before, when she and Danny had gone out trick-or-treating, she might have thought he was a mugger or a rapist, or that her former boss had finally sent someone to make sure she never talked about his close association with drug dealers. "The café's closed," she said. "We'll open up again at five."

He came no nearer, this man woven of shadows, and yet his presence was all around Neely, in and through her, like the very essences of time and space. "Don't be afraid," he said. "I'm not here to hurt you."

Neely figured a serial killer might say the same thing, but the idea didn't click with her instincts. She realized she *wasn't* truly afraid, but her stomach was fluttery, and she felt capable of pole-vaulting over the big neon sign out by the highway. "I don't think I caught your name," she said, finally breaking the odd paralysis that had held her until that moment.

"Aidan Tremayne," he said, keeping his distance. "And yours?"

"Neely Wallace," she answered, at last finding the impetus to start across the lot, the soles of her boots making tracks in the perfect snow. Idly she wondered if she would end up as a segment on one of those crime shows that were so popular on TV. She could just hear the opening blurb. *Ms. Cornelia Wallace, motel maid and waitress, erstwhile personal assistant to Senator Dallas Hargrove, disappeared mysteriously one snowy night from the parking lot of the Lakeview Truck Stop, just outside Bright River, Connecticut. . . .*

A high, dense hedge separated the parking area from the motel and trailer court beyond, and Neely paused under an arch of snow-laced shrubbery to look back.

Aidan Tremayne, clearly visible before in the glimmer of the big floodlights standing at all four corners of the parking lot, was gone. No trace of him lingered, and the new layer of snow was untouched except for Neely's own footprints.

She stood perfectly still for a moment, listening, but she heard nothing. She drew a deep breath and walked on at a brisk pace, making her way past the two-story motel and into the trailer court. Reaching the door of her tiny mobile home, which was parked next to Ben's larger one, she looked back over her shoulder again, almost expecting to see Tremayne standing behind her.

"Weird," Neely said to herself as she turned the key in the lock.

The trailer wobbled, as usual, when Neely stepped inside. She flipped on the light switch and peeled off her coat in an almost simultaneous motion. Then, as an afterthought, she turned the lock on her door and put the chain-bolt in place.

Her utilitarian telephone, a plain black model with an old-fashioned dial, startled her with an immediate jangle. She grabbed up the receiver, oddly exasperated.

"Damn it, Neely," her brother said, "I told you to call me when you were through closing up the café so I could come over and walk you home. Don't you read the newspapers? It isn't safe for a woman to be out alone so late at night."

Neely calmed down by reminding herself that Ben truly cared about her; except for Danny and her best friend, Wendy Browning, he was probably the only person in the world who did. She put away her coat, sat down on her hide-a-bed sofa with a sigh, and quickly kicked off her snow boots.

"I'm sorry, Ben," she responded, rubbing one sore foot. She frowned, spotting a run in her pantyhose. Even hairspray or nail polish wouldn't stop this one. "Yes, it's late, and that's exactly why I didn't call. I knew Danny would be in bed, and I didn't want you to have to leave him alone." She paused, drew a deep breath, and plunged. "Ben, what do you know about Aidan Tremayne, that guy who lives in the mansion down the road?"

Ben sounded tired. "Just that. His name is Aidan Tremayne, and he lives in the mansion down the road. Why?"

Neely was unaccountably disappointed; she'd wanted some tidbit of information to mull over while she was brushing her teeth and getting ready for bed. "I was just wondering, that's all. Danny and I went there on Halloween night. He struck me as sort of—different."

"I guess you could say he's a recluse," Ben said, barely disguising his indifference. "Listen, sweetheart, I'm beat. I'll see you in the morning."

Emotion swelled in Neely's throat. She and Ben had more in common than their late parents. He'd lost his wife, Shannon, to cancer a few years before, along with his job in a Pittsburgh steel mill, and he'd been struggling to rebuild his life and Danny's ever since. Neely had been forced to give up an entire way of life—her work, her apartment, her friends—because she knew too much about certain very powerful people.

"Good night," she said.

Neely's trailer consisted of one room, essentially, with the fold-out bed at one end and a kitchenette at the other. The bathroom was quite literally the size of the hall closet in her old apartment.

Resolving to dwell on what she had—her life, her health, Danny and Ben—instead of what she'd lost, Neely took off her pink uniform and hung it carefully from a curtain rod.

After showering, she put on an old flannel nightshirt and dried her hair. Then she heated a serving of vegetable soup on a doll-size stove and sat in the middle of her lumpy fold-out bed, eating and watching a late-night talk show on the small TV that had once occupied a corner of the kitchen counter of her spacious apartment in Washington.

Neely didn't laugh at the host's monologue that night, though she usually enjoyed it. She kept thinking of Aidan Tremayne, wondering who he was and why he'd stirred her the way he had. He was one of the most attractive men she'd ever met, and inwardly she was still reeling from the impact of encountering him unexpectedly as she'd left the café.

Not to mention the way he'd vanished in the time it took to blink.

She walked to the edge of the bed on her knees, balancing her empty soup bowl with all the skill of a good waitress, then got up and crossed to the sink. After rinsing out her dish, she returned to the bathroom and brushed her teeth. The thing to do was sleep; she would think about Mr. Tremayne another time, when fatigue did not make her overly fanciful.

Aidan was especially ravenous that night, but he did not feed. The hunger lent a crystalline sharpness to his thought processes, and as he sat alone in his sumptuous study, with no light but that of the fire on the hearth, he allowed himself to remember a time, a glorious time, when he'd been a man instead of a monster.

He closed his eyes and tilted his head back against the high leather chair in which he sat, recalling. Like most mortals, Aidan had not realized what it really meant to have a strong, steady heartbeat, supple lungs that craved air, skin that sweated, and muscles that took orders from a living brain. He had thought with his manhood in those simple days, not his mind.

Now he was a husk, an aberration of nature. Thanks to his own impetuous nature and unceasing pursuit of a good time, thanks to Lisette, he was a fiend, able to exist only by the ingestion of human blood. He longed for the peace of death but feared the possibilities of an afterlife too much to perish willingly.

Aidan could travel freely in time and its dimensions, but the Power that pulsed at the heart of the universe was veiled to him. He knew only that it existed, and that its agents were among his most dangerous enemies.

He could not bear to consider the fate that might await him should he succumb to the mystery of true death; he'd had enough religious training in his early years at school to sustain a pure and unremitting terror. Nor did Aidan choose to think of Neely Wallace, for to do that in his present mood would be to transport himself instantly into her presence.

He engaged in a sad smile, letting decades unfold in his mind, and then centuries. He'd been twenty-two when the unthinkable had happened. The year had been 1782, the place an upstairs room in a seedy English tavern, not far from Oxford. . . .

Lisette's waist-length auburn hair was spread across Aidan's torso like a silken veil, and her ice-blue eyes were limpid as she gazed at him. "Lovely boy," she crooned, stroking his chest, his belly, and then his member. "I can't bear to give you up."

Aidan groaned. They'd been together all night and, as always, as the dawn approached, she grew sentimental and greedy. He was amazed to feel himself turn hard, for he'd thought she'd drained him of all ability to respond.

Lisette was older than Aidan by a score of years, and her experience in intimate matters was vast, but other than those things, he knew little about her. One night a few weeks before, when Aidan had been out walking alone, a splendid carriage drawn by six matched horses had stopped beside him in the road. Lisette, a pale and gloriously beautiful creature, had summoned him inside with a smile and a crook of her finger. They'd been meeting regularly ever since.

Now she laughed at his reluctance to surrender even as his young body betrayed him.

She set the pace as the aggressor and the seducer. She took him, extracted yet another exquisite response from him, and left him half-conscious in the tangled bedclothes immediately afterward.

Aidan watched his lover through a haze as she paced the crude plank-board floor, once again clad in her gauzy, flowing gown, her hair trailing down her back in a profusion of coppery curls. He was glad it was nearly sunrise, that she would leave him then as always, because he knew that one more turn in her arms would kill him.

"See that you don't go dallying with a wench while I'm away," she flared. "I won't have it!"

He hauled himself up onto his elbows, but that was all he could manage. "You don't own me, Lisette," he said. "Don't be telling me what you'll have and what you won't."

She whirled on him then, and he saw something terrible in her face, even though there was no light but that of a thin winter moon fading into an approaching dawn. "Do not speak to me in that disrespectful way again!" she raged.

Aidan was a bold sort—indeed, his father's solicitor swore the trait would be his undoing—but even he did not dare challenge Lisette further. She was no ordinary woman, he'd guessed that long since, and she was capable of far more than ordinary mischief. He guessed that had been her appeal, along with her insatiable appetites and the envy her attentions generated among his peers.

Lisette cast a sullen glance toward the window, then glared at Aidan again, her eyes seeming to glitter in the gloom. They looked hard, like jewels, and they flashed with an icy fire. She made a strangled sound, a mingling of desire and grief, and then she was upon him again.

He tried to throw her off, for the sudden ferocity of her attack had unnerved him, but to his annoyance he discovered that she was far stronger than he was.

"Soon," she kept murmuring, over and over, like a mother comforting a fitful child, "soon, darling, all the earth will belong to us—"

Aidan felt her teeth puncture his neck, and his heart raced with fresh horror. He fought to free himself, but Lisette was like a marble statue, crushing him, breaking his bones. At that point he began to recede into unconsciousness; he was going to die, never see Maeve again, never laugh or paint or drink wine and ale with his friends.

He renewed his efforts, struggling to return to full awareness, even though there was pain and fear, mortal fear so intense that his very soul throbbed with it.

"Now, now," Lisette whispered, lifting her head to look into his eyes. "Your friends will think you're dead, poor fools, but you will only be sleeping. I will return for you, my darling, before they bury you."

Aidan was appalled and wildly confused. He felt strange; his body was weak to the point of death, and he could barely keep his eyes open, yet his soul seemed to soar on the wings of some dark euphoria. "Oh, God," he whispered, "what's happening to me?"

Lisette rose from the bed, but it made no difference that she'd finally freed him, for Aidan could not move so much as a muscle.

"You'll see, my darling," she said, "but don't trouble yourself by calling out to God. He turns a deaf ear to our sort."

Aidan fought desperately to raise himself, but he still had no strength. He could only watch in terrified disbelief as

Lisette's form disintegrated into a swirling, sparkling mist. She was gone, and even though Aidan was conscious, he knew full well that she had murdered him.

He could not speak, could not move. His heart had stopped beating, he wasn't breathing, and as the room filled with sunlight, his sight faded. His flesh burned as surely as if he'd been laid out on a funeral pyre, and yet Aidan knew the pain wasn't physical. He was dead, as Lisette had said, yet only too aware of all that happened around him.

A wench, probably come to fill the water jug and tidy the bed, found him later that morning. Her shrieks stabbed his mind; he tried to move, to speak, to show her he was conscious, but it was all for naught. Aidan was a living soul trapped inside a corpse.

He was aware of the others, when they came, for it was as though the conscious part of him had risen to a corner of the ceiling to look down on the lot of them. There were two men, the tavern owner and his burly, stupid son, but a priest soon arrived as well.

The boy took the door from its hinges, and they laid Aidan's helpless body out on that wooden panel. He could do nothing to resist them.

"Poor soul," said the priest, grasping the large crucifix he wore around his neck on a plain cord and making the sign of the cross over Aidan's mortal remains. "What do you suppose happened to him?"

"He died a happy man," the idiot-boy replied, leering. It didn't seem to bother him that he was addressing a man of God. "That's if the lady I saw him with and the sounds I heard comin' from this here room meant anything!"

Aidan returned to his wasted body from his vantage point near the ceiling, struggled to move something, anything— an ear, an eyelash, one of the tiny muscles at the corners of his mouth. Nothing. Blackness covered him, swallowed him up, mind and soul, and he was no one, nowhere.

When Aidan wakened, he still could not move. He knew, with that peculiar extra sense he'd acquired soon after Lisette's attack, that he was in the back of the undertaker's shop, laid out on a slab, with coins on his eyes. At first light he'd be closed up in a coffin and probably sent home to Ireland in the back of a wagon, no longer a troublesome responsibility to his prosperous English father. His mother, a dark-haired tavern maid, a woman of light laughter and even lighter skirts, would mourn him for a while, but Maeve would suffer the sorest grief. Maeve, his twin sister, his childhood companion, the counterpart of his personality.

Hope stirred in Aidan's being when he felt a cool hand come to rest on his forehead; his hope died when he heard his murderess's voice. "There now, I told you I'd come back for you," she said, placing a frigid kiss where her fingers had been. "Sweet darling, have you been afraid? Perhaps you'll remember, after this, what it means to defy me."

Aidan knew a pure anguish of emotion, but he could say nothing. He cried out inwardly when she bent over him again, when he felt her teeth puncture the skin of his throat like pointed quills thrust through dry parchment. In the next instant, liquid ecstacy seemed to flow into every part of him; he could see clearly again and hear with crystal clarity, even though he still had no breath or heartbeat. An unearthly and wholly incredible power was spawning inside him, growing, grumbling, surging upward like lava thrusting at the inside of a mountain.

His muscles were flexible again; he sat bolt upright on the slab and thrust Lisette aside with a motion of his arm.

"What have you done?" he rasped, for the joy that seemed to crush him from the inside was the sort denied to mere men. It was dark and rich and evil, and he yearned to throw it off even as he embraced it. "In the name of God, Lisette, *what manner of creature are you and what have you done to me?*"

Lisette thrust her arms up, as if he'd attempted to strike her again. "Do not speak of the Holy One again—it is forbidden!"

"Tell me!" Aidan bellowed.

There was a clamor beyond the door of the morgue, the sounds of rushing feet and muffled voices.

Lisette came to Aidan's side. Her mind filled the room, swirled around his like an invisible storm, swallowed it whole. When his awareness returned, when he knew that he was a separate entity, they were hiding together in a damp place with cold stone walls.

He was lying down once again, this time on an altar of sorts. In the flickering light of a half dozen candles, he saw Lisette, looming at his feet like some horrible angel of darkness.

"Please," he said, his voice a raw whisper. "Tell me what I am."

She smiled and came to stand beside him, smoothing his hair back from his forehead. He wasn't bound, as far as he could tell, and yet she must have been restraining him somehow, for he was utterly powerless once more.

"Don't be so anxious, my darling," Lisette scolded. "You are a most wonderful creature now, with powers others only dream of. You are a vampire."

"No," he protested. "*No!* It's impossible—such things do not happen!"

"Shhh," said Lisette, laying an index finger to her lovely, lethal mouth. "Soon you will adjust to the change, my darling. Once you've felt the true scope of your talents, you'll thank me for what I've done."

"Thank you?" Aidan trembled, so great was his effort to rise and confront her, and so fruitless. "If what you say is true—and I cannot credit that it is—then I shall curse you. But I will never, *never* thank you!"

Lisette's beautiful face became a mask of controlled rage. "Ingrate! You don't know what you're saying. If I thought you did, I would toss you out into the sunlight to burn in the sort of agony only a vampire can know! Count yourself fortunate, Aidan Tremayne, that I am mercifully inclined toward you!" She stopped, seemed to gather herself in from all directions, then favored Aidan with a smile made brutal by its sweet sacrilege. "Sleep now, darling. Rest. When darkness comes again, I will show you places and things you've never imagined. . . ."

In the nights to come, Lisette had kept her promise.

She had taught Aidan to hunt, and despise it though he did, he had learned his lessons well. She had shown him how to move as easily between eras and continents as a mortal travels from room to room. From Lisette, Aidan learned to find a safe lair and to veil his presence from the awareness of human beings.

From Lisette, Aidan learned pure, enduring, singular hatred, and all of it was directed at her.

He pitied his victims and often starved himself to the point of collapse to avoid taking blood. Then, one foggy winter night not so long after Lisette had changed him from a man into a beast, while sitting alone in a country tavern, pretending to drink ale, he'd been approached by another vampire . . . Valerian.

"Reminiscing about me? How touching."

Aidan started in his chair by the fire in his Connecticut house and muttered a curse. His unannounced and quite unquestionably arrogant caller leaned against the mantel, indolently regal in creased trousers and tails. He was even wearing the signature gold medallion, which meant he was in a mischievous mood.

Like Aidan, Valerian held the stereotypical media vampire in unwavering contempt.

"This is the second time in as many nights that I've taken you unawares," Valerian scolded, tugging at his immaculate white gloves. "You've become careless, my friend. Tell me, have you fed so well that your senses are dulled?"

Aidan raised himself from the chair and faced his visitor squarely. Valerian was ancient, by vampire standards, having been changed sometime in the fourteenth century. He was a magnificent monster, given to sweeping displays of power, but only the stupid showed fear in his presence.

When Valerian sensed cowardice, he turned dangerously playful, like a cat with a mouse between its paws.

"I am allowed some introspection," Aidan said, pouring a snifter of brandy and raising it to Valerian in an impudent toast even though he could not drink. "I was remembering how I came to join the ranks of demons, if you must know."

Valerian chuckled, took the glass from Aidan's hand, and flung the contents into the fire. A furious roar preceded his reply. " 'The ranks of demons,' is it? Do you hate us so much as that, Aidan?"

"Yes," Aidan spat. "Yes! I despise you, I despise Lisette, and most of all, I despise myself."

Valerian yawned. "You have become something of a bore, my friend, always whining about what you are. When are you going to accept the fact that you will be exactly this until the crack of doom and get on with it?"

Aidan turned his back on his companion to stand facing one of the bookshelves, running one hand lightly over the spines of the leather-bound volumes he cherished. "There is a way to end the curse," he said with despairing certainty. "There has to be."

"Oh, indeed, there is," Valerian said cheerfully. "You have only to tell some crusading human where your lair is and let him drive a stake through your heart while you sleep. Or you could find a silver bullet somewhere and shoot yourself." He shuddered, and his tone took on a note of condescension as he finished. "Neither fate is at all pleasant, I'm afraid. Both are truly terrible deaths, and what lies beyond is even worse, for us if not for mortals."

Aidan did not turn from his inspection of the journals he had written himself, by hand, over the course of two centuries. His musings had kept him from losing his mind and, he hoped, given some perspective on history. He had written a full account of his vampirism as well.

"I don't need your lectures, Valerian. If you have no other business with me, then kindly leave."

Valerian sighed philosophically, a sure sign that he was about to pontificate. He surprised Aidan this time, however, by speaking simply. "Lisette stirs again, my friend. Have a care."

Aidan turned slowly to study his companion. When he'd grown beyond the needs of a fledgling vampire, and spurned her affections, Lisette had first raged, then sulked, then gone into seclusion in some hidden den. She had emerged on occasion and busied herself with her usual dalliances, but she had not troubled Aidan in years. In fact, he seldom worried about her, although Valerian and Maeve constantly chided him for his carelessness.

"She has long since forgotten me," he said. "I am but one of many conquests, after all."

"You delude yourself," Valerian replied tersely. "Lisette has indeed taken many lovers, and made many vampires. But you were the only one who dared to resist her advances. It's a miracle you haven't perished long before this, and I honestly can't say why I keep trying to save you when you seem determined to die."

Aidan clutched Valerian's silk lapels in both hands. He was not afraid for himself, but he did fear for Maeve, and the human woman, Neely. "Have you seen Lisette?" he demanded. "Damn you, stop your prattling and tell me!"

Valerian shrugged free of Aidan's grasp and seemed to settle his garments closer to his skin, the way a raven might do with its feathers. "I have not been so unfortunate as to encounter Lisette," he said with ominous dignity, "but certain of the others have. She is weak and feeds only sporadically, according to my sources. Nevertheless, she has roused herself, and sooner or later, as mortals so colorfully put it, there will be hell to pay."

Aidan shoved splayed fingers through his hair, his mind racing. "Where? Where was she seen?"

"Spain, I think," Valerian answered. He'd shifted his attention to a mechanical music box on Aidan's desk; Valerian loved gadgets. He turned the key, and the tinkling notes of a long-forgotten tune echoed in the room. "If you say you're going there to look for her," he said distractedly, "I swear I'll wash my hands of you."

"You've made that vow often enough," Aidan said tersely. "What a pity you never keep it."

Valerian chuckled, but the snap with which he closed the music box lid was a more accurate measure of his mood. "What an insolent whelp you are. Who but Lisette would change such a difficult human into an immortal, thereby subjecting us all to an eternity of pathos?"

"Who, indeed?" Aidan replied. He sighed, and his shoulders slumped slightly. He was faint with the need for sustenance, but the dawn was too close now. There was no time for a proper hunt. "I'm sorry," he said, even though he wasn't, not entirely, and they both knew it. "If you see Lisette, will you let me know?"

The older vampire regarded him coldly for a long time, then said, "You may encounter the creature before I do, Aidan." He frowned, adjusted his gloves, and set his top hat at a dashing angle. "And now, adieu. Dawn is nearing. Sleep soundly, my friend, and in safety."

With that, Valerian vanished. He often indulged in dramatic exits.

Aidan banked the fire on the hearth, put the screen in place, and left the house, moving through the silent, snowy woods as noisily as a man, instead of with a vampire's stealth. Maybe Valerian was right; maybe he was courting destruction, in the unconscious hope that there was no heaven or hell beyond death, but only oblivion.

In oblivion would lie peace.

Aidan's hunger tore at him as he moved closer and closer to the long-forgotten mine shaft that was his lair. He glanced toward the sky, reasoned that he had about fifteen minutes before the sun would top the horizon. There was time to go to Neely, time for one look to sustain him in the deathlike sleep that awaited him.

He shook his head. No. He dared not approach her now, when he needed to feed.

He wended his way toward his hiding place, lowered himself inside, crouched against one dank wall, and folded his arms atop his knees. Then he yawned, lowered his head, and slept.

The mansion had looked spooky to Neely on Halloween night, but now that she stood before it in the dazzling sunshine of that November afternoon, it seemed very ordinary and innocuous, except for its size.

She wasn't sure why she'd come; Mr. Tremayne certainly hadn't invited her to drop by. All Neely really knew was that she was drawn to that house and even more so to its owner. It was as if she'd always known Aidan Tremayne, as if they'd been close once, very close, and then cruelly separated. Encountering him had been a reunion of sorts, a restoration of something stolen long before.

Wedging her hands into the pockets of her coat, Neely proceeded up the walk and climbed the steps onto the gracious old porch. Then, after drawing a deep breath, she rang the bell.

There was no answer, so she tried a second time. Again, no one came.

Neely walked around the large house once, thinking she might encounter the owner in the yard, but she didn't catch so much as a glimpse of him.

Finally, feeling both relieved and disappointed, Neely turned and walked back along the driveway toward the highway. She had already cleaned the motel rooms that had been rented the night before, and she wasn't due back at the café until the supper shift. Danny would be in school until three o'clock, and Ben was busy repairing a water pipe under one of the trailers.

Neely was a free woman, and she was at loose ends.

She decided to borrow Ben's battered old Toyota and head into Bright River. Her emotions were churning; she tried to put Tremayne out of her mind and failed.

She would stop by the local library, she decided. There she would surely find back copies of the Bright River *Clarion*; she intended to scan the microfilm records for interesting references to Aidan Tremayne or his family. After all, she rationalized as she bumped along Route 7 in her brother's car, she needed to keep up her professional skills—especially in research. God knew, she couldn't work as a waitress and maid all her life; her feet would never withstand the strain.

Besides, the project gave her a legitimate reason to think about Aidan on a more practical level, and it would distract her from the riot of emotions and needs that had been bedeviling her ever since their first encounter.

Neely adjusted the car's temperamental heater and shivered in spite of the blast of hot air that buffeted her. Aidan was going to change her life, and she was going to change his; she knew it as well as if an angel had whispered the fact in her ear. There was a magical mystery afoot here, and she yearned to learn its secrets.

The trick would be to stay alive long enough to investigate.

She sighed and silently reminded herself that she knew too much about her ex-boss's source of campaign funds, among other things. Five years working in the nation's capital had cured Neely of starry-eyed illusion—even though Hargrove was an easygoing sort who would not relish the prospect of ordering her death or anyone else's, he loved the power of his office, and the status it gave him. The senator would never sacrifice money, position, and his marriage, much less his personal freedom, for Neely's sake.

She must be more careful now and stop pretending to herself that all was right with the world.

Chapter 3

--•◦✗◦•--

When Aidan awakened, he was dangerously weak, a state that rendered him vulnerable to all manner of enemies. He had no choice but to hunt.

He rose slowly and stretched, this last being an unnecessary habit lingering from his days as a mortal. Aidan's muscles had long since atrophied to a stonelike condition beneath his skin. Even that was changed, he thought, extending his arms and gazing at his hands. The once-living flesh was now as cold and smooth and hard as marble.

Aidan did not stay long in his lair, for the hunger had grown merciless in its intensity, biting into his middle, sapping his strength, threatening his very reason. He climbed deftly up the smooth dirt wall to the surface of the ground. There, the moon shed a silvery light over a new layer of snow.

He thought first of Neely, and ached to be mortal and thoroughly ordinary so that he could be close to her, learn how her mind and heart worked, walk in sunlight with her. Most of all, he wanted to make love to her, feeling his own flesh warm and supple against hers, but that seemed the most impossible of all his dreams.

It was dangerous to think in such a fashion, he reminded himself. He would never be human again, and he would die at the hands of his enemies before he would turn Neely into what he was.

Aidan knew his vampire powers well, despise them though he did, and he feared that the fervor of his emotions would draw Neely to him. If he were to encounter her now, when he was so desperate to feed, when his vile hunger for blood would be coupled with the elemental physical and emotional passion he felt for her, he could not be sure of restraining himself.

As it happened, thrusting Neely from his mind was not enough, for she clung tenaciously to the innermost cords and fibers of his heart.

Maeve hid herself in the chilly mists of the evening and waited. Through the foggy windows of the Lakeview Café, she could see Neely Wallace, the woman Valerian was so concerned about.

Valerian was Maeve's mentor, after a fashion, and he had made her an immortal when Aidan refused. Thus, she trusted Valerian, as much as one vampire ever trusts another, and since he saw the Wallace woman as a threat to Aidan, so had she. Maeve had come to this backward country, this century she heartily disliked, prepared to confront and destroy an enemy. Instead she found herself drifting with the breeze in a parking lot, like so much smoke, and questioning Valerian's judgment.

Miss Wallace was an attractive young woman, between twenty-five and thirty, Maeve guessed, with short, shiny brown hair and large gamine eyes. She smiled a lot, and the café customers seemed to like her, but she was clearly an ordinary mortal with no special powers of any sort.

How could such a creature be a menace to any vampire, even a reluctant one like Aidan?

Maeve was irritated and not a little bored. She'd fed early so that the evening would be her own, and now she was missing at least one very important social event—specifically Columbine Spencer's supper-dance in Charleston, South Carolina.

"Bother," said Maeve. In a fit of pique she willed herself to Aidan's house, solidifying herself very dramatically in the center of his parlor.

He was there, remarkably, sitting behind the antique library table he used as a desk, bent over one of those interminable volumes of his. Even though there was electricity in this crass century, and his house was wired for it, he worked by the light of a smelly oil lamp.

He raised his eyes at Maeve's appearance, grinned, and stood, as befits a gentleman vampire.

"Kiss, kiss," said Maeve, making an appropriate motion with her lips. She placed her hands on her trim waist— she was wearing an elaborate white dress decorated with hundreds of tiny iridescent beads, because of the Spencer party—and tossed her head impatiently. Her dark hair was done up in tiny ringlets and curls, her flawless white skin prettily flushed because she'd taken nourishment soon after awakening. "Honestly, darling, you're becoming the worst sort of curmudgeon." She held out a slender gloved hand. "Come. I'm on my way to a ball, and I know the Spencers would be delighted to have you among their guests."

Instead of lowering himself into his chair, Aidan perched on the edge of his desk, his arms folded. "I suppose all the very best fiends will be in attendance," he teased, arching one dark eyebrow.

Maeve was not amused. "The majority will be mortals, of course," she said, raising her chin. "Stage actors, an opera singer, some artists of various sorts, I suppose—"

"Along with a vampire or two, a handful of witches and warlocks—"

Color flared in Maeve's alabaster cheeks. "When did you become such a snob?" she demanded. She didn't wait for an answer. "Valerian told me you were developing a dangerous predilection for the society of humans. Even after a firsthand look at the supposed object of your fascination, I still thought he was mistaken. Now I'm not so certain."

All friendliness had vanished from Aidan's manner. His eyes narrowed as he regarded his twin in the smoky light of the oil lamp. "What do you mean, 'after a firsthand look at the supposed object of my fascination'?"

Maeve gathered all her formidable forces, as she sometimes did when she wanted to intimidate a particularly brazen human. "I went to see Neely Wallace," she said.

Aidan didn't move, and yet every fiber of his being seemed to exude challenge. "*What?*"

Maeve began to pace, folding and unfolding her silk and ivory fan as she moved. "So it's true, then. You're actually smitten with a human being." She stopped and gazed at her brother with tears glittering in her stricken blue eyes. "Oh, Aidan, how could you do something so foolish?"

She saw conflict in her brother's remarkable face, as well as pain. "*Smitten* is hardly the word for what I'm feeling," he confessed. "Maeve, I've encountered the woman exactly twice, and it's as if she owns my soul. I keep recalling what the gypsy woman said that day Mother took us to have our fortunes told. Do you remember?"

Maeve flinched inwardly, wanting to recoil from the memory and all it might mean, even after so many years, but unable to do so. "Yes," she said grimly, "I remember it perfectly well. We visited a flea-infested camp, and Mama, bless her simple heart, paid an old, ignorant crone to predict our futures."

Aidan gazed at her in quiet reflection for a long moment, and Maeve saw something uncomfortably like compassion move in his eyes.

She was indignant. "All right," she conceded, even though her brother had not actually challenged her, "the witch was right about some things—our being cursed, if you want to think of it as that—but there is no reason to believe—"

"That Neely is the woman the sorceress mentioned?" Aidan finished gently. "The one who would mean either my salvation or my destruction?" He paused, evidently gathering his thoughts, and frowned pensively when he spoke again. "Oh, to the contrary, my dear, there is every reason to believe it. I know almost nothing about Neely, and as you've so often pointed out, she is a mortal. And for all of that, when I saw her, it was as though my very soul leapt out of me and ran to her, desperate to lose itself in her."

Aidan looked so haunted, so beleaguered, that Maeve wanted to weep. She began in that moment to fear the Wallace woman, and to hate her, for if Aidan's theory was fact and not fancy, then the situation was grave, indeed.

"What are you going to do?" Maeve whispered, struggling to restrain all the wild, violent emotions that suddenly possessed her.

"Do?" Aidan countered softly. "My dear sister, there is nothing to 'do.' It is something that must unfold."

"No," Maeve protested, shaken, remembering that long-ago day in the gypsy camp as if it were a part of last week instead of a remnant from a distant century. "The crone said it depended on your choices, yours and hers, whether you would be saved or destroyed!"

Aidan came to her then and laid his hands gently to either side of her face. "But I can only control my own choices," he pointed out with infinite tenderness. "What Neely decides is quite beyond me —" He must have seen the rebellion brewing in Maeve's eyes, for he smiled sadly and clarifed, "Beyond both of us."

Maeve was full of fury and fear. "You want to perish!" she accused. "Damn you, Aidan, I followed you into eternity, and now you would leave me to take refuge in death!"

He released her, stepped away, turned his back to stand at one of the tall windows, gazing out upon the snowy night. "To be parted from you would be exceedingly painful," he admitted, almost grudgingly. "Still, we are brother and sister, Maeve, not lovers. Perhaps we simply were not meant to travel the same path."

Maeve steadied herself, called on all her vampire powers to sustain her, as the agonizing truth of Aidan's words settled over her spirit. "You've decided, then, that you will pursue this madness?"

"Yes," he replied wearily, without turning to face his sister. For the first time in all the winding length of Maeve's memory, he seemed unaware of her feelings. "Yes," he repeated. "For good or ill, I will see it through and find my fate at the end."

At last Aidan abandoned that wretched window to look at Maeve again, though he kept his distance. She knew the span was not merely physical, but emotional, too, and she was further wounded by this realization.

"You are not to interfere, no matter how consuming the temptation may be," he warned quietly but with the utmost strength of purpose. "I mean what I say, Maeve—if you value my wishes, if you care for me at all, you will avoid Neely Wallace at all costs."

Maeve was stricken, for she could not doubt that Aidan was grimly sincere. If she meddled in this threatening affair, he might never forgive her, and the thought of his scorn was beyond endurance.

Still, she was angry as well, and suspicious. "Can you possibly believe there is a need for you to defend her against me?"

Aidan did not relent. "I don't know," he answered bluntly, "but aside from wanting to let this thing run its course, be it curse or blessing, I am concerned for Neely's safety. As you well understand, your presence could draw the attention of the others to Neely. Suppose, for instance, that Lisette should learn of her?"

Maeve had heard the rumors that Lisette, the most vicious and unfortunately the most powerful of all vampires, had come forth from her tomb, but she had disregarded them as alarmist drivel. "Don't be an idiot," she replied. "Even if Lisette is stirring abroad now and again, she surely has no interest in the likes of your pitiful mortal."

"She is *not* pitiful in any way, shape, or form," Aidan retorted tersely. "Neely is a magical creature, like most humans, and part of her splendor lies in the fact that she is quite unaware of her own majesty."

Maeve examined her ivory-colored fingernails, which were perfectly shaped and buffed to a soft glow. She was still in turmoil, and her outward calm was all pretense. "You're right to be afraid of Lisette," she said with a lightness she did not feel. She was injured, and in her pain she needed to be cruel. "If your enemies suspect you are fond of the woman, they may use her to make you suffer." She paused a moment for effect, then went boldly on, aware that the attempt was futile even as she made it. "There is one way to solve the problem forever, Aidan. 'If thy right eye offends thee . . . ' "

His rage was sudden and palpable; it filled the room with coldness. And it confirmed Maeve's worst suspicions.

"No." He whispered the word, but it had all the strength of an earthquake. "Neely is not to be touched, do you understand me? Her only sin is that she brought a child to my door one night, on an innocent errand—"

Maeve lifted one hand and laid an index finger to Aidan's lips to silence him. "You needn't raise your voice, darling," she said, again with a levity that was wholly feigned. "I will respect your wishes, you know that. Know also, however, that I love you and that I will do whatever I must to keep you safe."

They studied each other in silence for a long interval, equally determined, equally powerful.

"Please," Maeve cajoled finally. "Come to the ball with me. What better way to draw the attention of the others away from Neely Wallace?"

Aidan hesitated, then gave a grim nod.

He went upstairs to change into suitable clothing and quickly rejoined Maeve in the study. He was breathtakingly handsome in a top hat and tails, and for added affect he wore his silk cape.

Five minutes later, distracted and silent, he was entering the Spencers' antebellum ballroom with Maeve on his arm.

Once her shift was over, Neely lingered at one of the Formica-topped tables in the café, sipping herbal tea and poring over the information she'd collected earlier at the library. She became, by an act of will, the detached professional, putting her personal feelings about Aidan temporarily on hold.

She'd found a number of articles regarding the Tremayne family on microfilm and made photocopies of each one. According to the newspaper pieces, there had been an Aidan Tremayne living in the colonial mansion for well over a century. Each generation was as reclusive as the last, apparently marrying and raising their families elsewhere. There were no wedding or engagement announcements, no records of local births, no obituaries. The articles yielded only the most general information—in the summer of 1816, part of the house had been destroyed by fire. During the War Between the States, Union troops had moved into the downstairs rooms. In 1903 a young woman had disappeared after leaving a calling card at the Tremayne residence, and there had been a brief flurry of scandal, an earnest but fruitless police investigation. One of the earlier ancestors had been a painter of some renown, and several of his pieces had brought a fortune at auction in 1956.

Only when one of the chairs on the opposite side of the table scraped back did Neely bring herself out of her revelry. Lifting her eyes, she saw her brother sitting across from her.

Ben resembled nothing so much as a renegade biker, with his long hair, battered jeans, and black T-shirt, but in truth he was a solid citizen. He worked hard managing the motel, café, and trailer court, and he was a conscientious father to Danny.

"Digging up more dirt on Senator Hargrove?" he asked. The café was closed now, and the night cook and the other waitress had gone home for the night. They could talk freely.

Of course, Ben knew all about the discoveries she'd made while working in the senator's office as his assistant. She'd told him everything, from the very beginning, when she'd only suspected that her employer was consorting with criminals in general and drug dealers in particular, and he'd known about the documented proof she'd collected, too.

Neely shook her head in answer to his question; there was probably a lot more "dirt" to be dug up where Dallas Hargrove was concerned, but she was through playing detective. She'd given the FBI numerous papers and even photographs outlining the senator's exploits, and now she could do nothing but wait. And hope the Feds would bring Hargrove down for good before he decided to avenge himself.

"Not this time," she said, somewhat wearily. "I'm curious about the Tremayne family, but I haven't been able to come up with much. I'll try the courthouse tomorrow."

Ben looked puzzled and not a little uncomfortable. "Why, Neely? What interest could you possibly have in that place or those people? Hell, I've always thought it was a little spooky, the way that guy keeps to himself."

Neely propped one elbow on the table and cupped her chin in her hand. "I can't explain it," she answered, because honesty had always come easily with Ben. "It's almost like a compulsion. I've met Mr. Tremayne twice, and both times I felt some kind of paradigm shift—something I never even guessed it was possible to feel. Unless I watch myself, I think I could actually love him."

Ben shook his head and grinned, then got up to go to the pie keeper on the counter. He took out two slices of lemon meringue and returned to the table. Usually he wouldn't have stuck around, but Danny was spending the night in town with a friend from school, and there was no need to hurry home.

"Would that be so awful?" he asked. "If you fell in love, I mean?"

She picked up a fork and cut off a bite-size piece of pie. "When are you going to get married again, Ben?" she countered, purposely stalling. "Shannon's been gone for five years now. Isn't it time you had a romance?"

Ben chuckled, but there was sadness in the sound. "It isn't quite that easy," he said. "Nobody's likely to mistake me for Kevin Costner, for one thing, and for another, well, my job isn't exactly impressive. I have a young son who still looks for his mother to come home, a beat-up old truck that needs an overhaul, a small savings account, and medical bills roughly equal to the national debt. What woman in her right mind would tie up with me?"

Neely reached across the table and touched her brother's tattooed forearm affectionately. "None, if you're going to take that attitude," she scolded with a smile. "What about the fact that you're loyal—you stuck by Shannon through one of the worst ordeals a human being can experience, and you were there for her the whole time, even though you must have been reeling with pain yourself. You've raised Danny ever since, with love and gentleness, and you're resilient, Ben. A lot of other people would have given up, being widowed and laid off in the same year, but you kept going. You're a special guy, and there must be plenty of good women out there looking for somebody like you. All you've got to do is stop hiding behind that gruff exterior of yours."

A slight blush told Neely that her compliments had struck their mark. Ben concentrated on his pie for a time, chewing and swallowing several bites before he met his sister's eye and tried again. "How about you, Neely? Is it serious, what's happening between you and this Tremayne character?"

She looked away. "It could be," she admitted softly, after staring out at the snowy night for a long time. "At least on my side. For all I know, Aidan has never given me a second thought." It was time to steer the subject in another direction, however briefly. "The people Hargrove is involved with may wait years to strike, Ben, but sooner or later they'll see that I meet with an accident. It's bad enough that I'm hanging around here, in such an obvious place, endangering you and Danny. I can't drag some unsuspecting man into the situation, too."

Ben finished his pie and ate what was left of Neely's, since she'd pushed her plate away. "We're a pair, you and I," he said. "Still, the senator and his bunch are bound to go to prison, once the full extent of their sins comes to light.

Then none of them will be a danger to you anymore."

Neely gave her brother a wry look, carried their plates into the café's small kitchen, and returned to gather up her photocopies before answering. "We've had this conversation before," she pointed out. "We keep going over the same ground, again and again, as if we believe on some level that the situation will change if we just *discuss* things enough."

With a sheepish shrug Ben stood, taking his lined denim jacket from the brass coat tree next to the door and putting it on. "Who knows?" He waited while Neely donned her pea coat and fetched her purse from behind the counter. "It seems to me that it's taking the FBI a long time to pull the investigation together and make a move. Maybe you ought to give the material you gathered to the producer of one of those tabloid TV shows. I'll bet *that* would bring some action."

Neely passed through the open café doorway ahead of her brother, raising her collar against the cold wind while she waited for him to turn out the lights and lock the door. There were several big rigs in the parking lot, their drivers either staying at the motel or sacked out in sleepers in the backs of their truck cabs.

"I may approach a journalist or a reporter," she said, "if the FBI doesn't do something soon." Neely had another set of copies of the incriminating documents stashed away in a safe place, but she'd never told Ben or anyone else where they were. It was something too dangerous to know.

A hard crust had formed on the snowy ground, and the sky was clear, full of icy stars. Misty clouds passing over the moon made it look blurry and slightly out of focus. Neely's clunky waitress shoes made a satisfying crunching sound as she and Ben walked toward home.

Ben escorted her to her trailer and waited while she worked the lock, opened the door, and turned on the lights.

"Tomorrow's your day off," her brother reminded her, hands in the pockets of his jacket. "Do something constructive with it, why don't you, instead of rooting around in the courthouse files or straining your eyes at one of those microfilm machines."

Neely smiled. "Good night, Ben," she said.

He chuckled, shook his head, and walked away toward his own nearby trailer.

After locking up and performing her usual nighttime ablutions, Neely folded out her sofa bed and collapsed. She'd meant to go over the newspaper articles she'd copied at the library once more, just in case she'd missed something. Instead she barely managed to switch out the lamp on the wall above the couch before she tumbled into an unusually deep slumber.

Almost immediately she began to dream.

Aidan Tremayne appeared at the foot of her bed, even more handsome than before in the kind of beautifully tailored dancing clothes leading men sometimes wore in movies made in the thirties and forties. He even had on a top hat, set at a rakish angle, and his dark cape rustled in the draft.

As the dreaming Neely raised herself on one elbow to stare at him, he winked.

Neely laughed. "See if I ever have a chili dog with onions for dinner again," she said.

Aidan smiled and tipped his hat, tumbling it down his arm and catching it in one gloved hand.

Neely clapped, and he bowed deeply. She hoped the dream wasn't over, that the lemon meringue pie would pick up where the chili dog had left off.

"Is this dream a talkie?" she asked. "Or are we going to use subtitles?"

He held out one hand, and she felt herself rising effortlessly from the bed, floating toward him. "It's wired for sound," he answered. He caught her in his arms, and she felt tremendous energy in him, as well as danger, and, within herself, a tumultuous need. "I'm afraid I'm quite bewitched."

Neely reminded herself that she was asleep and decided to enjoy the night fancy as much as possible before real life intruded. She allowed herself to revel in being held close against him, to savor the melting warmth in her most feminine parts and the bittersweet ache that had taken root in her heart.

"You're dressed for dancing," she observed.

The walls of the trailer seemed to disintegrate; there was only Neely herself, and Aidan Tremayne, holding her, with all the universe silent and still around them. Stars fell in glittering arches and formed a twinkling pool beneath their feet.

Aidan's dark blue eyes sparkled more brightly than anything in the firmaments of heaven possibly could have. "Yes," he agreed. "You, on the other hand, are quite scantily clad."

Neely sighed. One nice thing about the imagination— a person could dance on the night wind in an oversize T-shirt without getting cold and give in to a scandalous attraction knowing that, come morning, it would no longer be real.

"This is wonderful," she said. "A girl can go her whole life without ever having a dream like this."

Aidan said nothing; instead, he drew her closer and bent his mouth to kiss her, and set her very soul to spinning within her like a skater on ice.

The kiss mended some parts of her that she had not guessed were broken, but shattered others, and Neely wept because she knew she loved Aidan Tremayne, that she would always love him, that this love was hopeless outside of her dream.

They waltzed along the treetops, up a staircase of stars, all around the moon. There was beautiful music, of course, for this was a celestial production number. The tune was unique, rife with a bittersweet poignancy, and it was still running through Neely's mind when she awoke with a thumping start, sitting up in the middle of her bed.

She was gasping for breath, feeling as though she'd been dropped from a great height. Her cheeks were wet with tears.

Neely hugged herself and rocked back and forth on her knees, possessed by a sudden and terrible sense of loss. The miraculous fantasy was evaporating, so she scrambled in the darkness for a pencil and a piece of paper in order to record it. She started to write, but the last of the memory faded, like a final heartbeat.

She switched on the light, trembling with this new grief, and read what she'd written on the back of her telephone bill. All that was left of her magnificent vision was a single, hastily scrawled word.

Aidan.

Chapter 4

—◦✦⊱※⊰✦◦—

Aidan slept profoundly all the following day, beyond the reach of dreams and nightmares that trouble mortals. He awakened only a few minutes after sunset and was still assembling his wits when Maeve appeared, resplendent in a flowing white toga.

She looked around the dark mine shaft, noting its lacery of cobwebs with mild but still obvious disdain. "Your capacity for self-punishment never ceases to amaze me," she remarked.

Methodically Aidan dusted the sleeves of his evening coat. He arched one eyebrow as he regarded his sister. Maeve was dressed for some kind of Roman celebration, but not the authentic article; like most vampires, she was forbidden to venture back prior beyond the instant of her death as a human being. He made a *tsk-tsk* sound and shook his head.

"On your way to one of those debauched Victorian parties?" he inquired, taking off his coat to shake out the dust, then putting it on again.

"It isn't 'debauched,'" Maeve snapped, her blue eyes fiery. "The Havermails are perfectly nice—"

"People?" Aidan teased.

Maeve looked away for a moment. "Vampires," she said distractedly. "They're vampires, of course." Her temper flared anew. "Stop trying to change the subject. You left the ball early last night, Aidan. Where were you?"

Aidan had a yearning for fresh air, even though he could not actually breathe the wonderful stuff. He pictured himself standing on the snowy ground overhead, and as quickly as that, he was there. Only a moment later Maeve was beside him.

The woods were quiet, except for the far-off hooting of an owl and the vague murmur of tires passing through slush on Route 7. Clouds hid the moon, and a sort of pale darkness had spread itself over the land.

"Where were you, Aidan?" Maeve persisted.

He started toward the house. He would change clothes and feed early that night, he decided, and then play his favorite, futile game by pretending to be a man again. "Assuming that's any of your business, which it isn't," he retorted without stopping, "why in hell do you care?"

Maeve stepped in front of him and glared up into his eyes. "You endanger all of us when you consort with humans, Aidan, you know that! If you truly want to throw away your own existence, I guess I'll just have to endure it, but you have *no right* to bring risk on the rest of us!"

Aidan winced, for her words stung. "All right," he said, feeling exasperated and weary, so unbelievably weary. He was like a guilty husband, hastening to explain a gap in his schedule, and he resented the comparison bitterly. "I left the ball, I came back here, and I settled in my lair to hibernate, like any good beast."

Maeve subsided a little and allowed Aidan to pass, rushing to keep up just as she had when they were children. "Valerian said you were dancing with—with that Neely creature."

"It was only a mental exercise, a shared fantasy," Aidan responded. He hated explaining even that much, but it was true that others might be threatened by his fascination with Neely. Too much association with mortals, for purposes other than feeding, of course, served to dilute a vampire's powers and dull his perceptions. Other fiends, such as Lisette, were frenzied by weakness, like sharks in bloody waters. "You don't think I'd dare to actually dance with her, do you, to hold her in my arms? A human woman?"

They reached the rear of the towering stone house and entered through the mudroom. In the kitchen, which contained almost nothing in the way of food, Maeve stopped her brother again, this time by reaching out and catching hold of his sleeve.

"Couldn't you simply put her out of your mind? Surely it isn't too late!"

Aidan gazed into his sister's face for a long time before answering hoarsely, "It was too late at the beginning of time," he responded. "Leave it alone, Maeve. There is no changing this."

"Put her out of your mind," Maeve pleaded, sounding frantic. "If you must play at romance, choose an immortal!" Tears glimmered in her eyes, and Aidan was touched; he was surprised that she'd retained the ability to weep.

He gripped Maeve's upper arms and squeezed gently. "I don't know what this is," he told her. "I don't pretend to understand what's happening to me. But I know this much—it can't be avoided. You, Valerian, the others—you must all stay away from me until it's resolved, one way or the other."

"No," Maeve said. "I cannot abandon you, Aidan—"

"You must!"

"I won't."

He hissed a swear word.

After a long interval of struggle, plainly visible in her expressive eyes, Maeve lifted one hand to touch his face. "Very well. I will do my best to keep my distance for as long as I can," she promised in a despairing whisper. "But hear this, Aidan, and remember it well: I will be guarding and nurturing my powers from this moment on. He—or she—who does you injury will feel the full force of my vengeance, and I will not trouble myself with mercy."

Aidan felt a mental chill. While his twin fed only on those humans whose souls were already damned, as he did, she did not share his aversion to the life of a vampire. To Maeve, the compulsion to consume human blood was a small price to pay for immortality, the capacity to travel through time and space at will, the heightening of the senses, and the fathomless physical energy.

"Stay away from Neely," he warned.

Maeve drew herself up, seeming to blaze with white fire. "If she brings about your destruction, she will die."

Before Aidan could respond, his sister vanished. He was alone in his shell of a kitchen, with its empty cupboards. He leaned against a counter, arms folded, full of despondency and yearning for ordinary pleasures, like the sound and scent of bacon sizzling in a skillet and the embrace of a woman, still warm from sleep.

What cruel irony it was, he reflected, that mortals never seemed to understand what a glorious gift it was, just to be human. If only they knew how they'd been blessed. . . .

Washington, D.C.

Senator Dallas Hargrove left his Georgetown house by a side door, wearing battered jeans, a T-shirt rescued from a bag of rags in the laundry room, sneakers, and a jacket so old that the leather had cracked in places. He pulled the collar up around his face and whistled tunelessly as he walked.

He was good at avoiding the press and other pests, and that night his luck held. He walked until he was some distance from the gracious room where his lovely, fragile wife slept, then hailed a cab.

The driver didn't recognize him—Washington was crawling with government types, after all—and drove him to a park at the edge of the city without question.

"Wait here," Dallas said. The snow was coming down harder, and not only was the wind picking up speed, but it also had a bite to it.

The man in the cab shifted uncomfortably. "I don't know, man," he said. "This ain't the *best* neighborhood in D.C."

Dallas handed over the fare, then flashed a fifty-dollar bill and a vote-getting smile. "Five minutes?"

The cabbie sighed, snapped up the fifty. "Five minutes," he agreed. "But that's all, and I mean it, man." He rested one arm in the open window of the battered, smoke-belching old cab and tapped the face of his watch with an index finger. "Once that sweep second hand has made five swings past the numbers, I'm out of here."

Dallas nodded, turned, and sprinted away into the park. There were a few derelicts sleeping on and under benches, but the wandering bands of thugs who usually frequented the place had apparently stayed in out of the cold. He walked quickly to the statue of a minor Civil War general mounted on a horse and stood in its long shadow.

His contact spoke up right away, though as usual Dallas didn't see more than a vague form. It gave him the creeps; the guy was like a ghost, moving without noise, materializing where he chose.

"It's time the Wallace woman was disposed of."

Dallas felt a twinge of guilt, even though logic told him Neely deserved whatever she got. She'd violated his trust, after all, sneaking around, going through his files and papers the way she had. Still, she was a pretty, vibrant thing and killing her would be like crushing an exquisite rose just opening to the sunlight. "Look," he said reasonably, "my friend at the FBI forestalled any problems we might have had. And Ms. Wallace hasn't made a move since or even tried to hide. She's living in Connecticut, for God's sake, helping her brother run a truck stop and motel. I say we leave her alone."

"She set out to bring us all down, Senator—you included. Who's to say she won't try again?"

Dallas ground his teeth, caught himself, and forcibly relaxed. He didn't want to see Neely die, despite the way she'd betrayed him, but he couldn't stand against these people. If he was foolish enough to try, he would be killed or crippled for his trouble, and then what would happen to Elaine? Who would take care of her if not him?

Once his beautiful wife had been vital and active, a successful journalist. Now she was confined to a wheelchair, suffering from a progressive muscular disease. Elaine's prognosis was grim, and he could not abandon her.

"You know where to find her," Hargrove said, rubbing his eyes with a thumb and forefinger. He had to think about his family, his backers, his constituents. What was one woman compared with so many others?

Almost five minutes had passed by that time, and Dallas was painfully conscious of the taxi driver's promise to leave when that small amount of time had elapsed. He handed over a packet of documents, and the man in the shadows reciprocated with a thick envelope.

It was all for Elaine, the senator told himself as he turned and hurried toward the curb. The cab was already moving when he landed inside.

*   *   *

Aidan washed, groomed his hair, and put on jeans and an Irish cable-knit sweater. He would hunt early, get the abominable task out of the way, and spend the evening next to the fire, working on his journal.

He guarded his thoughts carefully, for to think of Neely too intensely would be to summon her to his side. That would be embarrassing for him because he would have to come up with an explanation, and for Neely because she would suddenly find herself in his home with no memory of traveling there.

It was, he found, a little like that old schoolyard routine "Don't think of blue elephants." Fortunately the hunger was keen enough that night to provide sufficient distraction.

Aidan took a computer printout from a file cabinet against the wall, laid it on his desk, and ran his finger down the list of names. These men subscribed to the very basest of pornographic magazines, the kind even the most flagrant liberal would happily consign to the bonfire.

He selected a victim in the next county, closed his eyes, and vanished.

Only minutes later he was back.

Neely certainly didn't make a habit of walking alone along Route 7 at eleven-thirty at night, but she was too restless to stay inside her trailer. God knew, the place wasn't spacious, and that evening it seemed even smaller than usual. She'd felt like a grasshopper trapped in a pint jar.

As she walked, keeping to the far edge of the shoulder in an effort to avoid the headlights of passing cars, fat flakes of iridescent snow tumbled from the sky. She often found such weather peaceful, even festive, but just then it seemed eerie.

How ridiculous, Neely decided, to be so upset over a dream she could hardly remember. Aidan Tremayne had been part of it, she knew that much, and a wisp of weirdly beautiful music echoed in her mind.

As if all that wasn't enough, she had a sense that someone was stalking her, closing in slowly, watching and waiting.

She shivered and walked faster, stopping only when she reached the head of the Tremayne driveway.

"You're crazy," she told herself as a mud-splattered Blazer passed on the other side of Route 7, then slowed.

Neely's heart seemed to slide over an expanse of sheer ice, leaving her breathless. She bolted into the woods, stumbling in the deep snow. From the highway she heard the slam of a car door.

"Hey, lady, come back!" a man's voice called.

Neely ran on, tripped over a fallen birch limb, scraped her shin, scrambled to her feet again, and flung herself headlong toward Aidan's house. She could see the light on his front porch through the trees.

Behind her, the man from the Blazer crashed along in pursuit.

Neely looked back, half blind with unreasoning terror, and collided hard with something. At first she thought it was a tree, but then a pair of strong hands steadied her, and she looked up into the classically handsome face of Aidan Tremayne. She was too breathless to speak.

"You're all right now," he said in a low voice. For the first time she noticed a hint of a brogue in the way he framed his words. "No one's going to hurt you." He glared into the woods with a chilling intentness for a long moment, then shifted his gaze back to Neely again.

He smiled, and some of the starch went out of her knees.

Vaguely she heard running footsteps, the crash of a car door closing, the squeal of tires on wet pavement.

"What you need is a cup of tea," Aidan said, as though it were perfectly normal for the two of them to be standing out there in the woods at that hour. He wasn't even wearing a coat, just jeans and a fisherman's sweater. "Come along now."

Neely allowed him to escort her through the woods; he politely cupped her elbow in one hand.

"Do you always go out walking at such odd times?" he asked. There was no irritation in the question, only a companionable kind of curiosity.

"No," Neely answered, somewhat weakly. "No, I don't. It's just that I've been feeling very restless lately—"

"Any idea who the rascal in the woods might have been?"

Neely shook her head, embarrassed. She was making one hell of an impression. "I ran into the trees when he stopped and turned around, and he followed. He was probably harmless, but—"

"But you don't think so?" he asked. They had gained the edge of Aidan's sloping lawn.

Again she shook her head. "I have some formidable enemies," she said.

"So do I," he replied. They mounted the steps to the porch, and he held the door open for her, waiting politely while she passed over the threshold.

He led her into a parlor, where oil lamps burned cozily and a fire blazed on the hearth. "Here," he said, depositing her in a large leather chair. "Have a seat and catch your breath. I'll get that tea. Or would you rather have brandy?"

"Brandy," Neely said without hesitation.

Aidan smiled, went to a sideboard, and poured amber liquid into an etched glass snifter. He brought Neely the drink but stood well away from her chair while she sipped.

"I know I've already disrupted your evening," she began when her limbs had stopped quivering and her heart had slowed to its normal pace, "but I wonder if you'd mind driving me home. I'm afraid to walk, under the circumstances."

He was near the fireplace, arms folded, his back braced against the mantelpiece. The first two times Neely had encountered him, she'd been struck by the unusual fairness of his complexion, but that night his face looked quite normal, almost ruddy. "I'll bring the car around in a few minutes," he said in that refined voice of his.

Neely stared at him over the rim of her glass, wanting to blurt out that she'd dreamed about him, that she wondered why. But she only nodded.

"These 'powerful enemies' of yours," he said, watching her in a way that made her feel like some unparalleled work of art. "Can you tell me who they are?"

She sighed and sank back in the chair, slouching, running one index finger around the rim of the snifter. "It might not be wise to do that," she mused after a long time. "It's dangerous to know too much."

One moment he was halfway across the room, the next, Aidan was crouching beside her chair.

"It's often more dangerous not knowing enough, don't you think?"

Neely felt a purely elemental pull toward him and turned her head slightly in order to protect herself. She sighed. "I used to work for a United States senator," she said. "He was involved in some very crooked deals, and I gathered enough proof to put him, and the creeps he was dealing with, out of business. Or so I thought." Out of the corner of her eye she saw that he was looking at the base of her throat, and she felt a sudden and inexplicable desire to surrender to the dark magic she saw in his eyes. "Now it appears that they've decided to make sure I can't cause any more trouble," she finished shakily in a distracted tone.

He bolted away from her with unsettling swiftness. Had he been anyone other than who he was, Neely would have thought he hadn't heard her explanation, but she knew very little got by Aidan, whether he appeared to be paying attention or not.

"It will require some thought—your predicament, I mean," he said gravely, avoiding her gaze. "Please, make yourself comfortable. I'll bring the car to the front of the house in a few minutes. I don't use it often, so the engine will need some time to warm up."

Neely nodded, feeling both relief and disappointment at the prospect of being separated from him.

"Thank you," she said.

Aidan left the room.

Neely waited, then raised herself out of the chair, supporting her weight with one hand and clutching the empty snifter in the other. Her legs were still trembling, and the small injury she'd done to her shin earlier stung like crazy, but the brandy had definitely restored her. And none of those things were of any consequence at all in comparison to the emotions and yearnings Aidan Tremayne brought out in her.

She crossed to Aidan's desk and set the snifter down.

There was a music box sitting just to the left of the blotter, and Neely automatically reached for it, wanting to think of something else, if only for a moment, to shift her thoughts from the master of that spooky old house.

Besides, she had a collection of such boxes tucked away in a rented storage unit, along with most of her other belongings. The small mechanisms and delicate tunes had always appealed to her.

This one was clearly antique, perhaps dating back to the early nineteenth century. The case was carved of the finest rosewood, and there were tiny forest animals etched into its top.

Neely lifted the lid, and the tinkling notes of an old tune rose from inside. She trembled, and her heart lurched painfully.

It was the same melody she'd heard in her dream.

With a little cry Neely closed the music box and stepped back.

"Is something wrong?" an unfamiliar male voice inquired.

Neely whirled, one shock compounding with another. She had never seen the man standing behind her; he was enormous, imposing, and, she supposed, handsome, with his rich chestnut hair and discerning violet eyes. She clasped one hand to her chest and made an inarticulate sound.

"I've frightened you." With a calm, easy smile the man bowed his head. "I apologize."

Neely was still shaken, but she was beginning to regain her equilibrium. She would work out the music box thing later, she decided. As for the man's sudden appearance, well, that was easily explained. The Tremayne house was large, and Aidan hadn't said he was alone there. She had simply assumed that.

"My name is Valerian. Yours?"

"Neely," she said, still breathing fast. Could this man be the same one who had chased her into the woods? No— she'd been watching too much television and reading too many thrillers, that was all. This guy was hardly the sort to go rambling through the trees in the dead of night, and it was impossible to imagine him behind the wheel of a Blazer. "Neely Wallace."

"A pleasure," he said, taking Neely's hand, which she didn't recall extending, and barely brushing the knuckles with his lips.

A shiver went through her, part pleasure and part primal fear. She felt light-headed, almost as if she'd been hypnotized. She wrenched back her hand just as Aidan entered the room again, bringing the scents of fresh air and snow with him.

He looked at Valerian but spoke to Neely.

"The car is ready," he said. His tone was terse.

Neely nodded and scrambled into her coat, eager to be away. And, if she was to be honest, eager to be alone with Aidan again.

A white English sports car, a Triumph Spitfire with a canvas top and plenty of chrome, waited in front of the house. Aidan opened the passenger door for Neely before going around to the driver's side and sliding behind the wheel.

"What's going on around here?" she demanded, surprising even herself with the bluntness of the question. It seemed her troubled subconscious mind had decided to make a move on its own, bypassing the usual channels. "Aidan, I had a very strange, very vivid dream last night, about you. We danced, you and I, to an old-fashioned tune, one I'm certain I've never heard before. Tonight I lifted the lid of that music box on your desk, and out came that very same song."

Aidan shifted the expensive car into gear and stepped on the accelerator. The machine navigated the snowy driveway with ease. "Coincidence," he said, but he didn't so much as glance in her direction.

"No," Neely insisted. She was certain of that one conviction, if nothing else. "I couldn't remember the dream—it drove me crazy all day long—but when I heard that tune, everything came back to me. You and I were dancing. And—and I'm not sure now that it really *was* a dream. What's going on here, Aidan?" She paused to gather her courage. "Am I imagining the attraction between us?" she asked in a small but determined voice.

He shifted again, and the car fishtailed slightly but quickly regained its traction. "No," he said, with succinct reluctance, and in spite of all the danger she was in, Neely felt a rush of wild, flamboyant joy. She wanted Aidan to kiss her again, the way he had in the dream or delusion, whatever it had been, but he didn't even glance in her direction.

"We're playing for very high stakes, here—much higher than you can possibly imagine. You must keep yourself safe, inasmuch as you can, and most of all you have to trust me."

She sighed and settled back in the leather seat, clasping her hands in her lap and memorizing his profile. "Well," she said. "That was certainly cryptic. Why do I get the feeling you don't intend to explain?"

At last he looked at her, and even though he kept his distance, Neely had the oddest sensation that she'd just been soundly kissed. The incident left her dizzy and wanting Aidan with an embarrassing desperation.

"I will explain everything when I can," he said kindly.

Neely touched her fingertips to her lips, which were still tingling from a kiss that hadn't happened.

Aidan lifted one corner of his mouth in a teasing and damnably mysterious smile. "I can do other things as well," he said, leaving her even more mystified than before. "One of these nights I'll show you."

Neely blushed and barely kept herself from blurting out that she wanted him to show her all his tricks, then and there.

They had reached the highway, and Aidan made a right turn, chuckling to himself as if he'd heard her thoughts. She squirmed as the small, sleek car shot toward the Lakeview Trailer Court and Motel.

Neely looked around, forcing herself to think of something besides the inexplicable need Aidan had managed to stir in her.

There was no sign of the Blazer; the only other vehicle they encountered was a county snowplow.

Aidan turned onto the gravel road that wound through the trailer court and came to a stop at Neely's door.

She felt as awkward as a teenage wallflower at the biggest dance of the year. She wanted Aidan to touch her and at the same time was terrified that he would. She opened the car door hastily and climbed out. "Good night," she said cheerfully. "And thank you."

He left the car, walked Neely to her door, and waited patiently until she was inside. "Good night," he said formally, although something mischievous smoldered in his eyes all the while, as she closed the door.

It was only after Aidan had driven away, the taillights of his car blinking red in an otherwise white night, that she realized she'd never told him which trailer was hers.

"Hunt with me," Valerian pleaded as Aidan tossed his car keys into a china dish on the bookshelf behind his desk. His attention was focused on the music box.

"I've already fed," he replied, picking up the little rose-wood case and lifting the lid.

"Then feed again," Valerian said.

At last Aidan lifted his gaze. "Why? You know I abhor it."

Valerian sighed. "Yes," he agreed. "But a surplus may heighten your powers. It is more important than ever that you be strong, Aidan."

Now it was Aidan who sighed. "Another dire warning," he said, returning the box to its place. "What would you have me do? Become a hedonist as well as a heretic, like you?"

The other vampire slammed his hands down hard on the top of Aidan's desk, making the music box and several other items jump. "Spare me the moral discourse," Valerian rasped, his eyes seeming to burn like Saint Elmo's fire as he glared at Aidan from under his heavy brows. "Others have seen Lisette. She is beginning to circulate."

Aidan shoved a hand through his hair. "Perhaps the thing to do is confront her," he said.

Valerian shook his head. "In your present state, that

would be disastrous. Lisette is the queen of all vampires, the first female ever created. Even after a long sleep, her powers will be formidable."

Aidan's mind touched on Neely, on her softness and warmth. He had to protect her, and the best way to do that was to leave twentieth-century Connecticut entirely. "All right," he conceded raggedly, "I'll put myself in your hands, Valerian. We'll feed together, and I'll at least listen to your counsel. I want one promise from you first, however."

The elder vampire did not speak but simply raised one eyebrow in silent question.

"You must give me your sacred vow that you will not come back for the woman."

Valerian made an exasperated sound. "I presume you mean Neely Wallace."

"You presume correctly. I saw the way you looked at her, and I know what you were thinking. I want your word that you'll leave her alone."

Valerian laughed, but there was no mirth in the sound and certainly no joy. He raised one large hand as if to swear an oath. "I will not feed on the waitress," he said. There was a pause. "Just remember, Aidan. I cannot speak for the others."

"They won't bother Neely unless you call their attention to her."

"I could say the same thing to you, my friend." With that, Valerian raised both his arms high in the air and made a sweeping and wholly theatrical gesture.

Chapter 5

―•→✦✕✦←•―

V alerian was not without sympathy for Aidan, and a
number of other emotions in the bargain. Indeed, he
loved the younger vampire jealously, and with a devotion
and tenderness that transcended all earthly meanings of
the term.

Which was not to say he did not consider the poor fiend
to be wholly misguided. While he himself had been a
vampire for nearly six centuries, and a happy one for the
most part, Valerian also cherished certain recollections of
humanity. There was the warmth of spring sunlight on
winter-pale flesh, for instance, the oddly pleasurable sensation of an explosive sneeze, the sweet ache that followed in
the wake of unrestrained laughter, the solace of tears. Now,
as they sat in the rear of a dingy London pub, pretending
to consume ale and kidney pie, savoring those last precious
moments before they would be forced underground, Valerian reached out to touch his companion's arm.

Aidan, who had been staring morosely into space ever since they'd left the battlefield where they'd fed last, started slightly.

"Do you really hate it so much?" Valerian asked in a low and, for him, somewhat fragile voice. He could not credit Aidan's aversions; in all his wide experience he had never encountered another vampire who did not relish what he was.

Aidan forced a smile; he was a handsome lad, and he stirred things in Valerian's being that were probably better left alone, but he lacked the sensual abandon of most immortal creatures. "Yes," he said. He was pleasantly flushed from their recent feast, but there was a look of anguish in his eyes, of torment that far exceeded any felt by the dying soldiers they'd seen that night. "Yes, I hate it. I despise it. Hell itself cannot be worse than feeling this vile compulsion!"

Had anyone else made such a statement, Valerian would have asked archly why they had troubled to become a creature of the night in the first place, but this was Aidan. Aidan, the one blood-drinker he knew who had not made the transition willingly. He sighed, turning his plain wooden cup idly in one hand. "What would you have me do? What is it you want?"

There was a quickening in Aidan; he sat a little straighter in his chair, and his blue eyes glittered with something more than the temporary fever caused by feeding. "You are the oldest vampire in our circle, except for Lisette," he said quietly, "and among the most self-serving. If there is a remedy for this wretched curse, you either know what it is or how to find out."

Valerian looked away for a moment, toward one of two small, filthy windows. A subtle grayness permeated the black of night; dawn was near, and they must take refuge very soon, or the sun would catch them abroad. "I heard a legend once," he said in a ragged, distracted whisper. "Mind you, it was only a story, I'm sure of that—"

Aidan rose and seemed to loom over him. "Tell me!" he demanded.

Again Valerian sighed. "There is no time," he replied, hoping he'd disguised his relief in feigned regret. "It's almost morning." He rose and looked Aidan squarely in the eye. "Come. I know a place where we can rest safely."

He reached out, clasped Aidan's arm, and gripped it hard when the other vampire moved to pull away. In the space of a wink they were inside a crypt in a country churchyard, far from busy, suspicious London.

"Damn you!" Aidan cried, lunging toward Valerian with his hands out, as if to choke the life from him. Which was, of course, a macabre joke, since he was neither truly alive nor truly dead. "Tell me what you know of this legend!"

Valerian raised his arms, erecting a mental barrier between them, like a wall of glass. He smiled at Aidan's frustration and then yawned copiously. "I am too weary to tell tales," he said. "We will speak of it when the eventide comes again."

With that, Valerian turned to a stone slab, brushed away the bones and dust and the debris of a coffin that had rested there, and stretched out with a sensual sigh. He saw Aidan hesitate, then slowly, reluctantly recede, until his back touched the crypt's heavy door. He slipped into a crouch, his arms folded across his knees.

"Until evening," Aidan said. There was a warning in his tone, though his words were weighted with fatigue.

Valerian smiled again and slowly closed his eyes. Unlike younger, less sophisticated vampires, he was not totally lost to sleep; he often dreamed and sometimes projected his awareness to other places, leaving his physical self behind.

Such journeys were unquestionably dangerous, for the silver cord that anchored the spirit to the form could be severed in any number of ways. If that happened, the two could never be rejoined, and the traveler would be forced to contend with whatever fate awaited him in the next world.

The mere contemplation of such an event was a terror to sensible vampires, for even they could not see beyond the Veil to determine the true shapes of heaven and hell.

Far down in the deepest regions of his comalike rest, Valerian shuddered at the visions of eternal torment that had been impressed on his mind so long before, while he lived and breathed as a human animal. Since he had been born in medieval England, the images Valerian carried of the damned were especially horrible.

Still, he was an adventurous vampire, interminably curious, and he loved to explore the dusty little corners and pockets of time that generally went unnoticed in the great intertwining schemes of history.

And there was a secret.

Valerian loved secrets, and mysteries, and conundrums of all sorts, shapes, and sizes. All the better that only he and a handful of other old ones knew. By concentrating very hard, Valerian could cast his consciousness into the most remote folds and burrows of eternity, venturing back and back in time, passing beyond his mortal life and even his birth as a human being.

It was perilous work, utterly debilitating, often leaving him too exhausted to hunt for days afterward. Even so, Valerian could not resist occasional forays through the void, each time venturing closer to the Beginning.

That particular day he had an added impetus, bittersweet and compelling; he sought the oldest, most closely guarded secrets of the vampire, for only in finding those could he learn what Aidan so desperately wanted to know.

At nightfall Aidan stirred, opened his eyes, and raised himself slowly out of his crouch against the wall and into an upright position. Valerian still lay on his slab in the middle of the crypt, though he was awake, and he looked shrunken somehow. Even gaunt.

His flesh was a ghastly shade of gray, and there were great shadows beneath his eyes. He raised one hand weakly, to summon Aidan to his side, and even though there were no tears, it was plain that he was weeping deep down in the essence of himself.

Aidan clasped Valerian's upraised hand in both of his; they were not friends, but they were of the same brotherhood, they trod on common ground.

"What is it?" Aidan whispered. "What have you done?"

"I went back—to search—" He paused, made a strangling sound low in his throat. "Blood. I—need—blood." The plea rasped in Valerian's throat like a saw severing hardwood. He clutched Aidan's fingers so tightly that it seemed the bones would snap, brittle as twigs, drawing Aidan downward to hear, "Bring me blood."

Aware of an inexplicable urgency, and very little else, Aidan did not pause to question the gruesome request. He went to the door of the crypt, stopped to look backward once, and then willed himself to a time and place in London he'd often visited before.

He returned within minutes, burgeoning with the blood of a back-street thief and murderer. By instinct, or perhaps by some subliminal instruction from the still-stricken Valerian, he transfused the life-giving fluid into the other vampire by puncturing the papery neck with his fangs. The process left Aidan temporarily weakened, clutching the edges of the slab to keep from falling, and only partially restored Valerian.

The elder vampire sighed and slipped into a light, fitful slumber. His skin, which had looked as fragile as ancient parchment before, took on the faintest tinge of color, and his frame seemed to fill out slightly, having fewer hollows and sharp angles.

Now that the crisis had passed, whatever it had been, Aidan was wild with impatience. He paced at the foot of Valerian's slab, feeling confined and restless to the very core of his soul. The mere memory of his strange communion with the other vampire sickened him, and yet he could not deny, even to himself, that there had been some sort of fusion of their two spirits.

After a while Valerian stirred and opened his eyes. He seemed stronger, but his whisper was labored and raw. "Leave me, Aidan. I must rest."

It was all Aidan could do not to grasp his companion's lapels and wrench him upright, so desperate was his need. "You promised to tell me what you learned!" he blurted. "You *promised!*"

"And I will keep my vow," Valerian answered, grating out each word. "I cannot—speak of it now. Have pity, Aidan."

"Just tell me this," Aidan pressed, moving to Valerian's side, clasping his cold hand. "Is there hope? Can I be unmade, become a man again?"

The answer gurgled on Valerian's tongue, as though he were choking on the blood Aidan had given him. "It is too—dangerous," he gasped. With that he lost consciousness again.

Aidan was torn between a desire to stay and look after a fallen comrade and an almost uncontrollable urge to flee, to be as far from this place and this horror as possible.

He wanted Neely, wanted her to comfort him, to hold him tightly in her arms. He craved her humanity and her warmth, her very womanhood, but it was just that yearning that forestalled him.

Yes, he loved her, he knew that now, had begun to accept the realization. But he could not allow himself to forget that he was a beast, at least in part, and his need for blood was as great as that of any other vampire. He couldn't be certain, for all that his soul had already joined itself to hers, that his terrible thirst would not cause him to fling himself on her in a fit of passion.

The prospect of awakening from a frenzy, of finding Neely limp and lifeless in his arms, was worse than any punishment a demon could devise.

Frantically Aidan formed Maeve's image in his mind.

Neely had just finished the breakfast shift at the café when an ancient station wagon rattled into the parking lot, came to a shrill, steamy stop by the front window, and emitted a tall, gum-chewing blonde. The woman was wearing frayed jeans, an equally worn denim jacket, a tank top with a picture of a motorcycle on the front, and the kind of open, friendly smile that turns strangers into friends.

"Hi," she said, taking a seat at the counter and reaching out to pluck a menu from behind a chrome napkin holder. "My name's Doris Craig. I'm flitter-flat, down-and-out busted, and that old car of mine isn't gonna go much farther. You the manager here?"

Neely untied her apron, glancing past Doris's right shoulder, which bore a tiny tattoo of a bumblebee, to the loaded-down beater parked out front. But for its relatively modern vintage, the vehicle might have belonged to the Jode family of *Grapes of Wrath* fame, there was so much stuff tied on top and stuffed inside.

"No," she answered. "My brother manages the whole place. I just work here."

Doris closed the menu resolutely and gave Neely another of her guileless, openhearted smiles. "You aren't thinkin' of quittin' or anything, are you? If you are, I'd sure like to have your job."

Ben hadn't said he was looking for more help, but he hadn't said he wasn't, either. Neely poured a cup of hot, fresh coffee and set it down in front of Doris. "I think of quitting for the last three hours of every shift," she confessed with a grin, tapping her name tag with one finger. "I'm Neely Wallace. Glad to meet you."

Doris nodded cordially. "If you're not plannin' to quit," she said, blue eyes twinkling, "is there any chance of your gettin' fired?"

Neely laughed. "Sorry—like I said, the boss is my brother, and he's pretty well stuck with me. I'll be happy to send him over to talk to you, though. In the meantime, what'll you have?"

Doris pried two crumpled dollar bills from the pocket of her jeans and smoothed them out on the counter. "Soup and milk, if this will cover it," she said. While her circumstances were obviously desperate, there wasn't a trace of self-pity in either her voice or her manner, and Neely couldn't help being struck by such uncommon courage.

She nodded and went back to the kitchen, passing the teenager who was taking over for the afternoon and early evening shift. Heather was no unchained melody of ambition, but she showed up on time and did her job well enough, which meant she probably wouldn't be creating a vacancy anytime soon.

In the back Neely dished up a bowlful of vegetable-beef soup and grabbed a basket of soda crackers in individual wrappers. She set the food down in front of Doris, along with a spoon, and proceeded to the milk machine.

She was just putting the glass on the counter when the little bell over the door jingled and Ben came in. He'd been shoveling snow from the walk over at the motel, and his cheeks were red from the cold.

It seemed providential to Neely, his showing up at the perfect moment like that. "Ben, this is Doris Craig," she said. "Doris, my brother, Ben Wallace. Doris is looking for work."

Ben's ever-ready smile flashed instantly; he took off his plaid coat and came over to greet Doris, one hand extended. Neely poured him a cup of coffee, then grabbed her purse, said good-bye to Heather, and hurried out.

As far as she could tell, glancing back through the frosty café window, Ben hadn't even noticed that she was gone.

Neely was deep in thought as she crossed the parking lot. Maybe the fates were trying to tell her something, sending Doris along when they had. Perhaps it was time she got on with her life; she was only marking time in Bright River, and she could no longer overlook the fact that she represented a very real danger to her brother and nephew.

Because of her distraction, Neely all but collided with the dun-colored rental car that was parked just on the other side of the hedge, motor running. There was a whirring sound, and the window on the passenger side disappeared into the door. Senator Dallas Hargrove himself leaned across the front seat and said, "Get in, Neely."

In spite of all the senator had been a party to, and all she had done to ensure his intense dislike for all eternity, Neely still couldn't believe he would actually hurt her. She'd seen him with his wife, Elaine, who suffered from a degenerative muscular disease, and knew there was no violence in him. She drew a deep breath, let it out in a rush, and got into the car.

The senator was handsome, with well-cut blond hair and a square jaw, but there had never been an attraction between them. "That was pretty stupid," he said, steering the car onto Route 7 and away from Bright River. "For all you know, I might be planning to knock you over the head and dump you in some lake."

Neely relaxed against the seat and closed her eyes for a moment. She was so tired all of a sudden, so full of a longing she couldn't begin to understand. "You've made some terrific mistakes in your life, Senator," she said, "but you're not a murderer. Not a direct one, at least."

She could feel his tension; he was like tightly coiled wire, ready to come unwound. Still, she wasn't afraid.

"What do you mean, 'not a direct one'?" he demanded.

"We both know you've fixed it so that certain drug dealers can bring their wares into the country without the usual inconveniences," Neely answered with a sigh. "What do you think is happening to that garbage after it hits the streets? Real people are using it—kids, pregnant mothers, people who get behind the wheels of semi-trucks and school buses."

"If I didn't cooperate, someone else would." Hargrove's knuckles tightened on the steering wheel, relaxed again.

Neely reflected that her decision to get into the car with the senator might have been a bit rash after all. "That's a load of horse crap," she replied calmly. "Let's not waste our time debating the subject, since we'll never agree. What are you doing in Bright River? You can't be stumping for votes, since this isn't your district."

He turned the car off the highway onto a bumpy, unplowed road that snaked in behind a large Christmas tree farm. He stopped the car beside a weathered old mill spanning a narrow, silvery brook. His blue eyes were tormented as he looked at Neely. "Look, I came here to warn you. The people I deal with know you tried to bring the FBI down on their operation, and they want you dead. You've got to get out of here as fast as you can."

Neely regarded him in pensive silence for a time, her arms folded. "There's something I don't understand," she finally said. "I gave the government hard evidence of your involvement in a major crime syndicate. If your man on the inside hadn't managed to turn the tide—at least, that's what I *think* must have happened—you would have lost everything and gone to prison, maybe for the rest of your life. Why are you trying so hard to save me? How come you don't hate me and want me dead, like those hoods you've been hanging around with?"

Hargrove gave a despairing rush of a sigh and leaned forward, letting his forehead rest against the steering wheel. "I'm not a killer, Neely—I never meant for things to turn out this way. I needed money—there were so many debts— and then I was in too deep to get out."

"Debts? For Elaine's medical care, you mean? Come on. Thanks to the long-suffering taxpayer, you have a more than respectable salary and excellent health insurance."

The senator sat up straight, gazing out at the snow-laced mill wheel. The weathered building supporting it seemed about to cave in on itself. "There were all those special treatments, in Europe and Mexico," he said. "None of them worked, of course."

Impulsively Neely reached across the seat to touch his arm. She liked Elaine Hargrove, a brave and smiling person, liked the man the senator became whenever he was in his wife's presence.

"It wasn't just the treatments, though," Hargrove confessed wearily. "When Elaine was first diagnosed, I went a little crazy. I don't know what it was—the fear, the stress— I can't say. In any case, I was involved with a woman for a while, and then there were some gambling debts. . . ."

Neely had known about the woman, but the gambling was a new element. She closed her eyes for a few moments while she assimilated everything. "And I thought *I* was in trouble," she said.

"We're both in trouble," Hargrove replied. "Don't forget that for a moment, Neely. Get your things together and get out of here before they come after you!"

She nodded slowly. Although Neely wanted fiercely to live, just as she always had, it wasn't self-preservation that pushed her over the line, causing her to make the decision she'd been putting off. It was the knowledge that Ben and Danny would be in terrible danger as long as she stuck around.

From out of nowhere, like a careening vehicle, came the thought that she might never see Aidan Tremayne again. She tried to sidestep the realization, but it crashed into her full force, and she gave a soft cry of despair on impact.

Hargrove had turned the car around and was on the way back to the highway again before she could speak.

"You've got to turn yourself in," she said. "Sure, the sky will fall in, and there will be hell to pay, but at least you'll be alive—and free of those awful people."

The senator was shaking his head even before she'd finished the sentence. "No," he told her. "The publicity, the scandal, would be torture for Elaine. She'd never survive it!"

Sadly Neely thought of the once-vibrant Elaine Hargrove. She'd been a famous television journalist, still active and vocal about her opinions even after her sudden immersion into political life. Then, just two years before, she'd started feeling tired and having episodes of unusual awkwardness. The diagnosis was grim, the prognosis, terrible. Elaine had been going downhill, physically at least, from the very first. Neely looked out the window for a few seconds, struggling with emotions of her own—horror, pity, and, yes, God forgive her, a certain savage gratitude that *she* hadn't been the one to be struck down that way.

"I think your wife is a whole lot stronger than you give her credit for," she said.

"She's had to endure enough suffering as it is," Hargrove said. "Once it's all over, and she's—she's at peace, then I'll go to the authorities with the truth." The rental car bumped onto the highway and fishtailed slightly on the ice-coated asphalt. The senator's attention was fixed on Neely. "I'll do anything to protect Elaine," he told her. "Anything."

Neely understood. "You've done your duty by warning me," she replied, "and now I'm on my own. Does that about cover it?"

Hargrove nodded. They rounded a bend, and the café sign came into view, a symbol of everything ordinary. Just then Neely would have paid practically any price to have a mundane life again, uncomplicated by desperate politicians, vengeful drug dealers, and her unremitting fascination with Aidan Tremayne.

They came to a stop in front of Neely's trailer, and Hargrove looked around nervously. Then he reached into the inside pocket of his jacket and took out an envelope. "Here—take this cash and get as far away as you can, as quickly as possible."

Neely didn't want to accept the money, knowing only too well where it had come from, but her choices were limited. She'd put aside a little over the past few years, but it was mostly in long-term CDs, and she wouldn't be able to get to it without drawing unwanted attention to herself.

"Thanks," she said without checking the contents of the envelope or looking directly at the senator. She opened the car door and got out, and even before the sound of the engine had died away, Neely was packing a suitcase.

When that was done, she borrowed Ben's truck and went to town to pick Danny up in front of the school. He beamed when he saw her and broke away from his friends, who were boarding a bus.

"Hi," he said, flinging himself onto the springy leather seat beside her. "What's the deal?" Danny paused and frowned. "I don't have to go to the dentist again, do I?"

Neely shook her head and smiled, but at the same time she fought back tears. "No, you're done with dentistry for a while, kid. I do have news, though, and frankly I'm a little worried about how you're going to take it."

Danny's freckles stood out against his pale skin. "Those bad dudes are after you, aren't they?"

Neely drove down Main Street, past the drugstore, the Sweetie-Freeze drive-in, the library, and the bank. She was going to miss this town, but not as much as she'd miss Danny and Ben. She frowned. "What do you know about anybody being after me?"

"I heard you and Dad talking once."

Neely eyed the sheriff's office as they passed and wished she could solve the problem by stopping in and reporting the situation, but she knew that wouldn't work. If the FBI hadn't come through for her, she could hardly expect protection from an aging, overweight sheriff with one part-time deputy. No, her only real hope was to get her copies of the evidence against Dallas Hargrove and the others and turn it over to the media. The trick would be in staying alive long enough to pull it off.

She reached across the seat and ruffled Danny's soft brown hair. "I should have known I couldn't keep something like this from a super-detective like you."

There were tears in Danny's eyes. "You'll come back sometime, won't you?"

Neely was possessed of a sudden and rather ill-advised fit of optimism. Incredible as the prospect seemed, she had to make herself believe she was going to survive this mess—if she didn't, the terror of it all would immobilize her. "You bet," she sniffled. "Once the good guys get their licks in, everything will be okay again. In the meantime, I want you to promise me two things—that you'll say a prayer for me every single night, and that you'll look after your dad."

Danny offered a high five, and Neely completed the gesture. Now all she had to do was tell Ben good-bye, grab her suitcase, and hit the road. She wished she could see Aidan once more as well, but time was short. Besides, she hardly knew the man.

Five hours later Neely was headed north in the car she'd bought from Doris Craig. Saying good-bye to Ben hadn't been easy, but he'd urged her to disappear as quickly as possible, pressing all the money from the restaurant till into the pocket of her peacoat.

She'd turned her trailer and her job over to Doris and set out in Doris's old clunker of a car, making only one brief stop before leaving Bright River to ring Aidan Tremayne's doorbell. She'd hoped to bid him farewell, but he evidently wasn't at home.

Neely scribbled a note on the back of an expired registration found in the glove box of Doris's car, stuck the paper in the frame of Aidan's front door, and fled.

Twilight was gathering by the time the town of Bright River fell away behind her.

Maeve was visiting the Havermails at their estate in the English countryside, circa 1895. She was embroiled in a game of croquet, played by the light of thousands of colorful paper lanterns, when Aidan materialized at her elbow.

With a little cry Maeve started and accidentally tapped the croquet ball wide of the wire hoop she'd been aiming for. "Great Scot, Aidan," she hissed, "I hate it when you do that!"

He clasped her arm, heedless of the staring guests, and yanked her toward the shrubbery. "It's Valerian—he's found some way to change a vampire into a man," he told her.

Maeve stared at him, letting her wooden mallet topple forgotten onto the grass. "What?"

Aidan began to pace, unable to stand still because of the torturous agitation the knowledge had roused in him. "He's ill—I gave him blood—he sent me away without telling me—"

"Aidan, *stop*," Maeve pleaded, reaching out and clasping his shoulders in her extraordinarily white and graceful hands. "What in the world are you talking about? There is no way to change a vampire into a man—is there?"

"Yes," Aidan said. Now he couldn't contain his joy. Dear God, the very thought of it—breathing, having a heartbeat, living by daylight, loving Neely freely and fathering her children, and, when the time came, dying. In peace. "Yes! He says it's dangerous, but—"

"Would you truly become a mortal again, even if such a thing were possible?" Maeve whispered, plainly stricken.

He paused before answering, looking deep into his sister's eyes. He loved her with the whole of his being, and it was torment to think of such a chasm opening between them, but the bright, shining prospect of redemption blinded him to everything but itself.

"Yes," he whispered. "Oh, God in heaven, *yes*."

Maeve lifted her chin, but her lower lip was trembling. "You would leave me, Aidan? You want so much to be a mortal that you would turn your back on your own sister, for all eternity? Such a thing would make enemies of us." She stopped and with visible effort took control of her emotions. She even managed to smile. "I don't know why I'm worrying," she said, her voice brittle and bright. "Vampires are vampires, darling. They cannot be men just for wishing, any more than they can be angels. Come—I want you to meet the Havermails."

Aidan allowed Maeve to loop her arm through his and escort him across the lawn and into one of the estate's many fragrant gardens, where the mistress of the great house held court. Mrs. Havermail, like her husband and her two children, who gave new weight and substance to the term *brat,* was a creature of the night, and she showed her fangs and made a soft hissing sound as the newest guest approached.

Chapter 6

— ❧ ❧ —

Doris's rattletrap of a car seemed to stagger along the interstate, coughing, flinging itself forward in a wild, smoky burst of fumes and fervor, nearly stalling, then shuddering with the effort to begin the whole process all over again. A little after midnight Neely pulled into the parking lot of a tacky motel and, with no small amount of trepidation, turned off the engine. If the motor wouldn't start in the morning, she told herself wearily, she would abandon the heap with no real regrets and step onto a bus.

Maybe that would be better anyway, she thought, taking her purse and overnight case and heading for the front office. A neon sign burned dimly in the window, announcing a vacancy.

The clerk was a taciturn Yankee woman, clad in a chenille bathrobe and furry slippers that looked as though they might be developing mange, and she was none too pleased to be awakened.

Neely signed the register with a false name, purposely illegible, and paid cash. She was given a key with a red plastic tag emblazoned with a *6*.

The room was small and smelled vaguely of mildew and stale cigarette smoke, but Neely was far too tired and distraught to care about amenities. As long as the sheets and the bathroom were clean, she could overlook the rest.

After carefully putting the chain lock on the door, she undressed, put on a nightgown, brushed her teeth and splashed her face with warm water, then toppled into bed. She was exhausted, both emotionally and physically, and unconsciousness offered a welcome respite from reality.

Lying in the darkness, she found herself longing for Aidan. The desire was not merely sexual, though there could be no denying, at least in the privacy of her own mind, that she wanted him with a wild, primitive, even violent sort of ardor. No, there was much more to her yearning; it was complex, a living thing rooted in the very core of her spirit, spreading graceful vines into her mind and heart and even into the deepest recesses of her unconscious.

Despite her loneliness, life had never seemed sweeter or more precious to Neely. There were so many things she wanted to see and feel and do—not the least of which was to give herself to Aidan—and now she was probably going to die.

Neely turned onto her stomach, buried her face in the musty pillow, and wept, softly at first. Soon, however, her sniffles turned to unrestrained howls as she grieved for a future that might well be denied her.

In the charcoal-smudged hours just before dawn, something awakened Neely, a feeling rather than a sound. She lifted her head from the pillow, squinted into the darkness, felt a twinge at the realization that she was not at home in her trailer, but on the road, and running.

She groped for her watch, which was lying on the

nightstand, and peered at the numbers.

3:20 A.M.

With a sigh, Neely rolled onto her back and, in the next second let out a low, croaky cry.

A cloaked form towered at the foot of the bed.

"Oh, God," Neely whimpered. She didn't want to think the shadowy shape belonged to one of the senator's business associates or some serial rapist, but the possibilities had to be considered.

She had just made up her mind to fight the intruder with everything she had when a familiar voice spoke.

"Don't be afraid."

Neely snapped on the bedside lamp and gasped. She blinked hard, but when she looked again, Aidan Tremayne was still standing there, smiling at her.

She was at once wildly relieved and totally mystified. Had she conjured an image of him somehow, by entertaining all those scandalous sexual fantasies just after she went to bed?

Neely scrambled to the foot of the mattress, tugged at his cloak to assure herself that it had substance, and then hurtled back to the other end.

"It *is* you," she said in a tone that was almost accusing.

"Quite so," he replied gently, folding his arms.

Neely swallowed hard. She was at once terrified, sensing in her deepest being that Aidan had not entered her room by ordinary means, and at the same time wanting him to hold and caress and finally take her.

"Damn it, what's going on here?" she cried impatiently.

Aidan raised both hands, palms out, in a conciliatory, calming gesture. "I'm about to tell you the absolute and unvarnished truth. After that, you'll understand why I've been somewhat . . . secretive. First, though, I believe I'd best keep a promise I made not so long ago."

"What promise?" Neely whispered, but she knew. She

knew, and her body, suddenly shameless after a lifetime of relative modesty, was already burning.

Aidan arched one eyebrow to show he wasn't buying her attempt at ingenuousness. "Among my other talents, my darling, I can read minds. You want me to make love to you—is that not so?"

Neely gulped. "What if it is?" she finally managed.

He smiled. "Not good enough, Neely," he scolded. "If you want me to give you pleasure, you will have to say so, straight out. Whatever my other sins, I do not take women against their wishes."

Neely stared at him, fascinated, her whole body thrumming with the need of him and his intimate attentions. "I—I want you," she said.

Aidan did not move from his place at the foot of the bed, and yet Neely felt herself being pressed gently back onto the pillows. After that came light, tantalizing kisses, unseen lips grazing her mouth, nibbling at her earlobe and the side of her neck, tracing pathways of passion across the rounded tops of her breasts.

She moaned, overwhelmed by her need, too caught up in the sensations that were being evoked inside her to question the strange detachment of Aidan's lovemaking. Even as her nightshirt was gently removed, and her slender body lay bared to whatever magic he was working upon it, she could dimly see that he was still standing some distance away.

Impossible—he was touching her, kissing her, teasing her, everywhere. Wasn't he?

He told her to part her legs for him, and she did, though she could not have said whether the command had been spoken aloud or had simply come sauntering into her mind on its own.

Neely felt his hand, nimble-fingered and firm, brush the nest of curls hiding the physical center of her wanting. Incredibly she felt his touch in her soul as well, and the tension building there was even more tumultuous than the sweet, frightening eruption rising in her body.

She arched her back to welcome him and whispered, "Yes! Oh, yes . . ." as he uncovered the hidden nubbin of flesh and gently toyed with it. "Please," she whimpered, having lost all semblance of pride, tumbling toward a spiritual release of cataclysmic proportions even as an equally powerful physical climax loomed just ahead, waiting to consume her.

"Tell me what you want," Aidan said.

"I want *you*!" she cried out, not caring if anyone heard. "Oh, God, Aidan, I need you . . . the real you . . . inside me!"

Both her breasts were being suckled at once, and she felt strong, warm hands slide beneath her bottom to raise her high for the final conquering. She even felt him enter her with a hard, delicious thrust that made her cry out in ecstasy. Still, even through the fog of this all-encompassing passion, she could see that Aidan had not moved to join her on the bed, that he was watching her pleasure with a shimmer of tears in his eyes.

The crescendos were so violent, her body and her soul being satisfied in the same joyously terrifying moments, that Neely shouted aloud as she came, in involuntary triumph, lost in the glorious dual releases.

It was a very long time before she could speak or move, so completely, so thoroughly, had she been loved. But the moment arrived, finally, when the words that had been clamoring in her mind took shape on her lips.

"Why, Aidan?" she whispered. "Why did you make love to me that way, without actually touching me?"

He turned away from her briefly, and even though he held his head high, Neely knew he was overcome by emotion. Then he faced her again.

"I did not trust myself," he confessed hoarsely.

Neely managed to raise herself onto her elbows, but she

was still in a state of bliss and hadn't the energy to demand answers to all the obvious questions. "What do you mean, you didn't trust yourself?"

Aidan averted his gaze for a moment, then looked directly into her eyes again. "My passion for you is fathomless," he said. "It is wolflike, a thing of the darkness. I could not be certain of maintaining control."

She yawned, beginning to drift. "Most people lose control when they make love, Aidan," she observed. "That's the idea."

One corner of his inviting mouth lifted in a sad, rueful attempt at a smile. "Yes," he said. "But I am not a person. I am a vampire."

Neely sat bolt upright, as wide awake as if she'd just had an intravenous dose of pure caffeine. "Did you just say that you're a vampire?" she asked, sounding ridiculously cordial. A strange excitement rushed through her, along with a whisper of primitive fear.

At long last Aidan rounded the bed and sat down on its edge. "I'm afraid so," he said.

It was remarkable, incredible, his claiming to be a supernatural creature, but it made an odd kind of sense, too. After all, he'd disappeared that night, in the parking lot outside the Lakeview Café, in quite literally the blink of an eye. Furthermore, he'd just made love to her in a very extraordinary way, a way no normal man would have done.

Yes. There was surely some kind of magic at work.

He must have seen the beginnings of belief in her eyes, for his smile was less forlorn than the one that had preceded it, less weary.

"Let me see your teeth," Neely said impulsively. She was still a little afraid, but she was fascinated, too, and wildly curious.

Indulgently Aidan permitted her to lift his upper lip and peer at one shining, sharp incisor. It was obviously no ordinary tooth, so she checked its counterpart.

"Good grief," she whispered, marveling. She knew her eyes were wide with wonder as she drew back to look at him, and she felt a shiver of fear as she began the arduous process of letting herself accept the remarkable possibility that Aidan had spoken the truth. "Were you afraid you would bite me?" she asked, unconsciously laying her hands on his broad shoulders. "Is that why you didn't lie down with me?"

"That's a rather simplistic way of putting it," Aidan said, with a glint of humor in his eyes, "but yes. I was afraid of hurting you."

Neely frowned. "What about your own pleasure? Did you feel what we were doing?"

Aidan looked away, clearly embarrassed, but then met Neely's gaze again. "Holding you in my arms, entering you physically, would have been better, but yes, I took a certain amount of satisfaction from the experience."

Neely rolled her eyes. "You make it sound as if I gave you a back rub."

He smiled. "There are releases that are felt in the emotions, Neely," he said gently. "It was that way for me."

On an impulse she couldn't have explained had her very life depended on it, Neely put her arms around Aidan's neck and planted a light kiss on his cheek. His flesh felt cool and smooth beneath her lips, strangely like fine marble, and yet pliant, too. He flinched and started to move away, but Neely did not release her hold on him.

"If I trust you," she said quietly, "why can't you trust yourself? Lie down with me, Aidan. Sleep in my arms."

"I can't," he replied, and she heard unremitting anguish in his voice, felt it in his magnificent body.

Perhaps it was the ancient, elemental attraction she felt toward Aidan that made her behave so boldly in the instant that followed; Neely didn't try to analyze the decision. Still naked from his lovemaking, she raised herself onto her knees and brushed her left breast lightly across his lips which felt strangely warm and soft against her flesh. It was the only way she could think of to offer him her trust, as well as the intimate comfort he so clearly needed.

With a moan Aidan took her nipple into his mouth and suckled greedily, and Neely entangled her fingers in his dark hair and tilted her head back, feeling fresh ecstacy rise within her as she nurtured this man—this creature— that she had come to love.

"See," she told him softly as he moved to her other breast and took pleasure there, too, "you needn't be afraid—not of me, not of yourself."

He eased her backward onto the mattress and would surely have taken her, but just when Neely was ready, body and spirit, to receive him, he stopped, held himself utterly motionless, and listened with the intensity of some wild, exotic beast.

"Aidan," Neely pleaded softly.

But he raised himself from her, his attention so focused on some sound or feeling that he did not even seem aware of her presence.

"What is it?" she asked.

He gathered her into his arms and enfolded her warm nakedness within the whispering smoothness of his cloak. "I'll explain later," he promised, and then he bent and kissed Neely on the mouth. A drumming sound filled her ears, and it seemed that she was propelled outward into a dark universe, even while she lay helpless in Aidan's arms. She was made of thought alone, not flesh, and then she knew nothing.

Nothing at all.

Aidan laid the unconscious Neely gently on his bed in the house in the woods of Connecticut. The sound of her pursuers' approaching that faraway motel room still echoed in his head; by now the two men would be inside, ransacking the place, wondering how their quarry had managed to escape them.

He bent, kissed Neely tenderly on the forehead, and fought the awesome need to complete the dangerous process she had begun by taking him to her breast. The courage and sweet generosity of the gesture were beyond comprehension; he did not think he would ever fully understand why she had chosen to give him that singular joy.

"Sleep well," he whispered, tucking the blankets around her. Then he touched her cheek and whispered a command that would anchor her to the bed as effectively as the heaviest chains, for that was the only way he could think of to keep her safe. Then he vanished.

Aidan found the thugs in Neely's motel room, just as he had expected. They relished their criminality, he thought with disgust, and from what images he could glean from the recesses of their diseased minds, they hadn't even had particularly difficult childhoods. He filled the doorway, making no effort at all to hide what he was, or to be subtle about his powers.

They whirled to face him, and one of them cried out.

Aidan wanted to kill them, yearned to drain them of every glimmering red, droplet of blood, and then toss their husks aside to rot. This development unnerved him, for he was always coldly dispassionate about his victims, and what he felt now was a fiery and utterly ruthless appetite.

He crossed the room on the impetous of that thought, grasped a throat in either hand, and pressed his struggling captives to the wall.

"You may want to rethink this whole matter," he instructed politely. "It's a dangerous business, you see, involving forces and creatures you can't begin to grasp with those pitiful little snot-wads you fancy to be brains."

The thugs stared at him, mute with confusion. They were strong in a bullish sort of way and must have wondered why a lone man could render them powerless so easily.

"What the hell are you?" one of them managed to croak out.

Aidan showed his fangs then, although he personally thought it was a touch melodramatic—more Valerian's style than his own.

"Jesus Christ," murmured the first thug, while his partner fainted.

Aidan sighed. It was nearly dawn, and there was no time to go back to the Havermails and explain his sudden disappearance to Maeve, nor could he return to Neely. No, he must go to Valerian, who still lay stricken in that dusty crypt well outside of London, and it was imperative that he bring blood to give the other vampire sustenance.

Aidan eyed the two criminals before him, one awake and one unconscious. The bloodlust he'd felt earlier had turned to the purest disgust; he would have preferred to drink from rats. Regrettably, though, there was no real choice.

He fed on the larger one first, bringing him as close to death as he dared, and then lifted the smaller man and drank again.

The usual delirium of joy came over him, but it was nothing compared to what he'd felt when Neely had lain naked before him and cried out at the pleasure of his caresses.

But he could not think of her now.

Aidan blinked, and when he opened his eyes, he was in the crypt with Valerian. The sun had already risen by the time he arrived, although its light could not reach through the stone walls or the metal door, but the inevitable fatigue threatened to swallow his consciousness.

"Aidan," Valerian whispered in a hoarse, fitful murmur of joy, and groped for his hand. "Quickly—"

Aidan bent and, once again, found Valerian's throat. Black weariness clawed at him, pulled him downward, toward the filthy, bone-littered floor. He struggled back to the waiting vein and willed the blood to flow into Valerian, and it was still pouring forth when he collapsed.

Far away, yet near as the next heartbeat, Neely stirred in her soft, unfamiliar bed but did not climb toward wakefulness. She knew, on some level, that it was better to stay asleep, to wander in dark dreams. When she opened her eyes, after all, she would have to make sense of all that had happened to her in recent hours, and that was going to be virtually impossible.

Maeve found Aidan insensate on the floor of the crypt, his back to the high stone slab, his fine clothes speckled with blood. Ignoring Valerian, who stirred above their heads, she shook her brother and called his name in a frantic whisper.

He was empty and wasted, and Maeve knew he would perish if she did not save him. She ripped away the fitted cuff of her frilly shirtwaist and pressed the inside of her wrist to his lips. He resisted weakly, then drank.

After a few moments Aidan revived, opening his eyes. "Maeve," he said, giving the name the shape and substance of a sob.

She smoothed his lovely dark hair back from his wan face. "There now, you'll be fine after this. It's night, and you're strong enough to feed properly."

"Valerian," he said. "Is he all right?"

Maeve remembered the other vampire, her mentor and erstwhile friend, and rose slowly to her feet. Seeing Valerian's sunken cheeks and shadowed eyes, she clutched his hand and demanded, "What have you done?"

"Atlantis," he said. "Atlantis—"

Aidan scrambled up beside Maeve, fairly shouldering her aside to peer down into Valerian's tormented face. "What are you saying?" he rasped. "What about Atlantis?"

"That's—where it—began," Valerian managed. "The mystery lies on the lost continent—"

"Enough!" Maeve interrupted, her temper flaring. Having fed amply, she was by far the strongest of the trio, and she could afford to issue orders. "There will be no more talk of mysteries and lost continents! Can't you see that he's dying, Aidan? Don't you realize that you nearly perished yourself?"

Despair and frustration howled within Aidan like a spiritual storm. He grabbed at the bloody front of Valerian's shirt and wrenched the other vampire upward with the last of his strength. "*Tell me!*" he cried, and when Valerian remained silent, clearly too enervated to speak, Aidan wailed with all the forlorn grief of an animal caught in a trap.

Maeve whirled on him, her blue eyes, mirror-images of his own, flashing with pain. She raised one hand, fingers spread, and pressed it to his face. He felt her horrific power surge through him, like a double dose of lightning, and then he swooned.

When he awakened, he was lying on a wide-planked table, stripped to the waist. He turned his head—it felt as though a speeding locomotive had crashed into each temple at full throttle—and saw Valerian lying next to him.

"Maeve?" Aidan lifted his head. The room was dark and dank, and it had the oppressive feel of a dungeon.

"She's out hunting," answered a small, sweet voice.

Aidan relaxed for a moment, getting his bearings. Candlelight flickered over the ancient, moss-streaked walls, where rusted iron rings were bolted. "What is this place?"

A horrible parody of a child appeared at his side, a little girl with brown-gold ringlets, impossibly pale skin, and dark circles around her eyes. Her delicate fangs glinted in the candlelight.

"It's Havermail Castle," she said.

Ah, yes, Aidan recalled, despairing. The august home of Maeve's hideous friends, the Havermails—a mommy vampire, a papa vampire, and two absolutely vicious baby vampires.

He shuddered and tried to sit up, only to find himself too weak to rise.

The child laid a clammy hand on his bare chest. "You're not supposed to move," she said, and while this announcement was delivered ingenuously, it also reverberated with warning. "Neither is Mr. Valerian. You're to be our guests, until Maeve says otherwise."

"What's your name?" Aidan gasped the question, appalled at his weakness. As a mortal man, he had loved children and been able to communicate intelligently with them.

"I'm Benecia," the monster said. "And my sister is Canaan. She's gone out to hunt with Mummy, and when they come back, it will be my turn."

Valerian stirred next to Aidan, but it was plain that he was still in a stupor.

"How long have you been a vampire?" Aidan inquired of Benecia. This was a ludicrous conversation, in an even more ludicrous setting, but he was certain he would go mad if he tried to keep silent.

"Oh, a long time," Benecia replied sunnily. "Almost as long as Valerian, in fact—about five hundred and forty years."

Aidan stared at her, appalled that even a blood-drinking fiend would stoop to turning a child into a vampire. Surely hell itself could not boast of a crueler demon. "How did it happen?"

Benecia giggled, and the sound echoed eerily off the wet stone walls that had absorbed so much misery over so many centuries. "Papa was a scholar, and he joined a secret society. They met only in darkness, and he thought that was very curious, but nonetheless he was flattered to be invited, and he attended the meetings religiously. Finally he was initiated—the members made him into an immortal, like themselves. He came straight home and made Mama into a vampire, and she in turn transformed Canaan and me because she couldn't bear to be parted from us."

Aidan whispered a profanity because he did not dare to pray.

Valerian reached out and grasped his arm before he could express his opinion further, however, effectively silencing him.

Alas, Benecia was already offended. "I don't like you," she told Aidan in a sweetly vicious tone. "I don't like you at all."

"My friend is comparatively young, for a vampire," Valerian put in quickly, and with good nature aplenty. "Be patient with him, Benecia. Remember what it was to be foolish and impulsive."

Benecia's eyes were narrowed, and her searing gaze had not wavered from Aidan's face. "I'm much older than you are, and much stronger, and much smarter," she said with icy confidence. "Mind your tongue, fledgling, or I'll dangle you from a high window by your feet!"

Valerian laughed, though Aidan heard tension plainly in the sound. "Now, now, darling—is that any way to speak to a guest? Aidan is your aunt Maeve's favorite creature in all the earth. She will expect you to be pleasant to him."

Benecia subsided, but only after a snakelike hiss and a rather chilling display of her fangs. She turned and flounced away, a small horror in her pink ruffled dress; then a door slammed somewhere, and Aidan knew he and Valerian were alone.

Furthermore, Valerian was in a towering fury, the state

of his health notwithstanding. "You are truly remarkable, Mr. Tremayne, for your arrogant stupidity!"

Aidan was in no mood for a dressing-down. He'd been through enough as it was, what with all the high drama of recent nights. "I will not be threatened by a child!"

"That *child* was old when Shakespeare penned his sonnets," Valerian raged. "She can summon more power in a blink of her eyes than you've ever dreamed of attaining! Were she not mortally afraid of her beloved auntie Maeve, your head would probably be bouncing off an outside wall by now!"

Aidan gave a ragged sigh. He still had the psychic equivalent of a headache. "If Benecia is so terribly powerful," he began, "why is she afraid of Maeve?"

Valerian's chuckle was raspy, void of all humor, and hollow. "Do you know so little about your own sister, Aidan?" he scolded. "Maeve has special gifts—she lacks your aversion to the finer points of vampirism, you know—and it is said that she will someday replace Lisette as queen of the nightwalkers."

The thought made Aidan sick. He recalled Maeve as a human girl, warm and pretty and full of laughter and innocent mischief, and he came as near to weeping as a vampire is able. "You did it," he remembered as hatred pooled in his breast. "You made her into a monster, Valerian."

There was grief in the other vampire's voice, as well as resignation. "She pleaded with me," Valerian said. "She offered me her throat, and I was hungry."

Aidan had heard the story before, but even now, after two centuries, he couldn't fully accept the reality. "You might have resisted her. There were others about who could have slaked your thirst."

Valerian was growing weak again; Aidan could sense it because, for better or worse, their two beings were connected somehow, had been ever since that first sharing of blood. "We've been over this before," he answered wearily. "There is no changing it. I've been conscious for at least five minutes, Aidan. How is it that you have yet to hound me about what I learned of Atlantis?"

As incredible as it seemed, Aidan *had* forgotten about the miraculous secret that might be his salvation. His mind had been filled with thoughts of Maeve and of Neely. He rolled onto his side and reached over to clasp Valerian's arm, which was bare like his own. "Did you go there?"

Valerian shook his head slowly. "No, I tried, but I hadn't the strength. I caught glimpses of it, though, and heard the music—"

"But you discovered something."

"Yes," Valerian murmured. "Vampirism began on Atlantis, with a series of medical experiments."

"How do you know this?" Aidan demanded, tightening his grasp on Valerian's cold flesh.

"I'm not sure. The knowledge was just—there. Please, Aidan—I grow weary. Let me rest."

"Not until you tell me how to change myself back into a man!"

There was a long, horrible silence. Then Valerian answered, "You cannot. There is an antidote, but you would have to venture back even farther than I did to find it, and you are not strong enough. Resign yourself, once and for all, Aidan. You are, and shall remain, a vampire."

Chapter 7

—◦◦❋❳❋◦◦—

It took a long time to awaken, and Neely managed the task in stages, grappling her way from one level of consciousness to the next. The struggle required all the will she could summon, for the lethargy that pressed down on her was oddly blissful, a sweet sleep, peaceful and all-encompassing.

At last she persuaded her eyelids to rise.

She was lying in a strange, beautiful bed, an enormous four-poster of mahogany or some other dark wood. The canopy overhead was trimmed in exquisite ecru tatting, the sheets were the softest linen, and the coverlet was made of worn blue velvet.

Aidan's bed.

Neely remembered everything in a breathtaking rush—fleeing Bright River in Doris's old car, renting the motel room, waking to find Aidan standing at the foot of her bed. It all flooded back, the unbelievable lovemaking, his convincing claim that he was a vampire, all of it.

She gasped, stiffening beneath the covers. Aidan had wrapped her in his cape, and by some incomprehensible magic he had brought her here.

That was it.

Aidan must be a magician, and a very good one at that.

She began to make a case for her theory, in the courtroom of her mind. Yes, she *was* in his house in Connecticut, not a mile from the Lakeview Truck Stop, and she had no memory of making the trip; those were undeniable facts. But Aidan could have hypnotized her, or given her drugs, and planted the other recollections in her consciousness like seeds.

She would just get up, she decided, get herself dressed, and leave. Aidan Tremayne might be the most attractive man she'd ever met, and he'd certainly captured her heart, not to mention turning her inside out sexually, but that didn't mean she was going to let him kidnap her and play crazy games with her psyche.

Brave talk, she said to herself. The truth was, if Aidan came to her at that moment, she would let him—let him? she would *beg* him to—make love to her all over again.

She drew a deep breath and released it slowly in an effort to calm the dark, sweet excitement the memory of their strange intimacy stirred in her. In a more rational moment she faced another facet of her attraction to Aidan Tremayne, and that was plain, simple fear.

The man was probably just a very good magician, as she'd decided earlier, but suppose he'd been telling the truth? Suppose he really was a vampire, for God's sake?

Neely was confused and irritated, and besides that she figured her bladder was going to burst at any moment.

She moved to toss back the covers and sit up, but it was as if she were pinned to the mattress by some benign force. She ran a rather frantic mental check of her muscles and found them all in good working order. "Damn," she said and attempted to rise onto her elbows.

It was as if the ceiling had collapsed onto her, though there was no pain.

"Aidan!"

The name echoed in the large, empty room.

Neely waited, working up another burst of energy, fighting the urge to slip back into sleep. "Aidan!" she called again. "You get in here and help me out of this bed, damn it! I have to pee!"

There was no response at all, except for the hollow reverberations of her own voice.

Neely summoned all her will, which was formidable, and managed to make an inch of progress toward the side of the mattress. She waited, then moved again.

After ten minutes Neely was perspiring so heavily that the sheets clung to her skin. She reached the edge of the bed, spent a minor eternity gathering her strength, and then lunged again.

She landed on the cool hardwood floor with a thump and lay there dazed for an interval, exulting because she'd made it, yet so drained by the effort that she wasn't sure she could stand up.

The insistent complaint of her bladder forced her to try; she reached her knees, gripped the antique bedside table for support, and raised herself shakily to her feet. She stood there, trembling and drawing deep breaths, until she dared attempt a step.

To Neely's surprise, walking was easy. She went into the adjoining bathroom, which was fitted out in the costliest Italian marble, used the facilities, then draped an afghan around herself to keep warm and set about exploring the enormous bedchamber.

There were high casement windows on both sides of the suite, with built-in seats overlooking the snowy garden and the front yard, and the bureaus, closet, and armoires contained a wide assortment of men's clothing. The room boasted its own fireplace, fronted in priceless hand-painted tiles, and here and there an exquisite Persian rug graced the gleaming wooden floors.

Neely ventured out into the hallway. She was hungry, and a little reassurance from her mysterious host wouldn't have done any harm, either.

"Aidan?"

No answer.

She opened the double doors of the room across the hallway from Aidan's and found another suite, almost as big and grand as the one she'd just left. Here the closets and bureaus were empty, however, and Neely's hope of finding something to wear was dashed. She returned to the master chamber long enough to drop the afghan and put on one of Aidan's tailored white shirts, then ventured into the hallway and headed toward the rear stairs.

At the bottom of these was a kitchen, large and immaculate. The shelves of the cupboards and the pantry were bare even of dust, and there wasn't a plate or a glass or a butter knife to be seen.

Did vampires eat? Neely wondered. She immediately checked the silly thought. This whole setup was getting weirder and weirder.

Neely shifted her concentration away from her grumbling stomach and examined the rest of the massive house. In the movies it would have been filled with cobwebs and dust and spiders, she supposed, but instead the place was as tidy as a nun's dresser drawer. The massive crystal chandeliers glistened, the rugs and floors felt clean under Neely's bare feet, and the walls were decorated with fine original art. In Aidan's study, the only part of the house she had been in before, there were stacks of paper on the large table he used as a desk, and books lined the walls from floor to ceiling, on every side.

Neely gravitated to the music box she had discovered on her last visit, wound the brass key on its underside, and lifted the lid.

Sweet yet unbearably sad music flowed from the tiny, precise mechanism, arousing emotions so deep Neely could not even begin to identify them. She felt hot tears sting her eyes as she whirled round and round in a solitary dance, caught up in the sorcery of the tune, clutching the little chest in both hands. As she moved, twilight gathered at the tall, deeply set windows, and heavy flakes of snow waltzed past the glass.

"What a will you must have," Aidan said, startling Neely so badly that she stumbled and nearly dropped the music box.

He was standing in the doorway leading to the entryway, wearing a black overcoat, trousers, a white shirt, and a tie. Snowflakes glistened in his ebony hair and on the shoulders of his coat.

Neely stared at him, unable, for the moment, to speak. The impact of his presence was overwhelming; her soul trembled, her heart pounded. She didn't know whether to laugh or cry, whether to fling herself upon him in rage or seduce him on the spot.

Aidan's fine mouth tilted upward at one side as he indulged in a weary grin. "I guess I should have brought your suitcase when I carried you away from that dreadful motel," he said, pulling leather gloves from his hands and shoving them into the pockets of his coat. "Though you do look quite charming in my shirt. Tell me—how did you manage to get out of bed?"

She raised her chin. "No force can stop a woman who needs to go to the bathroom," she said.

Aidan laughed. "I see." He removed his coat and hung it from a brass coat tree.

"There's nothing to eat in this place," Neely said, her voice shaking a little.

"Oh, but there is," Aidan replied, disappearing into the entryway and returning momentarily with three cartons of Chinese take-out and a plastic fork wrapped in paper napkins. He smiled when she snatched everything from his hands and sat cross-legged on the hearth rug to rip open the boxes. Then he crouched beside her and said gently, "You're not a prisoner here, Neely, and you won't be mistreated. Please don't be afraid."

She gulped down a mouthful of fried rice. " 'Don't be afraid'?" she echoed, somewhat bitterly. "I'd be some sort of idiot if I weren't."

He smiled at her reasoning, touched her hair briefly, then drew his hand back. In the next moment an expression of infinite sorrow filled his eyes.

"I can't bear it," he whispered hoarsely, "knowing that you fear me."

Neely set aside the food, for even though her body still craved sustenance, her emotions had taken full control. She could not stop herself from touching Aidan, from laying her hands on either side of his face.

For one long moment they simply gazed at each other, exchanging some silent, mystical form of comfort. Then Neely said, "How did I get here, Aidan? Did you hypnotize me or something like that?"

He shook his head. "Nothing so ordinary, I'm afraid," he told her. "I really am a vampire, Neely, just as I said. And you were in rather grave danger last night, I might add. It was foolish of you to set out on your own like that."

She looked away because she wanted him so much, wanted to become one with him right there on the hearth rug, and out of the corner of her eye she saw him stand and distance himself from her.

"What kind of danger?" she asked, a little testily. She suspected Aidan had looked into her mind and seen her insatiable passion for him. His withdrawal struck her with the force of a blow.

"Two blighters came round to kill you," Aidan answered from the vicinity of his desk. He sounded distracted, like an ordinary man recounting the events of his day while flipping through the mail at the same time. "There's no reason to worry, though—I dealt with them."

So that was why he had suddenly stopped and thrust himself away the night before, when he'd been about to make love to her in the normal way. He'd heard someone approaching the room.

Neely allowed herself a slight shudder and took up her dinner again. "I'll bet you came as something of a surprise—especially if you let them see your teeth."

Aidan chuckled. "Yes, I daresay they weren't expecting to encounter me."

"Of course, it isn't over," Neely said with a sigh, reaching for one of the other cartons of Chinese food. "They're not going to give up quite so easily."

"Neither am I," Aidan remarked.

Neely could no longer resist looking at him, and when she did, she saw that he was watching her with a mixture of bewilderment and delight.

"What a hot-blooded little creature you are," he reflected.

Neely blushed. "What makes you say that?"

He laughed. "A few moments ago you wanted to make love on the hearth."

She didn't deny the thought; she couldn't. "I'm not normally so—amorous," she said.

"I should hope not," Aidan teased.

Her eyes flew to his face. She felt fury first, but the tender mirth she saw in his gaze stole her momentum, and she could not be angry with him.

"Have there been other men in your life, Neely?"

She was at once insulted and pleased by the question. "You claim you can read minds. Why don't you just look inside my head and find out for yourself?"

"Because it would be an intrusion," he said with a slight and very appealing shrug.

Neely sighed. "Fair enough," she replied. "The answer is, just one. He broke my heart, my first year in college." She decided that turnabout was fair play. "What about you, Aidan? How many women have you taken to your bed?"

His jaw tightened, and he looked exasperated. Then he murmured something that sounded like "This modern age!" A moment after that, however, he replied, "There were a number of tavern wenches in my youth—"

" 'Tavern wenches'?" Neely interrupted, struck by this old-fashioned turn of phrase.

Aidan was clearly growing impatient again. With quicksilver speed he changed the subject. "I will find you something more appropriate to wear," he said in a cool and formal tone. "Maeve must have left a few things behind—"

Maeve. Neely was troubled by the name, but she had enough to assimilate without pursuing yet another subject.

By the time Aidan returned, carrying a bundle of clothing with him, Neely had finished eating and stashed the leftovers in the big, hitherto empty refrigerator humming away in the kitchen. She was perched on a window seat, knees drawn up, the tails of Aidan's shirt tucked modestly beneath her, watching the snow fall.

"There's still some sweet and sour pork left. . . ."

He smiled. "Vampires don't eat, Neely. Not in the same way humans do."

She rolled her eyes, accepting the folded cotton garment he held out to her. "Please," she said. "You're no ordinary guy, I'll grant you that, but you can't really be a vampire. Can you?"

Aidan's laugh seemed to burst from his throat, rich and sensual and warm.

Neely slid out of the window seat and went to stand behind a high-back leather chair, her imagination running wild all of a sudden. "You don't actually drink blood?"

Again she saw that peculiar, fathomless look of mourning in his eyes. "Yes," he said miserably. "I despise it—I hate everything about being a vampire—but without blood I would die, and I am not quite prepared to do that."

She felt conflicting desires—to take him into her arms and to run away, as far and as fast as she could. She squinted, a habit she'd acquired in college, when she was trying to work out something that both intrigued and puzzled her.

"Show me your coffin," she challenged.

Aidan arched one dark eyebrow. "I beg your pardon?" he replied, looking and sounding genuinely bewildered.

"If you're a vampire," Neely said, trying to make reason of the unreasonable, "you have to sleep in a coffin."

He sighed, and his expression shifted to exasperation. "I most certainly do not sleep in a casket," he said, plainly insulted. "This is not the second feature of a drive-in movie we're talking about here, it's reality. I drink blood, I sleep during the day, and I can indeed be killed by having a stake thrust through my heart. And that, my darling, is the extent of my resemblance to a Hollywood vampire!"

She frowned, trying to remember if she'd ever encountered Aidan before sunset and failing to recollect a single instance. "Calm down," she said. She ran her tongue over her lips in a gesture of distraction rather than nervousness. "If you hate being a—a vampire so much, then why did you become one? Assuming, of course, that you really *are* a supernatural creature."

Aidan sagged into the chair behind his worktable with a great sigh, and that was when Neely noticed that he looked gaunt. There were faint smudges under his eyes, like bruises, and his skin was pale as marble. "You are impossible!" he muttered.

Neely smiled. "True," she claimed and promptly determined to show more appreciation. After all, no matter what Aidan was, or claimed to be, he had saved her from crooks who had almost certainly been ordered to assassinate her. And she still needed a place to hide.

Thinking it was a good time to take her leave, at least temporarily, she slipped out of the study. In the downstairs bathroom she exchanged the borrowed shirt for the graceful blue caftan Aidan had found for her. When she returned, he was standing at one of the windows, staring out at the dark, snowy forest edging the yard.

He turned to face her as she stood uncertainly in the arched doorway.

"I must go out for a while," he said solemnly. "Do not admit anyone to the house before I return." While Neely stared at him, trying to assimilate the news that he meant to abandon her, he lifted a fragile necklace over his head and placed it around her neck. A delicately shaped golden rosebud dangled from the chain.

"What is this?"

Aidan chuckled grimly. "Not the equivalent of a silver bullet or a crucifix, if that's what you're thinking. My sister and the others know it belongs to me, and that you would not have it in your possession except by my favor."

Curiouser and curiouser, Neely thought. She should be glad Aidan was leaving, she supposed, but instead she had to fight an urge to drop to her knees and fling her arms around his legs to make him stay. "What—what if those men come after me again? The ones who tried to break into my motel room."

Aidan made a gentle move in her direction, then drew himself back with a sharp, alarming motion. "They won't," he said. Raising his hands over his head, he slipped into a corner of the room and dissolved into the shadows.

Neely just stood there for a few seconds after he disappeared, staring, immobilized with shock. Then she broke her paralysis and hurtled across the room to the place where Aidan had been only a heartbeat before.

There was no trace of him, nor was there a door or a window near enough to accommodate such a dramatic exit. Murmuring, Neely knelt and felt the wainscotting with both hands, searching for a secret panel.

Nothing.

With a shiver Neely got to her feet. She was going to have to ask Aidan to show her how to do that particular trick—it might come in handy if those hired thugs ever caught up to her again.

Her glance strayed to the telephone on Aidan's table. She wanted to call Ben and let him know that she was all right, but she didn't dare. Dallas Hargrove's drug-dealing associates might have her brother's line tapped, and if they traced a call to this house, she was as good as dead.

With a groan Neely raised moist palms to her temples and rubbed. It would have been a relief to tell someone all that was happening to her, but who'd believe it?

Restless, Neely made a fire on the hearth and began examining Aidan's vast collection of books. A set of thick volumes, bound in Moroccan leather, drew her attention, and she reached for the first one on the left.

The thing was huge, and heavy, and Neely dropped into Aidan's desk chair before lifting the cover.

The paper was fine parchment, substantial and smooth, and the first few pages were blank. Neely flipped carefully through them until she came to one that bore an inscription in fading black ink. *This being the Record and Journal of Aidan Tremayne, Vampyre. Begun March 5, 1793.*

Neely felt something tickle the inside of her spine. She stared at the writing for a long time, then moved on to the

next page. Here she found a pen-and-ink drawing that practically stopped her heart; Aidan's laughing, handsome face
looked back at her from the parchment, while a beautiful
young woman, his female counterpart, peered smiling over
his broad shoulder. Both subjects wore clothing typical of
the eighteenth century.

For a while Neely just sat there, stunned.

Surely the man in the drawing could not be Aidan—the
sketches had obviously been done generations before—no,
it had to be one of his ancestors. Still, the image reached
out to her somehow, and the laughing eyes pleaded with
her to believe.

Just believe.

Shaken, she turned her attention to the woman, one of
the loveliest creatures she had ever seen. The resemblance
between the two was so strong that Neely knew they were
brother and sister, or perhaps cousins. . . .

Neely swayed and closed her eyes. Some primal instinct
insisted that this laughing young man in the drawing was
indeed Aidan Tremayne—her Aidan.

Impossible.

Believe.

Neely took a deep breath and held it for a moment.
Then, with a shaking hand, she turned another page and
began to decipher the neatly written but quaint script, with
its antique spellings and randomly capitalized words. "I,
Aidan Tremayne," she translated, "set Down this Tale for
the Sake of my own Sanity, and as a Warning to all those
who come after. . . ."

Soon Neely was so absorbed that she was unaware of
the passage of time. She devoured page after page, spellbound by the young Irishman's account of his meeting with
Lisette, the mysterious woman who had stopped for him in
a carriage one evening, along a muddy road, and quickly
captured his soul. Even though this other, earlier Aidan—

he could not be the one she'd held, the one she loved, could he?—was a shameless hedonist, mostly concerned with sex, music, and good ale, Neely felt pangs of despair and, yes, jealousy, as she read. She did not want another female to figure into the story at all.

When she came to the part where Lisette pounced on young Aidan and sank her fangs deep into his throat to virtually inhale his blood, Neely felt her own face go white and cold as window glass in winter. It was fiction, of course, a brilliantly conceived and quite horrible fantasy, but it seemed so *real*, the action so immediate and vital, that Neely almost became a part of the scenes herself.

The account only became more incredible. The boy Aidan had died in the bed of a flea-ridden eighteenth-century inn above a tavern, and yet he had *not* died. The innkeeper, his son, and a local priest had declared him dead, and he'd tried desperately to communicate somehow that he was alive, but to no avail. The men had taken the body, never dreaming that a spirit still occupied it, to the undertaker's establishment. He'd been abandoned there in that dreadful place, and forgotten.

Tears blurred Neely's vision as she read of Lisette's return, and how she had raised Aidan up as a monster, a *vampire*, by tapping into his jugular vein again, this time giving blood instead of taking it.

While she was fascinated and curious to a morbid degree, Neely found that she could not go on from there, not yet. She was deeply shaken, as if she'd witnessed the occurrences personally, in every gruesome detail. She felt true and abiding hatred for the heartless Lisette, along with an unholy resentment that the woman had lain with Aidan, had given him pleasure, and taken the same from him.

For a long interval she just sat, dazed by the intensity and variety of her emotions, staring into the fire but seeing instead the nightmare images so carefully outlined in the journal. How could anyone, even a vampire, do such a terrible thing to another, to condemn him, as Lisette had condemned Aidan, to an eternal nightmare?

"Neely?"

She started and guiltily slammed the volume closed.

Aidan was standing only a few feet away—she hadn't heard him come in—and he carried her suitcase, the one she'd been forced to leave behind at the motel the night before.

She felt such overwhelming love, just looking at him, that she could not get her breath to speak.

"I thought you might like to have some of your own clothes," he said innocently, sounding almost shy. His gaze dropped to the heavy book in her lap, and she saw both resignation and relief in his bearing. "You've found my histories, I see."

Looking up, Neely noticed that his skin, deathly pale before, was now healthy in color. A wild suspicion played in her mind; she chased it out and dropped her gaze to the suitcase in his hand. "Where did that come from? I thought we left it."

"We did. I went back."

Neely's eyes shot back to his face. "You couldn't have. It's too far."

Instead of replying, Aidan simply raised one of his aristocratic eyebrows.

She bolted out of the chair and grabbed for the case. "I have to let my brother know I'm all right," she blurted, desperate for any distraction from the threatening truth, the reality that was becoming too complex and too pervasive to be ignored or denied. "When the police visit that room and find no sign of yours truly, Ben will hear about it on the news. He'll be frantic. He might even think I'm dead."

Aidan folded his arms. "If you telephone Ben, we may soon have more of the senator's friends to deal with. That's all well and good, provided I'm here when they arrive, but what if you're alone, Neely? What if I'm hunting, or asleep?"

A chill, colder than the center of a snowman's heart, touched her stomach and seeped into her soul. " 'Hunting or asleep'? For God's sake, Aidan—you're really scaring me now. This vampire game has gone far enough!"

He took the book gently from her hands, laid it aside. "I was hoping I wouldn't have to resort to parlor tricks to convince you," he said in a quiet and damnably reasonable tone. "That's my story you were reading, Neely. The image in the drawing is mine, the girl is my twin sister, Maeve—"

"No!" She put her hands over her ears.

Aidan grasped her wrists, lowered them, pressed them to her sides. "You *will* listen," he said in a desperate whisper. "You know it's true—somewhere inside, *you know it's true*."

Neely uttered a sudden, wailing sob, because he was right. As incomprehensible as it all was, as much as she wanted to turn away from the evidence, she could no longer do that. It was no dream, and no one had given her drugs or induced any kind of hypnotic trance. All the strange things that had happened since she first met Aidan had actually, truly *happened*.

Aidan touched her elbows and then her shoulders, tentatively. After that, though, instead of taking her into his arms as she yearned for him to do, he retreated a few steps. "I'm sorry, Neely," he said gruffly. "I should have left you alone—"

"But you didn't!" she cried. She looked up at him, wiping angrily at her wet cheeks. "I'm fascinated, I'm entranced,

God help me, I think I'm in love—with someone who isn't even human! Tell me, Aidan—where do I go from here? What do I do now?"

He flinched, as if she'd hurled bricks at his broad back instead of words. He did not face her as he replied raggedly, "I could walk away, and you would get over what you're feeling now. But that wouldn't change the fact that there are more of those cretins out there, waiting for a chance to cut your throat!"

Neely moved to face Aidan and glared up into his face. She was wild with confusion, shock, and pain, and she spoke without thinking. "You could make me into a vampire, like you."

Aidan seemed to loom over her, taller for his fury. "Don't ever say that!" he cried. "You're asking to be damned, to be a fiend who feeds on the blood of living creatures! You're asking God Himself to turn against you, and for all eternity!" His anguish lay naked and vivid in the words, and Neely's first real comprehension of its extent took her breath away.

She approached him, laying her hands gently on his face. "Aidan—" she whispered, longing to comfort him, knowing there was no way to do that.

He wrenched free of her and moved away. "Didn't you hear me, Neely?" he growled, reminding her of a wolf that had just chewed off its own paw in a desperate effort to save itself from the metal teeth of a trap. "I am cursed for all time, and to care for me is to blaspheme against Creation itself!"

She was shaking her head again. "No, Aidan—no." It couldn't be a sin to love, could it? But, yes. The act of adoring something evil did not transform it into good, but instead poisoned what was holy.

They both stood still, the silence ringing around them like the deafening toll of some horrid death bell, for the longest time. Then, unable to bear it, Neely muttered, "My brother—"

Aidan moved to his desk, keeping his back to her. "Write him a letter, then, and explain as best you can. Just remember that he will have to live with your words until the end of his days."

Neely nodded distractedly, well aware of Aidan's meaning. She could tell Ben only that she was in hiding—it would be an outright lie to say she was safe, and there was no plausible way to describe the terrible truth.

She went upstairs to the room where she had awakened hours before, switched on a lamp, and sat down at a small desk to stare, unseeing, at a blank piece of paper.

Aidan paced his study, too restless to work on his journals, not daring to follow Neely upstairs and continue their conversation. He had fed sparsely that night, and he had yet to look in on the still-ailing Valerian, who was his only hope of finding redemption and, with it, peace. Maeve, adore her though he did, was embroiled as usual in adventures of her own and could not be depended upon to look after wounded ones.

He rubbed his temples with a thumb and forefinger, slouched back against the edge of his desk, and sighed. Then, with the utmost reluctance, he took himself to the dungeon of Havermail Castle.

Valerian still lay prone and ill, his long frame covering the length of a trestle table. In the flickering lights of the candles Aidan saw a small, snarling creature spring out of the shadows and attach itself to Valerian's throat.

Horror rocked Aidan as he realized that this abomination, this greedy fiend, wore the person of a child. He plunged forward and tore the small, wiry body away from Valerian's neck as though it were a leech. The little girl—this had to be Canaan, Benecia's sister—twisted in Aidan's grasp, baring her lethal fangs and making a vicious sound low in her throat, like a starved she-wolf.

Valerian moaned and rolled onto his side. "Stop," he pleaded. "Please—*stop!*"

Remarkably, the hellion went still, but when she raised her sherry-colored gaze to Aidan's face, he saw the most abject hatred there that he had ever encountered. Coming from a being who looked for all the world like a sweet and warm-blooded five-year-old, the experience was particularly chilling.

"She was merely trying to help me," Valerian said gently.

"Shall I leave you alone with this one, Valerian?" the fiend-child inquired, in a voice as delicate as the chimes of an exquisite little clock. "I do not favor him, you know."

Valerian gestured affectionately toward the door. "I am quite safe with Aidan," he insisted. "Go now, please, and tell your mama and papa that we have a guest."

Aidan's gaze sliced to his friend's face. He had no real desire to socialize with the elder Havermails; they were innately horrible creatures, like their daughters. When Canaan had swept from the room, he bit out, "Honestly, Valerian, I can't think what you and Maeve see in this family of monsters!"

"We see ourselves," Valerian answered quietly.

The words left Aidan stricken, for no weapon could wound as deeply and as savagely as the truth.

"This is what we *are*, Aidan," the elder vampire insisted in an urgent whisper.

"No," Aidan rasped, shaking his head, trying to pull free of Valerian's grasp. "*No!* You went back, almost to Atlantis—so will I. I will find the antidote for this curse or die seeking it!"

Incredibly, Valerian smiled. "What a passionate specimen you are. Come with me, my friend, and let me show you other realities." He paused, patting Aidan's hand fondly. "You might have been a stage actor, with your flair for the dramatic. Together we could write plays that would outshine the words of the Bard himself. We could—"

"Damn it, Valerian, you're dreaming!" Aidan broke in sharply. He hadn't meant his tone to be harsh, but it was, cruelly so, and the momentum carried him farther. "I want nothing from you, do you hear me, *nothing*, except for the secret that would restore the life that was stolen from me!"

Valerian turned his head to one side, and it seemed that he was caving in on himself again. He looked much as he had that first terrible night in the crypt, when he had come so close to perishing. His suffering was tangible; it swelled in the room, choking Aidan, crushing him.

Because of their bond, Aidan felt Valerian's pain as keenly as if it were his own. And maybe, since he had caused it, it was. With a cry, Aidan let his forehead fall to Valerian's concave chest. "I cannot offer you the devotion you want from me," he whispered in agony. *"I cannot!"*

Slowly, and with tenderness, Valerian raised a trembling hand to the back of Aidan's head and entwined cold fingers in his hair. "Yes," he said brokenly. "I know."

Just then, a nearby door swung open with a *thunk,* and Aubrey Havermail swept in, accompanied by his small, demonic daughter. He smirked as he watched Aidan step back from Valerian's side, dazed by despair.

"Such a touching, tender scene," Aubrey drawled.

Chapter 8

———◦❦◦———

"We were just about to sit down to dinner," Aubrey Havermail went on after a brief, charged interval of silence had passed. "Won't you join us?"

Under other circumstances, Aidan might have laughed at the idea of vampires taking a meal in the human way, but he sensed that his host was in deadly earnest. When Valerian reached out to grasp Aidan's hand and squeeze, silently urging him to accept, Aidan inclined his head in polite assent.

"We'll just go on ahead, then," Havermail went on, when it was clear that Aidan didn't mean to leave the dungeon before he had a private word with Valerian. "Come, darling." He took Canaan's tiny, snow-white hand. "I'm sure our guest will be able to find his way on his own."

When the pair had gone, Valerian raised himself onto one elbow and regarded Aidan with sunken, shadowed eyes. "Is there any way," he began, "that I can dissuade you from attempting to uncover the secret that would make you mortal again?"

Aidan shook his head. "No," he said.

"I thought not," the stricken vampire replied in a rasp of despair. He struggled for a time, grappling visibly with some fathomless fatigue, and finally went on. "My advice to you, as you already know, is to turn from this foolish pursuit and never look back. Clearly, though, you are not wise enough to heed my counsel—in which case, I offer you what little information I have to give."

Aidan leaned closer to his companion; had he been a man, he would have been holding his breath. "I beg of you, Valerian—tell me."

Valerian closed his eyes for a moment and was taken by an almost imperceptible fit of trembling. Then he met Aidan's gaze and said, "You must learn to *listen*, my friend, if you are to survive! Do you not recall what the other child, Benecia, said before, when you asked how an entire family had become vampires? *She stated that her father had joined a secret society.* I've been thinking about it ever since and exploring this dreary castle with my mind whenever I could manage the effort, and I've come to a conclusion. Benecia spoke of one of the oldest fraternities on earth, Aidan—the Brotherhood of the Vampyre. This fellowship can trace its origins back to Atlantis itself!"

Now it was Aidan who trembled, for the implications of Valerian's words were, to him, profound. The Brotherhood, an organization Aidan had heard of only once before, when Maeve had mentioned it in passing, might well possess some clue to the secret of his own redemption—if not the means itself.

"Thank you," Aidan said, his voice hoarse. He enclosed one of Valerian's large, elegant hands between his own. "I will come back to speak with you before I go."

Valerian held him fast when he tried to walk away. "What of that mortal woman you became involved with? Have you set her free, Aidan?"

"She was never my prisoner."

"You are hedging!"

Aidan forced himself to meet Valerian's gaze. "Neely is living in my house. I cannot take the time to explain everything now; suffice it to say that I can neither hold her nor let her go."

Valerian stared bleakly up at Aidan, saying nothing.

"You have fed?" Aidan inquired quietly. At Valerian's nod, he went on. "Are you recovering your strength?"

At this, the elder vampire turned his face away from Aidan and remained stubbornly silent.

Reluctantly Aidan left Valerian's side, left the dim candle-glow of the dungeon for the torch-lit passageway beyond. Instinct led him up a curving flight of stone stairs, worn to slippery smoothness by centuries of use, through a dusty corridor, and into the castle's great hall.

There was every probability that all manner of knights, nobles, ladies, and wenches had dined and celebrated in this yawning chamber in some distant century. Now, however, the place was empty, except for the four Havermails, who sat around a long wooden table next to an enormous fireplace, their empty plates and glasses making clinking sounds, their horribly beautiful faces bathed in the crimson glow from the hearth.

Aubrey, head of this ghoulish family, rose from his chair when Aidan approached. "Our guest has arrived. We wondered at the delay."

Aidan reminded himself that this posturing creature he so despised might be the very one who could solve his dilemma. "I hope I did not inconvenience you," he said evenly. "I was concerned for my friend."

Benecia looked up at him with large, malevolent eyes, her tarnished-gold ringlets capturing the firelight. "Valerian is not your friend," she said. "No vampire is, truly, for you are not one of us. Why do you pretend?"

"That is quite enough," Aubrey interceded. He was a slender, finely built man, obviously a product of generations of aristocracy. "Do join us, Mr. Tremayne."

Aidan was, for the first time in recent memory, mildly embarrassed. He took the only empty chair at the table, situated between Mrs. Havermail—Maeve had introduced her as Roxanne during his last visit—and Canaan, who looked as fragile as a kitten and was clearly about as well-mannered as a white shark in frenzy.

Roxanne gave a trilling laugh that tripped down Aidan's backbone, leaving patterns of frost as it passed. She had rich, dark hair, uncomfortably reminiscent of Lisette's, perfect bone structure, and practically no color at all to her skin. "Please don't be alarmed by our strange custom of sitting down at table together, Mr. Tremayne," she said. "It is the one semblance of family life that remains to us."

Aidan nodded, his eyes moving from one lovely monster to another. Despite differences in size and in human age, all the Havermails were no doubt equals in their powers and experience as vampires. Roxanne's reasoning made a grisly sort of sense; while seated around a table, they could *pretend* to be flesh and blood again.

And that was something Aidan understood.

"Do you miss being mortal?" he inquired, just to make conversation.

Roxanne's chuckle was wicked enough to curdle a saint's blood. "Miss being mortal?" she echoed. "Dear me, Aidan— I feel that I know you well enough to address you informally, since dear Maeve has spoken of you so often—why would anyone *miss* head colds and bunions and broken hearts?"

"And having to die," Benecia put in.

Canaan wrinkled her delicate, freckle-spattered nose. "And sitting in the schoolroom hour after hour, learning dull lessons."

Aubrey called the group back to order by raising both hands, palms out, making a silly smirk, and turning his head slightly to one side. "Here, now. Let's not be rude."

Rude, Aidan thought. Amazing. These were beings who surely stalked their mortal counterparts by night, drained them of their life's blood, and slept off the kill by day in perfect contentment. And Havermail was concerned about their table manners?

"I don't like you," announced Canaan, as her sister had before, regarding Aidan with cheerful disdain.

"I feel much the same way about you," Aidan replied cordially.

The other Havermails were amused by his audacity and cackled among themselves, putting Aidan in mind of the three crones in *Macbeth*. *Double, double, toil and trouble,* he thought, *fire burn and cauldron bubble*.

Roxanne startled everyone by picking up a silver spoon and setting it clattering against the side of a crystal goblet. "Canaan, Benecia—you will atone for your poor manners by entertaining. Canaan, you may recite. Benecia, you will sing."

Inwardly Aidan groaned. Was this atonement, or was it free rein to torture a hapless captive?

"Jolly good idea," said Aubrey Havermail, leaping up from his chair with such suddenness that he overturned his empty wineglass. "To the main drawing room, then, where we shall find the pipe organ."

Aidan smiled, already in acute pain, and followed the family of vampires across the great hall and into another, smaller chamber. There was indeed an organ, along with tarnished candelabras and dingy chandeliers, all dripping cobwebs, and rugs so long neglected that wisps of dust floated up from them as they were trod upon.

Canaan took her place next to the organ, while Roxanne sat down at the discolored keyboard. Aubrey sank into a leather chair and drew Benecia onto his knee, just as a human father might have done. Aidan perched gingerly on the arm of a settee, trying to comprehend the fact that his sister deliberately spent time with these beasts.

The younger daughter, not even three feet tall, clasped her tiny white hands together and held forth, reciting Shakespeare's poem, "Venus and Adonis," with chilling precision. "I know 'The Rape of Lucrece,' as well," Canaan said, upon finishing.

"Sit down, dear," Roxanne told her fondly.

Aidan held himself still, though he wanted to fidget and, even more, to flee.

Benecia slipped off her father's lap and sashayed forward to stand in front of the small company. She and her mother conferred, in whispers, and then Roxanne struck an introduction on the stained organ keys, and Benecia began to sing.

The lyrics were Latin—something quite ordinary, concerning bluebirds and meadows and sparkling streams— but it was the child-vampire's voice that struck Aidan. It seemed to move in the chamber like the eddies, swirls, and undertows of some vast, invisible river.

When the performance was over, when the last quavering note had fallen away into silence, Aidan remembered to clap. This drew a look of scathing reprimand from Canaan, whom he had neglected to acknowledge in quite so formal a fashion.

Roxanne rose from the organ bench and gathered her children close. "Come, darlings—there are still several hours left in which to hunt," she said in the same tones a human mother might use to summon her brood to the station wagon for a trip to the nearest shopping mall. "Say good-bye to Mr. Tremayne."

Benecia and Canaan stood primly before Aidan and curtsied in unison. Then they chorused, "Good night, Papa," kissed Aubrey on either of his waxen cheeks, and scampered out, their mother following.

"Am I keeping you from anything?" Aidan asked when he and Havermail were alone in that odd room. The place might have come from the pages of a Dickens novel, he thought; all it really lacked was a spoiled cake being nibbled on by rats, and a demented old woman in a rotted wedding dress.

Aubrey sat back in his chair as Aidan went to stand next to the fireplace, where an old clock stood on a mantel beneath a drapery of spider weavings.

"No," Havermail replied, studying his guest thoughtfully. "I fed some hours ago and have no desire to gorge myself, as my wife and daughters often do. Tell me, Mr. Tremayne—what is it you want from me?"

Aidan thrust his hand through his hair, fingers splayed. "According to your elder daughter, you became a vampire some five hundred and forty years ago, when you joined a select fellowship and undertook their initiation."

Havermail's countenance darkened, and his mouth pursed for a moment. Clearly the lovely, vicious Benecia had spoken out of turn. "What is your interest in the Brotherhood?" he asked after a long and somewhat awkward silence. "It cannot be that you seek immortality, since you are already a vampire."

Aidan framed his words carefully, setting them out like so many fine porcelain plates. "I seek—mortality. In short, I want to be a man again."

After staring for several moments, Havermail burst out laughing. "You cannot be serious!" he howled when he'd recovered just a little.

"I have never been more sincere about anything," Aidan replied evenly. "I was robbed. I want the forty-odd additional years of life that were my due."

Aubrey stood, all vestiges of mirth gone from his expression. "Who made you a blood-drinker?"

Aidan hesitated. "A powerful female called Lisette."

Havermail made a sputtering sound and moved one hand as if to make the sign of the cross over his chest, before stopping himself. An old habit, evidently, that had died hard. "Powerful, indeed," he murmured. "All sensible vampires fear Lisette, Tremayne. Why should I risk incurring her wrath?"

"You needn't risk anything," Aidan snapped, barely keeping himself from grasping Aubrey by the lapels of his cutaway coat and lifting him onto his toes. "I want to know about the Brotherhood, that's all. Is it true that the fellowship has existed since before the fall of Atlantis?"

Aubrey looked patently uncomfortable. "Yes," he said, "but that is all I will tell you without permission from the elders." He moved to the fireplace with that quick, gliding motion typical of vampires, took a poker from its place on the hearth, and jabbed at the burning logs until sparks rose toward the chimney in a crackling shower. "Leave this house, Tremayne. Go on about your business, whatever it is. If the Brotherhood wishes to grant you admittance, you will be contacted."

Desperation filled Aidan, along with a certain fragile elation. The Brotherhood existed, and he would be given audience only on the approval—perhaps the whim—of these mysterious elders.

Still, the fellowship might well possess the knowledge he needed, the secret that would set him free. He must bide his time and be patient. He started toward the doorway. "I will be back again tomorrow night to look in on Valerian," he said in passing. "Thank you for a most interesting evening."

Down in the dungeon, Aidan was surprised to find Valerian sitting up and looking a bit more chipper. He was wearing a snow-white shirt, buttoned halfway up his chest, dark trousers, and boots.

"I've decided to go back to Connecticut with you," he announced.

Aidan stopped cold, felt the smile freeze on his mouth, and let it fall away. "What?"

"I'm bored with this place, and you plainly need a guiding hand, given your reckless ways." He was rolling down his sleeves, fastening cuff links made from Roman coins. "Don't worry, Aidan. I won't corner your lovely mortal and bite her neck. I only want to help you."

Aidan sighed. "I suppose there is no persuading you to stay here?"

Valerian smiled fondly. "It would be easier to make a bat love daylight," he said.

And so it was that when Aidan returned to his house outside of Bright River, Valerian was with him.

Not surprisingly, considering the many recent upheavals in her life, Neely hadn't been able to sleep. She had taken a long, hot bath in Aidan's tile-lined tub, dressed in jeans and a sweatshirt taken from the suitcase he'd recovered for her, and finished off what was left of the Chinese leftovers she'd stashed in the refrigerator. Then she'd meandered back to Aidan's study, taken up the first volume of his journal again, and tumbled headfirst into the story.

She'd read, spellbound, of Aidan's early adventures as a vampire. Early on, he'd traveled to the north of England by night, intending to visit his twin sister in her convent school. He'd stopped at an inn along the way and there been approached by an imposing vampire who called himself Valerian—

"His lucky night," a masculine voice commented.

Neely jumped in her chair and had to grab at the book to keep it from toppling to the floor. Before her stood the towering, graceful creature she'd met once before, the night the man driving the Blazer had chased her into the woods. The night she'd found the music box.

"Yes," he said drolly, with a slight bow. "It is I—Valerian—in person. So to speak."

Neely tried to melt into the chair cushions, her eyes rounded, her heart flailing with the purest sort of terror. "Stay away from me," she whispered, holding out the rose medallion Aidan had given her, hoping it had some power to ward off intruders.

Valerian laughed. "What? No garlic? Such is the shameful state of vampire lore in this modern and wholly unromantic age!"

Just then, when she thought panic would surely consume her, Neely caught sight of Aidan. He smiled at her but spoke sharply to the intimidating Valerian.

"I meant what I said. Leave her alone."

Valerian yawned. "Of course I will obey your every wish," he said convivially. "It's almost dawn, in case you haven't noticed. What assurance can you offer that this delicious gamine will not drive stakes through our hearts as we slumber?"

"None," Aidan answered wearily, "except that the task would be a nasty one, and she's probably not up to it. Stop your teasing and retire, Valerian. I want a word alone with Neely."

The great vampire sighed in a long-suffering way, raised his arms over his head, and disappeared without a trace.

Neely stared at the space Valerian had just vacated, blinked, and then passed a hand slowly back and forth in the vacuum, certain her eyes had deceived her.

Gently Aidan took the book from her and set it aside. Then he bent to kiss her forehead. "I know what you're thinking, but you mustn't tax yourself with conundrums about smoke and mirrors," he advised. "What you just saw was neither a trick nor an illusion. Vanishing is elementary vampire stuff."

"Elementary vampire stuff," Neely repeated. By that point she was almost completely overwhelmed, through no fault of her own, and that irritated her. She flushed and looked up at Aidan with defiance in her eyes. "Tell me, Aidan— what else can vampires do?"

He sat down on the hassock, next to her feet, and folded his graceful hands. He looked forlornly amused as he regarded her. "They can travel through time—back to the point of their own death as a human being, though not forward past the present. The future is as much a mystery to them—us—as it is to you. They are able to communicate mentally with other creatures like themselves, across great distances, and move so rapidly that they cannot be seen."

Neely eased past Aidan and stood, her hands on her hips, her mind filled with dangerous puzzles. "Can they—can you—reproduce?"

Aidan sighed and rose to his feet. "Not the way mortals do. But rest assured, vampires are quite capable of making love."

Neely felt the familiar heat, along with a measure of fear and a storm of loneliness that rushed through her spirit like a wailing wind. "I know," she said, remembering.

He reached out and touched the base of her throat with the tip of a cool index finger. "You know far less than you think you do," he said, not unkindly. "We're greedy, violent creatures, quite fond of pleasure—which explains the typical penchant for immortality."

"Vampires marry, then?"

"They sometimes mate, though it's rare," Aidan clarified, and although one corner of his mouth was raised in the slightest smile, he looked sad. "For the most part, Neely, we nightwalkers tend to keep to ourselves. We mistrust even our own kind, and especially other sorts of fiends." He glanced uneasily toward the window, where dawn was beginning to thin the darkness.

Neely took hold of his arm when he would have turned from her. "You—you mean there are other things"—she paused to blush—"*monsters*—walking around among regular people?"

"Yes," Aidan answered, sounding mildly impatient now. "There are werewolves and ghosts, angels and fairies— lots of 'things.' And then there are the other dimensions, overlaying this one. Were you truly so vain as to believe that humanity has the universe all to itself?"

The question required no reply.

"I don't want you to leave me," Neely blurted out when he moved to pull away. "Please, Aidan—I want to go wherever you're going."

He laid his hands lightly on her shoulders and looked deep into her eyes. "I cannot allow that," he said gently. "Go upstairs and try to rest. I will come to you through your dreams if I can."

She had to be content with that, for it was almost morning; any minute the sun would spill over the horizon and flood the world with light.

Aidan traced the outline of her jaw with one finger, then raised his arms and disappeared.

Neely lingered for a time, trying once again, and wholly in vain, to make sense of what she had just experienced. Her insomnia left her, she was infinitely weary all of a sudden, and felt as if she could sleep for a century.

After returning the first volume of Aidan's journal to the shelf, she slowly climbed the stairs, entered the bedchamber, took off everything but her T-shirt, and tumbled into bed.

Soon after she closed her eyes, Neely found herself float-ing serenely on the dark inner waters of her mind. She allowed her consciousness to drift, too weary to anchor it in reality.

Aidan was in his lair, at least physically, crouching against the wall as he always did, but that day he left the husk of himself behind and sought Neely. He was inexperienced at such travel, unlike Valerian; he could not feel the sunshine or the wind, and he could see only dimly. With practice, he knew, his senses would sharpen.

He found Neely easily, saw her as the dimmest of shad-ows, sprawled in the middle of the large bed he had never actually slept in, her arms and legs askew.

He thought her name, and she stirred, uttering a soft, despairing sound that made him yearn to console her. All the while, Aidan was aware that he should not be testing the limits of his powers in this way, without first taking instruction from Valerian or Maeve. He was in danger because of his wandering, but there was a much greater peril to be considered now—Neely's. As fiercely as he wanted to protect her, she was at risk, for Lisette and perhaps even Valerian would not hesitate to use her, should the opportunity arise.

Valerian was given to dalliances; he would drink from her, toy with her for a time, as cats do with rubber balls and cloth mice, and then toss her aside when his fickle interest waned.

Lisette, and a few others who had reason to hate Aidan, would delight in destroying Neely or, worse yet, turning her into a fiend.

Imagining Neely as a vampire made Aidan cry out softly, in anguished despair. He had to let her go, he thought, to walk away and not look back, to forget her and pray that she would go unnoticed by his enemies.

But could he do that? Did he have the strength, needing the woman as he did? The comfort and affection and love she gave him were as necessary to him as the blood he was condemned to drink, and her whispered gasps of passion engendered in him an ecstasy he had never felt before.

Yes, he admitted to himself, at last, he loved Neely Wallace, fully and completely, as he had never loved anyone else before, in all his two centuries of existence, but he had no right to such tender sentiments. No right on earth, or in heaven.

It was torture, the wanting, the needing and, worst of all, the knowing.

Aidan caused the covers to slide slowly downward, to the foot of the bed, and Neely groped for the pillow next to her and sighed his name.

With that simple, innocent sound the last vestige of Aidan's already tenuous self-control faded. Easily, using only the mental power at which all vampires are adept, he arranged her on her back and removed the T-shirt, drawing it off over her head.

Neely didn't open her eyes, but she was aware of his presence, and she welcomed him, crooning softly and arching her wondrous, supple body once, as if to entice him.

Still, Aidan cherished this fragile, independent creature too much to press his advantage. *May I touch you, Neely?* he asked, exerting no other power now beyond being mentally present in that room. *May I give you pleasure?*

A fine sheen of perspiration glistened on her skin, and the tips of her lush breasts shaped themselves into buds. "Yes," she whispered. "Oh, yes."

" . . . yes . . ."

Neely had never had a more sensual, more downright delicious dream. It seemed that Aidan was lying with her in that huge bed, naked and warm and gloriously passionate.

She felt his hands stroking her, moving over the length of her, learning the curves and hollows of her body, taking their time. When it seemed that her every pore was open to him, he narrowed his caresses to her breasts, weighing them in his palms, fondling them with a gentle reverence that made her want to weep, chafing their nipples with the sides of his thumbs.

She wanted *this* to be real, this tender, fiery loving. *Oh, please,* she wished in silence, *let all the rest of it, the vampires and the men who want to murder me, let those things be the dream.*

Neely cried out in nearly unbearable pleasure when Aidan moistened one nipple with his tongue, then began to suckle. She tried to put her arms around him, but there was nothing to hold, for he was a phantom lover.

Neither waking nor sleeping, Neely responded without restraint as Aidan pressed her breasts together and somehow teased and tasted the straining tips of both. Her body began to undulate, and she felt her hair clinging to her face in moist tendrils. Again she reached for Aidan, again she failed to find him, though he was undeniably *there*, loving her more fully than she'd ever been loved.

She clawed and clutched at the bedclothes as he continued to worship her, rose high off the mattress with a cry of primitive surrender when he burrowed through the silken delta between her legs and nibbled greedily at the very core of her femininity. At the same time he continued to enjoy not one breast, but both, and then—then he added the final element to her conquering. He thrust inside her, hard and hot, while still subjecting her to all the other sensations, too.

Neely was not inexperienced—she'd been deeply in love once before, after all—but she'd never felt anything like this before Aidan. He, and only he, was touching her, and yet all her erogenous zones were being attended at once. She thought the pleasure would surely kill her, and didn't care one whit if she died, if only she could have the promised satisfaction first.

Her release was savage in its intensity, seeming to draw her up onto her elbows, the rounding of her heels, the crown of her head, where she hung suspended, uttering one ragged shout of ecstasy after another. Aidan plied her senses mercilessly, the whole time refusing to allow her to fall after scaling only one peak. No, he took her to another pinnacle, and then another, still higher, and when he finally allowed her to rest, she was mute with exhaustion. She curled up in a corner of her own heart and slept a fathomless sleep.

When she awakened, it was late afternoon. Somewhere deep inside her a chord still resonated with the last sweet music of Aidan's caresses. Neely smiled, stretched, reached for him . . .

And remembered.

She had only dreamed that Aidan had made love to her.

Tears blurred Neely's vision as she turned onto her side and gazed toward the row of windows on the other side of the room. Winter would soon arrive in earnest, and the first faint shadows of twilight were already gathering. She lay there, watching the daylight fade, mourning for the dream world where she and Aidan had become one.

An hour passed, and part of another. When the room was bruised with darkness, Aidan came to her. She saw him, felt him with her outstretched hand, and his weight pressed into the edge of the mattress, gloriously real.

"Aidan."

"Yes, my love."

She reached up, smoothed the sleek, raven-dark hair at his temple with her palm. "I had the loveliest, most scandalous dream."

He smiled that sad, poignant, beautiful smile again, the one that never failed to pierce her heart. "Did you?"

Chapter 9

—◦◦◦)◦(◦◦◦—

As he sat beside Neely on the bed, looking down at her and remembering her responses to his purely mental lovemaking, Aidan again acknowledged the most difficult and treacherous reality of all. She was safe from human enemies while in his house, but in the gravest of danger from immortal predators. Valerian would see her as a plaything, Lisette, as a tool of revenge—even Maeve, in her reckless sisterly and somewhat possessive affection, represented a threat to Neely.

Besides, whatever loyalty Maeve and Valerian might feel toward him, they were vampires, first and always, and as such they could not be trusted with a mortal.

Aidan felt starved and enervated himself, for he had expended tremendous energy pleasuring Neely, and he knew better than anyone what a temptation she offered. Even though he was certain now that he could make love to her, with his body as well as his mind, without fear of doing her harm, he was still terrified for her.

He stood, then retreated a pace. "I'll return in a little while," he said gruffly. "While I'm gone, I want you to remember—to go over every hour, every moment of your past—until you think of some place where you might hide from the senator and his friends until I can deal with them."

She sat up, regarded him with round eyes, unconsciously covering herself with the sheets. "You were really here, making love to me, weren't you? It was some sort of—of vampire magic, like before—and like the night we danced."

Aidan could not look at her, could not bear to reply. He'd done a vile, damnable thing, tainting her delicate purity with his own foul passions. By loving her, he might well have condemned her to a fate that was quite literally worse than death.

"Aidan," she persisted.

"Yes," he admitted, fairly sobbing the word. "Damn it, *yes*, it was real!"

She left the bed, the top sheet wrapped around her slender figure and trailing behind her like a bride's train, and came to him.

"Are you still afraid?" she asked. Her voice was like balm to his tormented spirit, a drop of water on the tongue of a sinner suffering in hell.

"Oh, yes," Aidan ground out, visibly forcing himself to look at her. "Not of bedding you, my lass—I know now that the love I feel for you is far greater than any lust for blood—but there are other dangers."

She stood on tiptoe and kissed him with a tenderness that broke his heart.

"Then let us have whatever time together that we can," she said. "Come, Aidan, and lie with me."

He had never wanted anything so much, with the possible exception of his lost mortality, but he forced himself to draw back from her, knowing that every moment they spent together made her doom more likely.

"There are things I must do," Aidan said, leaving her alone again.

Neely took a quick shower and donned yesterday's jeans and one of Aidan's sweaters, then dashed down the stairs. In a moment of panic, she considered bolting out the front door and running—just running—until she collapsed. The problem was, there was nowhere to run to, and there was certainly no place to hide.

Anyway, she couldn't tolerate the thought of being separated from Aidan—she would rather become a blood-drinker herself than to lose him.

She stood in the dark entryway, breathing deeply, until she'd calmed herself a little. Then she marched resolutely into the kitchen. A bowl of fresh fruit and a loaf of French bread had materialized on the counter; Neely wondered, with grim amusement, if Aidan had conjured the food for her.

Vampire magic, she thought, gazing at the stuff, and doubted that she'd ever feel like eating again.

Although Valerian was ambulatory, he was still too weak to hunt in his usual flamboyant fashion. For exactly that reason—and because Aidan did feel a degree of compassion for the older vampire—he wasn't about to leave his charge alone with Neely.

Instead, at Valerian's suggestion, they visited a bar on a back street in a modern American city, where the local deviants gathered. Here, in the Last Ditch Tavern, drug dealers congregated, along with pornographers of every description, and others who preyed upon the uncertain, the weak, and the naive.

It was a crowded dive, too warm and too dark, filled with

shrillness and smoke, harsh music with indecipherable lyrics, and the intangible specters of lust and hatred and fear.

Aidan despised the Last Ditch instantly, but Valerian surveyed the place as though it were a superb gourmet restaurant. The elder vampire nudged Aidan and pointed to a lonely figure seated at a corner table. He spoke mentally, since it would have been futile to address anyone in the ordinary way in the midst of such chaos.

That pale, skinny creature, there in the shadows, Valerian said. *He's a serial killer, specializing in teenage prostitutes. Likes to make them suffer a little before he finally snuffs them out.*

Aidan regarded the quarry with revulsion. *Scum,* he replied.

Precisely, Valerian answered, beginning to weave his way through the howling, oblivious crowd toward his prey—who undoubtedly, and quite mistakenly, considered himself to be the predator.

Aidan followed, albeit reluctantly, reflecting as he went that there were indeed many kinds of monsters abroad, and relatively few of them were supernatural. *Are there other vampires here?* he inquired of Valerian's broad back.

No, came the sharp retort, rapid-fire, *and you'd damn well better learn to sense their presence on your own.*

We're the only immortals, then? Aidan asked, feeling only mild chagrin. He hated being a vampire and saw no reason to polish the attendant skills.

Valerian turned his head and pinioned Aidan with a brief glare. *There are two warlocks at the bar. Go ahead and look at them. They've been watching us since we came in.*

Aidan tried to resist, but he could not. He glanced toward the long bar, with its brass rails and milling crowd, and immediately spotted the male witches. They stood out in a subtle way, being taller and handsomer and of brighter countenance than most humans. One lifted his glass to

Aidan in an elegant salute and smiled benignly.

Valerian was already closing in on his quarry, the sullen killer sitting alone and feeling sorry for himself. *Don't be fooled by their friendliness,* he warned as a hasty aside, already concentrating palpably on his imminent feeding. *The warlock's blood is poison to us, as I've told you many times before. They envy our powers and use their own to thwart us whenever they can.*

Aidan shifted his attention to the measly specimen Valerian had chosen to feed upon. The elegant vampire smiled his most charming smile, pulled back a chair, and sat down at the table.

"Hello, Udell," he said to the pockmarked boy.

Aidan sat, too, although he could hardly tolerate the psychic stench that rose from the lad's diseased soul. To his amazement, Udell smiled at the beast who would consume and perhaps kill him.

"How'd you know my name?" he shouted over the perverse celebrations and the grating music.

Valerian looked as handsome as an archangel as he settled back in his chair and regarded the monster with apparent fondness. "By magic," he said.

Watching the interchange, Aidan felt sickened, even though he had no pity at all for the hapless Udell. He'd already glanced into the little worm's mind and seen his favorite forms of amusement firsthand. No, it was Valerian's blithe amorality that troubled Aidan now, that hardened hazy suspicions into fact. Here was a creature who, in the final analysis, would indulge his own dark appetites, wherever the opportunity arose. Whether the victim was good or evil, male or female, old or young, might not matter at all.

Suddenly Valerian's gaze sliced to Aidan's face. *It isn't true, what you're thinking,* he told him, in the same silent way they'd communicated before. *I am capable of love and the purest devotion, just as you are.*

Aidan looked away, uncomfortable. *Just get on with it*, he replied. One of the warlocks was moving through the throng toward them, smiling. *I don't want to stay here any longer than I must.*

Valerian held out a hand to Udell, who took it, smiling foolishly, like an old maid who has finally been asked to dance. Together, vampire and witless victim disappeared, blending into the grinding, sweating mass of humanity choking the dance floor.

Great, Aidan thought, watching the warlock. *Now I get to make small talk with somebody who wants to turn me into a toad.*

The warlock laughed. He was attractive, with soft brown hair, impish hazel eyes, and a quick grin. "I want to do nothing of the sort," he said, holding out his hand. "My name is Cain."

"Figures," Aidan replied, ignoring the gesture. He looked toward the other ghoul, still standing at the bar, and arched one eyebrow. "Is that your brother, Abel?"

All the mirth had drained from Cain's manner. "Not funny." He grabbed a wooden chair, wrenched it around, and straddled the seat, his sinewy arms folded across the back. "You cannot possibly be so naive as you seem," he declared. "Do you know what goes on in this bar?"

"Every sort of depravity, I would imagine," Aidan answered coolly. "Look, I'm not out to make friends or bridge any philosophical gaps between your kind and mine, all right? I'm here to feed, and for no other purpose."

Cain's smile returned. He turned his head slowly and pulled down on the collar of his expensive sweater with one hand to bare his throat in invitation.

Aidan wondered if it was possible for a vampire to vomit. "Thanks, anyway," he said, rising from his chair. He scanned the crowd, looking for Valerian, enjoying a brief fantasy in which he drove a spike through that particular vampire's heart with a croquet mallet.

That night Aidan made a point of selecting a female victim, a very disturbed creature who had left her children with an abusive biker boyfriend to come to the Last Ditch for an evening's diversion. Minutes before Aidan approached her, she had sucked the week's grocery money up her nose through a rolled-up dollar bill. Her name was Fay, and she was more than neglectful, she was a sociopath, untroubled by the dimmest flicker of conscience.

They danced for a while, moving against each other, and then he led her through the hallway at the rear, past the rest rooms, and into the alley.

It certainly wasn't a sexual encounter, but when Aidan bit into Fay's narrow throat to drink, he felt the usual jubilation—and an almost paralyzing rush of guilt.

He left the woman half-conscious, but very much alive, huddled beside an overflowing trash bin, and went in search of Valerian. At first, seeing no sign of the other vampire only annoyed Aidan, but then, when a single, grim possibility struck him, he was alarmed.

Neely was alone, unguarded. And Valerian surely saw her not only as a tempting delicacy, but as a rival.

There, on a snowy street corner, Aidan raised his arms over his head, clasped his hands together as if to pray, and vanished.

Neely had found Aidan's car keys after an impulsive search. She was bending over his desk, hastily penning a note, when there was a rippling stir in the air. Catching her breath, she looked up to see Valerian standing only a few feet away.

She laid one hand to her heart, willing it to slow down to its regular pace, and managed a shaky smile. "I was just going to the market," she said, feeling foolish even as she uttered the words.

Valerian folded his arms and tilted his magnificent head to one side. He had a mane of chestnut-colored hair and mischievous violet eyes, and he grinned as he regarded her, as if he were mildly puzzled.

Neely reminded herself that this was a vampire she was dealing with—an ancient and very accomplished one, according to Aidan's journals. She took a step backward. "Where is Aidan?"

Valerian sighed. "He's occupied with other matters just now. You shouldn't go out. It's very dangerous."

She put her hands on her hips, figuring bravado was a better bet than sniveling cowardice, though it was the latter she was inclined toward. "Don't look now," she said tartly, "but I'm not exactly safe and sound as it is."

He chuckled, his arms still folded and his expression still curious. "It's hopeless—loving Aidan Tremayne the way you do, I mean. He can never be a husband to you in any fashion you would even begin to understand."

Neely's temper, an unwary and impulsive force in its own right, flared with all the fury of the fires that burned at the center of the earth. She forgot all about Valerian's supernatural talents and went to stand directly in front of him, looking straight into his eyes. "You want him for yourself," she accused quietly. "You want him for a lover."

Valerian's eyes flashed, and he seemed to grow taller, fiercer, and much more dangerous. "You cannot possibly comprehend my feelings for Aidan, with your pitiful mortal brain," he growled. "*I am a vampire*, and my affections transcend such trivial concepts as sexuality! Do you think you can categorize me into your narrow human view of what a lover should be? Well, you are wrong!" He paused and, to Neely's enormous relief, made a visible effort to restrain his temper. "Once Aidan comes to terms with who and what he is—"

"No," Neely interrupted quietly, almost gently, shaking her head. "You're the one who needs to get in touch with reality, Valerian. Be careful, or your delusions will destroy you."

The legendary vampire actually looked crestfallen, as well as enraged, just for the merest flicker of a moment. He turned aside and shoved a hand through his thick hair. "To be a creature of the night," he said in a hoarse voice, "is to feel every emotion that mortals feel, a hundredfold, a thousandfold, be it an admirable one or not. In the immortal world, gender has no real bearing on matters of the heart—it is the individual, the object of one's love, who matters."

Neely hugged herself and turned away, hoping Valerian would not sense what she was feeling just then—pity. She reached into the pocket of her coat and jingled Aidan's car keys with her fingers, in a nervous and singularly impotent gesture. She wasn't going anywhere now, that much was clear.

"Perhaps we're both fooling ourselves," she reflected miserably. "I'm as guilty of it as you are."

Before Valerian could offer a response—maybe he had never meant to anyway—Aidan arrived. His appearance wasn't subtle, but violent, and the very force of his rage seemed to shake the room like an earthquake.

"What are you doing here?" he demanded, seeming to tower over the gigantic Valerian, like a mountain about to spew lava.

Neely shrank back, taking refuge behind Aidan's desk.

"Calm yourself," Valerian said good-naturedly, laying his hands on Aidan's shoulders. "I was finished before you left the woman."

Aidan flung Valerian's arms aside while Neely sagged into the desk chair, stricken. She had no claim to Aidan's fidelity—and certainly no sane person would expect loyalty—but she was wounded all the same.

"Damn you," Aidan spat at Valerian, as fierce and ferocious as an angry panther, "get out—leave us!"

Even though she'd witnessed the phenomenon before, it still left Neely shaken, the way Valerian just dissipated into the air like so much smoke. Unconsciously she had raised both hands to her face, and now she gazed at Aidan through splayed fingers, unable to speak.

He crossed the room, then stood just on the other side of the desk, looking down at her with an unreadable expression. His words startled Neely further, for she had expected, hoped for, some explanation. Some impassioned defense.

"Well?" he asked impatiently. "Have you thought of a place to hide?"

Neely felt shattering despair at the idea of leaving him, even though she'd been telling herself earlier in the evening she must do just that. Like Valerian, she had been whistling in the dark, making-believe that she and Aidan could ever have any sort of sane relationship. "I really have to go, then?"

Aidan nodded, looked away. She saw her own anguish reflected in his countenance, mirror-perfect. "Yes," he said raggedly. "Involving you in my life was an unconscionable thing to do, Neely. My enemies—good God, even my friends—are infinitely more dangerous to you than any human criminal could ever be."

She wanted to go to him, to clasp his arm and rest her head against the outer length of his shoulder, but she held herself back. "Valerian, Lisette, the others—yes, I can believe they might do me harm. But you, Aidan?"

He whirled on her, imperious in his pain, taller and fiercer for it. "No," he said in a bitter hiss. "But I am not a man—I have no literal, physical heart, no lungs to breathe with, no stomach to fill. I cannot give you children or walk with you in the light of the sun. My passion for you is an unholy thing—" Here he held his hands up, white and strong and elegant, as if offering some monstrous display. "Don't you understand that I am, first and foremost, a beast, cursed by man and by God?"

Neely felt herself go pale, and she wanted to faint from sheer grief, but she would not let it happen. "It's impossible, isn't it?" she mourned with quiet dignity.

Aidan's eyes were bleak indeed as he regarded her. "I made love to you with my mind, Neely," he said despondently, "not my hands, my mouth, my body. I am a monster, and I beg you not to forget that, even if I should. Although I would not hurt you, ever, I endanger you simply by the fact of loving you. Now, is there a place you can go to hide?"

Glumly Neely nodded. "Yes," she said. "There's a cottage on the coast, up in Maine. It belongs to a college friend of mine, Wendy Browning. She's in London now, studying drama."

"Very well," Aidan agreed reluctantly. "I will take you there."

Neely shook her head. "I don't want to be beamed anywhere," she replied. "It's too hard on my nerves. If you would just lend me your car, or I could rent one under another name—"

Aidan stood still, visibly debating the idea in his mind. "You will take mine," he finally conceded. He arched one dark eyebrow and smiled slightly, his gaze fixed on the pocket of Neely's coat, which she'd forgotten she was wearing. "You were going to, anyway, weren't you?"

"I didn't know what I was going to do." The words were fragile, and several splintered and broke as Neely uttered them.

He moved, as if to approach her, then visibly held himself in check. He went the long way around to reach the desk, giving Neely a wide berth, and took a handful of cash from the one drawer. "Here," he said. "Take this."

"Will—will I see you again?" Neely hated herself for

asking, but she had to know. She had enough on her mind without wondering about that, too.

"Yes," Aidan answered, albeit reluctantly. "I have certain hopes for myself, for us, though I can't discuss them with you now. And wonderfully independent Yankee that you are, I think you'll need my help to completely resolve your problem with the senator and his buddies."

It was incredible, Neely thought, the exultation she felt at being told she wasn't seeing Aidan Tremayne for the last time. She was, logically speaking, in no position to be exulted about anything. "I'll make a map—so you can find the cottage," she offered, perhaps too eagerly, and with a sniffle.

Aidan smiled, very sadly. "No need, my love. There is no place, time, or dimension where you could hide from me. Your beautiful, brave spirit shines as brightly as if it were the last star in the universe."

Neely sniffled again and wiped her eyes with the back of one hand. "You know, if you ever get tired of the plasma business, I think you could make it big as a poet."

He chuckled, but the sound was hollow and desolate. "Go," he said.

Neely went, taking his car, the money he'd given her, and her toothbrush.

When Neely had gone, Valerian reappeared. Undoubtedly he'd folded himself into some nook or corner and watched the whole melodrama with acute interest.

"If you know what's good for you," he told Aidan, going to the liquor cabinet to pour a brandy he could not drink, "and for that fetching little creature who just left, you'll never go near her again."

Aidan was standing at the parlor window. He'd seen the sleek white car move into the driveway, watched until its foggy-red taillights had disappeared into the snowy gloom. "I have never known what was good for me," he answered.

"That's why I ended up in this fix."

"What are you going to do now?"

Aidan sighed, but he did not turn around to face the other vampire. "Two things: make myself available to the Brotherhood, should they decide to pay me a call—and find Lisette."

The brandy glass clattered to the floor and broke, and Aidan felt a certain triumph in the knowledge that he'd startled the great Valerian. That wasn't an easy thing to do.

"Are you mad?" Valerian demanded.

"You know I am," Aidan answered.

"How will you find her?"

"Easily. I mean to put myself directly in her path."

Valerian's voice trembled with rage. He gripped Aidan's arm and wrenched him about so that they faced each other. "She will destroy you!"

"Maybe," Aidan agreed, lifting his shoulders in a distracted shrug. "I mean to find out, as soon as possible."

"It's this girl," Valerian cried, waving his arms wide in a gesture of fury, "this Neely Wallace, who has brought all this grief and trouble down on our heads! I should have destroyed her long ago!"

Aidan narrowed his eyes as he looked into Valerian's strained features. "You have that power," he agreed. "No one can dispute that. But if you harm Neely, my friend, you will have to destroy me as well. For if you do not, I will plague you with every step you take, until the last trumpet sounds!"

Valerian's expression was one of grief and subsiding fury. "Doesn't it matter, that I care for you?"

"No," Aidan answered. "Your kind of caring is perversion to me. There is a bond between us, because of the blood communion, but I cannot give you anything more than loyalty and friendship. The sooner you accept that, Valerian, the sooner we can go on to other things."

The elder vampire did not reply but instead turned his back to Aidan without a word and made himself into a shifting wisp of smoke.

Aidan sat down in a leather chair near the fire, closed his eyes, and mentally followed Neely's progress through the town of Bright River and northward, toward New Hampshire and, beyond that, Maine.

Neely stopped at an all-night café just before dawn and put a call through to her brother. She had not been watching television or even reading newspapers, but she knew her disappearance from that tacky motel room several days before had probably drawn some media attention. Although she'd finally written a note, which Aidan had delivered by some means she hadn't asked him to explain, she wanted to reassure Ben and Danny that she was still alive and well.

"Hello," her brother said, sounding alert even at that unholy hour of the morning. He was an ambitious sort and had probably been up long enough to shower and make coffee.

"Ben," Neely whispered, hunching close to the pay phone, which was situated in a narrow hallway, next to the café's rest rooms. "It's me. I can't talk long, in case someone traces the call, but I wanted to tell you that I'm okay, and that I love you and Danny—"

"Neely." Ben sighed the name; it resonated with sadness and relief. "Thank God. I thought maybe they'd gotten you, those bastards from the Capitol."

"Not yet," Neely said. She smiled grimly, glad her brother didn't know what *else* might be stalking her. "Look, don't worry about me, Ben, because I've got at least one very powerful friend. Gotta go now."

"I love you," Ben said in parting, understanding as always. "Take care."

With that, Neely hung up. Tears stung her eyes as she turned around and nearly collided with a smiling truck driver, who was waiting to use the phone. He was tall and good-looking, and the name "Trent" was stitched on the pocket of his shirt in red thread.

Neely was hungry, but she was afraid to linger too long in one spot, just in case Senator Hargrove's henchmen were following her. She found a McDonald's, bought a breakfast sandwich and some orange juice at the drive-through window, and headed back out onto the freeway.

Spain

Lisette was feeling stronger with every fall of twilight, every fevered feeding. Her favorite victims were innocents; their blood gave her the most energy and the greatest euphoria, and she always pressed them as close to death as she dared.

She slept in a hidden crypt by day, a safe nook tucked away in the cellar of the villa she'd bought generations ago. Every fifty years or so, she'd willed the place to herself, along with the fortune that had been hers ever since she'd arrived in Europe, many centuries before, and married a very rich mortal. She was feared and revered by all but a few very foolish vampires; she had everything.

Almost.

Seated on the stone railing of the terrace outside her bedchamber, gazing out at the star-dappled water, Lisette thought of the one scalawag in all her long history who had managed to break her heart.

Aidan Tremayne.

She smiled a fragile smile, remembering. She'd given him immortality, the ungrateful wretch, and taught him to stalk and kill, to navigate through time and space, to protect himself from other immortals and veil his presence from humans and lesser vampires. In return for her kindness, he had betrayed her.

Lisette sighed and tossed her head, so that her rich dark hair tumbled back over one alabaster-smooth shoulder. She wore a Grecian dress, strictly for the sake of drama. Her mistake, she reflected, had been in making Aidan into the splendid fiend he was. Instead she should have used him until he bored her, like the multitude of handsome young mortals who had preceded him, and then consumed his life force and discarded him.

"Fool," she said to herself in a bitter whisper. A soft breeze carried the word out over a warm Spanish sea.

Lisette stepped up onto the terrace railing and stood there, her arms spread wide, her white gown flowing and billowing wonderfully around her slender figure. For a century and a half she had lain dormant in her hidden tomb, rising only when she knew she would perish if she did not feed, languishing in her despondency, too distraught to function.

Then, during one of her brief, slightly frantic forays into the world of humans, she'd caught a glimpse of another female vampire, Maeve Tremayne. Maeve was Aidan's twin, and her resemblance to him had stirred some sudden and harsh violence deep in Lisette's being.

From that night onward, Lisette had forced herself to rise and feed. She had been practicing her powers and regaining her former strength for months. Soon she would be immune to the light of the sun as she had once been, able to track errant vampires to their lairs.

She was still queen of the blood-drinkers, among the oldest on earth, and she intended to show them all that she had no intention of abdicating. After that she would deal vengeance to her enemies, one by one.

Valerian would be first, that despicable traitor. After him, Maeve, who, Lisette was convinced, secretly aspired to reign over the nightwalkers herself. And when Maeve and Valerian were nothing but smoldering piles of ash, shifting in the sunlight, Lisette vowed, she would turn her full attention on Aidan.

By the time she was through meting out her myriad punishments, the very fires of hell would look good to him.

"Lisette."

The voices came from behind her, speaking in chorus and startling her so that she nearly toppled off the high terrace onto the rocky shore below. The fall would not have done her bodily injury, of course, but her dignity might have been hopelessly wounded.

She turned slowly and looked down into the white, upturned faces of her visitors.

Canaan and Benecia Havermail stood before her, wearing identical dresses of yellow satin. Lisette was glad they would never grow to adult size, for their natures were at least as vicious as her own, and she would not relish the competition.

"What do you want?" she snapped, irritated.

Again the child-fiends spoke in eerily perfect unison, their fangs glinting in the starlight as they chattered. "We've come about Mr. Tremayne. He's been to Havermail Castle, you know, inquiring about the Brotherhood."

Lisette floated down from the railing to stand before the horrid little pair. "What does Aidan want with the Brotherhood?" She raised a hand when they both started to talk again. "Only one of you need answer."

Benecia, after a triumphant glance at her younger sister, went on alone. "He desires to be mortal again," she said. At this oddity she giggled, and so did Canaan.

Lisette, however, was not amused. She turned away from her visitors and grasped the terrace railing in both hands. No vampire, to her knowledge, had ever made such a transition, but Aidan was just brazen enough, just fanciful enough, to try.

Perhaps she would be forced to resolve the matter sooner than she'd planned.

Chapter 10

—◦◦◦✕◦◦◦—

Neely drove until midafternoon, when she simply could go no farther. She rented a room somewhere in New Hampshire, this time choosing one of the large chain motels, and secured all the locks carefully before collapsing onto the bed. After an hour or so she awakened just long enough to remove her coat and kick off her shoes, then sank back into an exhausted sleep.

When she opened her eyes, feeling as if she'd just risen from the depths of a coma, there was no light except for the red numerals on the clock radio on the lamp table.

3:47 A.M.

Neely would have been glad to sleep another twelve hours, at least, but she didn't dare linger in one place for too long. Although she was fairly certain no one was following her, she couldn't afford to depend on luck.

She stumbled into the bathroom, showered, and put yesterday's clothes back on. Later, she promised herself, she would buy jeans, sweaters, underwear, and the like. For now she was traveling light.

At 4:14, Neely left the motel room. She was starved, but the fast-food places weren't open yet, and the idea of wandering into a big, well-lit truck stop for oatmeal and toast made her feel too vulnerable. In the end she stopped at a convenience store for high-octane coffee and a sweet roll.

As she had the day before, Neely drove until she was blind with fatigue. Then she stopped at a shopping mall, entered a crowded discount store, and bought the clothing she needed, along with a hot dog and a bag of popcorn. That afternoon she checked into a motor court beside a frozen lake. She propped a chair under the doorknob, since the locks didn't look all that secure. After devouring her scanty supper, she bathed and toppled into bed.

Sleep didn't come as readily this time, even though Neely was every bit as tired as she had been the night before. She switched on the television set, turned to one of the cable networks, and settled in to watch a tabloid program.

"This is Melody Ling," a sharply dressed reporter was saying, "reporting from Washington, D.C., where Mrs. Elaine Hargrove, wife of the prominent senator, is allegedly recovering satisfactorily from emergency surgery."

Neely sat bolt upright against the musty pillows at her back, staring at the screen, willing Ling to say more. Unfortunately the piece was over.

She grabbed up the remote, then sought and found the twenty-four-hour news channel. She'd had the car radio on all day while she traveled, but she'd heard nothing about the Hargroves.

Neely watched three segments—a scandal concerning the sale of arms to some hormonal Third-World country, a piece on distraught dairy farmers, and the latest tidbit out of Buckingham Palace. Then, finally, Senator Dallas

Hargrove appeared on the screen, striding out of a well-known Washington hospital, looking harried and impatient.

Although Hargrove was definitely a skunk and a moral lightweight, Neely thought, it was impossible not to feel sorry for him just then. Reporters barred his way, the portable lights deepened the lines and shadows in his face, and microphones stabbed at him like drawn lances.

"Senator Hargrove, can you tell us anything about Mrs. Hargrove's accident?"

"Is she resting comfortably?"

"Will she recover?"

"Was she driving when the accident occurred?"

The senator stopped and held up both hands in a bid for order. "Elaine—Mrs. Hargrove—is conscious," he said tersely. "We have every hope that she will survive. And no, my wife suffers from a chronic illness and does not drive. She was riding with our chauffeur when the limousine was forced off the road by a reckless driver."

"Has an arrest been made?" a reporter called out, but Hargrove was plainly finished with the interview. He forced his way through a throng of newspeople and got into the backseat of a waiting car.

The camera switched to an anchorwoman in the network newsroom, where the scanty details of Elaine Hargrove's accident were reviewed. She had been on her way to a luncheon, where she was to be presented with an award of some sort, when, according to the chauffeur, another car had come up behind them and crashed hard into the bumper. The driver, already traveling at a fairly high speed, had been startled and lost control of the wheel. The limo had sideswiped a concrete abutment and then swerved into the path of an oncoming semi-truck.

No one else had been injured besides Elaine Hargrove.

Chilled, Neely hobbled in and took another bath, soaking in the hottest water she could stand. When she got out of the tub, however, and wrapped herself in a rough towel, she was still as cold as ever.

Obviously the senator had run afoul of his drug-dealing friends, and they'd made a cruel example out of Elaine. Hargrove would be desperate to appease the mob now, which meant he would make no further efforts to protect Neely.

All thoughts of sleep deserted her, even though she was half sick with weariness. She was on her own, and if she wanted to stay alive, she'd better move fast.

She tore the tags from her new clothes and wrenched on panties and a bra, stiff jeans, and a starchy sweatshirt. Then she groped for the telephone and dialed New York information.

Ten frustrating minutes later, Neely was speaking to someone in Melody Ling's department at the television network. Ms. Ling was still out on assignment, and it would probably be impossible to reach her before morning.

Neely slammed down the receiver, snatched up her few belongings, and rushed out to the car.

She tried twice more to get through to Ling, the following morning and the one after that, and was unsuccessful both times. Finally, in the midst of a blizzard, she reached Timber Cove, a tiny town on the winter-bleak coast of Maine. Wendy Browning's summer cottage was five miles north, and after buying a few supplies in a small grocery store, Neely took refuge there.

The front door key was under one of the legs of the picnic table out on the snow-mounded deck, as always. Neely had been a guest in the cottage many times, and before flying off to London, Wendy had told her she was welcome to use the place whenever she wished.

She let herself in, turned up the gas heater, and lifted the telephone receiver to her ear. There was a dial tone.

Neely carried in her bags of clothing and her groceries, set a pot of coffee to brewing, and stood at the glass doors leading to the deck, looking out at the rocky, snow-streaked shore.

When she had had a cup of coffee to warm herself, she put on her coat and trekked outside, through the grayness of late morning on a stormy day, to the woodshed. There she knelt in a corner and raised a loose floorboard with both hands.

Underneath lay a fat manila envelope, wrapped in plastic, just exactly where Neely had left it.

She carried the packet back to the house, opened it, and saw that all the documents and recordings were still there. Trembling slightly, Neely returned to the telephone and dialed Melody Ling's number.

This time she got lucky.

Aidan found Maeve easily, for once. She was at her house in London, in her beloved nineteenth century, enter-taining a drawing room full of guests. A string quartet played Mozart in one corner, while elegantly dressed visi-tors mingled, some sipping champagne and nibbling clam puffs, others only pretending.

It was an interesting mix of vampires and humans, jaded writers and artists who probably knew full well that they were socializing with fiends. In Aidan's experience the right-brain types found such things stimulating.

"Darling." Maeve swept toward him, her crisp satin dress rustling as she moved, both hands extended. Her dark blue eyes were alight with surprise and pleasure, both swiftly displaced by worry. "What a lovely—surprise. Aidan—?"

He kissed her cheek and smiled wanly, but that was the extent of his effort to appear normal. He had not fed for three days, he'd been so grieved over the parting with Neely, and he was faint with the lack of nourishment.

Maeve frowned, still holding his hands, and he felt some of her abundant strength flow into him. She pulled him through the strange crowd and out onto a stone terrace with high iron railings.

The wind was bitingly cold, but it did little to revive Aidan.

"What's happened?" Maeve demanded. "Honestly, Aidan, if this has something to do with that wretched woman—"

He looked directly into his sister's angry eyes. "It has everything to do with Neely," he said. "I love her. I'd rather perish than lose her, and I would sell my soul, if indeed I have one at all, to live with her as a man."

Maeve's face tightened, and for a moment her fury pulsed between them, but then she let her forehead fall against his shoulder and wept disconsolately.

Aidan held her in a gentle embrace. "I'm sorry," he whispered raggedly.

She looked up at him, after a long time, her beautiful eyes glimmering with tears. Aidan was heartbroken to see his sister in such a state.

"There is no turning you aside from this course, is there?" Maeve asked, lifting her chin. "You'll either succeed in your foolish enterprise or perish in the attempt."

Aidan laid his hand gently against her cheek. "Anything is better than being what I am, darling," he said. "Even eternal damnation."

Her alabaster skin grew even paler, and she clutched at the satin lapels of his dinner jacket. "Don't say that!" she pleaded in an agonized whisper. "To think of you burning forever and ever—oh, Aidan, I can't bear it!"

"Shhh," Aidan said, laying his hands on her glowing shoulders and giving her just the slightest shake. "Then don't think of that."

"How will I know what's happened to you?" Maeve pleaded. "How will I know whether you're alive or—or dead?"

He kissed her forehead. "Wait until you hear the first rumors," he told her with a sad smile. "Then visit my house in Connecticut. If I've managed to make the transition, I'll leave a bouquet of white roses on that round table in the entryway, as a sort of signal."

Maeve studied his face for a long moment, then nodded. "You haven't fed. Surely you know you cannot hope even to survive if you do not guard your strength."

Aidan let his hands fall to his sides, though he still studied his sister with affection. He wanted to remember her always, whether he writhed in hell or was allowed to live out his allotted number of years as a man.

"The hunger makes it possible to think more clearly, Maeve," he said. "You know that."

She touched his cheek, and her lips moved, but no sound came from her.

"Good-bye," he said.

Valerian crashed Maeve's party half an hour after Aidan left, looking distracted and a little frantic. He grabbed her hand and pulled her out onto the same terrace where she'd stood with her brother, her heart broken at her feet.

"Have you seen that idiot sibling of yours?" Valerian demanded.

Maeve bridled, but not because Valerian had called Aidan an idiot—she quite agreed, just now, that the description suited. "Who do you think you are, dragging me away from my guests like this and speaking so familiarly?"

He paused, then shamed her with a languorous smile.

Maeve looked away, remembering things she would rather have forgotten. Valerian had taught her much more than how to travel through time and read minds during their long association. "That's over," she said.

"Perhaps," Valerian agreed. Then he grew impatient again. "Tell me—have you seen Aidan?"

"Yes," Maeve said, leaning back against the terrace railing and studying her mentor in the cold light of the stars. "He was here earlier, to bid me farewell."

"*What?*"

She nodded, and when she spoke, her voice was lined with tiny fractures. "He would rather die than be what we are, Valerian—he would choose oblivion, even hellfire, over the life of a vampire. He despises himself, and us."

Valerian gave an explosive sigh and shoved one hand through his mane of rich brown hair. "I should never have left him alone," the magnificent monster fretted. "It's just that he exasperates me so, and he has no compunction whatsoever about breaking my heart—"

"You don't have a heart," Maeve snapped, annoyed. As usual, Valerian was thinking only of himself. "And why *did* you leave Aidan alone?"

"He was moping about over that woman, and I needed to hunt, to rebuild my strength," Valerian said, flinging his hands out wide in a gesture of angry resignation. "I spent a few nights indulging myself—I admit that—and when I returned to Connecticut to look in on Aidan, he was gone."

Despair swelled up inside Maeve. "He's not coming back, Valerian. The sooner we both give up and accept that, the better it will be."

"You don't understand!" Valerian cried. "Somehow he's learned to veil his whereabouts from me. Maeve, without me he has no defense against Lisette!"

"Some defense you offer," Maeve accused. "She despises you almost as much as she does Aidan. Leave my brother alone, Valerian—let him work this out for himself."

"Damn it, Maeve, do you have any idea what she'll do to him?"

Maeve closed her eyes. "I have to believe he'll escape her," she said. "I cannot think otherwise and still go on living." With that, she turned and would have gone back into the house to rejoin her guests, but Valerian forcibly stopped her, gripping her shoulders and wrenching her around to face him.

"Perhaps you are willing to let Lisette play vile games with Aidan until she finally decides to kill him, but I am not. And I am more powerful than you are, Maeve—don't forget that."

She trembled, this female vampire who was afraid of nothing, save seeing her brother suffer. "What do you want?"

"Look deep inside yourself," Valerian ordered, his voice low and hypnotic, but urgent, too. "There you will see Aidan's reflection. Tell me where to find him, Maeve."

Maeve began to shiver. "He's standing on a terrace— like this one—" She gave a small, involuntary cry and raised curled fingers to her mouth. "Oh, Valerian, Aidan has gone to Lisette's villa, on the coast of Spain!"

Valerian released her so swiftly that she sank to the tiled floor of the terrace, too weakened by horror to rise. He held out his cloak and spun around, and before he'd completed a single turn, he'd vanished.

Maeve sat dazed on the tiles for a few minutes, sobbing inwardly, longing to rush to Aidan's rescue, as Valerian had, and knowing that her brother would never forgive her if she did. As rash and ill-advised as Aidan's decision had been, no one, not even Valerian himself, would be able to sway him from it.

"You *are* the adventurous type."

Aidan whirled, though he knew the voice behind him wasn't Lisette's, and saw a youth leaning against the stone wall of the villa, his arms folded. He was dressed all in black, like a cat burglar, and wore a cocky grin. By Aidan's guess, the lad was no older than seventeen.

"Who are you?"

The sleek young vampire pushed himself away from the wall with one foot. "The name is Tobias—Aidan. You ought to be more alert, you know. It's nothing but luck that Lisette is hunting elsewhere tonight."

"Yes," Aidan said, "it's luck, all right. Bad luck." He tugged at the cuffs of his dinner jacket. "What do you want—Tobias?"

"Not a thing. I'm here because of what *you* want. Or, at least, what you told Aubrey Havermail you wanted—a chat with a representative of the Brotherhood."

Aidan was taken aback, but he smiled and offered his hand. "Aren't you a little young to be part of such an august group?"

Tobias gave a slow grin. "I guess that depends on how you define the word *young.* I was among the first vampires created." The sudden stunned expression on Aidan's face seemed to please him. "Come. Even we old ones don't enjoy tangling with the likes of Lisette. She can be such a bitch."

In the next instant everything went dark, and Aidan heard a rushing sound. When he was conscious again, he found himself standing with Tobias in a natural tunnel, beside an underground river. There was no light, but that didn't matter, of course, for a vampire's vision is at its best in the blackest gloom.

"Where are we?"

Tobias sighed. "You don't need to know that," he answered with cordial impatience. He sighed again. "I'm afraid Aubrey was quite right about you. You're not much of a vampire."

"No," Aidan said evenly. "I'm not."

"He says you want to be changed back into a man." The words echoed in the dank chamber, hollow with disbelief. "Is that true?"

"Absolutely," Aidan answered. He felt a thrumming excitement deep inside, as well as a certain well-founded terror. "I did not willingly become a vampire. I was forced."

"You are not the first," Tobias pointed out, clearly unmoved.

"Perhaps not," Aidan agreed mildly. "But I am a weak link in the chain. You saw for yourself, back there on Lisette's terrace, how easy it is to catch me unawares. Suppose I fall into the hands of those who are enemies to all vampires—the Warrior Angel, for example. What's his name again? Ah, yes. Nemesis. What if I were to be captured by Nemesis and forced to tell all I know about blood-drinkers such as yourself? The Dark Kingdom would crumble then, wouldn't it, like a castle of sand?"

"I have only to destroy you, here and now, to prevent such a tragedy," Tobias said coolly. Aidan was aware of the creature's tension, however; he was like a string on an instrument, pulled tight and ready to snap.

Aidan smiled. "I am an insignificant vampire," he admitted, "but there are those who would miss me, and even dare to avenge my destruction."

"Valerian," Tobias said despairingly. "And Maeve."

"You know them, then," Aidan chimed, in a pleased tone that was meant to be irritating.

"They are rebellious and cause the elders a great deal of consternation."

Aidan made a *tsk-tsk* sound, well aware that he was on proverbial thin ice. "I don't know what vampirism is coming to," he said. "Do you?"

Tobias glared. "This way," he growled. Then he turned and moved along the stream's edge, headed into the very heart of the darkness, and Aidan followed.

Eventually they reached a large, torch-lit cave, where ancient scenes and symbols had been painted onto the walls, among the earlier sketches and scrawls of prehistoric man. Aidan would have been fascinated if his business in that place hadn't been so crucial.

The vampires assembled themselves from particles of dust in the air around Aidan, it seemed to him, the oldest blood-drinkers on earth, some fresh-faced like Tobias, others with flowing silver beards and skin as crinkled and weathered as aged leather.

"This one would be mortal again," Tobias announced to the gathering, his bewilderment plain in his voice. "He says he was made against his will."

The elders murmured among themselves as they walked around Aidan, examining him, but their language was unfamiliar.

Aidan kept his shoulders straight and looked each one, in turn, directly in the eye. He caught the name "Nemesis" in the conversational drift, and knew Tobias had reported his threat.

They might well destroy him now, Aidan thought. He was mildly surprised to realize that he didn't care; having met Neely, and been reminded of what he was missing, he knew he would rather perish by the most horrible of means than live for all eternity knowing she could never be his.

If he could not be restored to his humanity, if he could not love Neely freely, and without fear, he wanted only destruction.

At long last the circling ceased. One of the elders leaned close to Aidan and rasped in English, "Do you follow Nemesis?"

Aidan showed his fangs, in a rather impudent and theatrical way. "I am no angel," he pointed out in the next moment.

The ancient vampire's glacial blue eyes narrowed, and he made an angry gesture with one age-gnarled hand. "Confine this unmannerly whelp where he can do no harm to himself or the rest of us. We will decide his fate later."

Vampires closed in on either side of Aidan, taking his arms, and he struggled, but in vain. Still, he did not regret the course he'd taken, for he was willing to risk anything, undergo any ordeal, in order to be with Neely.

Aidan was dragged to a barred chamber and flung inside. His fine clothes were torn away without ceremony or apology, and he was given a monk's robe, made of some coarse brown cloth. He put the garment on, for the sake of his own dignity, and when his jailers had left him, he tried the bars.

They were immovable.

"I trust you're happy now," a familiar voice said.

He turned to see Tobias standing just behind him, inside the cell, and scowled. "Overjoyed," he replied.

Tobias shook his head, clearly amazed. "Such infernal audacity."

"There's nothing worse than a smart-ass vampire," Aidan agreed.

Tobias laughed outright at that. "If you say so. You're the first blood-drinker ever to ask for transformation—did you know that? That's why you're not staked out in some desert somewhere, waiting for the sun to cook you by degrees, you understand. Because you're an oddity."

Aidan was careful not to let his trepidation show, although to be forced to endure the cruel ministrations of the sun was among the worst fears of nearly every vampire. "Have they destroyed others that way?" he asked.

"Oh, yes. Over the centuries certain rebellious ones have had to be . . . dealt with," Tobias answered. "We learned that particular trick from Nemesis."

An involuntary chill passed through Aidan at the mention of the Warrior Angel, and Tobias chuckled, recognizing it for what it was. There was no mercy in Nemesis, despite his ties with the Kingdom of Heaven; he had been conducting a personal vendetta against blood-drinkers for thousands of years.

"Is there a way?" Aidan whispered, his voice hoarse. "Is it possible to go back to what I was?"

For the first time since their arrival in that pit, there was a glimmer of compassion in Tobias's deceptively youthful face. "Some of the oldest ones wanted to try, for the sake of learning, but it was always forbidden. After all, those who failed would logically be brought before the Throne of Judgment. If Nemesis is as he is, can you imagine what his Master must be like?"

Aidan squeezed his eyes shut for a moment and nodded. "Yes—yes, I can imagine. And I'd rather face even Him than go on as I have been since Lisette changed me!"

"Then you are either a vampire of uncommon courage or a mad one! Which is it?"

He sighed, ran a hand through his hair. "I don't know," Aidan said. "I honestly don't know."

"Why do you want the transformation so much?"

Aidan knew he could not hide Neely's image from this ancient vampire, and he did not try. "I love a human woman."

"You must care a great deal," Tobias marveled, "to take such a risk as the one confronting you now." Having offered this observation, he watched Aidan in troubled silence for a few seconds, then vanished.

Aidan slept, dreamed fitful dreams of Neely, and awakened believing they were together. His despair at the discovery that he was still alone, and a prisoner in the bargain, was a crueler burden than any he had ever borne.

Twenty-four hours later, when Aidan was half-mad with thirst, he was given three enormous rats, scrabbling inside a picnic basket.

Aidan broke their necks, one by one, and tossed their blood-filled bodies through the bars.

When another twenty-four hours had passed, he was in a fever, crouched against a wall of his cell, his mind loose inside his skull, hot with delirium.

A form appeared before him, wavering and slender.

"Go away," he moaned, turning his head.

"So stubborn," a feminine voice scolded, and the sound of it was like cool water pouring gently over his parched spirit.

"Neely," he rasped.

She laughed at him. "No, silly." He felt her cold lips nuzzle the burning flesh of his throat, started when her fangs punctured it. Blood flowed into Aidan, reviving, sustaining blood, and he was helpless to resist. He drank, all his dried and empty veins leaping greedily to life, and when at last it was over and he could focus his gaze, he saw Roxanne Havermail kneeling beside him.

She ran her fingers through his dirty hair, and he felt the sticky pressure of her lips where she kissed him on the forehead, undoubtedly leaving a smudge of blood.

"How did you get in here?" Aidan rasped, resisting the urge to push her away.

Roxanne smiled, then touched his mouth tentatively with her own. "What does that matter? I am well able to escape and I will take you with me." She laid her hand to his face, and he felt its hardness and its chill. "Close your eyes, darling. Think of candlelight, and soft music, and—"

Aidan lost consciousness, mesmerized by her words, her tone, her caress.

When he awakened, he was lying on silk sheets, stripped of the rough robe his captors had provided, and Roxanne was washing him tenderly with warm, perfumed water.

He tried to sit up, found himself too weak. Obviously the one feeding had not been enough to restore his full powers. Instead it had merely drawn him back from the brink of either blessed oblivion or the unbridled wrath of God.

Roxanne bent and kissed his bloodless chest.

"No," he said.

She drew back, looked at him with wide amber eyes, then narrowed ones. "What did you say?"

Vampire sex, a cataclysmic and usually violent joining of two immortal bodies, was not without a certain appeal at that point, but Aidan wasn't about to indulge. His love for Neely, however hopeless, wouldn't permit it.

"You heard me," he told Roxanne. "Nothing is going to happen between us—Mrs. Havermail."

Roxanne sighed and continued to bathe him. "Honor among fiends," she said. "Tiresome. Plain tiresome."

Valerian, Aidan thought. *Help me.*

Chapter 11

—◦◦◦〉⊱◦←

Melody Ling, the television reporter, agreed to a rendezvous, but only after a little fast talking on Neely's part. Although Neely refused to identify herself directly, she had to do some pretty heavy name-dropping in order to establish credibility—*and* hint that someone inside the FBI had obstructed justice. The site of the proposed meeting, an isolated, long-unused wooden bridge in the woods of central Maine, was chosen by mutual consent, during half a dozen fragmented calls from as many different telephones.

Neely left Aidan's car parked in the small garage behind Wendy Browning's beach cottage and took the bus to the village, stopping off on the way to purchase a long red wig and big sunglasses. Of course she was taking an enormous chance, trusting a total stranger to meet her alone in an out-of-the-way place, but it seemed like a better bet than heading for New York and strolling into network headquarters with the packet of proof under one arm.

When the bus stopped in snowy Danfield Crossing, Neely remained in her seat, toward the back, watching everyone else get off. Once she was fairly sure no one was lurking outside, waiting for her, she made her way up the aisle, her purse under one elbow, carrying a disreputable old duffel bag she'd found in the shed behind Wendy's cottage.

There was no need to ask directions to the old bridge; Neely and Ben and their father had fished for brook trout there, years ago, and the place shimmered brightly in her memory. After a quick glance around, she set off for the woods, not following the county road, but keeping to the narrow, hard-packed trails left by cross-country skiers.

Melody Ling was waiting patiently behind the wheel of a rental car, looking intent in the chilly afternoon sunlight. Her dark hair was moussed, her makeup too heavy and artful for the occasion, and she seemed poised to go on camera immediately. None of which mattered to Neely.

Seeing her mysterious contact come trundling out of the woods beside the road must have been disconcerting, but Ling didn't flinch. She opened the car door and stepped out onto the icy road in high heels.

Neely glanced around nervously, but no gun-toting criminals or FBI men burst out of the bushes, and it was still too early in the day for vampires.

She approached Ling and held out the manila packet, which was still wrapped in plastic. "Here's the evidence we talked about," she said, considering a preamble unnecessary.

Ling took the offering. "You'll grant me an exclusive interview, once everything has gone down?"

Neely nodded. "I'll be in touch," she said. She smiled. "Good luck—and thanks."

The reporter nodded back, got into her car, and left.

Neely immediately returned to the village, by way of the woods. She bought a fish sandwich and a diet soda in a convenience store and hitched a ride back to the coast with a trucker who wore a T-shirt with a picture of his three toothless children on the front.

It had all gone so well, she reflected, settling into the passenger seat of the big rig to watch the night scenery go by.

So amazingly well.

"What happened to him?" Valerian demanded, arriving in the guest wing of Havermail Castle with an unceremonious crash.

Roxanne turned from Aidan's bedside, one hand to her throat in a gesture of gracious alarm. She was a vile strumpet, without a shred of loyalty to adorn her nature, and Valerian despised her.

She simpered. "Mr. Tremayne actually dared to challenge the Brotherhood," she marveled. "Was that your idea?"

Valerian approached the bed and peered down into Aidan's sleeping face. The basement chamber was completely dark, since the windows were sealed, and tallow candles provided an eery, wavering light. Gently the elder vampire laid a hand to a pale but well-sculpted shoulder.

"Aidan," he said, despairing, ignoring the female.

"He's weak," Roxanne said with a saintly sigh, "but he'll recover with proper care."

Valerian was at last able to lift his eyes from Aidan's still features to Roxanne's chillingly perfect ones. "He was a captive, and you rescued him." The statement was meant as a question, and it held no note of praise.

Roxanne nodded. "In a manner of speaking. The Brotherhood had thought to break Aidan by punishment, and they failed. No one tried to stop me when I went to him."

"What punishment?" Valerian rasped, furious. He held tightly to his anger, knowing he would give way to utter despair if he loosened his grip for even a moment.

"Poor Aidan. He was confined in a small space and sub-sequently starved." Roxanne spoke matter-of-factly, making her way around to the opposite side of the bed and taking one of Aidan's limp hands into her own. She ran the pad of her thumb thoughtfully over the protruding knuckles. "It was his own fault that he nearly perished for want of feeding—he refused the rats they offered."

In that moment Valerian felt such contempt, not only for Roxanne, but also for the Brotherhood, that he could barely contain it. "Rats," he rasped. "They gave him *rats*?"

Roxanne shrugged. "It's not such a terrible shame. Most of us have subsisted on vermin at one time or another," she said. "If anything destroys our Aidan, Valerian, it will be his own stubborn refusal to follow the rules."

Valerian sensed that dawn was nearing; they would all be safe from sunlight in this dark cellar chamber, but he did not want to sink into the near-coma of sleep in that place. He didn't trust any of the Havermails, including the children.

He wrapped Aidan's inert form carefully in the bed-clothes and lifted him into his arms.

"What do you think you're doing?" Roxanne cried, incensed. "I found Aidan, and *I* fed him and brought him home. He's mine!"

Valerian held out one hand, fingers splayed, and pressed it to Roxanne's morbidly beautiful face. "Sleep," he said in a sort of crooning drawl, and she dropped to the floor with a thumping sound.

The fiend would succumb to her vampire slumber, there on the cold stones, and awaken just a little the worse for wear when night came again. Only her dress and her temper would be ruffled.

Valerian lowered his magnificent head, until his fore-head touched Aidan's fevered one, and together they van-ished.

*   *   *

Aidan dreamed that he was a Viking, that he'd died bravely in battle, and his comrades had arranged his body in the curving belly of a dragon ship. He was covered with straw, which someone set ablaze with a torch, and the small, flaming craft was pushed out onto the still blue sea. It burned brightly, a majestic pyre, and Aidan burned with it, but he felt no pain, only joy and the most poignant sense of freedom. . . .

When he opened his eyes, realized that he'd only been dreaming, that he was still trapped in the immortal, marble-cold body of a fiend, the disappointment was crushing.

He was lying on a flat surface, in a dark place that he didn't recognize, and he was so thirsty that he felt raw inside. "Neely," he whispered, the word scraping painfully from his throat.

Then he saw Valerian looming over him, his face twisted with anguish. He started to say something, this enigmatic ghoul with the looks and countenance of a favored angel, then stopped himself. Instead Valerian bent, gently plunged his fangs through the skin of Aidan's neck, and gave him blood.

Aidan moaned in a combination of ecstasy and revulsion; he wanted to resist this macabre salvation, but his will to survive, which seemed a wholly separate entity at the time, refused to surrender itself. He felt Valerian's tears on his flesh but decided fitfully that he must have imagined that.

"Where—what is this place?" he managed as the new blood surged through him, vital and warm, as intoxicating as the finest brandy on a cold night.

"Never mind that," Valerian answered shortly, his voice gruff. "Your thoughts are generally written in neon letters five feet high. If you don't mind, I'd prefer that every other vampire between here and the gates of Hades wasn't able to pinpoint us by reading them."

Aidan chuckled, but the indulgence cost him dearly. "You saved me," he said. "Shall I thank you for that, Valerian, or call you cursed?"

"Neither. I didn't truly save you, except from the wiles of that witches' spawn, Roxanne Havermail."

Aidan's laugh was soblike. "Thank you for protecting my virtue," he said. "You'll understand if I consider the gesture a little dubious."

Valerian scowled down at him, but the expression didn't hold. He gave a throaty chuckle, wholly involuntary, and then turned away—ostensibly to compose himself. When he met Aidan's gaze again, his manner was as coldly remote as that of the Grim Reaper. "Fool!" he spat. "Do you realize how close you came to being destroyed?"

"Not close enough, evidently," Aidan reflected, looking past Valerian to the ceiling, which was lined with dusty beams. "What can you tell me of Neely? Is she safe and well?"

Valerian's jawline tightened for a moment, then he bit out, "I wouldn't know. I have only one use for humans, and the fascinating Miss Wallace's association with you puts her off limits. For the moment."

" 'For the moment,' is it?" Aidan asked, reaching up, clasping the front of Valerian's flowing linen shirt in one fist.

Valerian slapped Aidan's hand away. "What an arrogant pup you are," he snarled, "issuing challenges to me— *me!*" He paused to thump his own chest angrily. "If I desired the delectable Neely, I would have her, and no force on earth could stand in my way, including—*especially not*—you!"

Aidan's strength, so temporal, was waning again, but he found enough to press the argument. "Get a grasp on your emotions," he said. "I grow impatient with your constant histrionics."

The great vampire gave a snarling shriek of frustration and rage and disappeared completely.

Inwardly Aidan sighed. He'd probably just offended the only friend he had, besides Maeve, but fruitless acts of impulse seemed to be a part of his nature of late.

He'd failed miserably with the Brotherhood, he reflected, absorbing the knowledge like a series of painful blows. He'd found out nothing and had managed to infuriate the elders in the process. It probably wouldn't be long before they came for him, he supposed, and dispensed their vampire justice.

Valerian had obviously been right in refusing to tell him where they were. Aidan's mental state was such that he probably would have broadcast the information for any passing ogre to pick up on.

Neely shrieked and sent the magazine she'd been reading fluttering into the air like some ungainly bird. Valerian stood between her and the television set, glorious in the usual fine evening clothes, his arms folded, his big head tilted to one side.

"Are you quite through?" he inquired scathingly, retrieving the magazine and setting it neatly on the coffee table.

Neely's gasps slowly slackened into regular breaths. She gave one violent hiccough, in a spasm of residual terror, and Valerian rolled his violet eyes disdainfully.

"Well, you scared me!" Neely said, more angry, all of a sudden, than afraid. Then even the anger faded away, and she got awkwardly to her bare feet, pulling Wendy's pink robe close around her, like chenille armor. "This is about Aidan, isn't it? What's happened to him?"

Valerian looked down his perfect nose at her for a long interval, then answered, "*You* have happened to him, more's the pity. He loves you, and that foolhardy affection may well cost him his very existence."

"Where is he?"

"I wouldn't dream of telling you that," Valerian said sharply. "Like all humans, and some vampires as well, unfortunately, you have a billboard for a mind—complete with loudspeakers and sweeping searchlights. Suffice it to say that Aidan needs comforting very much just now. Besides, you are probably the only being in the world who can cause him to see reason at this point."

"You'll take me to him, then?" Neely's heart was wedged into her throat. She clutched the lapels of the borrowed bathrobe in one trembling hand.

Valerian nodded grudgingly. "Put on some decent clothes."

Neely turned and hurried into the cottage's closet-size bedroom, where she hastily donned jeans, sneakers, a pink bulky sweater, and her coat. Back in the living room, she looked up into Valerian's face with wide eyes. "Is this going to be a Superman sort of thing? I mean, are you planning to tuck me under one arm and just—fly?"

Valerian only shook his head, came a step closer, and swirled his cape around Neely like some whispering, perfumed cocoon. She fainted, only to revive seconds later and find herself in a place so dark she thought she had gone stone blind.

"Just a moment," Valerian barked impatiently, as if she'd complained aloud. A match was struck, a tallow candle lit.

Neely was taken aback to find herself inside a crypt, an old one, judging by the looks of the disintegrating caskets and random bones lying about.

In the center of it all, on a high Roman couch upholstered in ugly maroon velvet, lay Aidan, as white and still as a corpse.

"He will awaken soon," Valerian said, his voice passing Neely's ear from behind, like a fall breeze moving through dry leaves. "If you love Aidan, then make him see that there can be no future for the two of you. Should you fail to reach him, he will continue on his present course, careening toward destruction. He will be executed, Neely, as an example to all vampires—staked out in the sun and left to die in the most horrible agony imaginable. Do you want that for him?"

Neely forgot her surroundings and stumbled forward, her white-knuckled hands clasped together. She would rather suffer the death Valerian had just described herself, she thought, than see Aidan endure such torture.

She touched her beloved's still face. "Aidan?"

He opened his eyes, and she felt a sweet seizing in her heart as he looked at her, apparently dismissed her as an illusion, and then realized she was truly there. "Neely," he said and groped for her hand.

She pressed her palm to his, and their fingers interlocked. "What's happened?" she whispered.

Aidan stared up at her, mute, clearly bursting with a sorrow he could not begin to articulate.

She kissed him lightly on the forehead, and then on the mouth, and felt his fever sear her own skin. She laid her head against his chest then, but heard no heartbeat thumping away beneath her ear, no breath flowing in and out of his lungs.

He entangled his fingers in her short hair, holding her close. They were simply *together* in those moments; it was as simple, and as complicated, as that.

After a long interval had passed, Neely raised her head and looked into Aidan's soul, her vision glittery and blurred, as though she were seeing the world through melted diamonds. She could not leave him now when he was so broken, but deep inside Neely knew Valerian was right. By loving Aidan, by dreaming an impossible dream, she could only destroy him.

And that was unthinkable.

Resigned, heartbroken, Neely climbed onto the Roman couch with Aidan, stretched out beside him, held him close in her arms. Soon enough, they would be parted, for all of time—alpha to omega, world without end, amen.

Amen.

For now, though, nothing would put them asunder.

Valerian's grief howled within him, like a storm wind, but he dared not release it there in the crypt, however oblivious Aidan and Neely might seem. Brashly, too driven by pain to think, Valerian fled to an earlier century, the eighteenth, and hid himself in an isolated lair. It was little more than a mouse's nest, really, a hollow place in the wall of an ancient abbey, mortared over so long ago that there was no demarcation between the old stonework and the new.

Now he curled up in that space, as fragile as an unborn chick still cosseted in its shell, and he wept.

It wasn't as though Aidan hadn't warned him, more than once, that there was no hope. Still, Valerian had heard what he wanted to hear and forgotten the rest. But now he had seen the true state of matters between Aidan and Neely, and he could no longer ignore the evidence.

Somehow, even without the sacred exchange of blood, the pair had forged that most intimate and unbreakable of all bonds.

Valerian sobbed like a stricken child, his anguish as deep and unbridled as his devotion. What he felt for Aidan was indescribably sensual, and yet it transcended gender and completely overshadowed the simple animal gratification humans know. No, it was communion with the other vampire that Valerian craved, something far more profound than mere sex, for he loved Aidan as he had never loved another creature.

Save one.

He threw back his head and cried out in torment, the sound as shrill as the cry of a wolf on a clear winter's night. When that wail had died away, he loosed another, hoarser this time, and full of despair. Finally, when he could weep no more, when he had purged himself of all emotion, Valerian closed his eyes and slept.

Twelve hours later he awakened and wafted through the cracks and chinks in the old abbey wall like so much pale smoke.

Inside the crypt where he had left Aidan and the woman, Valerian assembled himself again.

Neely was asleep, curled up against Aidan's side like a kitten. Her pale skin was flushed from some dream, and Valerian could hear her heart beating, and he wanted so desperately to drink of her warmth and vitality.

He must not indulge, he told himself. It would be a poisoned victory and, thus, a defeat.

Aidan opened his eyes and spoke to his friend, but with his mind instead of his voice. *Take her away from this place,* he pleaded. *If you ever cared for me, Valerian, put Neely back where you found her and make sure she's safe. Now, before she awakens.*

Valerian nodded, but he could not answer, not even silently. He laid his hand over Neely's face, and her breathing deepened, and she was pulled by her own inner forces into that shadowed place well below simple sleep. That done, Valerian lifted her into his arms and thought grimly of the little cottage on the coast of Maine.

The television set was still on when Neely opened her eyes to find herself lying chilled and cramped on the couch in the cottage living room, an open magazine spread under her cheek. She was wearing her nightshirt and Wendy's chenille robe, and there was a blizzard blowing up outside.

Neely tossed the magazine aside, and her fingers were smudged with ink after she rubbed her cheek. She rolled onto her back and stared up at the ceiling, mourning. It had all seemed so real—Valerian, practically giving her a heart attack by appearing from out of nowhere, in all his intimidating splendor. Aidan, lying helpless and sick in that terrible place.

It couldn't have been a dream.

They'd been so close, she and Aidan, so connected, as they lay innocently in each other's arms, their souls fused. She would have given him her very blood, had he asked, and willingly, as a mother gives breast milk to an infant. Such sharing could not have been a travesty, for in those precious hours they were as one being, with but one heart and a single soul, and all their veins were interconnected.

Neely was too numb and too stricken to weep. She rolled off the sofa and raised herself drunkenly to her feet. She went to the thermostat, sent heat booming through the vents with a dusty *whoosh*. Then, shoving her fingers through her sleep-rumpled hair, she made her way into the kitchen and put coffee on to perk. Maybe a jolt of caffeine would get her confused brain back on track, and she would be able to untangle dreams from reality.

Valerian had definitely paid her a visit the night before, she assured herself later as she sipped hot coffee at the window and watched the snowstorm obliterate the ocean from view. She had put on jeans and a sweater, and he had taken her to Aidan. . . .

Neely hurried into her bedroom and opened her dresser drawers, one by one.

The pink sweater was neatly folded and tucked away in one section, the jeans in another.

She unfolded the jeans, felt a whisper of relief when she saw that the denim was embedded with white dust. She made a face and, conversely, held the garment close against her chest, glad of the proof it offered.

She *had* been with Aidan the night before, and for a moment she was joyous.

Then Neely remembered what Valerian had said: Other vampires viewed Aidan as a threat. They might well tie him down in the night and leave him for the brutal sun to find with the morning. He would suffer horribly, devoured by the same light that nurtured virtually every other living thing on earth, and the fault for this would lie, at least partially, with Neely herself.

Desperate for some distraction from her thoughts, she went into the living room and switched on the TV again. The news channel came up immediately.

There was no word of a scandal involving Senator Hargrove and his friends in the drug cartel, and Neely's uneasiness, already considerable, grew significantly. Once before, she'd tried to right a wrong, to stop a gross misuse of authority, and her contact inside the FBI had betrayed her trust. Suppose Melody Ling did the same thing?

Neely glanced at the telephone, but she was afraid to try contacting the network from the cabin. Technology being what it was, the call could probably be traced right back through the circuits to the cottage, and she certainly wasn't ready for that.

She dressed, put on her warm coat and some rubber snow boots she'd found on the floor of the laundry room, and took the keys to Aidan's Spitfire from the hook beside the back door. She might have worn the wig and sunglasses again, but she'd dropped them into a trash bin the previous night, just before catching a ride back to Timber Cove with the good-natured trucker.

Snow had been falling all night, and it was deep enough to make the tires of the sports car spin helplessly in the driveway. The sky was clear by then, however, a soft blue dusted with wispy clouds, and the sun shone brightly.

Neely fetched a wide shovel from the shed and worked industriously to clear a path to the road, which had, fortunately, been plowed and sanded. She went back inside the cottage for her purse and keys, and when she did, she found herself paralyzed by what should have been a very ordinary sound.

The telephone was ringing.

Neely had not given the number to anyone, and she hadn't even contacted Wendy in London to let her know the cottage was in use. No one—besides Valerian and Aidan, who had no use for telephones anyway—was supposed to know she was there.

She hesitated, her hand poised over the receiver. The jangling continued, and Neely thought frantically. Had she given the number to Ben, or to Melody Ling, and simply forgotten? No. A person didn't let things like that slip her mind, not when her very life depended on secrecy.

Finally Neely snatched up the receiver, to end the terrible ringing if nothing else, and said, "Hello?" She hoped she sounded like a man, annoyed at the disturbance.

"Neely?"

Her blood turned to small, jagged shards of ice, piercing her veins in a thousand tender places. The voice was feminine and vaguely familiar, but Neely couldn't match it with a face or a name.

"Neely, are you there?"

She closed her eyes and let out a long breath. She'd already given herself away by staying on the line so long, even though she hadn't admitted to her identity. "Who is this?" she asked.

"My name is Lisa Nelson—I'm Senator Hargrove's personal secretary—"

What a fool I've been, Neely lamented silently, *actually telling myself they wouldn't track me down.* Before she could say anything, think of a lie to tell, or even just hang up, Lisa went on.

"Senator Hargrove asked me to tell you that some mutual friends are on their way to pick you up for the services."

"What services?" Neely asked, glancing accusingly at the blank screen of the television set. The remark had to be a warning; if Elaine Hargrove had succumbed to her illness or her recent injuries, there would have been some mention of it on the news.

"He just said, well, that there's going to be a funeral. Didn't some mutual friend of yours pass away?"

Neely's heart was pounding. She was glad Mrs. Hargrove was still alive and, at the same time, painfully aware that her own days—maybe even her hours and minutes—were numbered. "Right," she said. "Thanks, Lisa." With that, Neely hung up with a crash, flung her few belongings back into her suitcase, and ran for the car.

She'd traveled a considerable distance before she realized that she was headed toward Washington, D.C. She'd chosen an out-of-the-way place to take refuge before, by going to live with Ben and Danny in Bright River; now she would try hiding in plain sight.

Too afraid to check into another motel, Neely drove until she was blind with exhaustion, then pulled into a rest area and slept with the car doors locked, slumped over the steering wheel like a drunk. She chose to have breakfast in a tavern, hoping to throw off any pursuers, and gulped down German sausage and a diet cola while the morning drinkers nursed their beer.

There were two bikers at the pool table, big and hairy, with every visible part of their anatomies tatooed, but they didn't bother Neely. They just poked coins into the jukebox and sang along with various artists in off-key voices.

Nobody in the place, least of all Neely, was stupid enough to protest.

There was a television set behind the bar, but the proprietor had tuned it to a game show, and he didn't look like the type who would switch to the news channel just because somebody asked. Neely paid for her food, used the rest room, and started out again.

Aidan's car radio picked up nothing but static for the next few hours, so Neely bought a newspaper when she stopped for gas, along with a plain seltzer. Normally she would have been hungry again by then, but she was scared and upset, and the sausage she'd consumed at the tavern that morning was still roiling in her stomach.

The store's parking lot was empty, except for a few teenagers, so Neely took time to scan the newspaper. There was nothing about Senator Hargrove's shady doings, but in the upper right-hand corner of page five she found an interesting item.

MYSTERIOUS BLAST DESTROYS BEACH COTTAGE NEAR TIMBER COVE, the headline read. Neely folded the paper, then folded it again, and braced the article against the steering wheel. Sometime during the night, the eager reporter had written, an explosion had leveled the Browning cottage on Blackberry Road. It was not known if there had been any casualties, but investigators were sifting through the wreckage.

Neely pushed open the car door, ran behind the store's giant garbage bin, and was still retching long after her stomach was empty. If Senator Hargrove hadn't warned her, however indirectly, she would have been blown to smoldering fragments, perhaps in her sleep.

She went into the public rest room when the bout of sickness was over, rinsed her mouth, and splashed cold water on her face until she figured she'd recovered her senses. Maybe, she thought, leaning shakily against a graffiti-scarred wall, she should rethink the idea of returning to Washington. It might be smarter to find a circus, climb into the tiger cage, and juggle a couple of raw pot roasts until the cats noticed.

Chapter 12

※ ❀ ※

Even separated from Neely by time and distance, Aidan felt her turmoil in his own spirit. He knew she was in the gravest danger, and yet his weakness pinned him to the couch in that lonely crypt, far more effectively than any physical bond could have done. He struggled, but the effort was fruitless.

"Valerian!" he shouted into the dry darkness of the tomb. He waited, listening as the echo of his voice slowly faded away, but the other vampire did not appear. Aidan's pride would not let him call out again.

He closed his eyes, tried to calm himself. In his mind, he saw Neely standing next to a garbage bin, behind some roadside shop, retching. He watched her hurry into the women's room, tasted the rusty water she used to rinse her mouth, felt the cool relief as she splashed her face. Then he frowned, trying to make sense of a sudden vision of Neely venturing inside a tiger cage at a circus, juggling ugly chunks of raw meat.

The ludicrous image disappeared; Neely was behind the wheel of a car—he recognized the interior as his own Spitfire. He felt her quick, shallow breaths as if he'd drawn them himself, and the warm moisture of tears on her cheeks.

She was afraid and confused, and not being able to go to her was among the greatest agonies Aidan had ever suffered.

Neely, he thought, his soul reaching for hers. She didn't consciously hear him, he knew, but she sniffled and squared her shoulders.

"Okay, Wallace," she said aloud. "No more panic. It's time for some straight thinking."

Atta girl, Aidan encouraged, still seeing the world through her eyes and picking up her emotions and physical sensations.

"I can't go to the police, and certainly not to the FBI. I don't know if Melody Ling is going to break the story or if she's going to cave in to pressure and pretend it never happened." With one hand she mussed her pixie hair in frustration, and Aidan felt the softness between his own fingers, and the tugging wiggle of her scalp. She sighed— he shared that, too—and his eyes filled with tears because he had been deprived of such simple, sweet nuances of humanity for so long. "If I go back to Bright River, then Ben and Danny will be in danger again. Which leaves my original plan—I'll take the proverbial bull by the horns and head straight for Washington. I'll confront Dallas Hargrove, either in his office or in the Capitol Building, and if the mob shoots me, they might just have to do it on the floor of the Senate." With that, she started the car engine, shifted deftly into first gear, and guided the Spitfire back onto the slush-covered highway.

No, Aidan protested, but it was to no avail, of course, for Neely apparently wasn't aware that he was with her, even though he was conscious of her every pulse. He noted the electrical activity of her brain, along with other subliminal processes, like digestion and the manufacture of all sorts of chemicals and hormones. He warmed his own frozen soul at the silver spark of divinity shining at the core of her, the mysterious gift that was given to all mortals with the first tentative *tha-thump* of their hearts.

Aidan rode with Neely for an hour or so, but the effort sapped him, and he withdrew. He had been foolish, he realized now, to squander his strength so recklessly by seeking out Lisette and the Brotherhood the way he had. Now, when his powers might have made a positive difference, he was all but depleted.

He began to drift, now fully conscious, now only half aware. He slept, finally, and awakened to a ravenous hunger and a sense of terrible urgency.

He had to rise, feed, and go to Neely, and the fact that those things might well be impossible had no real bearing on anything. Aidan was fresh out of choices.

He shook his head, fighting the disorientation, the infernal weakness.

After a painful struggle Aidan managed to raise himself onto one elbow. The effort left him grimacing, bruised with exhaustion, but he refused to lie down again. He used all his will to rise to a sitting position and then to stand, knees trembling, beside the couch. The piece of furniture, so absurdly out of place in that old crypt, was high and curved at one end. Aidan gripped that part for support.

He needed blood, a lot of it, and fast.

Aidan thought frantically. The tightly mortared stone walls of the crypt admitted neither the light of the sun nor that of the moon, but he knew it was night simply because he was conscious. What he did *not* know was whether the dawn was hours away, or just seconds, for he carried no watch. How much time had he lost to delirium?

Should he miscalculate and be caught abroad at sunrise, the result would be an interminable and hideous death. That possibility was terrible enough, but there was a very real danger that this cruel passage would be only the beginning of his suffering. If there was indeed such a place as Hell, beyond the mysterious veil that separated the known from the unknown, Aidan would surely be condemned to everlasting torment.

Remembering Neely, Aidan sought and found a forgotten reservoir of courage within himself. He began to pace, stiff-legged, from one end of the crypt to the other, forcing his woodlike limbs to function.

He wanted to tune in to Neely again, to find out where she was, and how she was, and what she was feeling, but he didn't dare waste energy. Before he attempted anything else, Aidan reminded himself, he must feed.

All three floors of Senator Dallas Hargrove's elegant Georgetown house were brightly lit, even though it was nearly three in the morning when Neely arrived. She'd driven for thirteen hours, on and off, and she was hungry, drained of all but the last quivering dregs of energy, and badly in need of a hot bath. For all of that, just the knowledge that she'd reached her destination gave her a second wind.

She glanced around, saw designer Christmas wreaths on some of the doors. Getting out of Aidan's car, Neely felt a stab of chagrin. Had Thanksgiving gotten by her somehow, when she wasn't looking?

She didn't even know the date, she realized, with a sense of quiet shock. She just hoped Ben and Danny had roasted a turkey for the occasion, and maybe invited Doris, the new waitress, to dinner.

Staunchly Neely moved up the front walk, climbed the brick steps, and rang the bell. The senator himself answered the door, and when he saw Neely, he swore and made a move to block her way, but she was too quick. She pressed past Hargrove and stood facing him in that spacious entry hall, with its parquet floors, cherrywood grandfather clock, and marble-topped credenza.

"You must be suicidal!" the senator snapped. He had taken off his jacket at some point and opened his shirt, and his tie hung in a long loop, like a noose about to be jerked tight. There were shadows under his eyes, his cheeks were gaunt, and it was anybody's guess how long it had been since he'd shaved. "Damn it, Neely—I did everything I could to warn you—it's a miracle you're alive—"

Neely didn't retreat, even though Hargrove's stance was intimidating because of his superior size and strength. "I'm tired of running," she said. "I won't be tracked and hounded like some pitiful creature wanted for its hide!"

After regarding her in stricken silence for several moments, the senator groaned. "No, Neely, you won't be hunted anymore," he said. "You won't be hunted because they've *found* you, you little fool!"

At this, four large men in dark, high-quality suits appeared, one from the room on the right side of the hall, two from the left, and another from the curved staircase. Neely dived for the door, but she was tired and her reflexes were poor.

The smallest of the thugs caught her easily, pulling her arms back, hooking his own beneath her elbows.

Neely struggled and screamed, but the man held her easily. One of the others came over and slapped her hard across the face, and the coppery taste of blood covered her tongue.

"There's no need for violence," Hargrove protested, but his tone was weak, like his character.

Neely stomped on her captor's instep with one heel, and he howled in pain and released her. In a movie the trick might have worked, she thought fancifully as the other three bad guys rushed forward. In real life, however, two of the trio of stooges held her, while the third one brought a syringe from the pocket of his coat.

"For God's sake," Hargrove pleaded, as ineffectually as before. Neely wondered how he'd ever attained high office in the first place, let alone held on to his seat in the Senate and married a topflight person like Elaine. "I see no reason to—"

Neely struggled, making an inarticulate sound as she tried to avoid the needle. She felt a minute puncture in the side of her neck, then a stinging sensation as the drug, whatever it was, entered her system. After that, reality dissolved into a colorless, shifting mass of nothingness.

When Neely came to her senses, she was surprised and alarmed to find herself lying on the hard, bare floor of a pickup truck or a van, her arms tied behind her back, her feet bound at the ankles. Her throat felt raw and dry.

Senator Hargrove lay beside her, also tied.

He glared at her. "I hope you're happy now," he whispered.

Neely didn't answer immediately; her thoughts were still pretty incoherent. Her head ached, and so did her right hip and knee. She saw a metal roof a few feet overhead and decided the vehicle was probably a van.

"They're going to kill us," Hargrove said in a stage whisper.

Neely tried to sit up and failed miserably. The floor of the van was as hard and cold as marble and, worse, it was corrugated, making a new bruise every time they went over a bump.

"And you thought they were such nice guys," Neely drawled, shifting in a restless effort to make herself more comfortable.

"Shut up," snapped her former employer.

She tilted her head back, caught glimpses of shadowy hulks in the passenger and driver's seats. It was still dark, and snow swirled against the dark windshield, while the wipers went *thumpety-thump, thumpety-thump*.

"You aren't going to get away with this," she called out cheerfully, toward the front. "I turned all the proof over to a television reporter, and she's going to make household names of the lot of you. Who knows? Maybe they'll show your trial on cable. . . ." Neely was well aware that she was ranting like an idiot, but she didn't give a damn. Her only other option was screaming in hysteria.

The driver crumpled a paper bag in one meaty hand and tossed it over his shoulder. His aim turned out to be pretty good; the wad struck Neely on the chin, and she caught a whiff of stale french fries. "Put a sock in it," he said in classic Brooklynese.

Neely didn't stop talking, she couldn't, but she lowered her voice and directed her comments to the senator. For once in his life, she thought, he was going to have to actually *listen* to an unhappy voter.

"I can't believe you ever got involved with these people!" she hissed.

Hargrove closed his eyes for a moment. He looked sick, and Neely scooted back a ways, until she felt the cold steel of the wheel-well against her bottom. "I had to," he said. "Elaine—needed so many things—"

"Do me a favor and don't blame this on your wife, all right?" Neely interrupted furiously. "I know the lady, and I can't imagine her cooperating with a drug cartel for any reason or any amount of money!"

"Keep it down back there," grunted the guy in the passenger seat. He sounded as though he needed adenoid surgery.

Neely bit her lower lip to keep herself from talking back. These creeps were for real, and if she made them mad enough, they might just pull over to the side of the road and blow her brains out with an illegal handgun.

Hargrove gave a low, strangled sob, and his face contorted into a mask of grief.

Neely felt sorry for him, but there was no way to lend comfort. Her hands were tied behind her back, and, besides, she wasn't sure she wanted to touch the senator anyway. "I heard about the accident," she said moderately. "How is Elaine?"

He made a broken sound, deep in his throat, and it was terrible to hear. "She—she isn't going to make it," he managed.

Neely ran the tip of her tongue over her lips and tasted dried blood. Perhaps because she was half out of her mind with fear, she wondered what Aidan and Valerian and the others liked so much about the stuff. The flavor was salty and metallic.

"I'm sorry," she said gently. "About Elaine, I mean."

Hargrove nodded. "It's selfish of me, I know," he confessed in a miserable rasp, "but I'm almost glad. She would be destroyed if she knew what I've done."

Neely followed the old rule of saying nothing when she couldn't say something nice. She wanted to console the senator, yes, but she also ached to condemn him.

The van bounced violently over what must have been a cattle-guard, and then Neely heard branches scraping the vehicle's sides. They were in the countryside somewhere, maybe deep in a wood, but she had no idea where because she didn't know how long she'd been knocked out.

"I have to go to the bathroom," she called out.

Hargrove sighed. "Don't try any stupid tricks, Neely," he whispered. "This is no time to be a hero!"

"It's no trick," Neely replied. "I really have to go."

The driver cursed—more fluent Brooklynese—but he wrenched the van over to one side of the road, and it jolted to a stop. "I told ya we shoulda just shot 'em both dead," he muttered to his partner. "Next thing you know, this broad is gonna wanna pick up a frozen yogurt someplace."

"Keep goin'," the other thug replied. "She can just hold it."

"I can't *hold it*!" Neely protested.

"Look, lady, I ain't gonna fall for any of that TV stuff and untie your hands so's you can go to the john in some blackberry thicket, awright? Only other option is, I go out there, too, and pull your pants down for you. You want that?"

"No," Neely snapped. "Of course I don't."

"Then shut up."

"I wouldn't mind pullin' down the lady's pants, Sally," volunteered the driver.

"Ain't you been payin' attention, Vinnie? You can catch bad diseases doin' stuff like that. And don't use my name again!"

"Right, Sally," grumbled Vinnie.

They went over a particularly large bump, and Neely's head thumped hard against the floor. She closed her eyes and fought a wave of dizzy nausea with all her strength of spirit. This was no time to pass out, even if she did find oblivion more appealing than reality.

The van soon ground to a stop, and the front doors slammed almost simultaneously. On Hargrove's side there was a click as a latch was lifted, a grinding rush as the panel was shoved aside.

Vinnie and Sally showed no inclination toward gentleness or mercy as they wrenched their captives out onto the snowy ground, the senator first, then Neely. She pressed her thighs together, desperate to relieve herself.

They were propelled forward, toward a shadowy, boxlike house, passing an ancient clothesline and a mossy, snow-dusted cement birdbath. Time and neglect had tilted the structure to one side, and it reminded Neely of a tomb-stone.

The way things were going, she thought, it might turn out to be her own.

Vinnie, who was at least eighty pounds overweight and probably on the fast track to a triple bypass, lumbered up a set of creaky wooden steps and produced a jangle of keys from the pocket of his pants. Maybe he was a slob, and he'd certainly made poor career choices, but he dressed well.

They entered a room, and the lights blared on, revealing a kitchen with a sagging floor and one of those old refrigerators with the motor on top, among other things. To the left, at the end of a long, narrow hallway, Neely saw the glimmer of white porcelain.

"Please," she said.

Surprisingly, Sally gripped her by the back of the neck and marched her toward the bathroom. "I never nabbed nobody that was more trouble than you," he griped. He wrenched the ropes off her wrists and flung her through the doorway. "Don't try nothin' stupid, neither. That window over the toilet is painted shut, and even if you broke it, you wouldn't even get across the yard before I caught you. You got it?"

"Got it," Neely said with a sigh. She went into the bathroom, switched on the light, and quickly attended to her business. While she was doing that, she scanned the small cubicle for a weapon, such as an old-fashioned razor or maybe a plunger with a thick handle. There was nothing visible except for a scrub brush that had been stuck bristles first into a rusty coffee can.

Neely flushed, fastened her jeans, and washed her hands at the stained sink. When she came out, Sally was waiting. He didn't bind her wrists again immediately but instead gripped her elbow and double-timed her into what had probably been a living room at one time.

There was a piano with a warped keyboard on one side of the room, a wood stove on the other. On the wall over a filthy, rat-chewed sofa was a maudlin portrait of some martyred saint, suffering big time.

Aidan, Neely thought.

The distinctness of the answer startled her so much that she jerked, as if someone had touched her with something hot. *Hang on, love. I'm on my way.*

Such relief swept through Neely at the clarity of the thought, and the knowledge that it had not been her own, that she swayed on her feet.

Vinnie thrust her into a chair and wrenched her hands back, to be tied again. The senator was beside her in another chair, also bound. He looked strangely detached, as if he'd managed to move out of his body and watch the evening's events from a distance.

Inwardly Neely sighed. Given all the things Dallas Hargrove had done, it wasn't surprising that he was a master of denial. No intelligent person could have betrayed so many trusts, public and private, without practicing a great deal of self-delusion.

Calmer now—although her senses told her Aidan was nowhere near, she *had* heard his voice—Neely watched as Sally built a fire in the stove to take the chill off the room, with its wavy, linoleum-covered floor. Vinnie wandered over to the opposite side of the room and opened a battered old cabinet that looked as if it might contain a Murphy bed.

Instead there was a big-screen TV set inside.

Vinnie switched it on, tuned it to the news channel, and cursed. Melody Ling's carefully madeup face loomed on the screen; she was standing in front of the Capitol Building in Washington.

Neely listened with gratitude and relief. Quietly, professionally, the journalist blew the lid off the whole scandal, listing crimes and naming names.

Senator Hargrove was still in a stupor; he didn't look up or react at all to the mention of his part in the complicated, ugly matter. Officers of both the DEA and the Bureau wanted to talk to the politician, Ling said; the head of an eastern crime syndicate and two FBI agents had already been arrested.

As if as an afterthought, she went on. "Added to this tragic perversion of justice is the fact that Elaine Hargrove died tonight at Washington Hospital. She never regained consciousness, following a recent automobile accident, and was surrounded by friends and family at the end—except, of course, for her husband, Senator Dallas Hargrove. . . ."

The senator emitted a wolflike howl of grief that tore at Neely's heart. *Godspeed, Elaine*, she thought sadly. She had sincerely admired the other woman's professionalism and courage, and nothing could change that.

Vinnie and Sally were in a panic. "Did you hear that?" one of them demanded of the other—Neely wasn't paying enough attention to notice which. "They brought down the Boss, for God's sake!"

The voices became distorted, seeming to pulse and echo through a tunnel.

"I say we kill 'em both!"

"The hell with that! You wanna stay here and play wise guy, you do it, but I'm getting out."

The senator began to sob, but for once he probably wasn't worried about his own hide. He'd just learned that his wife was dead, he had not been with her at the moment she'd most needed him, and in spite of all the terrible things he'd done, Neely sincerely pitied him.

Chapter 13

—◦◦✕✕◦◦—

Vinnie and Sally were still arguing under the painting of the martyred saint when Aidan materialized in a corner of the room.

Neely grinned, being both glad to see him and fairly used to his theatrical entrances and exits. He was wearing the uniform of a Nazi officer, of all things, and he slapped one gloved palm with a riding crop as he stood glowering at the two crooks from Brooklyn.

"Holy shit," said Vinnie.

"Where did *he* come from?" Sally asked.

Aidan gave Neely a sidelong glance and a wink, though no one else seemed to notice the gesture. "So," he began, the word properly guttural and Germanic. He took the greatest care to show his teeth. "You have taken these people captive."

Sally was blathering by then. "God," he moaned, "it's that guy Max kept talking about, the one that drank his blood!"

"You don't believe that crap, do you?" Vinnie asked his partner, but there was a distinct lack of conviction in his tone. Aidan was backing the two of them slowly across the torn linoleum floor.

Senator Hargrove came out of his daze just long enough to mutter, "Who the hell is that?"

Neely didn't answer but instead glanced nervously toward the windows, then around the room, searching for a clock. If dawn happened to be imminent, the rescue would be spoiled, to say the least.

Aidan tossed the riding crop aside when he was face to face with Vinnie and Sally, who were now cowering against the wall.

Neely braced herself, suddenly terrified of what he might do. She loved Aidan Tremayne with her whole soul, but that would certainly change if she witnessed the true reality of vampirism.

As if hearing her thoughts, Aidan looked back at her over one shoulder, favored her with a half-grin, and turned again to his prey. Raising both hands, he pressed a palm to either man's face, and a strange energy seemed to move through his body, along his arms, and into the crooks.

When Aidan drew back, graceful and cool, but visibly weakened, Vinnie and Sally glided to the floor, both staring stupidly at nothing.

"What did you do to them?" Neely whispered. He hadn't bitten their necks, but the night was still young. She hoped.

Aidan turned, straightening his tunic. "Not much, really. They're just taking a little nap—one that will last three or four weeks. They'll remember you one day, it's true, but given the recollection of tonight, they won't be anxious to look you up to reminisce."

In the chair beside Neely's, Senator Hargrove sat with his head lolling. He moaned something incoherent.

Aidan untied Neely but regarded the senator with a pensive expression. "What about him?" he asked, frowning.

Neely was rubbing her sore wrists and, at the same time, heading in the direction of the bathroom. She gave Vinnie and Sally a wide berth, even though they looked about as dangerous as a pair of carrots. "Don't do anything till I get back," she called to Aidan.

When she returned, he was pacing.

Ah, Neely thought whimsically, *the vampire I love.*

"What's with the Nazi threads?" she asked.

Aidan shrugged, stopping his pacing to lay another thoughtful frown on the senator. "I had to wear something," he answered distractedly, "and this was what came to hand. This is the infamous Senator Hargrove, is it not?"

"You know who he is." Neely sighed, folding her arms. "You're psychic, along with all your other talents."

Aidan walked around the senator's chair once, pondering the slumped figure. "He's not all bad, you know," he reflected, as though reading an in-depth dossier. "Just weak."

Neely nodded, then looked again toward the window. "Yes," she agreed. She explained about Dallas Hargrove's great, destructive love for Elaine. "On top of everything else," she finished, "Mrs. Hargrove died tonight, and he wasn't able to be with her. My guess is, he's probably having the kind of breakdown a guy doesn't come back from. So maybe he doesn't need prison, too."

Aidan paused, silently considering, and Neely would have given anything to read his thoughts. Was he thirsty, for instance?

"He's gone," the vampire said finally. "The senator has retreated so far inside himself that he may never find his way out."

"What if the prosecution needs him to testify?"

Aidan untied Hargrove and draped the man's inert frame over his shoulders, fireman-style. "Their tough luck, I guess.

Come now, I'll load your friend here into the van for you, but you'll have to get yourself back to Washington because the sun will be up in about forty-five minutes." He nodded toward Vinnie and Sally, who were still sitting on the floor, staring vacantly into the distance. "The fat one has the keys—they're in the inside pocket of his jacket."

Neely approached the men gingerly, fully expecting them to jump at her, but they didn't even seem to see her.

"Even if you're right, and they don't come looking for me when their memories return, I still won't be completely off the hook," she said, fishing a key ring from the appointed pocket and withdrawing quickly. "I'll still have to deal with their bosses, won't I? Am I going to have to be part of the Witness Protection Program or something?"

"Yes," Aidan answered, hauling Senator Hargrove's limp person toward the back door. "The Aidan Tremayne Witness Protection Program." He looked very solemn for a moment. "Frankly, my love, these thugs are the least of our problems. They're far easier to deal with, after all, than some other creatures abroad on this earth."

Neely rushed after him, but she didn't offer a reply to his remark, though it had reminded her of the grim truth. She would probably have to give Aidan up one day soon, in order to protect him from the outraged indignation of his own kind, among others, but she wanted to pretend, for a little while at least, that it wasn't so.

Aidan gave her a wry look over one shoulder, turning so that he could see around the senator's rear end. He'd obviously been reading her mind again. "Come, now," he scolded gently. "You're not going to give up so easily as all that, are you? Where's that Yankee persistence I've heard so much about?"

"I used up a lot of it tonight," Neely answered, but she managed a smile.

They trudged through the deep snow in the backyard

passing the clothesline and the leaning birdbath. The van was parked behind a looming, weathered shed.

The snow had stopped, but there was no moon. Still, Neely could see Aidan as clearly as if he were giving off some inner light all his own. He put the senator in the back of the van, taking care not to hurt him, and closed the door.

Aidan and Neely stood facing each other in the cold chill, Neely's breath making a white cloud between them.

"Thanks," Neely said. Again she noticed that he seemed enervated, as though the evening's events had been unusually taxing for him.

Aidan leaned forward and kissed her forehead. "Anytime," he answered with tender irony. "Can you find your way back? You just follow this road west until it intersects with the main highway, then turn left. After that, there will be plenty of signs to point the way."

Neely started to speak, but her voice came out as a croak, and she had to begin again. "What about Senator Hargrove? What am I supposed to do with him, Aidan?"

"Take him to the emergency room at the first hospital you see. He'll be looked after."

Neely glanced toward the van. It had seemed so sinister before, but now she saw that it had a few dents in the fender and green fuzzy dice hanging from the rearview mirror. It looked, well, innocuous.

"Is the senator going to be some kind of vegetable?"

"I can't answer that," Aidan answered with a weary sigh. "I don't think you'll ever have anything to fear from him, though—my guess is, he never really wanted to see you harmed in the first place."

Neely recalled the times the senator had warned her, both directly and indirectly, and nodded in agreement. She would feel pity for him after that night but never fear. She worked up a faltering smile and jangled the keys. "I'll be in Bright

River, at my brother's place," she said. She wanted to ask if she was ever going to see Aidan after that night, but she was too afraid of the answer. "Thanks again."

Aidan lifted his hand in farewell. "Take care," he said, and then he simply faded away, boots, swastika and all.

Neely stared at the place where he'd stood until a moment before and wondered if she was in any better shape mentally than Vinnie and Sally and the senator. Then she climbed resolutely into the van, started up the engine, and ground the gearshift into reverse.

Aidan barely reached the sanctity of his lair behind the Bright River house before he collapsed. He slept sprawled on the dirt floor of the old mine shaft, and when he awakened, he was sick with weakness.

He had been lying on his stomach, but when he sensed another presence, he rolled quickly onto his back.

Tobias was crouching beside him, grinning his ancient, teenage grin. "You seem to be feeling poorly," he observed. He ran his eyes over Aidan's dusty tunic, cobweb-laced breeches, and smudged boots. "Can't say I care much for your taste in clothes, old fellow."

Aidan struggled to raise himself to a sitting position, found that he could manage no more. If Tobias had come to destroy him—and he might well do just that, being an elder and therefore exceedingly powerful—then he, Aidan, was done for.

"What do you want?"

Tobias stood gracefully. His garments looked medieval— he wore leggings, a long tunic, and leather shoes that curled at the toes. "You didn't think you were finished with the Brotherhood just because Roxanne Havermail carried you off to her castle, did you? Come, now, Aidan, this isn't a fairy tale, and there may well be no happy ending."

"If you're trying to be witty," Aidan replied, groaning a

little, "you're only half successful. Get to the point."

Tobias laughed. "Such audacity. That, you know, is both your greatest blessing and your worst curse, Aidan. I suggest you curb the trait if you want the tribunal to decide in your favor."

Aidan got slowly to his feet, swayed, but was steadied by Tobias's quick grasp on his shoulders. "What tribunal is this?"

"You might say it's the vampire version of the Supreme Court," Tobias answered. "They're interested in you and want to know what makes you tick, so to speak."

"Am I to be tried for some crime?" Aidan felt no fear, so none showed in his manner or his words. He was through running; he had to confront his personal demons and be done with it, for better or for worse.

Tobias shrugged. "Not really, though the tribunal does want to determine firsthand whether or not you're a threat to the rest of us. Suppose you turned traitor, for instance, and somehow made contact with Nemesis? We might all be destroyed then."

Nemesis, Aidan recalled foggily, was the Warrior Angel so feared by lesser supernatural beings. "I, too, am a vampire," he reasoned. "If I were to go to Nemesis, it would surely be the end for me." He sighed, ran a hand through his hair. "Or worse yet, the beginning."

"The elders are worried that you might sacrifice yourself in some fit of heroism or despondency. You must admit, Aidan, that you are a very reckless vampire at times."

Aidan sighed, then gave a half-hearted grin. "All right," he said wryly. "I'll go peaceably."

Tobias spread his hands. "You don't have much choice, it seems to me." He ran his gaze over Aidan's stolen Nazi uniform. "You'd better change first, though. Some things are too disgusting even for vampires."

Aidan blinked, and when he opened his eyes, he was

standing in the cold bedroom of his great house, the room where Neely had once slept, so warm and womanly. Tobias was right beside him and sat down in the window seat with a sigh.

"I do want one assurance before I submit to questioning," Aidan said, taking jeans and a heavy sweater from his bureau. He strolled into the adjoining bathroom to change.

"And what is that?" Tobias inquired companionably, as if he didn't already have the upper hand.

"I'm concerned about my sister, Maeve. And Valerian. They have no part in my discontent with vampirism, and I don't want the Brotherhood bothering them."

Tobias rose from his seat with another sigh, this one philosophical and slightly martyred. "The elders have no quarrel with them, for the time being at least."

"But you know exactly where they are at all times," Aidan deduced.

"Of course we do," Tobias answered. "Maeve has taken to her loom and hunts only enough to keep up her strength. As for Valerian, well, he's curled up in the wall of an old abbey, whimpering over his wounds."

Aidan felt a stab; he didn't need to ask what injury Valerian had suffered, because he knew only too well. "He's strong," he murmured. "He'll recover."

"I have no doubt of that," Tobias answered, "but it may be a hundred years or so before Valerian is truly himself again. Vampires can lie dormant, except for an occasional feeding, for centuries—but of course, you know that."

"Yes," Aidan answered distractedly, thinking of Lisette and feeling a chill grasp his psyche. "I know. But Valerian is different. He'll sulk awhile, but once he realizes that the world is going right on without him, he'll come back. He won't be able to bear the thought that he might be missing something."

"I hope you're right," Tobias said, without evident conviction one way or the other. "Let us go now, Aidan. The tribunal awaits."

Aidan remembered the cell he hadn't been able to escape on his own, the hunger, the filthy rats he'd been given as sustenance. A part of him wanted to feel the upcoming confrontation, but he accompanied Tobias without struggle.

Although Ben and Danny were ecstatic at Neely's return, the hole her leaving had left had already knitted itself closed again. Ben was in love with Doris, as were half the regular customers at the café, evidently, and business was thriving.

"All that trouble," Ben had asked, the night Neely arrived in Aidan's sports car. "It's over?"

Neely had nodded. "I can't explain it, Ben, but my part in the Hargrove thing is history. I wouldn't have come back here if I didn't know it was settled."

Ben had taken her into his arms then and hugged her.

At first Neely had slept a lot, and taken a great many hot baths, and helped out by cleaning motel rooms and occasionally waiting tables with Doris. She yearned for Aidan even as she tried to forget he'd ever existed, but there was no putting him out of her mind. Waking and sleeping, he haunted her.

She took to breaking and entering, letting herself into Aidan's house through a window off the mud room, and spent night after night reading the chronicles he'd written. In truth, of course, she was waiting for him to return—but he didn't.

His sister did appear, however, two nights after Christmas, when Neely was sitting by Aidan's hearth and gazing at the flames.

Her heart wedged itself into her throat and hammered there, for Neely knew from the drawings in the first journal that this was the legendary Maeve. Aidan's twin was stunningly beautiful, with her rich ebony hair and dark blue eyes, and she was also a vampire. An accomplished one, if Aidan's written accounts meant anything.

This is it, Neely thought with a strange sense of calm resignation. *She's going to drink my blood and leave me flat as an old tube of toothpaste.*

Maeve laughed, obviously sharing her brother's ability to read minds.

"Are all vampires telepathic?" Neely heard herself ask.

"More or less," Maeve answered. She went to the desk, picked up the music box, and listened thoughtfully as it played its quaint familiar tune.

The ditty left Neely stricken with love and longing for Aidan. She had not been able to bring herself to lift the lid of the small box and wind the key, for fear she would fall apart.

"Do you know where Aidan is?" Maeve asked, quite cordially. She was dressed in a simple muslin gown, and she sat down on a nearby settee, folding her arms and regarding Neely pensively.

Neely gulped, then shook her head. "No," she replied honestly. "I wish I did."

Maeve fiddled with the brocade upholstery on the arm of the settee, not looking at Neely. "He's been taken before the elders of the Brotherhood," she mused, revealing none of what she was feeling. Her blue gaze rose, linked with Neely's. "They may destroy him."

Neely sank back in her chair and closed her eyes. She'd never felt so helpless before, not even when she'd been tied up in the back of Vinnie and Sally's van and slated for a mob-style execution. Somehow she'd known she would survive.

This was different; Neely couldn't return the favor and rescue Aidan, as he had done for her. She had none of his powers.

"I see you're wondering how you might be of help to my brother," Maeve went on. "There is a way, Neely."

Neely leaned forward, still afraid, but curious, too. It wasn't every day, after all, that one sat and chatted with a lady vampire. "What?"

"You could become one of us," Maeve said bluntly. "Then perhaps Aidan could forget this nonsense about being human again."

Maeve's pronouncement brought about an emotional earthquake, and almost a minute must have passed before Neely was able to reply.

She shook her head. "Not that," she said. "I love Aidan more than I've ever loved anybody, but I won't sell my soul even for him. And he wouldn't ask it of me."

"You're right," Maeve said coolly. "He would be furious at first, but he loves you desperately. Can you honestly say it holds no appeal for you, the immortality of being a vampire? The power?"

Again Neely shook her head. "All I want to be is a woman, a plain, ordinary woman." She paused, waited a heartbeat, then dared to ask, "Aidan really wants to be human again?"

"He'd do anything to accomplish it," Maeve answered in a rush of confounded annoyance. She arched one eyebrow, studying Neely, paying a little too much attention to the pulse point at the base of her throat. "I don't have to give you a choice, you know. I can make you into a vampire without your consent."

Neely thought of the early entries in Aidan's journals, the despair and anger he'd felt. "That was what was done to your brother," she answered evenly, fingering the golden rosebud on the pendant Aidan had given her. "He despises the one who changed him, and he would be outraged if it happened to me as well. Do you want Aidan to hate you, Maeve?"

The impossibly blue eyes widened at the sight of the pendant, then were averted. "I adore him," she said brokenly. "I became a vampire so that Aidan and I would not be separated. Now he wants to change back."

Neely folded her hands in her lap and spent a few seconds gathering her courage, which, it seemed to her, was mostly bluster. Since that was all she had to work with, she proceeded. "Is that possible, for a vampire to be turned back into a human being?"

Maeve stared into space for a long time, then shrugged. "To my knowledge, no one has ever done it. But there are secrets and rituals only the elders know."

Neely bit her lower lip and offered a silent prayer, not for her safety, but for Aidan's redemption.

Abruptly Maeve rose from her seat and stood glaring down at Neely, her expression imperious and completely chilling. "You cannot stay here," she announced. "If I found you, so might the others."

Neely shivered as horrible images from books and movies flooded her mind. "What quarrel do any of you have with me?" she dared, setting aside the last volume of Aidan's journal, the one that mentioned his love for her, and getting shakily to her feet.

"You are a threat to all of us," Maeve answered. "Vampires and humans do not normally mix, beyond the obvious feedings and an occasional brushing of shoulders."

"But what could I possibly do to you?" Neely pressed.

"You have already done it," Maeve said, and her words rang with an infinite and eternal sorrow. "You have taken Aidan's heart and made him into a weak link. He might betray us all, not intentionally, of course, but simply because he's lost a large part of his reason."

Neely put a chair between herself and Aidan's twin, although she knew only too well that no such puny effort would save her if Maeve decided to follow through on her original idea and make this troublesome human into a vampire.

"My crime, then," she whispered, "is that I love your brother with my whole heart. As you do, Maeve." Neely watched as the majestic creature of the night turned her straight, slender back, apparently struggling to contain some emotion. "We aren't enemies, you and I. We're on the same side."

When Maeve turned to face Neely again, there were tears glittering in her sapphire eyes. "What will become of him?" she murmured. "Of all of us?"

Neely actually wanted to touch Maeve, to comfort her, but of course she didn't dare make any such move. To do so would be like petting a wild tigress. "I don't know," she said honestly. "But there is one thing you can count on. I truly love Aidan, and I will never purposely hurt him."

Maeve assessed Neely in silence for a long time, probably weighing her words. In the end she evidently found them true. "I have promised not to interfere in this other madness of Aidan's, this transformation he so foolishly seeks. But there is one thing I can do, and that is protect the woman he loves more than his own soul."

Neely waited, having no idea how to respond. For all she knew, making her, Neely, into some immortal, blood-drinking monster was Maeve's idea of protecting her. Or perhaps the beautiful vampire would simply kill her, angering Aidan but at the same time saving him and a lot of the mysterious "others" mentioned earlier.

As it happened, Maeve stepped back to the desk, found a pen and paper, and scribbled something. "Come to this address, in London, as soon as you can. It is perhaps your only hope, to be under my protection."

Neely swallowed. "London?" she echoed.

"Yes," Maeve snapped, shoving the scrap of paper at her. "And be quick about it. The housekeeper will let you in. You do have money?"

Neely nodded. Dallas Hargrove had given her a healthy sum in cash, and so had Aidan. She'd spent very little. "Is that where Aidan is? In London?"

"Would that he were," Maeve said with a bitter sigh. Having so spoken, she raised both her arms, as Neely had seen both Aidan and Valerian do, and vanished.

"London?" Neely muttered to the empty room.

The next day, after saying good-bye to Danny and Ben and Doris, who had begun to assemble themselves into a tight family unit, Neely got into Aidan's car and drove to New York City. She carried only her passport, a toothbrush, and her wad of cash; she was getting very good at traveling light.

Another day passed, and then Neely flew out of JFK Airport, aboard a 747 bound for Heathrow. She sagged numbly in her seat, now sleeping, now staring out the window at the clouds blanketing the Atlantic. She held one shimmering, fragile hope close to her heart: that she would see Aidan again soon.

The flight was interminable, and when the plane finally landed, there was still Customs to be gotten through. Neely managed the task, practically dead on her feet. Outside, in the gray, slushy twilight of an English winter, she found a cab right away.

Neely gave the driver the address Maeve had written for her and ignored the gregarious cabbie's whistle of exclamation.

"Pretty fancy real estate, that," he said.

Neely wasn't up to chatting, but as it turned out, that hadn't been a problem. The driver had talked nonstop from Heathrow to the quiet, elegant neighborhood that was her destination.

He brought the old cab to a lurching stop in front of one of the most impressive mansions Neely had ever seen, Washington and New York included. The place was three stories high, made of gray stone, and surrounded by a high iron fence.

Even as Neely sat still in that tattered backseat, wondering how she was ever going to get inside the place and what she would do when she got there, a figure came hurrying out to open the gate.

Neely paid the driver, stepped out onto the sidewalk, and was immediately grateful for the bracing bite of the wind. The cab sped away, leaving its former passenger to stand there with her hands in her pockets, gaping.

"Miss Wallace?" the figure asked, clattering a key in a great lock and then swinging open the gate.

Neely blinked. She'd been expecting Frankenstein's monster, but Maeve's housekeeper was instead a plump, genial woman with rosy cheeks and bright, mischievous brown eyes.

"Yes," Neely answered.

The housekeeper beckoned. "Well, come along then," she prompted, with good-natured impatience. "No sense in our standing out here, freezing our bums off, now is there?"

In spite of herself, Neely laughed, drawn by the woman's ordinary kindness.

"No sense at all," she agreed.

Neely made little note of the inside of the house that first night, for she was too tired and too distracted. She simply followed the housekeeper, whose name, to Neely's delight, was Mrs. Fullywub.

"Call me Mrs. F.," the woman ordered benignly, depositing Neely in a guest suite on the second floor. "I'll bring up some tea and scones shortly. There's a robe and nightgown, folded all neat and tidy on the bench in

the water closet—through that door." She pointed a pudgy
finger. "A hot bath can resurrect the dead, I always say."

Neely made no answer, since none seemed to be needed.
She took off her peacoat, looking around at the unbelievably sumptuous room in a state of mild shock. There was
a fireplace, with glistening brass andirons, and a bed that
probably dated from the reign of Elizabeth I. The couches
and chairs were upholstered in mint-green silk, to match
the spread and pillow shams, and there was a Chippendale
desk in one corner.

It was like stepping into a layout in a high-tone decora-
ting magazine, but Neely was too far gone to appreciate
her surroundings. She soaked in the guest bath, which was
roughly the size of a Scottish loch, then put on the waiting
nightgown and robe. She brushed her teeth, stumbled back
into the bedroom, and collapsed.

Mrs. F. brought tea and scones, which Neely ignored, and
built a fire on the pristine hearth. Soon shadows danced on
the high, molded ceiling, taking the shapes of vampires and
angels.

Chapter 14

—◆◆◆❳❲◆◆—

In the morning Mrs. F. brought Neely breakfast in bed—orange juice, oatmeal, buttered wheat toast, and a slice of melon. Tucked under the housekeeper's right arm were two newspapers, which turned out to be the London *Times* and yesterday's *USA Today*. Neely might have enjoyed the small irony, not to mention the luxury, under other circumstances.

"Thank you very much," she said after forcing herself to take a sip of the orange juice, for her fearful yearning for Aidan was a shrill, relentless thing that left no room for food. "But you needn't wait on me after this. I can look after myself."

Mrs. F. beamed, looking bright-eyed and matronly with her salt-and-pepper hair arranged in a loose but tidy bun. She wore a flowered dress, along with a pristine white cobbler's apron. Neely wondered if Mrs. F. knew that the lady of the house was a vampire.

"Nonsense," said the good woman, in her brisk and lively accent. "You've great dark circles under your eyes, you have, and if you don't mind my saying so, miss, it's apparent that you could do with a little seeing to. Besides, there's the jet lag to consider. You'll enjoy your visit more if you give your mind and body time to adjust to the changes."

For a moment Neely wanted to weep. She couldn't remember the last time anyone had treated her with such tenderness, except for Aidan, of course, and that made the experience bittersweet.

She blinked back tears of terror that Aidan would be hurt or destroyed by forces she couldn't begin to understand, let alone combat, but there was an element of self-pity in her sorrow as well. She *was* exhausted, not to mention confused, scared, and more than a little heart-sore, and she could use some time to heal, gather her scattered thoughts, and make plans for the future.

After a few moments of inner struggle, she managed to compose herself.

Neely pretended to nibble at her toast as Mrs. F. toddled over to the hearth and stirred a cheery fire from ashes and embers. "Have you been working for—?" She stopped. How was she supposed to refer to Mrs. F.'s employer—as Maeve? Miss Tremayne? That woman with the fangs? She redirected. "Have you been here long?"

"A few years," Mrs. F. replied. "Madam isn't around much, so it's quite an easy job, really. Which is good, since my knees aren't what they used to be. The heavy cleaning is done by a service, once every fortnight, regular as teatime. I putter, for the most part—dusting, answering the telephone, the like of all that. Once in a while, the Madam decides on a party, and then there's a flurry, I don't mind saying."

Neely smiled, though she still felt as if she'd been broken to bits and glued back together with some of the pieces missing. This gregarious, talkative woman knew nothing of Maeve's other life, and wouldn't believe the truth in any case. Who could blame her?

"How did you come to be acquainted with the Madam?" Mrs. F. inquired, catching Neely off guard.

No longer pretending to an appetite, she set the tray aside. "I'm a friend of her brother's," she said.

Mrs. F. looked disapprovingly at Neely's untouched breakfast but refrained from comment. In the next instant her face was alight. "Oh, you're one of Mr. Aidan's lot. Now, there's a lovely gentleman for you. As handsome a rascal as the Lord ever turned from His hand, he is. Makes me blush with his teasing, and me twice his age."

Neely thought of Aidan's birthdate—the spring of 1760— and sighed wistfully. She didn't know if she'd ever come to understand the mystery that was Aidan Tremayne; she just hoped she'd get the chance to try. "You're younger than you think, Mrs. F.," she told the other woman.

The housekeeper took the tray and left, and Neely immediately reached for her newspapers. At that point she was in dire need of a distraction, a way to avoid further thoughts of the dangers Aidan faced.

USA Today said nothing about the Hargroves—Elaine's funeral and the senator's subsequent "nervous breakdown," which had rendered him temporarily unfit to stand trial, were old news. The London *Times*, however, contained an update on Dallas Hargrove's condition, tucked away in a corner of page 14.

The senator had contracted pneumonia, and while everything possible was being done for him in the way of medical treatment, he did not seem to be responding. Neely suspected that he'd simply decided to die; without Elaine, without his freedom and his reputation, he might well feel that he had nothing left to live for.

Feeling even sadder than before, Neely refolded both papers, set them on the bedside table, and tossed back the covers. A yellow-gray fog was curling at the mullioned windows, and there was a distinct chill in the air, even with the fire popping in the grate.

"Vampire weather," Neely mused fancifully.

Soon enough she realized that even though she was weary to the point of collapse, inactivity would be the worst thing for her. Perhaps if she just kept moving, she reasoned whimsically, then disaster would not be able to overtake her.

Half an hour later, bathed and clad in a gray cashmere pants and sweater set that probably belonged to Maeve, she ventured out of her room. She would explore the house first, then call her friend, Wendy Browning, who was in London studying theater arts, and make arrangements to meet. Maybe that afternoon, if she felt up to it, Neely would go shopping for clothes. As it was, she had only the outfit she'd worn on the plane, and she couldn't go raiding closets and bureaus for more of Maeve's things.

Neely found the stairway leading to the third floor and climbed it. Here, instead of a nursery or servants' quarters, as many such houses would have had, there was one great, drafty room.

Neely's footsteps echoed off the walls of that lonely chamber as she approached the object that dominated it—a huge old-fashioned loom. Someone, Maeve surely, had been weaving a tapestry in delicate pastels and deep earth colors, though all that was visible was the hem of a pale, gauzy dress, a carpet of brown and crimson maple leaves, and a fallen rose, shedding its ivory petals.

A chill tickled Neely's spine, and she hugged herself.

Aidan, she mourned silently. *Where are you?*

Tilting her head back, she saw that huge skylights had been cut into the roof, and the fog brushed against the glass like an affectionate cat.

There was a stack of completed tapestries on a table next

to a far wall, but Neely didn't approach. She felt as if she'd seen a private part of Maeve's life as it was, and besides, this was a place of sorrow. Suddenly that huge room seemed as barren of life and hope as a cemetery.

She turned and hurried out of the attic studio.

On the second floor were a number of bedrooms and baths, along with a sitting room that overlooked the sumptuous garden at the rear of the house. Neely proceeded to the first floor, where she found an old-fashioned and purely elegant drawing room, a combination library and study, a formal dining area, the kitchen, of course, and a gallery.

Neely was even more drawn by the paintings on the walls of the gallery than she had been by the curious tapestry in Maeve's attic room. These works, at least, had purposely been put on display, and because of that, Neely could look without feeling that she was prying.

The morning dawdled by, it seemed, and promptly at one o'clock Mrs. F. served a luncheon of deviled eggs, fruit compote, and salad in the kitchen. Neely forced herself to eat a little, then went off to the study to call Wendy Browning.

An answering machine clicked on. "Hi, this is Wendy. Jason and I are probably in class, acting our brains out. Leave a message, and one of us will call you back at the first opportunity. In the meantime, break a leg. Bye."

Neely grinned as she left her name and the number where she could be reached. The thought of seeing Wendy again lifted her spirits, though she wasn't looking forward to explaining why her friend's seaside cottage in Maine had been blown to splinters. This might just be one of those rare incidences where it truly was better to lie, or at least go on pretending she didn't know what had happened.

Feeling restless as the gloomy day wore on and twilight approached—Neely realized that she was both dreading the coming of darkness and looking forward to it because it might bring Aidan to her side—she called for a cab. While she waited for the car to arrive, she reflected on her own mixed emotions.

True enough, Aidan could appear. On the other hand, so could Maeve or Valerian or other vampires she wouldn't even recognize. The cab appeared before she'd worked out the problem in her mind, and Neely put on her coat and rushed down the walk and through the gate to meet it.

It was time for a little therapeutic shopping.

She avoided the posh places, like Harrod's, the designer shops, and the trendy boutiques, and spent the remainder of the afternoon in a fascinating establishment called Tea and Sympathy, which dealt in secondhand clothing. It was upscale stuff but definitely used.

In that hectic, cheerful, crowded atmosphere, Neely felt wonderfully safe and ordinary; she was even able to forget, at least during that brief, shining interval, that vampires were real creatures and that she'd fallen hopelessly in love with one.

She bought a black skirt that had supposedly once belonged to the princess, along with several pairs of equally royal-looking woolen slacks, some sweaters in soft colors, and a black, sparkly dancing dress. On the way home she had the cabdriver stop at a neighborhood shop, where she purchased a supply of underwear, some pantyhose, and three soft cotton nightgowns.

Later, Neely settled into the guest suite, back at Maeve's house. Mrs. F. brought tea and "biscuits," which were really cookies, and built up the fire. Neely couldn't ignore her hunger any longer, so she sipped from a bone china cup, ate exactly one biscuit, and reviewed the day's loot. Briefly she entertained a wry, bereft hope that someday she would have steady access to her own wardrobe again, instead of having to rush out and buy things everywhere she went.

Wendy called just before dinner, and she and Neely made plans to meet for lunch the next day, near the theater academy.

"Anything exciting going on?" Neely inquired, winding an index finger nervously in the telephone cord. She imagined herself blurting out the gist of her own situation. *Guess what? I'm in love with a vampire.*

Wendy's voice was bubbly and cheerful, like always. "Well, the police in Timber Cove did call to say my cabin in Maine had been reduced to ashes. I'll have it rebuilt with the insurance check. What are you doing in London, anyway?"

Neely suppressed an urge to tell all.

Of course, she didn't talk about Aidan, or his mysterious mission, or the other vampires who threatened to demolish any whisper of a chance that they could ever be happy together. "You've read about the big scandal stateside, involving Senator Hargrove and the drug cartel, haven't you?"

Wendy laughed. "All I read is *Variety* these days, and Shakespeare." She paused, and there was a worried note in her voice when she went on. "Sounds like pretty dangerous stuff. Are you okay, Neely?"

Her friend's concern warmed Neely, reassured her that there were still regular people in the world, affectionate, funny people who didn't believe in the Undead.

"I'm terrific," Neely lied, feeling her hard-won facade starting to slip. "I'll explain it all tomorrow."

"Great," Wendy responded. "Now remember, twelve-thirty at Willy-Nilly's."

"I'll remember," Neely promised. But a nervous tremor struck her as she hung up the receiver, there in Maeve's august study, a new and very frightening feeling came over her—the absolute conviction that someone was watching her.

Now, she thought with bravado, *if I can just make it to tomorrow.*

This time the Brotherhood did not mistreat Aidan physically, though his mental powers and his emotional strength were both severely tested.

He was given an austere chamber in the cellar of a remote hunting lodge in Scotland and allowed to come and go as he pleased, feed in his own way, and wear his own clothes.

Each night, however, as soon as he'd fed, Aidan was expected to present himself in the lodge's main hall, where he sat in a great carved chair of medieval oak, facing the five members of the tribunal.

The elders lined a long wooden table, sometimes just staring at Aidan, but mostly they interrogated him. They asked seemingly limitless questions about every corner and facet of his life, explored his most private thoughts and beliefs with their probing minds. Since there was nothing Aidan could do to stop them, for his puny powers were laughable beside theirs, he endured the inspection as patiently as he was able.

The experience was intensely painful on a psychic level, and the Brotherhood made no particular effort to be merciful. They saw Aidan as a potential threat to themselves and all other vampires, and half of them argued openly and heatedly for an immediate execution. That, the angry ones claimed, would settle the problem once and for all.

Others, however—Tobias among them—spoke for simple justice. Tremayne had not, after all, committed any crime, and surely he should not be destroyed on the mere speculation that he *might* betray the others. Besides, if he passed through the ancient purging process—even in his suffering, Aidan was jubilant to learn that such a process existed at all—his memory of life among blood-drinkers would vanish, along with all the powers and demands of vampirism.

The group seemed to be deadlocked, and there came a time when Aidan's impatience and fear and unceasing mental pain made him reckless. He finally demanded some answers of his own.

"Tell me," he dared, believing he had nothing to lose, on the twelfth night of the inquisition, "which of you would make a vampire of a mortal man, if that man did not ask you to do so?"

The five members of the court turned to each other and communicated for several minutes. He did not hear what they were saying because they veiled their words by some mysterious means of their own. There was much Aidan didn't know about vampires, for all his two hundred years among them, because he'd spent most of that time rebelling against his fate.

Finally the archaic creature on the far right stroked his white beard and muttered, "There is no ordinance among us forbidding the making of new vampires, be the mortals involved willing or unwilling. I personally would like to witness the results of such an experiment as we speak of here, however, and for that reason I vote that we allow it."

Aidan started to speak, but the elder cut him off with a look and a warning. "The process is extremely painful, and most dangerous. It is possible, for example, that the silver cord connecting your spirit to your physical being will be severed during the transformation. If this happens, you will be neither vampire nor mortal, and it may be that such a fate is even worse than the Judgment of Heaven."

There was a hush in the great chamber, for this was an eventuality inherently feared by every vampire, warlock, shade, and specter.

Aidan rose slowly from his chair, gripping the armrests,

weakened by the ordeal and all that had gone before it. He did not dare to think of Neely, though her image was safely hidden in his heart, sustaining him, giving him courage, making it possible to bear the pain of the Brotherhood's unmerciful poking and prodding.

"How?" he whispered. "How is it done?"

"Be seated," ordered one of the elders, obviously stunned by such audacity on the part of a mere fledgling.

"I will not," Aidan answered, standing squarely now. He was trembling inwardly, and there was an echo in his brain—*difficult . . . painful . . . dangerous*. He didn't care about those things; what was important was that the transformation was *possible*. Besides, the name nestled in his heart made him bold. "I have cooperated with you. I have answered your questions and opened my mind, my very spirit, for your inspection. Now you must tell me how to become a man again!"

More murmuring ensued, then another member of the vampire court stood and rounded the table. He wore coarse, monklike robes that rustled when he walked, and had long, flowing red hair and fierce features.

"In early times on Atlantis," he said ponderously, "great medical experiments were carried out. Scientists discovered a means of immortality, through a change in the chemistry of the blood, and we, the first vampires, were created by a special system of transfusion. We thought, in the beginning, that our—appetites—could be satisfied intravenously. Soon, however, we learned that it was not so. We had to drink the blood of living beings or perish of a terrible starvation.

"Some chose this fate, rather than prey upon man-creatures, while others allowed the sunlight to burn them to ashes. Most of us, however, chose to go on, for it was eternal life we sought in the first place."

Aidan listened, and waited, with all his being.

"We escaped the Catastrophe because of our unique powers and brought some of the knowledge with us. Alas, much was lost. There is an antidote for what is to you a curse, and to us a blessing. One receives a transfusion, after the blood has been treated with several chemicals and herbs. The experiments were interrupted by the great Disaster that befell our beloved continent, but some things are known. For one, the procedure is an enervating ordeal, probably as painful as being staked out to burn."

Aidan did not flinch. No suffering could be worse than what he already felt. He loved a human woman and dared not be close to her, and he drank blood to survive. He clung to life with an involuntary fervor, and yet he called himself monster—abomination—devil.

"I don't care," he said hoarsely after a long and echoing silence. "I will risk anything—suffer any torment—to be a man again!"

The vampire who had been speaking—none of them, besides Tobias, had deigned to give Aidan their names— uttered a sigh and turned to stare at his comrades for a long moment. Then he looked upon Aidan again.

"Be aware, fledgling, that should this mad enterprise succeed, you will indeed be wholly human. You will live an undetermined number of years, you will grow old and sick, and *you will die*. With the transformation you will lose all the special powers you possess now and, gradually, all memory of those abilities as well. In time you won't even believe in us any longer."

Aidan said nothing.

"You must also remember," the older vampire went on, seeming stunned and bewildered by Aidan's determination, "that when you perish, as all men must perish, you will then face eternity—either oblivion or the wrath of a God we all rightly fear."

Aidan nodded. Hidden away, in a secret fold of his being,

was the hope that with the transformation would come some
sort of absolution. All sensible creatures, good and evil,
trembled at even the mention of God, but was He not
known for forgiveness and mercy, as well as damnation
and fiery rage?

"I'll take my chances," Aidan said.

The elder sighed again, heavily. "Very well. Such a thing
cannot be undertaken lightly, however, and we must debate
the matter further among ourselves. We will send Tobias
when we have reached a decision."

"Thank you," Aidan replied with cool dignity. He wanted
to scream with frustration and impatience, but of course, to
give free rein to such emotions would be foolhardy. He rose
again from the chair, turned, and walked out of the hall
without once looking back.

Outside, in the rich black-velvet embrace of the night, he
allowed Neely's cherished image to rise from his spirit into
his mind.

He wondered how he had come to love her, while no
other woman had touched his heart in all his two centuries
of living, and knew that there was no real answer. Why
did any man or immortal fall in love with another? It was
a timeless mystery that would probably never be solved,
and in any case, he didn't care. All that mattered to him
was the shining, eternal reality that his soul was somehow
linked with Neely's, and that as long as he existed as a
conscious being, in whatever form, inhabiting whatever part
of the vast universe, he would love, adore, *worship* this one
woman.

He had forgotten that intense thoughts of Neely would
either draw her to his side or carry him to hers, and thus he
was surprised to find himself in the elegant bathroom adjoining one of Maeve's guest rooms. Neely sat in the tub
up to her chin in soap bubbles.

She gave a little squawk when she saw him, and for a

moment he thought she was going to slide right under the water. "What are you doing here?" she sputtered, sending suds skittering with her breath. For all her shock at seeing him, there was a light in her dark sprite's eyes that said she was glad of his appearance.

Aidan shrugged. "I might ask the same thing of you, love," he answered somewhat gruffly. His adoration of her swelled inside him, like another being trying to burst through his skin. It was a sweet agony, and he wondered that he'd never dreamed, in two hundred years, that it was even possible to cherish one woman so thoroughly, so hopelessly.

He saw her love for him in her wonderful eyes and knew it for an emotion as elemental as his own. Such joy, such beauty—what an irony that it might well be doomed.

"Maeve invited me here," she explained in an uncertain voice. "In case you're wondering, I came by plane. Look Ma, no magic."

Aidan chuckled, and the sound held both marvel and despair. At no time had he ever yearned more desperately to be a man again than he did in those moments. If he had been he would have taken off his clothes, climbed into that big bathtub, and made love to Neely until there was nothing left for either of them to give to the other, but he was not a man. He was a fiend, and he was afraid that if she saw his body, pale and statuelike in its hardness, she would be repulsed.

He leaned against the framework of the bathroom door with an indolent impudence that was wholly feigned, his arms folded, one eyebrow slightly elevated. "I didn't know you and Maeve were acquainted."

"We're not, really," Neely answered, making nervous waves under the water by flapping her hands back and forth. "She claimed this would be a safe place for me to stay—I guess it's the old trick of hiding in the open—lest any of your vampire friends decide they want me instead of a V-8. There is, of course, a glaring possibility that she just wants to kill me personally, so she knows the job has been done right."

Aidan shoved splayed fingers through his hair. "Maeve won't do you any harm," he said with quiet certainty.

"Don't be so sure," Neely responded, and very quickly, too. "She worships the ground you walk on, and she also thinks I'm the worst thing that could have happened, not only to you, but to the whole vampire community." She drew a deep breath and let it out again, sending more soapsuds tumbling, and looked at Aidan warily out of the side of her eye as she reached for a sponge on the tiled shelf bordering the tub. "Did you ever like being a vampire, Aidan? Even for a moment?"

He sat down on the lid of the commode, resting his forearms on his knees and leaning toward Neely. She was watching him now, with a fragile hope in her eyes. "There was never a time when I didn't want to be a man, if that's what you mean," he answered. "I did enjoy making love to you, and I will always cherish the memory of the night we danced on a carpet of stars."

Tears glimmered along her dense lashes. "Can you— can you make love to me again—this time in the regular way?"

Aidan felt his heart splinter and fall into assorted pieces. "It's possible—mechanically, if you'll excuse the expression—but—"

"But what?" She sounded impatient. Irritated. "You said yourself that you're not afraid of—of biting my neck anymore, and we almost made love once, if you'll remember. Is it that you don't want me, Aidan? Is it because I don't look and feel like a vampire?"

"No," he said, his voice gravelly with the frustration of wanting her so much and, at the same time, struggling to keep himself from indulging. "It's because *I* do look and feel like a vampire."

She stared at him, her gamine eyes even rounder than usual. "I don't care," she said. She raised one toe out of the water and poked at the spigot with it. "What if I said the whole idea turns me on a little? Hell, call me kinky, it turns me on *a lot!*"

He averted his gaze, for although he knew this woman thoroughly, her frankness still surprised him. His last experience with love had happened in the eighteenth century, after all, when young ladies of Neely's quality and station would have burned at the stake before admitting to such an attraction.

"Neely," he reasoned finally, making himself meet her eyes again. "Even though I would never willingly hurt you, I am much stronger than you are, and I want you in a way that is almost frenzied. In my passion I might not be gentle."

"What if I say I'm willing to risk it?" she asked in a tremulous tone.

Aidan felt conflicting urges to laugh and cry. "Then I would reply that you are a damnably stubborn, if very beautiful, woman."

Neely just looked at him, full of defiance, silently daring him to take her.

In spite of himself, in spite of the ordeal he faced and all his misgivings, Aidan laughed. An instant later he had composed his features into a solemn expression.

Then he simply held out one hand to her.

She blushed furiously, and the very splendor of her made his soul ache within him. She rose, dripping soapsuds and water, and their fingers intertwined.

In order to lighten the moment a little, Aidan glanced at the tub and mentally pulled the plug. A gurgling sound ensued, but Neely wouldn't be distracted by showmanship;

she wanted, plainly and simply, to be taken to bed.

Even the prospect filled Aidan with ecstasy, but now that he had made the decision to express his love to Neely in the most intimate way possible, he would not be hurried.

He stepped back to allow her to pass into the bedroom before him, and she did so regally, with all the haughty dignity of some beautiful pagan queen. Her skin was still wet and shiny from her bath; it would be slippery to the touch.

Once Neely was standing beside the bed, however, she lost some of her aplomb. She was, for all her bluster, a virtual innocent where such matters were concerned— even if she'd been with a thousand men, she would have been pure, for her spirit was the sterling sort, rare as golden pearls—and Aidan thought his adoration for her would be his undoing, so intense was it.

He went to her instead of touching her mentally from across the room, as he might have done had he not been so thoroughly bewitched. And when he stood face to face with her, so close that he could literally feel the beat of her heart in his own senses, she reached out and began lifting his heavy fisherman's sweater up, revealing his midsection, then his chest. Finally she pulled the garment off over his head and tossed it aside.

Aidan braced himself for her horror when she saw the alabaster whiteness of his chest, but it never came. Instead there was a sort of reverent tenderness in her eyes as she touched him, spreading her soft palms over musculature as hard as the finest marble.

She looked up at him in loving surprise. "Oh, Aidan," she whispered. "You're so beautiful—it's like touching one of Michelangelo's sculptures."

He was unbearably moved by her acceptance—he was the Beast being transformed by the Beauty's tenderness— and he feared for a moment that he would break down and weep. But then Neely opened his trousers and boldly stroked him. Aidan's senses, all of them, were infinitely keener than any mortal's, and he groaned in ecstatic misery as she grew even more brazen and closed her strong fingers around his staff. When she teased the tip with the pad of her thumb, he thought he would go wild with the need of her, but he took care to remember that she was flesh and blood, that the bones and tissue beneath her moist, supple skin were fragile. He drew her close against him and kissed her, softening his lips by a trick of the mind, and knew a stunning joy when she whimpered in pleasure and fell onto the bed, pulling him with her, as eager and wild as a female panther in her season.

Aidan kissed her deeply, once, twice, a third time, but his control was tenuous indeed, for he felt as though he'd dreamed of this woman, yearned for her, since the foundation of the world.

He tasted her breasts, frantically, and delighted in her cries of pleasure as he nipped at their hard, sweet little peaks.

"Take me," Neely pleaded finally. "Oh, Aidan, take me, or I'll die—"

He found the musky, warm entrance to her body and prodded gently with his rod, as much to warn her of its size and its hardness as to tease her into wanting him even more.

"Now, then," Aidan said gruffly as he glided slowly, carefully into Neely's tight depths, "we can't have you passing on for want of something I would so willingly give you—"

She clutched at his shoulders, spread her fingers over his chest, stroked his buttocks in fevered urging. "Aidan," she whimpered. "Do it to me—really do it to me—"

He began to move upon her, and her magic encompassed him, and her sweet sorcery tormented him, and he was a man again, not a fiend. His tears—tears born of a joy so fierce he feared he could not contain it—fell softly on her cheekbones and sparkled like diamonds in her hair.

Neely arched beneath him, pleading, in stark Anglo-Saxon terms, for what he and he alone could give her. And when she came, Aidan climaxed as well, and lost his mind in a maelstrom of light and sound and pleasure so intense that it seemed, for a few moments at least, that he had been pardoned and admitted to Heaven after all.

"I love you," she whispered breathlessly when their love-making was over and they lay still, their limbs entangled.

Aidan kissed her forehead, wanting to hold the truth at bay as long as he could. "And I love you," he answered. "Whatever happens, Neely, I want you to remember that."

Her fingers traced a pattern on his chest, and she gave a combination sigh and moan, since they were still joined and he was still steely. The tip of his staff rested against that very sensitive place deep within her, the one scientists had only just given a name to, though lovers had known of it forever.

"Can I—can you—?" Neely paused, and gave an involuntary shiver of rising pleasure. "Can we make a baby together, Aidan? Is that possible?"

Aidan felt a grief as expansive as his earlier jubilation. "No," he said raggedly, grateful that he could not plant an abomination such as himself in the receptive, nurturing flesh of a mortal woman.

She stirred again, her body deliciously soft under his, and spoke shyly, breathlessly. "I—I think I need you again—" He rotated his hips, and she gasped and clutched at his shoulders. Soon the maiden had turned into a demanding little wench once more, and Aidan marveled at the way she abandoned herself to pleasure and at the same time gave it with such generosity.

Aidan loved Neely again and again that night, until she was exhausted, her lush body flexing with climaxes even in sleep. He withdrew from her gently, kissed both her plump, well-suckled breasts, and rose from the bed. For a time he stood there in the moonlight, admiring her, worshiping her, lusting after her even though she had satisfied him over and over.

He sat in a chair near the bed and watched over Neely, a guardian angel from the wrong side of the universe. Aidan did not leave Neely's side until just before dawn, when he took himself off to the dark chamber in Maeve's cellar.

There he crouched against the wall, lowered his head, and slept.

Far away in his lair, within the crumbling ruins of the abbey, Valerian stirred uneasily in his own comalike slumber. She had found him, he could feel her presence stretching over his prone form like a smothering fog.

Lisette, he thought, despairing.

Valerian heard her laughter. *So you remember me, do you?* she trilled, her voice seeming to come from within his skull. *Isn't that touching.*

Having been dormant for several weeks, swallowed whole by his despair, Valerian was feeble. His strength was gone; he had no means of self-defense.

What do you want with me? he asked. *We were never lovers. Never friends.*

You poisoned Aidan's mind against me, Lisette's voice answered, burrowing deeper into Valerian's head like some hard-shelled parasite. *You loved him. Deny it if you dare!*

Valerian's sigh was not physical; it came from the very depths of his spirit. *I deny nothing, least of all my affection for Aidan. I would have died for him.*

How very dramatic. As it happens, my darling, you shall both die. Horribly.

Do what you will to me, Valerian responded, *but leave Aidan be. You've already robbed him of the one thing he held most dear, his humanity. How can you ask more?*

The whole of the supernatural world seemed to quake with the ferocity of Lisette's fury. Her final words reverberated through Valerian's wasted soul. *I ask. And I will not be denied.*

Chapter 15

—◦◦✗◦◦—

Neely awakened bemused, hardly daring to believe that Aidan had truly visited her the night before, fearing that she might have dreamed the entire encounter. Whether real or strictly fantasy, however, the experience had left her with a vibrant sense of well-being, and she was already up when Mrs. F. knocked at the door of the suite and entered with a tray.

The housekeeper took in the princess's skirt and the soft blue sweater Neely wore with it, and smiled. "Very nice," she confirmed. "Are you going out again today, then?"

Neely nodded. She wanted to visit at least one museum before her lunch date with Wendy Browning and Wendy's boyfriend, Jason.

Mrs. F. set down the tray and glanced toward the windows, where a gray mist was shifting and flowing, a cloud come to earth. "Well, it's typical London weather we're having, and that's for certain. Have a care that you dress warmly, miss, because an English wind will go straight to your marrow and take hold there, if you let it."

"I'll be very careful," Neely promised, feeling at once mellow and energetic. She knew a fresh, fragile new hope that things would be all right, though she couldn't imagine how.

By the time Neely left the house for a waiting cab, having fortified herself with one of Mrs. F.'s substantial breakfasts, the wind was mixed with icy slush, and the charcoal skies promised snow. The trip into the heart of the city was harrowing because of the narrow, perilously slick roads, and Neely felt lucky to be alive when she finally stepped out onto the sidewalk in front of a famous art museum.

She paid the driver hastily, rushed up salted stone steps, and, inside the building, paused to rub her reddened ears with her palms in an attempt to restore circulation.

"Good morning," a gracious gray-haired woman said from behind a podium. "We ask all our visitors to sign our guest book."

Neely nodded, handed over the price of admittance, and signed with a flourish. When she stepped into the museum itself, she was stricken by a kind of delighted reverence. It had been a long while since Neely had visited such a place.

She viewed sculpture and paintings of various sorts, along with furniture from the medieval period and pottery from the time of the Romans. Neely indulged herself that day, reading every sign and studying each piece closely, and before she knew it the morning was gone.

She had about twenty minutes to find Willy-Nilly's, the club where she and Wendy and Jason were to meet for lunch, but even so, Neely didn't rush. There were still some tapestries she wanted to see.

The first three were pretty prosaic—plump, cherry-cheeked maidens with flowing hair and crowns of flowers, frolicking with unicorns, angels, or fairies—but the fourth creation all but wrenched Neely forward onto the balls of her feet.

She stared up at the eight-by-twelve-foot hand-loomed tapestry in amazed fascination. It showed a beautiful, dark-haired woman—plainly Maeve Tremayne—enfolded in the flowing cape of a handsome vampire—plainly Valerian. There was a castle or an old monastery in the background, along with an oak forest so realistically wrought that delicate veins were visible in the leaves on the trees.

Neely raised one hand to her mouth, both fascinated and repulsed. She studied Maeve's face, creamy white with the merest hint of pink in her cheeks, and saw joy in the wide blue eyes, as well as a touch of fear.

The tapestry was a cruel reminder that there was much to be resolved before Aidan and Neely could hope to share a life; it left her stricken and supplanted her lingering satisfaction with the old, familiar terror.

"Isn't it magnificent?" asked a woman standing beside Neely, startling her anew. Neely was flustered and would have babbled if she could have spoken at all, which she couldn't. She bit her lower lip and nodded instead.

The woman, wearing a severe brown dress, pearls, and a name tag that identified her as Mrs. Baxter, an employee of the museum, smiled, showing large grayish teeth that arched high into mauve-colored gums. "This tapestry is close to two centuries old, you know. We've taken great pains to preserve it."

Neely finally found a fragment of her voice. "It's—it's—"

"It's quite horrible," said Mrs. Baxter cheerfully. "But the weaving itself reveals an almost supernatural talent, don't you think?" She paused, studying the ominous work of art solemnly. "One would almost believe in vampires, when looking upon such a piece."

"Almost," Neely agreed, shaken. She knew from Aidan's journals that it had been Valerian who had transformed Maeve from a woman to a vampire, and that Maeve had wanted to be changed. Still, it was jarring to see a near-perfect rendering of the actual event, as if the moment were frozen in time, existing, always, as an unutterably tragic truth.

It was knowing that the art depicted a very real event—that the travesty had happened before and would happen again, no doubt—that nearly crushed Neely's spirit on the spot.

She made her way out into the museum lobby, fearing she would either vomit or faint, her program rolled tightly in one sweaty hand, and found a fountain. After several sips of tepid water, she felt a little better and, by means of grim resolve, set out to find Willy-Nilly's.

She had to keep functioning, stay in touch with the ordinary world, give herself time to assimilate facts she had been taught since infancy to regard as fables.

A blizzard greeted her at the threshold of the museum's outer door, and Neely was actually grateful for its biting chill. She drew the shocking cold into her lungs and was a bit less light-headed.

There were no cabs, but fortunately the combination club and restaurant she sought was only a few blocks away. By the time Neely rushed down a set of stone steps to a basement establishment swelling with music, she was numb.

Wendy was there, however, smiling her brilliant smile, her long auburn hair gleaming under the fluorescent lights. Wearing a funky black chiffon dress, a flowered vest, and high-top shoes from some thrift store, she looked delightfully theatrical.

They embraced, and Wendy's dark blue eyes shone as she introduced her tall, handsome actor-student-bartender boyfriend, Jason Wilkins.

Neely felt sane again, and real. She knew the sensation might be temporary, but she grasped it and held on tightly.

Over mugs of dark amber beer and orders of fish and chips served on newspaper and sprinkled with malt vinegar, Wendy and Neely chatted, being sure to include Jason in their conversation. Wendy described her life in London, then propped one elbow on the table, cupped her chin in her hand, and demanded, "Okay, so what was this you mentioned on the telephone, about the senator and some drug cartel?"

Neely drew a deep breath, then told the story, beginning with her first suspicions, a year after going to work as Senator Hargrove's assistant, that something shady was happening. She told of copying files, letters, and memos, and finally turning everything over to the FBI.

Wendy's eyes were bigger than ever. "They didn't help you?"

"I approached the wrong people the first time. The evidence I gave them probably went no further than the office shredder."

"Did you contact the police?" Jason asked.

Neely shook her head. "No. After the debacle with the Bureau, I was afraid to trust anyone else. I hid the duplicates I'd made of everything—" She paused, blushed, then met Wendy's gaze. "I drove to your cottage up in Maine and hid the papers under a floorboard in the shed. Then I took a bus to Bright River, Connecticut, where my brother lives. I wanted to lay low for a while, for obvious reasons."

"Maybe it wasn't smart to go straight to Ben that way," Wendy observed. If she'd caught the connection between Neely's purloined evidence, the cartel's determination to silence her, and the explosion that had leveled the cottage, she didn't let on. "I mean, that would be the first place they'd look."

"I know." Neely sighed. "I wasn't thinking straight—I was so scared and confused." She would leave the most astounding part of the story—falling wildly in love with a true vampire—for another time. Say, some future incarnation, when such phenomena might be commonplace.

With regret Wendy glanced at her watch. "As fascinating as this is," she told Neely, "Jason and I have a class in ten minutes." She nodded toward the narrow windows that afforded a view of passing feet and deepening snow. "Have you noticed that we're having the storm of the century? You'd better stay in the city tonight—public transportation will be hell."

Neely nodded distractedly; a little snow was the least of her problems.

"I'd invite you to stay at my flat, but all I've got is a fold-out couch," Wendy said, rising from her chair. Jason helped her into her coat before donning his own, and Neely felt a stab of envy. Jason and Wendy were living ordinary lives, sharing days as well as nights. They would probably grow old together, unlike Neely and Aidan; only Neely would age. Aidan was immortal, for all practical intents and purposes, though he was not invulnerable.

Neely said good-bye and promised to call soon, and then her friends were gone, and she felt as if she'd been abandoned in an empty universe.

All her carefully cultivated bravado deserted her.

She toyed with the remains of her french fries for a while, then left the restaurant to brave the frigid streets. She rented the last available room in a shabbily elegant old hotel across the street—apparently quite a few Londoners had decided not to risk the commute—and called Mrs. F. to let her know she wouldn't be returning that night.

The doting housekeeper warned her to keep her feet warm and put extra lemon in her afternoon tea, and Neely promised to follow instructions.

After hanging up, she ventured as far as the gift shop in the hotel's gilt-trimmed lobby, where she purchased several newspapers, that week's issue of *Time,* and a paperback romance novel. Back in her room she ordered hot tea and biscuits from room service and settled in to wait out the storm.

The air in Valerian's cramped hiding place fairly throbbed with Lisette's presence. He felt her energy and her boundless hatred, but he was half-starved now, and far too ill to do battle with such a powerful creature.

She became visible at twilight, curled up beside him, as if they were twins sharing a stony womb. He looked at her bleakly, too spent to speak aloud or with his mind.

It made everything infinitely worse, the fact that Lisette was so beautiful. Valerian had always cherished beauty, whether he found it in a woman-creature or a male, and the reminder that sometimes pure evil was lovely to look upon was like a fresh wound to him.

Lisette laughed, curling a finger playfully under Valerian's chin, where the flesh was paper-thin and dry as fine ash. "So you think me evil?" she chimed in a merry voice. "How very hypocritical of you, Valerian—you, who have always sought pleasure wherever it was to be found."

Slowly, and at great cost, Valerian shook his head. "No," he croaked. "I have no taste for innocence."

She smiled, but her aquamarine eyes were hard with anger. "So very noble," she taunted. "Wasn't the lovely Maeve Tremayne an innocent when you found her? And what of your many and varied lovers, Valerian? Were they all vampires when you seduced them, or were some of them hapless humans who had no idea what sort of fiend they were consorting with?"

Valerian closed his eyes for a moment. "Stop," he rasped. "You will gain nothing by torturing me."

"I will gain everything," Lisette snapped. "And the torture has only begun." With that, she glared at the outer wall of Valerian's narrow lair, and the stones themselves seemed to explode, bursting outward into the purple-gray chill of a winter evening, scrabbling onto the ground.

Briefly Valerian yearned for life, and for mercy, but these frail wishes were soon swamped by his despair. What good was there in saving himself, even if he had been able? What right had he, who had fouled what was holy, to live forever?

He did not move but remained curled up inside the crumbling wall.

Lisette scrambled over him, being purposely ungraceful, he was sure, and stood in the soft, powdery snow, the night wind playing in her coppery hair. With a murmur of irritation she reached into the chasm and clasped Valerian in both hands, using her legendary strength to wrench him out like a baby torn too soon from its mother's belly.

He was fragile, like something broken, and lay helpless in her arms, his head against her cold breast. For a time she just stood there, cradling him, crooning some demented lullaby, but then she began to glide over the ground.

They must have traveled that way, a hideous pair abroad on a winter's night, for the greater part of fifteen minutes. Then Valerian recognized the unsanctified ground beyond the outer walls of the abbey, the forgotten place where heretics and murderers had been buried. The weeds and the soft ground had long since swallowed up all but one of two of the few crude markers that had been there in the first place, but Valerian was aware of the moldering skeletons and half mummified corpses beneath the earth, and he shuddered.

Lisette laid him in the center of that desolate place, and he still had no strength to resist. She spread his arms and legs wide of his wasted body and pinned him there, with a mental command, a bond stronger than any steel manacle. He felt the first faint stirrings of fear.

She smiled down at him when she'd completed her work, her arms folded. "Aidan will sense your despair and come to save you like the fool he is. And when he does, I will destroy him."

Valerian moaned, blocking Aidan's image from his mind with the last shreds of his strength. If he didn't cry out to Aidan, didn't think of him, the other vampire might not be drawn into the trap.

Lisette knew Valerian's efforts and laughed, flinging her head back in a fit of mirth. "You're all idiots," she said after the terrible, shrill sound of her amusement had faded away into the night. "Since when do vampires behave like besotted humans, rescuing each other, pretending to honor and chivalry? Where is your white charger, Valerian?"

Valerian didn't reply. He was losing consciousness; he could feel his spirit seeping into the cold ground, curling like smoke around the bones of the long-dead and eternally unforgiven. As terrible as the experience was, he knew he would long to be as insensate as those corpses when morning came and the sun found him. The hot rays would consume his flesh like a rain of acid, but slowly. Long after his physical body was nothing but a smoldering shell, he would still be imprisoned inside himself, and he would feel agony until his thoughts were snuffed out like the flame of a candle.

And after that he might find himself in Dante's version of Hell, on the threshold of an eternity of suffering.

He groaned aloud at the prospect, and Lisette laughed again, then shrieked into the night sky, "Let all vampires see, and remember, what it means to betray me!"

In the next moment a soft, cool snow began to fall. Flakes covered Valerian's closed eyes, the hollows in his gaunt face and body, and suddenly, vividly, he recalled being a human boy, no older than eight. He remembered the drawing of breath and the steady thump of his heartbeat; he heard his own laughter, felt it in his throat, felt the warm, pliant muscles in his legs as he ran, in just such a snowfall as this.

For the merest fragment of time, Valerian was innocent again. He was free and whole, and the greatest powers of heaven looked upon him with benevolence.

Just before he swooned, a smile touched his mouth.

Aidan awakened in Maeve's cellar, well-rested from a day of slumber and determined to avoid Neely for as long as he possibly could. He knew the Brotherhood was keeping an account of his whereabouts and his actions, allowing him an illusion of freedom while the members decided his fate among themselves, and the last thing he wanted was to draw their attention to the woman he loved.

His soul still hummed with the joy Neely had brought him by offering herself in passion and in trust.

In a blink he transported himself to his room on the second floor of the mansion. He seldom used the chamber, but there were fresh clothes in the wardrobe, and he felt like sprucing himself up. He would hunt in nineteenth-century London, perhaps among the riffraff along the waterfront, and then look in on Valerian. Surely the other vampire would be over his sulk by now, and they could talk. Aidan was eager to tell his friend that it was possible to be mortal again; he wondered if other vampires would step forward and ask to be changed, if he succeeded in making the transformation.

Aidan whistled as he put on his most elegant evening clothes—black trousers with a glistening silk stripe down either leg, a cutaway coat with tails, a ruffled white shirt of the finest linen, a narrow string tie, and a top hat. He wore spats over shiny shoes and completed his ensemble with a long cape lined in gold.

He looked down at himself, decided he looked like a proper vampire, raised his arms above his head, and disintegrated into a wispy vapor.

I'm going to miss doing that, Aidan admitted silently when he reassembled himself in a filthy, rat-infested alleyway behind a combination brothel and opium den within a stone's throw of London's waterfront.

Snatches of fog curled around him, around empty crates and whiskey barrels and piles of garbage, like dancers in a spectral ballet troupe. Aidan sighed and waited; there was a corpse sitting upright, just a few doors down, crouched against a brick wall with its head resting on its updrawn knees.

He shuddered in distaste and tried to ignore the thing, but that was difficult. Out of the corner of his eye he saw the ghost rise from the body, heard it wail in despairing protest.

Suddenly it flew at Aidan, a bluish-gray blob of wavering light, keening and shrieking. The creature was—or had been until about half an hour before—a seagoing lad, barely fifteen years of age. He'd been robbed of the few pence he possessed, then stabbed under the ribs with a fisherman's knife.

"Go on," Aidan told it, speaking kindly but in a tone that would brook no argument. "There is nothing for you here. Look around you for the Light, and follow where it leads." He was no more certain that there was an afterlife than the shade itself was, he supposed. He said the words because he had heard his mother say them to a dying man when he, Aidan, was a small boy. The unlucky fellow had gotten in the way of a runaway coach, and his legs, pelvis, and rib cage had been crushed beneath the horses' hooves and the wheels, but he'd taken comfort from a tavern maid's pretty assurances and passed on peacefully.

Aidan was just about to move along when a great, loud hoyden of a woman burst through a rear doorway, dragging a gawky, half-starved child along with her. Gripping the young girl's hair—she was twelve, Aidan saw, by glancing briefly into her mind—the drunken harridan flung her victim hard against the brick wall.

The child sobbed, almost hysterical, as helpless as an animal with one limb in a trap. She'd stolen from the kitchen, a piece of bread, a crumbling morsel of moldy cheese, and the woman had caught her.

"Now I'll box your ears for you!" the drudge shrilled. "See if you dare steal from Dorcus Moody again, you workhouse brat!"

Aidan stepped out of the shadows, resplendent in his gentleman's clothes, and both the old witch and the child stared at him, obviously confounded.

"What is your name?" he asked the girl gently.

Mistress Moody did not move, for Aidan had frozen her in place.

"Effie," came the whispered response.

"You took the cheese and bread for your mother," Aidan said, having already discerned the fact.

Effie nodded.

"She's sick."

The child nodded again. "We got throwed out of the workhouse—my brother made trouble when one of the blokes as looked out for us there tried to put his hand down me dress."

Aidan gestured for Effie to wait, slipped inside the tavern's gloomy kitchen, and gathered up two loaves of bread, a block of cheese, and a joint of venison. After dropping the loot into a cloth sack, he brought it outside and silently offered it to the girl.

Dorcus Moody was still facing the wall with one meaty hand raised to slap, eyes staring, muscles as rigid as if rigor mortis had set in.

Effie snatched the bag of food, turned on her bare feet, which were blue with cold and encrusted with the filth of the street, and ran, without giving Aidan, Mistress Moody, or the sailor's corpse a second look.

Aidan walked around Dorcus Moody's hulking frame and smiled into her senseless face. She had a wart beside her nose, and a thin trail of spittle trickled down her chin.

"May I have this dance?" Aidan asked with a slight bow. He put his hands on her, as if for a waltz, then bent his head to her jugular vein and drank.

He left her beside the dead sailor, staring witlessly into space, her pulse thready but regular. She was a vile creature, was Mistress Moody, Aidan observed to himself as he walked away, but her blood was as potent as a fine Madeira.

He turned, there in the gloom of the alley, and took his hat off to her. "May you live to nourish another vampire, Gentle Dorcus," he said.

She made a soft, whimpering sound, low in her throat.

The image struck Aidan from out of nowhere as he left the alley; he saw Valerian, staked to the ground in some snowy cemetery, awaiting the dawn.

Aidan muttered a curse, then focused all his powers into one single thought. *Valerian!*

The reply was faint, but it formed instantly in Aidan's mind. *Stay away. I beg you, stay away!*

Aidan was on the point of ignoring the injunction and seeking Valerian out in the same way he would have sought Maeve, or Neely, when someone on the fringe of a passing mob of drunken swabs bumped into him, hard.

"I wouldn't if I were you," Tobias said good-naturedly. "You could never save Valerian alone."

Tobias was right, but Aidan could not turn his back, even though the scale was balanced between himself and Valerian, and all debts had been canceled. Yes, the other vampire had cared for him when he was ill, nourished him, even brought Neely to his side, but Aidan had saved Valerian once, too, after the attempt to travel too far back in time.

"I can't leave him to burn," Aidan answered.

"Suppose I told you that you have one chance to become a man again, and that you must take that opportunity now, this moment, or lose it for all of eternity?" Tobias asked in a reasonable tone. He, too, wore evening clothes, and the two of them strolled down the street together, an odd sight indeed in that grim, desolate part of London.

Aidan thought of Neely, of all his dreams. He wanted to come to her as a man, not a monster. He wanted to lie beside her in a real bed, make love to her as often as possible, and work in the sunlight every day, until his skin glistened with sweat and his muscles ached. He wanted to vote and attend PTA meetings and drink beer on the beach and complain about taxes.

For all of that, he still could not desert Valerian. Aidan knew only too well that, if their positions were reversed, the older vampire would try to help him.

"I guess I'd say I have rotten luck, and you and the Brotherhood have lousy timing," Aidan finally replied. "So long, Tobias."

With that, he did his vanishing number, and almost immediately found himself standing on the ruined wall of an old abbey. His cape floated in the wind, in true vampire tradition, and Aidan felt a certain bitter amusement. Damned if Valerian hadn't found a way to screw up his plans after all, even if it had been an inadvertent move.

Aidan focused his powers into a single invisible beam and found Valerian almost immediately. He was on the hillside, well beyond the outermost wall of the abbey, and he was helpless.

"Damn," Aidan said. He closed his eyes, opened them again, and found Valerian spread-eagle at his feet.

The other vampire seemed delirious, drifting in and out of consciousness, and when he saw Aidan crouched beside him, he moaned. "I told you," he rasped, "to stay away. She's—she's here—waiting."

"Lisette," Aidan said. "Yes, I figured as much."

Just then, a weird, shrill music filled the cold night air, and Aidan raised his eyes from his stricken friend to see Lisette pirouetting gracefully atop a crude stone slab.

Valerian began to weep. "Why, Aidan—why did you come? I could have borne anything but what she will do to you—"

"Stop whining," Aidan instructed him lightly. He discerned the mental bonds that held his friend, tried them with his mind, and found them strong. "If there's one thing I truly despise, it's a sniveling vampire."

Lisette ceased her hideous dance and held out her arms to Aidan. She seemed to waver in her white, shroudlike robe, a specter with substance.

"Come waltz with me, my precious."

Aidan approached her. He supposed he should have been scared, but he was well beyond that, well beyond cold terror and even outright panic. A strange calm possessed him. If he was never to be a man again, never to hold Neely in his arms, then he wanted to perish.

"Release Valerian. You have no quarrel with him."

Lisette pouted prettily, and Aidan recalled an innocent time when he had believed her to be a flesh-and-blood woman and had taken unabashed pleasure in her embrace. "I do have a quarrel with him," she insisted. "He plotted to be your companion for all of eternity!"

"He's since found me uncooperative. Let him go, Lisette."

She pirouetted again on top of the gravestone, her auburn tresses blackened by the gloom, moving like living strands woven of the night itself. She laughed, and the sound was silvery, sparkling, and brimming with madness.

"Foolish boy," she scolded. "Valerian is going to die screaming with the sunrise, and so are you, my sweet darling."

It was not an idle threat, but Aidan was still calm. If his existence was to end this way, then so be it. No doubt, from a cosmic point of view, his fate was a just one. "I thought you wanted to dance with me," he said evenly.

Lisette descended to stand facing Aidan in the snow. There was a mischievous glint in her cool blue eyes. "Do you imagine for a moment, Aidan Tremayne, that I don't know when I'm being patronized?"

He simply held out his arms as he had long ago, when they had danced on summer grass, under bright stars, and he had not yet guessed what horror he courted.

She batted her thick eyelashes coquettishly, then drifted into Aidan's embrace. He began to turn around and around, and her shroudlike gown billowed out around them, as did his cape, and after a while Lisette began to hum softly.

He thought, once or twice, of the spectacle they all made—he and Lisette, a pair of monsters, waltzing in a moonlit graveyard, Valerian staked out on the ground like some hapless character in an old Western. Aidan might have laughed, had he dared, but dawn was already approaching, a faint grayish glow shimmered along the horizon.

"You were such a delightful creature in the beginning," Lisette fretted, running the tip of an index finger from Aidan's throat to the top of his cummberbund. "I should never have changed you, though. That was my fatal mistake."

Privately Aidan agreed, although he was glad he'd stayed alive long enough to know Neely. That wouldn't have happened, of course, if he'd lived out his normal span of years. "Did you create others?" he asked on a sudden hunch. "Valerian, for instance?"

She sighed and tossed a disparaging glance in the other vampire's direction. "That insufferable pest? I should say not. I don't know how he was made, much less why, and I don't care if he screams in hell from now until the end of eternity."

"Why do you hate him so much?"

"Because he dared to love you."

"Do you hate yourself as well, then?"

Lisette stopped cold and stared up at Aidan, her face rigid. "I do not love you."

"I think you do."

She was silent for a time, utterly motionless, her expression unreadable. "It changes nothing!" she screamed in sudden, wild fury. At the same moment a border of golden light formed between earth and sky.

It was almost morning.

Chapter 16

—◦✴〉⊱◦—

An unearthly shriek rent the air, and Aidan didn't know if Lisette had made the sound, or Valerian, or even he himself. Full sunrise was minutes, perhaps only moments, away, and already he felt as though a miniature fire blazed in every pore. Pain seared his eyes, and he stumbled slightly, blinded.

Neely, he thought, involuntarily unleashing all the power of his love for her, of the dreams he'd cherished, and the hopes. The soul-cry was not offered in an effort to save himself—it was surely too late for that—but because he could not bear to leave her.

Whatever his intentions, the name sent him plummeting through time and space, and he landed with a hard thump on a carpeted floor.

He rolled, still unable to see, as the morning sunlight licked at him like the very flames of hell.

"Aidan!" Neely cried, and he was aware that she'd

dropped to her knees beside him. "Aidan, what is it?"

"The light," he managed; it was all he could do to speak without screaming.

She bounded away for a moment; he heard a rushing *whoosh* as she yanked the drapery cord to cover the offending window, and he actually chuckled, impressed by her quick thinking, even though he was suffering the purest agony he'd ever imagined.

Neely returned to him, and he felt her hands against him, pushing. He was sheltered beneath something then, and the pain lessened ever so slightly. Still, he could see nothing but the blazing light of the fire that was consuming him.

Aidan lay gasping, realized that the cooling touch of darkness surrounded him, eased the pain. "Where—what is this place?" he whispered.

"You're under my bed at the Majestic Arms Hotel," she answered breathlessly; he could tell she was rushing about, doing something. "Nice of you to pop in."

He made a groaning sound. "This is no time for morbid humor," he said.

She dropped to the floor and crawled under the bed frame to lie beside him. The mischief was gone from her voice; she sounded fragile, worried, and very sad. "Are you going to die?"

"Probably not, thanks to you," Aidan answered. "For someone who hasn't been trained to administer emergency aid to vampires, Neely, you did rather well." He sensed that she wanted to touch him but hesitated because she feared causing him further discomfort.

"I untucked the blankets and sheets from the mattress and arranged them so the light couldn't get in," she said earnestly. She was about to cry, Aidan thought, and he was at once touched that she cared so deeply and fearful that he would find her sorrow even more torturous than the sunlight.

"Very good." He sighed the words. "It feels as if—I'm going to lose consciousness for a time. There may be changes—please don't be frightened. . . ."

A sheen of tears glistened in her eyes. "Is there anything more I can do?"

"Yes. You can stand guard, so to speak, and make sure I'm not exposed to the sunlight."

She was silent for a few moments and made no move to leave his side. In fact, she cuddled close and cautiously put an arm around him. "There's a storm outside, you know," she finally said. "A blizzard, actually. The sun is mostly hidden."

Aidan was slipping, though he didn't know whether death and judgment awaited him or an ordinary, healing sleep. "A stroke of good fortune, that," he mumbled, "though the light always gets through—no matter what." He opened his eyes, but Neely was only a faint shadow beside him; his vampire vision, ordinarily sharper than a cat's, was gone.

In the next moment oblivion closed around him like dark, cool water.

Aidan might only be resting, and he might be dead of his injuries. Neely had no way of knowing, since the usual signs of life—a heartbeat and breath—didn't apply in this case. Being careful to let in as little light as possible, she slipped from beneath the bed and got to her feet.

The room was gloomy, since she'd closed the drapes and turned out the lights, but it was a poor substitute for the kind of deep, encompassing darkness Aidan needed.

Neely put the DO NOT DISTURB sign on the door and locked the room from the inside, just to be extra careful. Then she snatched all the towels from the bathroom racks and draped them over the sides of the bed, along with the heavy blankets, sheets, and bedspread, in an effort to shelter Aidan as completely as possible. When that was done, she crawled underneath the bed again, on the side opposite the window, and lay beside him, trying by an effort of sheer will to transfer her own strength to him.

The telephone rang once, but Neely ignored it, leaving the improvised lair only when she needed to use the bathroom or get a drink of water. Since she didn't want to leave Aidan, and was even less willing to call room service, Neely breakfasted on half a candy bar, found adrift in the bottom of her purse, and reminded herself there were worse things than an empty stomach.

Like seeing Aidan die, for instance.

Maybe it was the jet lag Mrs. F. had spoken of, but after a while Neely nodded off into a half-sleep and drifted along the moving surface of dreams yet to be dreamed and hopes yet to be recognized.

Maeve awakened at sunset, in the corner of what had once been the abbey's wine cellar, and saw that Tobias was already conscious. Perhaps he had never slept at all; he was a very old vampire, despite his youthful appearance, and she had heard that some of the old ones did not require rest or even very much blood.

She shifted her gaze toward Valerian's prone form. His skin was lumpy and gray, as if bubbles had arisen beneath. He was utterly motionless, and Maeve sensed no vitality in him, no power. "Is he dead?"

Actually she was much more interested in finding out what had happened to her twin, her beloved Aidan, but caution guided her words. She was not used to these elder vampires, did not know enough of their ways and habits to predict the things they might do. This was not the time for a faux pas.

"Perhaps we were too late."

Tobias laid one hand lightly on Valerian's disfigured forehead. "He wanders somewhere far from here," he mused, "keeping his distance from the pain."

Maeve shuddered, the memory of the nightmare unspooling itself in her mind in the course of seconds. She had sensed Aidan's distress, being so attuned to him, and raced from her den, where she'd been about to settle down for the day, to find her brother on the hillside behind the old abbey.

If she lived to be a thousand, Maeve reflected, she would never forget the terror of reaching his side, only moments before the sunrise. Seeing Lisette, she'd screamed in fear and rage.

Maeve had heard, or perhaps only felt, Aidan's cry. *Neely*. In the next instant, he was gone, utterly vanished, and then Lisette had fled as well.

"Come," a voice had commanded from behind her. "Quickly!"

Maeve had whirled, seen the stranger crouched beside Valerian's inert body, watched mutely as he lifted the fallen one into strong arms. She'd felt the first acid sting of the sunlight then, and hurried to the other vampire's side.

The next thing she remembered was the blissful, chilly safety of the wine cellar. There she had learned that Valerian's rescuer, and perhaps hers as well, was called Tobias, and that he was an ancient one, a member of the Brotherhood.

"What of Aidan?" she whispered now as the night stirred around them. Indeed, she could withhold the question no longer. "Where is he?"

Tobias arched an eyebrow. "Don't you know? The two of you are twins, are you not? Linked by some unseen and unbreakable cord?"

Maeve's eyes burned, but she told herself that was only a residual effect of her close call with the sunrise. "It used to be that way," she said woodenly. "Before—"

"Before the woman?"

Maeve looked away. "Yes. Her name is Neely, and Aidan is a fool for her."

"I know," Tobias said easily. "He was never meant for this life in the first place, in my opinion. He thinks too much like a mortal."

"Yes," Maeve agreed sadly. Eternity yawned ahead of her like a great void, and she knew some of Valerian's fathomless despair, though she had been slightly contemptuous of it before. She had become a vampire to keep from losing Aidan, but now it appeared that it had all been for naught. Even if he had escaped Lisette and found safety somewhere, he was bent on either destroying himself completely or becoming human again. The very fact that she couldn't locate him in her mind meant he was veiling himself from her.

"Tell me, please. Where is my brother?"

Tobias sighed. "London, I believe. It was a near miss for him, and he's blinded—though that condition is probably temporary—but the woman is looking after him."

Maeve's relief was so great that she nearly swooned under the force of it. "What will happen now?"

The other vampire shrugged. "Nothing has been decided, really. There are those in the Brotherhood who want to agree to the experiment, merely for the sake of learning. Others feel that rebellious vampires should simply be destroyed, for the protection of all, and as an example to those who would digress from our code."

"I see," Maeve whispered. So there *was* a way to be mortal once more, and Aidan had found it. Inwardly she grappled with the staggering realities of what her brother meant to attempt.

"In either case, Maeve," Tobias said kindly, "there is nothing you can really do besides accept whatever course he chooses."

"And Lisette?"

Tobias sighed. "I must go now," he said, nodding toward Valerian, "and hunt for this one, since he cannot hunt for himself. As for Lisette's whereabouts, I know not, but she has surely taken refuge in some lair. She will not return for a while."

"Why not?" Maeve asked. She had never feared another vampire, had in fact grown stronger herself with every night's feeding, exercising her powers, learning, practicing, but she knew Lisette was a dangerous adversary.

"She wants no truck with the Brotherhood," Tobias said. "And now, adieu."

With that he was gone, and Maeve was alone with the cobwebs, the rats and spiders, and Valerian's insensate hulk. She ventured to his side, touched his warped, discolored skin, and remembered a time when she had loved him. Even after she'd come to despise Valerian, she'd thought him beautiful.

"Come back," she said softly.

One of Valerian's eyelids twitched, just slightly, but he did not look at her or speak.

She stroked his singed hair, half burned away now, but once so glorious and thick. "You mustn't leave me, Valerian," she whispered. "I've lost Aidan—I can't spare you as well."

The wounded vampire did not stir.

Maeve watched him for a long time, remembering. Soon her own hunger drove her out of the hiding place to hunt.

Night came, finally, and Neely crawled out from under the bed and sat cross-legged on the carpet, biting her nails and waiting for Aidan to rouse. She didn't think about what she would do if he was dead—weren't vampires supposed to be immortal?—but she did consider his need for blood.

She even thought of offering him some of her own, though she hoped it wouldn't come to that.

Ten minutes passed, and there was no ruffling of the edges of the blankets. Neely gathered her courage, lifted the covers, and peeked.

Aidan was gone.

Neely was relieved—surely this meant he was alive—but she was annoyed, too. Why, if it hadn't been for her, that vampire would be nothing but a mysterious pile of ashes waiting to be vacuumed up by the maid, and how had he repaid the favor? By vanishing without so much as a good-bye or a thank-you!

She dropped to her knees and peered under the bed again, just to make sure. There was nothing there, not even a dustbunny.

Soon Neely became restless, her emotions in a tangle, and the half candy bar had long since worn off. She showered, dressed, brushed her teeth, and put the bed back into a semblance of order, so the maid wouldn't speculate, then went out for some fresh air and food.

The night was dark and cold, and, though the storm had abated a little, the great city was still essentially paralyzed. Neely called Mrs. F. again, from a corner pub. She was safe and sound, she told the housekeeper, and taking plenty of extra lemon in her tea.

After eating, and warming herself with said tea, Neely braved the sidewalks again. A part of her wanted to go back to the hotel room and wait for Aidan there, but she discarded the idea. When the time was right, she would see him again.

She bought a ticket to a foreign movie and whiled away a couple of hours in the dark theater, but she never really saw the film itself. She was busy thinking about what it meant to be a vampire, not just to drink blood, but to be a creature of darkness, never stirring into the daylight.

Tears brimmed along Neely's lashes. She was a day person; if she ever traded her flesh and blood for immortality, she would always yearn to see the sun, even as she lived in terror of its rays.

She was pondering this when suddenly the empty seat beside hers was filled.

Wild hope stirred Neely's heart, but in an instant she knew that her visitor was Maeve, not Aidan. The vampire was clad in a hooded cloak of dazzling dark blue velvet, and she brought along with her an ambience all her own, one rife with tension.

"Where is Aidan?" she asked moderately.

"I don't know," Neely answered in a mild state of shock. She'd bought popcorn, but so far she had just held the carton in her lap and played idly with the kernels. She told Maeve about Aidan's sudden appearance the night before, his condition, and her own clumsy efforts to help him.

Maeve was silent for a few moments, probably absorbing the images and emotions Neely's account would stir in a sister's heart. "I see," she said finally.

The remark sounded ambiguous to Neely, but she wasn't foolish enough to say so.

"It was wise, your leaving my house, although I wouldn't have recommended it," Maeve announced presently. "Perhaps this is the safest place for you after all, in the very heart of London, among the throngs."

The theater was more than half empty—not much of a throng—but again Neely kept the opinion to herself. "Am I really in such terrible danger?" she asked.

Maeve looked at her in silence for several seconds, then answered gravely, "Yes, you are. After this I recommend that you stay in at night, however. These are, after all, the hours when vampires stalk their prey."

Neely suppressed a chill. She was well aware that Maeve Tremayne could turn vicious at any moment, like a once-wild wolf thought to be a pet, and tear her apart. "Is there anything you'd like me to say to Aidan if I see him before you do?"

The beautiful creature stiffened, her face glowing pale as alabaster inside the graceful hood of her cloak.

A heartbeat too late, Neely realized her mistake.

Maeve leaned close, so close that Neely squirmed, and whispered, "Aidan and I took root in the same womb. We grew together, each of our hearts beating in perfect unison with that of the other. No one will ever, *ever* displace me in his affections."

"I don't want to be his sister," Neely pointed out, wincing inwardly at her own bravado, especially since it came on the heels of a blunder. Some instinct told her, however, that since she was in for a penny, she might as well be in for a pound. Maeve wasn't the sort to respect any person less forceful than herself.

"No? And what would you be to him, if you are not willing to become a vampire?"

Neely was defiant, angry that the most basic, the most cherished, of her emotions should be questioned. "I love Aidan. He is a part of me, and I am a part of him. And if he succeeds in making the change, I will be his wife—more than that, his mate, for all of eternity if I have anything to say about it—and I will bear his children."

Maeve was silent for an uncomfortably long time. "Tell Aidan not to forget the white roses," she said in a very sad tone, and then she vanished again.

Neely gave up trying to watch the second feature, tossed her popcorn into a trash bin in the lobby, and walked out into the snowy street. Even at that late hour the traffic was still tangled and angry. Accompanied by the sound of honking horns and insults shouted between cars, she hurried back to the hotel.

It was something of a disappointment to find that Aidan had not returned, a conclusion Neely didn't fully accept until she'd looked under the bed as well as behind the shower curtain and inside the closet.

Unable to sleep, too proud to keep a vigil, Neely opened her romance novel and began to read. She visualized the hero as Aidan and the heroine as herself, and for a brief, tenuous time the story kept her distracted from her own problems.

The return of Aidan's vision was gradual—the patrons of the Last Ditch Tavern were mere shadows, shifting and swaying—but his other senses compensated quite nicely. He circulated, catching a scent here, picking up a snatch of conversation there.

That night, feeding, and feeding well, was a matter of survival.

Finally he selected his prey, a young thug named Tommy Cook, who made his living snatching purses and holding up the occasional convenience store. Tommy's mind was a greasy, unpleasant place, but Aidan planted an idea there, and it soon bore fruit.

Cook wandered into the gloomy hallway leading to the rest rooms, stopped in front of the cigarette machine, and fumbled in the pockets of his jeans for change.

Aidan closed in, rendered Tommy unconscious with a strategic tap at his nape, and caught him before he slumped to the floor. Though several people passed while Aidan was taking the pint or so of nourishment he needed, no one looked twice, let alone interfered.

Tommy's blood was powerful stuff, like potent wine. Although Aidan hated it, just as he always had, he felt a sweet, dizzying ecstasy, unlike anything he'd experienced before. A moment after he'd hauled Tommy to a chair at a corner table and left him there to sleep it off, however, it was as though someone had just injected him with a syringe full of raw sunlight. He was on fire, but this time his insides burned, not his flesh.

Aidan's knees buckled; he fought to remain upright.

Tommy, stuporous before, was now smiling up at him, his dark, impudent eyes flashing with triumph. Aidan's vision sharpened, dulled, and sharpened again, in sickeningly rapid sequence, and he gripped the table edge to keep from falling.

"What is it, Vampire?" Tommy drawled. "Are you ill?"

Warlock, Aidan thought. Too late, he remembered Valerian's injunction to beware of other supernatural creatures when he ventured into such cesspools of consciousness as the Last Ditch Tavern.

Tommy laughed. "Yes," he said.

The pain rose up around Aidan now, as well as within him, like a smothering vapor. He turned, staggered, fell.

The warlock's taunting laughter echoing in his brain, Aidan struggled back to his feet. Mostly by groping, for the vivid world of the night was branded into his injured eyes one moment, hopelessly black the next, he found a side door and thrust himself over the threshold.

He gasped, then fell unconscious into a new, powdery snow.

"Look," said Canaan Havermail, giggling as she pointed a small, chubby finger. "He's a snow angel."

"Do hush!" Benecia hissed as she knelt beside Aidan Tremayne's inert frame and turned him over onto his back. It always made her impatient when Canaan behaved childishly, for she had lived quite four centuries as a vampire and that was enough to mature anyone. She brushed the soft snow from his scarred but still handsome face and felt a broken yearning in her heart, long since withered and atrophied though it was. She was fond of Aidan, though she hadn't admitted the fact to anyone else, but she could never have him for a lover. In his eyes she was not an adult female with powers equal to and even exceeding his own. Instead he saw her as a monstrous mockery of a child. "We've got to take him to Mother or Aunt Maeve. I believe he's been poisoned."

Canaan sighed, irritated to have the night's adventures interrupted by duty, especially when it was still early. "Oh, bother. What do you suppose it was that got him—a warlock?"

"Probably," Benecia said, speaking tenderly as she lifted Aidan's upper body into her plump, dimpled little arms. "Are you coming with me, or must I do this alone?"

Canaan tapped one delicately shod foot, her head tilted to one side. "If I help you, might we have a tea party?"

"Yes," Benecia agreed wearily.

"With our dolls?"

"With our dolls!" the elder sister snapped. In the next instant she turned herself and Aidan into a wafting mist.

The trio arrived at Havermail Castle seconds later, only to find that both Aubrey and Roxanne were still out hunting.

Canaan wanted to dump Aidan in the dungeon and indulge in the promised tea party, but Benecia wasn't about to let him out of her sight. Thus it happened that the three of them gathered around a low, square monument to a long-dead contemporary, in the oldest part of the castle's cemetery. Aidan slumped in his chair, still unconscious, while Canaan arranged her dolls in little chairs around the improvised table. Her china tea set, complete with miniature silver spoons, was carefully arranged.

"Have some tea, Benecia dear," Canaan urged, her voice chiming with delicate malice. "Don't you think your friend would like a cup?"

Benecia rolled her eyes. "Does he look thirsty to you?"

Canaan pretended to pour, then handed her sister a fragile cup filled with nothing. "You needn't be so tiresome," she scolded. She might have had the body of a little girl, but there was something of the fussbudget spinster in her as well. "It's not as if I'm asking you to do anything terrible."

The elder sister suppressed a sigh and pretended to sip from the cup. Their mother, Roxanne, liked to play the same silly game with plates and glasses and silverware, as if they were all still human and required the sustenance of food and drink.

Aidan moaned and moved his head slightly.

"There, see!" Canaan cried. "He *does* want tea!"

Benecia set her cup and saucer down with a clink and rushed to his side. "Good heavens, Canaan, get a hobby. He doesn't want tea, you ninny—he's dying!"

"Poppycock," said Canaan in a crisp tone. "Vampires don't die."

Before Benecia could respond to the contrary, they were surrounded by dark, shifting forms. She and Canaan huddled close together, trembling slightly, for they did not recognize these creatures.

"Look," Canaan whispered. "We have guests for our party."

"Who are you?" Benecia demanded of the robed figures, pretending to possess courage that had long since deserted her. "What do you want?"

A fierce-looking vampire stepped forward, his hair and beard as red as fire. He resembled a Viking, with his hard features and strong build.

He did not trouble to answer Benecia's questions but instead bent and draped Aidan's lifeless arm over his massive shoulders, then lifted him to his feet.

"Wait!" Benecia cried, rushing forward, grabbing at the sleeve of the vampire's tunic. "Where are you taking him?"

Still, the Viking offered no reply. Supporting Aidan against his side, he disappeared into the darkness, and the others filed after him.

Canaan gripped Benecia's arm when she would have followed. "Let them go," she said quietly. "We'll find another plaything."

Benecia was trembling. "I wanted *him*."

"Don't fuss," said Canaan, shaking a finger in her sister's face. "He's gone, and as far as I'm concerned, it's good riddance." Purposefully she refilled Benecia's cup with emptiness, and there was nothing to do but drink of it.

Lisette crouched in a corner of her lair, deep in the bowels of the villa on the coast of Spain, whimpering. Her hands and arms were piteously scarred, and her face misshapen, disfigured. Her once beautiful hair now hung in hanks and wisps, and her scalp was black and crumbling.

She tossed her head from side to side, wailing in her grief. She had been such a fool to dally with Aidan those extra minutes, caught up in the old fascination, forgetting her own vulnerability to the glaring sun. Now he'd escaped her vengeance, as had that miserable specimen, Valerian, and she found the knowledge virtually unbearable.

Lisette collapsed onto her side, too aggrieved to stand, and curled herself into a tight little ball. Inside she was shrieking, but all that came from her parched throat now were soft, squeaking mewls.

Her body was an unbearable place to be, and she left it to wander in happier places, knowing all the while that she would return, stronger and more beautiful than ever. And when she did, both Valerian and Aidan would know the depth and breadth of her wrath.

Neely awakened with a start, sending her book tumbling to the floor. "Aidan?" she whispered, even though she knew he wasn't with her in the hotel room. In fact, she had a feeling that he was in terrible trouble.

She rushed to the window and pushed aside the curtain. Dawn was still several hours away, but the snow had stopped, and there were cabs and buses moving along the streets.

Neely gathered up her belongings, put on her coat, and took the elevator to the lobby, where she settled her bill in cash. Flagging down a cab took longer than she would have liked, and she was numb with cold by the time one stopped for her. She sat shivering in the back seat, her teeth chattering as she gave the driver Maeve's address.

The going was slow, given the state of the roads, but roughly forty-five minutes later, Neely found herself standing outside the high iron gates in front of the mansion. The cab scooted away, and she pressed anxiously at the button that would alert Mrs. F. to her presence.

A considerable interval went by before the housekeeper came bustling out, wearing galoshes, her nightdress, and a huge woolen overcoat. "You might have telephoned ahead," she scolded, fumbling with the lock and key on the other side. "At least that way you wouldn't have had to stand out here like a lost soul!"

"I'm sorry for waking you," Neely said, hugging herself, feeling very much a lost soul. Mrs. F opened the gate, and she slipped through. "I came on an impulse, and I didn't think to call first. Is Miss Tremayne around?"

"Well, now, that she is, miss," said Mrs. F., hustling Neely up the walk and through the gaping front door. In the entry hall she set about brushing the snow from Neely's coat. "It happens that she's up in the studio, on the third floor, hard at her weaving. Why, she's working that loom as if all that mattered in this universe hung in the balance."

Chapter 17

—◦⋊ ⋉◦—

Although Valerian's body was all but ruined, some essential part of him crouched inside the husk, a small spark of consciousness able to recognize itself and, however laboriously, to reason.

Fact by fact, Valerian pieced together what had happened to him. It had all begun with his love for Aidan, an emotion born long before, on that night when they'd met for the first time, in an eighteenth-century inn. Aidan had been new to blood-drinking then, bitter and afraid, wanting only to say farewell to his sister before seeking a way to destroy himself—actually believing it would be so easy to find peace and oblivion.

Soon after, Valerian had met the beautiful Maeve, still warmly human then, and been tempted to his limits. Maeve, after all, had been a female version of Aidan, and for that Valerian had adored her. When she learned what had happened to her beloved twin—convincing her of the truth had been no small task—Maeve had demanded a transformation of her own.

She and Aidan had argued violently, because Aidan despised what he was from the first and could not fathom why his sister would willingly choose such a fate. Maeve had wanted to be close to her brother for eternity, but there were other reasons for her aspirations as well.

Valerian had recognized in her a fierce hunger for immortality, for the singular powers Aidan so reluctantly demonstrated, and from the very first he had taken note of her wild and adventurous nature. She was greedy for life, like Valerian himself, wanting to test every sense, explore every emotion.

After the shouting match, which took place in the moonlit orchard of the convent where Maeve had been raised since the age of seven, Aidan had vanished in a rage. Some things never changed; Aidan was forever acting on impulse and then living to regret whatever he'd done.

Maeve had turned to Valerian and begged him to make her into an immortal, and heaven forgive him, he'd done it. He'd taken her blood and then restored it to her, changed.

It still bruised him to remember how Aidan had hated him for that.

For a time Valerian and Maeve had traveled together. He'd taught her to hunt, to sense the presence of other vampires or such enemies as angels and warlocks, and to hide herself from the sun. They had been lovers, as well, in that unique mental way of nightwalkers that was so much more profound than the frantic, messy couplings of humans.

Eventually, however, Maeve had caught Valerian playing similar games with a fledgling vampire named Pamela. After that, they had not been truly intimate again, though they had finally established a bristly truce. For the most part, Maeve and Valerian had avoided each other, but their common weakness for Aidan often caused their paths to cross.

The glow of awareness inside Valerian's devastated hulk began to gather strength, though the process was torturous and awkward, rather like trying to gather scattered buttons with bandages swelling one's fingers.

His fundamental fascination with Aidan Tremayne had never truly left him. Perhaps, he reflected, Maeve had known that all the while, known the real reason for her appeal to Valerian.

Of course, Valerian had not been the only one obsessed with Tremayne; Lisette, Aidan's creator, had regarded the lad as her own plaything. Had Aidan's angry spurning not wounded the vampire queen to the point that she'd sought dormancy, open warfare between Lisette and Valerian would probably have erupted immediately.

He'd been such a self-pitying fool, he thought now, to curl up in a hole like a wounded rat and let his strength seep away into the rubble around and beneath him. If it hadn't been for that very embarrassing mistake, he would still be a powerful vampire, and not this little flash of sensibility trapped inside a drying corpse.

It came to him then that perhaps, just perhaps, he wasn't imprisoned after all. Suppose he could transmit himself to other places and times, as he'd done so often in dreams?

Valerian gathered his being together into a small, whirling nebula of light and remembered Aidan fiercely. If any bond still linked them, he wanted to travel along it, hand over hand, until he found his friend.

His friend.

That was all that would ever be between him and Aidan, and Valerian found surprising peace in accepting the bittersweet truth. In the next instant he felt himself spinning through space, through dark, mindless oblivion, and then crashing against something hard.

That something was the stone wall of a crypt or cellar.

For a few moments Valerian was disoriented. He collected and calmed himself. There was a creature huddled before him, and he recognized it, though just barely.

Lisette raised her head, aware of Valerian even though his presence was purely mental. She was a hag, charred and almost hairless, incomprehensibly ugly, and she shrieked and raised her hands, as if to hide herself from his view.

You've failed, Valerian told her. *Plainly, I am not destroyed.*

If you've come for vengeance, then take it! Lisette responded in torment. *I have no spirit for battle.*

I will have my revenge, Lisette—you may be assured of that. For now, however, I have more important things to attend to.

With her thoughts, not her melted, misshapen hands, Lisette clutched at Valerian. *Does he live? Does Aidan live? Tell me!*

I don't know, Valerian answered, *but hear this, Queen of the Vampires: If you've harmed him—and I swear this by all that is unholy—your suffering will be without end.*

Lisette snarled and batted at the ball of light that was Valerian with one blackened claw. It was the movement of an animal, cornered and vicious. *You dare to threaten me? You are an even greater fool than Aidan!*

Valerian offered no reply; he was impatient to move on to find the vampire he had originally sought. It didn't trouble him that he'd willed himself to Aidan's side and ended up facing Lisette instead. That was probably just some sort of psychic short circuit.

Once again Valerian focused all his energies on finding Aidan. On this second attempt he was successful.

Aidan was in a cavern, far beneath the surface of the earth, a dank place echoing with the sound of water dripping. He lay naked, except for a loincloth, on a table formed of natural stone, his still, pale form surrounded by robed members of the Brotherhood. The light of a few torches flickered eerily through the chamber, dancing with shadows.

The redheaded Viking whirled, sensing Valerian's arrival, and called out, "Who is it?"

There would be no eluding these, the oldest and most formidable vampires on earth. Valerian volunteered his name readily.

"Leave this place," ordered one of the elders with an impatient wave. "We have important rites to perform."

I want to stay, Valerian responded. He could not speak audibly as they did, for he had no body, and thus no throat muscles or voice box to form the words.

For a few moments there was utter silence, except for the incessant *plunk-plunk-plunk* of water droplets striking stone.

"What is your business here?" one of the other elders demanded. They were being remarkably patient, but Valerian took nothing for granted.

The wounds Aidan suffered, he suffered because of me, Valerian said. *I was Lisette's prisoner, tied down to be burned alive in the sunlight, and he tried to help me.*

The Viking gestured toward Aidan with a meaty, hair-covered hand. "Would you have us stand about yammering with you while he perishes? He, too, was injured by the sun, but that is the least of his problems. The Vampyre Tremayne drank the blood of the warlock, and he is filled with poison."

Valerian would have sworn it was impossible to feel more pain than he already had—until now, that was. Through a new and excruciating baptism in despair, he learned that he had not even begun to suffer. He receded into a corner, pulsing with private anguish, to watch the proceedings. *Damn you, Aidan,* he told the inert being on the slab of stone, furious in his grief, *I warned you about warlocks. I warned you!*

Just then Tobias appeared, sparing not so much as a glance for Valerian. He took Aidan's limp hand into his own, but his question was addressed to his companions. "Are we ready?"

One of the others sighed heavily. "Yes."

While Valerian watched, helpless, yearning as he never had for his lost right to petition favor from heaven, the mysterious ceremony began. A golden chalice was taken from a blue velvet bag, along with a gleaming knife with a whisper-thin blade.

The Viking was the first to grasp the knife, slice deeply into his own wrist, and allow some of the blood to drip into the chalice. After that, the others did the same, one by one. Then, when the cup brimmed with crimson nectar, Tobias took a small vial of distilled herbs from his tunic pocket and added the contents to the cup.

That done, he lifted Aidan's head and held the chalice to his lips.

Nothing happened at first—Valerian was certain Aidan had already perished. Then Tobias muttered some quiet urging. Aidan began to drink, though in the vampire way, drawing the liquid through his fangs instead of over his tongue to be swallowed.

Valerian drew nearer—he could not help himself—and hovered just behind Tobias's right shoulder. Aidan had taken all the chalice held, and there were crimson specks of blood on his mouth. Before Valerian's eyes, he turned the blue-gray color of death.

What will happen to him? Valerian demanded. Tobias was not truly his friend, for vampires did not generally form such maudlin attachments, but the elder had been Valerian's rescuer not so long ago. There must be a shred of pity or understanding somewhere inside the ancient creature.

Tobias heaved a mental sigh. *I do not know—we had to act quickly to counteract the effect of the warlock's poison. Even if our efforts have succeeded, Aidan must endure other ordeals and move through passages none of us can imagine.*

Valerian wanted to take the potion and walk through the Valley of the Shadow at Aidan's side, though he did not form the desire into words, even in his mind.

The wise vampire, so deceptively youthful in appearance, read the emotion and responded, *Come, Valerian. Would you truly give up all that you are, all that you have, even now, to be a man again? To live a few brief years and then perish? I think you are neither so noble, nor so stupid.*

Valerian recognized the truth in Tobias's words and was shamed by it. He drifted into the shadows again and fretfully kept his vigil.

Aidan wandered, as if in a dream, back and back, through foggy drifts of time and memory. He did not suffer, and yet he was suffering itself, pain and struggle embodied. While on some level he knew exactly what was happening—his body was lying in a cavern, with the blood of the oldest vampires on earth sustaining it—other elements of the experience were more nebulous. This other self, this mental energy gone traipsing on its own, was as much his true being as the form on the stone slab.

He saw himself, long ago, lying in the undertaker's back room, undead and yet certainly not alive, either. He felt the horror again, and the helplessness, and cursed Lisette from the core of his soul.

Aidan did not expect to travel farther; he'd always understood that such a feat was impossible, except to the most accomplished and reckless vampires, like Valerian. To his surprise, he heard a whistling sound, shrill and harsh, and felt himself plunging through wisps of moonglow and sharp, splintered stars.

His stopping was a collision, not an arrival, and it was several moments before he recovered his equilibrium. He was in a pit, dark and cold, echoing with the screams and rustlings of beings he could not see.

This, then, was hell, or its anteroom. Aidan stifled a wail of his own, for his despair was crushing, unbearable, and worst of all, almost surely eternal.

In desperation he dared what no vampire would and cried out from his heart, *God of Light, have mercy on me—I was condemned on the whim of another, and not by my own choice!*

Silence. Even the moaning of the lost souls haunting the darkness was stilled.

Aidan waited.

Valerian remained in the cavern as long as he could, keeping watch, but he soon discovered that this separate, mental self could not long survive apart from the body. He returned, or rather was wrenched back, to that lonely, moldering place, and there he waited. There, almost against his will, he began to heal.

Neely did not trouble Maeve at her weaving, but instead took a bath, put on one of the nightgowns she'd left behind, in the guest suite, and collapsed into bed. She slept deeply, dreamlessly, and awakened to a foggy morning and a ringing telephone.

The jangling stopped and presently there was a tap at Neely's door. "For you, miss," Mrs. F. called breathlessly from the other side. "Your friend Miss Browning, I think."

Neely sat up and reached for the receiver on the bedside table. "Hello?" she mumbled, rumpling her hair with one hand and feeling as befogged as London itself. Beneath that murky layer was the terrible longing for Aidan, and the unfaceable fear that something was dreadfully wrong.

"Hi, Neel," chimed Wendy. "I hope you enjoyed the blizzard. We gave it in your honor, you know."

Neely laughed, though the sound scraped at her throat and made swallowing difficult. "Thanks a whole lot," she said. "Next time, how about a hurricane?"

"Done," Wendy agreed cheerfully. "Listen, we're doing a sort of showcase thing at the academy tonight—scenes from different classic plays—and I'd like you to be there. I do a mean Lady Macbeth."

"Is there any other kind?"

Wendy's smile was transmitted over the wire, warming her voice. "Such a wit. Will you be there? We could have dinner afterward."

What Neely really wanted to do was hibernate and wait for Aidan to reappear, but she forced herself to accept the invitation. She made a mental note of the time and address, rose, and dressed in slacks and a sweater.

If she remained in her room, watching the fog shift in front of the windows, she knew she would go insane. So she went to the kitchen, where Mrs. F. was dutifully assembling a tray, and insisted on eating there.

Neely and the housekeeper chatted, though Aidan's name certainly didn't come up, and neither did Maeve's.

After clearing away her dishes, Neely went to the down-stairs gallery, though she'd been there before, feeling drawn by the art. Mrs. F. chose that room to dust, probably for want of company.

Neely inspected each painting again, marveling. Some were portraits—Maeve, Aidan, Valerian—but most were landscapes. Intuitively she knew these green rolling hills and harsh rocky cliffs overlooking tempestuous blue-gray seas were glimpses of Ireland. Her practiced eye told her that all but a few of the works had been done by one artist.

She dragged a wooden stool over and climbed onto it to peer at a signature. "Tremayne," she muttered. Neely turned, still poised on the stool, to look at Mrs. F., thinking of the beautiful tapestry she'd seen at the museum. "Did Maeve do these?" she asked.

Mrs. F. laughed as she orbited a lampshade with her fluttering feather duster. "Oh, no, miss. Those are old paintings, for the most part—look closely and you'll see that they're done on wood instead of canvas. Priceless, they are, and not just because they were painted by an ancestor of the Madam."

Neely swallowed, feeling strangely moved. She touched one of the paintings tentatively, with just the tips of her fingers. Somehow she knew the truth even before Mrs. F. cleared up all vestiges of the mystery.

"The artist's name was Aidan Tremayne," she said proudly. "Just like our own Aidan he was, dark and handsome and full of charm, if the stories are to be believed."

Just like our own Aidan, Neely repeated to herself, and then she smiled. Very like our own Aidan indeed, she thought. She had not known that Aidan painted—there wasn't a word about it in his journals—but she should have guessed because of the sketch of him and Maeve on the first page of the original volume, far away in that Connecticut study.

"It's where all their money comes from, you know," Mrs. F. confided in a whisper, her feather duster shedding sparkling particles of dust. "They've sold a painting from time to time, and Mr. Tremayne is very good with investments— another family trait."

Neely turned her face to hide her smile, which might have been a bit secretive and perhaps even a touch smug. "Fascinating people," she said. The compulsion to explain that Maeve and Aidan were immortal, that they were in fact their own ancestors, was almost overwhelming, but of course Neely kept the information to herself. It would be a betrayal of trust, and besides, the housekeeper wouldn't believe a word.

Neely lingered a while, to be polite, and went on her way only after Mrs. F., settled in with a cup of tea to look at her favorite morning program on "the telly." Neely was drawn to the third floor, the very place she'd avoided the night before, when she'd known Maeve was there. It was a contradiction, of course, but Neely's life had been fraught with such things since Halloween. That was what she got, she supposed, for hanging out with vampires.

Reaching the studio's high, arched door, which was made of glowing English oak and beautifully carved with tiny birds and acorns, Neely paused and knocked softly, even though she knew Maeve would not be inside. Although the day was cloudy, and the atmosphere gun-metal gray, the sun was shining as brilliantly as ever beyond the earth's shroud of fog. Maeve, like all the other vampires, would be sleeping in some dark and hidden place.

Neely turned the brass handle on the door and stepped inside the great drafty room. She wondered if Maeve had woven the tapestry of herself and Valerian in this room, the one that was on display at the museum in the center of London. The house, like the tapestry and those paintings downstairs in the gallery, was old, and so was the loom.

She approached it cautiously, as though it might spring suddenly to life and chastise her, then touched its rough-hewn wooden frame in wonder. How beautiful and spare it was in its rustic simplicity. It was so plain, that loom, and yet it could mirror the visions of an artist in fine detail.

Neely walked around to look at the emerging tapestry again. There was the hem of the gauzy dress, the toe of one black slipper, the leaves, the ivory rose with its scattered petals. Something about this incomplete scene gave Neely a sense of deep sorrow, almost of mourning, and she had to turn away from it.

She moved to the windows, which stretched from floor to ceiling, their diamond-shaped panes lined with lead. The fog had gone, but now there were fat, soft flakes of snow drifting down, draping the metal gate out front, trimming the square tops of the old-fashioned lampposts, disguising cars and other evidence of the modern age.

It might have been 1894, Neely reflected fancifully, as she stood there looking out, or even 1794. She imagined, for a moment, that she could travel through time, as the vampires described in Aidan's journals did, and the idea sent a chill skittering up her spine.

Neely bit her lip as she turned away from the windows. Between getting herself mixed up with Aidan and his crowd and playing chase with the drug cartel back in the States, she'd had all the adventure she needed for one lifetime. She wanted what Aidan did—for him to be a man again, so that they could both live in the sunshine. She wanted to make love to him and to bear his children.

The possibility seemed remote, impossible, and yet Neely clung to it with all the tenacity of her being. She loved Aidan too deeply to give up now, even in the face of incomprehensible odds.

Still, Neely was used to taking action, and waiting was not her strong suit. She needed to be busy, building a life somewhere, carving out a place where she and Aidan could begin again.

He would find her, she thought as she left the studio, closing the door quietly behind her. Aidan would come to her when he could, and she would be waiting for him with an open heart.

One tear slipped down Neely's cheek as she descended to the second floor, for despite her faith in her love for Aidan and his for her, she knew that their happiness would be won only after a fiery battle.

In the guest suite she found her passport, opened it, and wondered at the innocence of the face in the photograph.

After the lonely, whispering darkness came the fire. Aidan felt its heat pulsing all around him, and yet he was oddly detached, untouched by the flames. He was silent now, for he had offered his prayer, and there was nothing left to say.

Then, suddenly, the flames became a living presence, not God Himself, but Someone. Definitely an individual, thinking Someone.

Vampyre, a silent voice boomed. *By what name are you called?*

Aidan quaked. Now it would happen, now he would tumble into the bowels of hell, to be consumed, and not consumed. So be it, he decided. At least he wouldn't be a blood-drinking monster anymore, preying on humans, passing himself off to the dying as an Angel of Mercy.

I am Aidan Tremayne, he answered at length. Then some spark of his old arrogance prompted him to ask, *Who are you?*

There was a thunderous hush, followed by amusement. *I am the Warrior Angel, Nemesis,* the voice replied. *Do you know that you are damned?*

Aidan was awe-stricken now, beyond fear into an emotion so profound that he could not call it by name. *Yes,* he replied when he could recall his own language and once again shape its words in his mind.

You have asked for absolution, Nemesis replied. *What right have you, a vampyre, a fiend and a demon, to expect the mercy of Heaven?*

None, Aidan answered. *But what right have they, those humans your Master so cherishes, to their redemption? And yet the choice between Heaven and Hell is their birthright, is it not?*

Nemesis was silent for a time, considering. *You are bold, Vampyre,* he said.

At this point, what else would serve me? was Aidan's response.

Again the Warrior Angel, dreaded from one end of Creation to the other, was amused. *True enough. What is it that you would have me do?*

There was no other course but to brazen it out. *None are to be snatched from His fingers,* Aidan challenged. *So say the holy words. But I am the exception, for my soul was stolen, not given willingly.*

Another pause, long and thoughtful, dangerously charged. *I will consider,* Nemesis replied.

Neely put on her black dancing dress, borrowed an evening cape from Maeve's closet, with Mrs. F.'s permission, and took a cab to the address Wendy had given her. The theater academy was in London's West End, and the ride was a long one.

She arrived just five minutes before curtain time, clutching a bouquet of yellow roses she'd sent out for earlier, but her thoughts were with Aidan, of course, and the need of him was raw within her.

Tomorrow or the day after—as soon as she could get a seat on a plane—Neely would return to the United States. The danger from the drug cartel was past, and she was determined to live constructively while she waited for Aidan to return to her.

When he was ready, he would find her.

She went into the theater, took her assigned seat, and was, for a time, lost in the performances of her friends,

Wendy and Jason, and their talented classmates. Between scenes, however, Neely's mind groped for images of Aidan and clung to them.

She figured she was going to need some therapy once this whole thing was over, one way or the other, though God only knew how she would explain her obsession with vampires. Any normal shrink was certain to see that as a neurosis, plain and simple, and classify Aidan and the others as unconscious archetypes.

Once the evening's presentation was over, Neely met Wendy and Jason in the lobby, near one of the stage doors. She handed Wendy the roses and gave her a congratulatory hug, then embraced Jason as well.

They had supper three blocks away, in an elegant club where the music was soft and smoky. Neely surprised herself by actually choking down a reasonable amount of food.

When Jason left the table for a few minutes to speak with friends, Wendy gently squeezed her friend's hand. "What's wrong, Neel? I've never seen you look so miserable."

Neely wished she could confide the whole truth, but of course that was impossible. Even the artistic, talented Wendy, with her fertile imagination, would not be able to take in the undiluted facts of the situation. How could Neely explain that she was hopelessly in love with a vampire?

"I guess I'm just tired. I've been through a lot in the last few months."

Wendy nodded sympathetically, her blue eyes wide with compassion. At least she knew about Neely's adventures with the drug cartel. "You certainly have," she agreed. "What you need is a good rest. You should go somewhere warm, where the sun shines, and think things through."

Neely sighed in agreement. "I don't know where I'll wind up, just yet," she answered, "but I feel ready to leave London now and make a lasting niche for myself somewhere. I'll be in touch with you as soon as I get my bearings."

Wendy patted her hand. "You'll be all right, Neely. You're the bravest, most resilient person I know."

"Thanks," Neely said. She knew her friend had meant the compliment, but at the same time she couldn't really take it in. The days and nights ahead looked bleak to her, for as badly as she wanted to, she could not ignore the possibility that Aidan might never return to her.

She finished out the evening, cried all the way home in the cab, and spent much of the night composing a letter to Aidan. She wrote that she loved him, that she would always love him, that she would wait for him, even into the next lifetime, if that proved necessary.

Neely left the letter on the mantelpiece in the gallery the next morning, beneath one of Aidan's paintings, said good-bye to Mrs. F. and set out in another cab for the airport.

Chapter 18

—◦◦✦ ◦✦◦—

For four days and three nights, Aidan lay upon his slab, motionless and pale as death. Valerian came, in spirit, to watch over him and stayed as long as his limited energy would allow, before scurrying back to his own ruined and unwelcoming body to regroup. The old ones returned every twenty-four hours, always at nightfall, to fill the golden chalice from their wrists as they had on that first occasion, and add their concoction of herbs. The only sign of life Aidan ever showed was when he opened his lips to draw from the cup.

Each night, as Valerian kept his helpless vigil, a new fissure traced itself over his heart. He would gladly have taken the beloved one's place on that cold bed of stone, borne all his pain, argued his case for him in that other world, the mystical one, where some part of Aidan surely wandered. None of these courses were open to Valerian, however; all he could do was wait.

When the fourth sunset came, Valerian was there in the cavern even before the elders appeared. It was as if he were the heart of some giant unseen entity, pumping fear, like blood, into veins and limbs and organs beyond his awareness.

He drew near Aidan, but it seemed that a wall of cold surrounded the still form, now as rigid and gray as a cadaver. Valerian withdrew again, scorning his vampire powers for the first time since his making. *Smoke and mirrors,* he thought furiously. *What good are my tricks and secrets if Aidan does not live?*

The others arrived, one by one, solemn in their dignity, wearing it as tangibly as their robes. They made a circle around Aidan, then, in a single motion, lifted him up in their hands.

Valerian was jolted out of his angry reverie; he rushed back to Aidan, shimmering above his bare middle like a firefly.

Wait, he demanded of Tobias, seeing no sign of the chalice. Something had changed; the ritual had taken a new turn. *What are you doing? Where are you taking him?*

Tobias sighed, and his effort at patience was lost on Valerian for the moment because he was too frantic to recognize it. The older vampire responded in the language of the mind, though there was never any question that the others could hear and understand.

We can do no more for the fledgling, Tobias said. *The sunlight must now be his final judge.*

Valerian felt horror batter against him, then surround and absorb him. *What?*

We will lay him out in a place once holy to mortals. If he survives the full rising of the sun, the transformation will be complete. If he cannot be changed, and we have failed in our efforts, he will be destroyed.

Valerian became a scream, since he could not utter one without his body. *No!*

It is done, Tobias responded.

In the next instant they were gone. All of them—Tobias, the other elders, Aidan.

Valerian's strength was already waning—his body claimed much of it, being determined to renew itself—but he used all his will to follow the elders and their unconscious burden.

The small, hideous company reassembled itself in the center of a circle of ancient pillars, not far from Stonehenge. Moonlight splashed the ruined monument to some long-forgotten deity and turned the crusted snow to iridescent silver.

Aidan made no sound or movement as the elders laid him in the exact center of the ring of giant stones and stepped back, each one fading slowly, slowly, until they'd all vanished.

Valerian shrieked soundlessly, wild in his frustration and fear. He could not bear it, seeing Aidan left to await the sunrise and suffer the terrible cruelties reserved just for vampires, but there was nothing he could do.

Still, Valerian lingered as long as he was able, and when he saw dawn trim the distant horizon in golden lace, he tried to form himself into some kind of shield, to cover and protect his friend. Alas, he was made of nothingness, and he could offer no protection.

He was wrenched back to his own faraway body, just as the light tumbled and spilled over the snowy hills and into the circle of stones where Aidan lay.

Neely sat numbly on the postage-stamp-size terrace outside her hotel room in Phoenix, sipping iced tea and staring at the shifting patterns of turquoise light playing over the pool below. The sun was dazzlingly bright, and its warmth teased the very marrow of her bones.

She sighed, reached for her ice tea, and took another sip. She didn't know a soul in Arizona, and Ben had made it plain when she telephoned him, on her first night back in the country, that he thought she needed looking after—at least for a while.

Neely didn't want anyone fussing over her, for in those freaky times when the numbness wore off, she was hypersensitive to pain, and the very currents in the air bruised her. During these periods, the slightest sound seemed deafening and hammered against her senses until she trembled.

She needed to think. That was what she'd told her brother. She had money, now that the drug people weren't tracking her anymore and she could tap her personal funds. She wanted to wait, and later, if necessary, do her grieving, in peace and privacy. Before she could go on and begin making some sort of life for herself and Aidan, however, she must finish putting herself back together and smoothing away the rough places where the breaks were mended.

As soon as possible, Neely planned to find herself a job as an assistant to some executive, rent an apartment, buy a car, make new friends. She wasn't planning to sit on the sidelines while she waited for Aidan, though she certainly didn't intend to date other men, either, for Neely knew one thing: For the rest of her natural days and, most probably, throughout eternity as well, she would love no one but Aidan Tremayne.

Neely closed her eyes, leaned back in the chaise lounge, and sighed, letting the sun caress her winter-whitened skin. It frightened her that sometimes she could almost convince herself that she'd imagined the whole fantastic experience—encountering Aidan for the first time, sleeping beside him under a hotel-room bed in London, Valerian and the paintings and the tapestries and Maeve's grand mansion. The memories always returned, vivid and sharp, and wore well in her mind like a bright picture on a bar of novelty soap, one that would never wash away.

The last thing she wanted was to forget.

Often she awakened in the night, thinking Aidan was there beside her, and weeping when she found herself alone. She tried hard to accept reality: Aidan was a vampire, with all the attendant gifts. If he had not perished in that strange experiment of his, or been grievously injured, he would find her.

Neely waited, suspended, swinging back and forth between one emotion and its opposite, reminding herself to eat and sleep and even breathe.

She would hold on, though—she was determined to do that.

The first thing Aidan was conscious of was light. Dazzling, fiery light. He waited for the glare to consume him, but instead it played sweetly over his skin like some intangible ointment. He slowly opened his eyes, saw nothing but the luminous glow, and closed them again.

The next sensation he recognized was cold. Saints in heaven, he was lying in snow, bare as a pauper's purse, and freezing his ass off in the bargain.

He raised his eyelids once more, only to be driven back a second time into the comforting darkness.

Aidan tried to lift his hands after that, but they were heavy at his sides. Where was he? In Hell? It would be some joke, he reflected, if the place turned out to be an ice pit instead of an everlasting pyre.

"Great Scot, Martha," a male voice boomed from somewhere above him. "He's quite naked, isn't he? And him out here in the weather and all. Might be he's a Druid or something like that."

Someone crouched beside Aidan. He felt a woman's hand come to rest on his shoulder, strong and blessedly warm.

"Druid or none, he's in a bad way. Run and get the woolen blanket from the car, Walter, and we'll wrap him up snug in that. Then we'll try to lift the poor man between us."

He felt the blanket go round him, and the awkward angels wrested him onto his feet. He could neither see nor speak, but as he stumbled along between his rescuers, a momentous realization came upon him.

He was *breathing*.

Aidan's spirit soared even higher when he explored his chest and found a living heart beating there. "Neely," he whispered as tears slipped down his half-frozen face. "Neely."

When he awakened again, he was in the hospital, and the numbness of hypothermia had worn off, leaving a raw, scraping pain in its place.

Aidan exulted in that pain, however, for it was more proof that he'd been given a second chance.

He was a man.

He lifted one of his hands to his mouth, with no small amount of struggle, and felt his teeth. His fangs were gone, leaving an ordinary pair of incisors in their places.

Aidan tried to sit up, only to be gently pressed back to the bed again.

"There, now," a woman, probably a nurse, said gently, "just rest and don't be trying to rise. You came very near to meeting your Maker, you know."

He felt tears gather in his lashes, hot and wet. *You can't imagine how near,* he thought. He'd been forgiven, it seemed, or at least given an opportunity to redeem himself. He meant to make full use of whatever time was left to him.

"Thank you," he whispered as the pain took hold and started to drag him under again. The nurse thought he'd been speaking to her and assured him that she was just doing her job.

In the days to come, Aidan tried to keep track of time, but the task proved impossible, since he was conscious only in bits and snatches. During those brief intervals, he reveled in the steady beat of his heart, the ragged but regular meter of his breathing, the ache in the back of his hand, where an intravenous needle was lodged. Even the need to relieve himself in a cold steel urn brought by a nurse was cause to celebrate.

When he found the strength to lift his eyelids for the first time, he saw gray-green walls, uninspired hospital art, a tiny television set that seemed to huddle in a corner of the room, near the ceiling. His bed was the crank-up sort, an iron monstrosity that might well have been a relic of some war.

A moment passed before Aidan realized that it was night, and he was seeing clearly. The knowledge frightened him; he thought for a moment that he'd only dreamed of being a mortal.

Then he saw the vampire, standing motionless and majestic at the foot of the bed. Aidan did not recognize the creature, and that only increased his alarm. He drew back against the pillows and held his breath.

The stranger raised a stately hand. Like his face, it glowed white in the darkness, illuminating him, so that he appeared to have swallowed the moon itself. "Do not be afraid, Mortal," the creature said, sounding mildly exasperated. "I have not come to change you, but only to bring a message from the Brotherhood."

Aidan's heart had risen to his throat and was pounding there. He was frightened, and yet the mere existence of his pulse caused him almost incomprehensible joy. "What is this message?" he managed to ask, and as vulnerable as he was, there was a note of challenge in his voice.

The vampire chuckled. "Tobias was right," he said. "You are certainly brave to the point of idiocy, Aidan Tremayne."

He took several items from inside his coat, then rounded the bed to lay them on the stand and look down into Aidan's defiant eyes. "I've brought you a passport, credit cards, some money. You have lost your powers as a vampire, of course, so you will have to make a place for yourself in the world of humankind now."

Aidan glanced at the leather packet on the bedside stand. He'd had no use for identification and money before, but they were quite necessary to mortals. "Did Maeve ask you to help me—or Valerian?"

"Neither," the fiend replied, moving away to stand at the window, looking out. "No one knows where that pair has gotten themselves off to, as a matter of fact. The Brotherhood simply felt that matters should be brought full circle—your mortal life was taken from you, now it is restored. In these modern times it is difficult to function without passports and the like."

Aidan was silent for a moment, absorbing the knowledge that Maeve and Valerian had both disappeared. He felt his limitations as a man sorely—he could do nothing to help his sister or his friend—and then he accepted the new reality.

"How long?" he asked. "Am I going to live a day—a decade—another fifty years?"

The vampire smiled, then shrugged. "How long would you have lived before, if your life had not been interrupted? Only those beyond the Veil of Mystery possess such knowledge." He sighed, tugged at the sleeves of his elegant coat, and approached the bed again. "I must go soon and feed." He laid one of his cold alabaster hands to Aidan's head. "You will forget what you were, in time, and, someday, even laugh at those who believe in such creatures as vampires and warlocks."

Aidan caught at the corpse-like hand with his own warm fingers, tried in vain to throw it away. "Wait—there is a woman—I want—I *have*—to find her—"

"You will always be Aidan Tremayne," the monster said. "Although your mind will soon dismiss her image, your heart will remember forever."

"But—"

"It is done," decreed the vampire quietly. And then he was gone, and Aidan tumbled into sleep, as if he'd been pushed over the edge of an abyss.

The next morning he ate solid food for the first time in more than two centuries and wondered why he was so excited over milk toast and weak tea. Wild, macabre images played chase in his mind; he told the pretty nurse he'd dreamed a vampire came to his room the night before, and she smiled and shook her head and pronounced the human brain a strange organ indeed.

Aidan had to agree, at least privately, for he held another picture in his mind, that of a lovely woman with short hair and large pixie eyes. He knew the gamine's name was Neely, but that was the sum total of what he remembered about her. It was miraculous, considering that he'd had to take his own identity from the packet of identification that had turned up on his bedside table one night while he slept.

He grew strong in the days to come, and his mind manufactured a complicated and quite viable history for him. Soon Aidan believed the assortment of facts and actually thought he remembered the corresponding experiences.

He was alone in the world, having been born to his Irish parents very late in life. He had money, a grand house outside of Bright River, Connecticut, and an impressive career as an artist.

Certain mysteries remained, however. Aidan still did not know where he'd been before he was discovered lying in the middle of that ancient circle of stones, naked as a newborn, or how he'd gotten there in the first place. The police were equally baffled, but after an initial interest and a barrage of questions in his hospital room, they'd stopped coming round. No doubt they'd written the patient off as a head case, and Aidan had to admit there were ample grounds for the idea.

He left the hospital in borrowed garb, bought himself new clothes, luggage, and toiletries, none of which he seemed to possess, spent one night in a London hotel, took a cab to the airport, and then flew to the United States.

In New York he rented a car and drove the rest of the way to Bright River.

Upon arriving in that small Connecticut town, he went immediately to the big house in the country. He didn't remember the place being so gloomy, he thought, as he went from room to room, flinging back the heavy draperies to let in the sunlight.

The snow was melting, and spring wasn't far off. He opened a few windows and doors to let in some fresh air.

Aidan wandered into the kitchen, humming. His breakfast, a muffin and a cup of coffee he'd grabbed at the airport, had long since worn off.

He opened one cupboard after another, amazed to find that there wasn't so much as a can of chili or a box of salt on the shelves. There were no plates, no cups, no knives, forks, or spoons.

Puzzled, he shrugged his shoulders, found a leather jacket in one of the closets, and left the house. There was a truck stop just down the road; Aidan was sure he remembered eating there once or twice.

He set out on foot, his hands jammed into the pockets of his coat, reassuring himself as he walked. Although the doctors in London had insisted that the gaps in his memory would surely close someday, he was still troubled.

For one thing, there was that name that haunted him, and the sweet face and figure that went with it. *Neely.* Who was she? She had touched his life, he was certain of that, but he couldn't remember where he'd known her, or when.

On the most basic level of his consciousness, a driving, urgent need to find the mysterious woman raged like a river at flood tide.

Aidan reached the truck stop, a noisy, cheerful place where the jukebox played too loudly, and felt better for having people around him. He took a seat at the counter and reached for a menu.

A friendly waitress—her name tag read "Doris"—took his order right away. While Aidan was sipping his coffee, a boy rushed in, waving a sheet of pink paper and beaming. He was about seven, Aidan guessed, and he had freckles and one missing tooth.

"Look, Doris!" the child cried, scrambling onto one of the stools, right next to Aidan. The lad glanced up at him, smiled with what could only be amiable recognition, nodded a greeting, and then turned his quicksilver attention back to Doris. "There's a letter from Aunt Neely!"

Aidan's heart somersaulted at the mention of the familiar name. It was unusual, after all, and it followed that he'd known her here in Bright River.

"What does she say, Danny?" Doris asked, grinning as she set a dinner of chicken-fried steak, mashed potatoes, and green beans in front of Aidan. She winked at him before turning her full attention on the boy.

Danny still clutched the letter in one grubby hand, and it was all Aidan could do not to reach out and snatch it away from him. "She isn't in Phoenix anymore—she's in Colorado," the kid announced importantly. "She was working in an office for a while, but now she's got a job in a steak house. Aunt Neely was bored sitting behind a desk. She says she's got all kinds of—all kinds of—" He paused and consulted the paper. "Nervous energy," he finished.

Aidan felt warm inside, and oddly amused, and he could explain neither emotion. He stuck his fork into his food, but his ravenous appetite was gone.

"And look at this great stamp!" Danny said, slapping a pink envelope down on the countertop.

Aidan strained, saw the return address: 1320 Tamarack Road, Pine Hill, Colorado. "I used to collect stamps when I was a lad," he commented casually.

Danny beamed at him. "I must have a thousand of them. Aunt Neely sends them to me all the time. I've got a whole boxful from England."

England. That produced another vague recollection, more a feeling than an image. He'd been so certain that he'd met the elusive Neely in Bright River, but the mention of the country he'd just left touched a resonant chord in his spirit.

1320 Tamarack Road, he repeated to himself. *Pine Hill, Colorado.*

"This Aunt Neely of yours must be a pretty interesting lady," Aidan commented when Doris had given Danny a cup of hot chocolate and bustled off to wait on some new arrivals.

Danny's eyes were alight. "She is. She used to work for a real senator. He was a crook, and she almost got killed because she told the FBI what he was doing, but she's okay now."

Aidan frowned, for the child's words stimulated still another memory that wouldn't quite come into focus.

He finished his meal, returned to his huge, echoing house, and wandered restlessly from room to room.

In the morning, after a virtually sleepless night, Aidan called the car rental company and asked them to pick up the vehicle he'd driven from New York. Then he went out to the garage where his white Triumph Spitfire awaited him.

He smiled when the engine caught on the first try, and sped into Bright River. His first stop was the supermarket, where he purchased staples—milk and butter and bread—along with tea and potatoes, both fresh and frozen vegetables, and a thick steak. Passing a florist's shop, he suddenly stopped, grocery bags in his arms, oddly stricken by an enormous bunch of white roses on display in the window.

Aidan felt yet another tug at his deeper mind, and this one was patently uncomfortable. The flowers had some significance, he was certain, but that was all he knew.

Walking slowly, Aidan took the bags of food to the car and set them on the passenger seat. Then he returned to the florist's window and stood there, looking at the roses, trying to work out why they stirred him so.

He swallowed, fighting an unaccountable desire to weep.

A gray-haired woman put her head outside the door of the shop and called, smiling, "Hello, there, Mr. Tremayne. Aren't those the finest roses you've ever seen? I buy them direct from a nice man upstate—he raises them in his own greenhouse. They smell wonderful, too, unlike those poor anemic things they sell in the supermarkets these days."

Since the woman had called Aidan by name, he probably knew her, but her identity eluded him. He smiled and went into the shop, drawn there by some curious force buried in his subconscious.

The scent of the roses was delicate, but it seemed to fill the small shop, overshadowing the perfumes rising from bright splashes of colorful flowers grouped in buckets and pots and vases.

Aidan selected eight of the roses, which were still tightly budded, and put money on the cluttered counter.

"Good day, Mrs. Crider," he heard himself say as he left the shop with the strange purchase. So he *had* known the woman's name, after all, though he still had no recollection of meeting her before.

How odd, he thought.

At home Aidan found a crystal vase in a cabinet in one of the bedrooms and put the roses in water even before bringing the groceries in from the car. He set the flowers on the marble top of the round antique table in his entry hall and then stood staring at them for a long time, his arms folded. He wondered why the sight satisfied him so much, and at the same time stirred in him a seemingly fathomless sense of loss.

He supposed he was probably a little crazy, which wasn't really surprising, considering that he'd been found naked in the middle of an English snowstorm, lying inside a circle of stones like some kind of sacrifice.

He'd get over it, he assured himself, turning from the roses and heading outside for the bags he'd wedged into the passenger seat of his car. One of the few things he knew for certain was that he was a resilient sort, not easily broken.

Still, the scent of those flowers haunted him, and he kept going back to them, wondering and trying to remember.

Something else troubled him, though, even more than the roses did. It was the name Neely and the newfound knowledge that she lived in a place called Pine Hill, far away in Colorado.

After a steak dinner, which he devoured, Aidan retired to his study. The place was crammed with books, some of which he remembered reading and many that he didn't. The paintings on the walls were only vaguely familiar, though he knew he'd done them with his own hands.

He sighed, took an atlas from the shelf, and flipped through until he located a map of the United States. Bewildered, fascinated, *driven,* he sought and found Colorado, then traced the distance between that place and Connecticut with the tip of one finger.

Once again Aidan whispered the name of his private ghost: "Neely." Once again he searched his mind for something more than the fading image, but it was no use. Nothing came to him, except for a sensation of sweet sadness, and a yearning so keen that it brought tears to his eyes.

Suddenly Aidan was seized with a terror that he would forget the face, and even the name, as he had forgotten so many scattered details of his past.

He rummaged for paper, scrounged up a pencil, and bent over his desk, in such a hurry to sketch the features wavering in his thoughts that he wouldn't even take the time to sit down. He finished in a few strokes, wrote "Neely" beneath the rendering of the beautiful young woman with large, inquisitive eyes and short dark hair, and gave himself up to the sweeping relief of having captured her likeness before she vanished from his mind's eye.

Aidan sat looking at the drawing for a long time, memorizing every line and curve.

Neely huddled in the big leather chair facing her therapist's desk, her blue-jeaned legs curled beneath her. She bit her lower lip, silently reminding herself that she wouldn't be able to come to terms with the events of the past few months unless she talked about them. Still, getting started was hard.

"You work at the Steak-and-Saddle Restaurant, don't you?" Dr. Jane Fredricks prompted kindly, reviewing Neely's information sheet.

Neely nodded, grateful for the gentle push. "I wait tables there. I like being busy all the time—that way, I don't think so much—and since I work the night shift, I'm always with other people when it's dark."

"You're afraid of the dark?" the doctor asked.

Neely bit her lip again, then forced herself to go on. "Not exactly," she said. "I'm afraid of—of vampires. Except for one, I mean, and—oh, hell." She bit down hard on her right thumbnail.

Dr. Fredricks didn't grab the telephone and shout for help, or even gasp in surprise. "Vampires," she repeated, with no inflection at all, making a note on Neely's chart.

Neely's voice trembled. "Yes."

Dr. Fredricks met her gaze directly. "Go on," she said.

Neely stared at her for a moment. "I suppose you're going to say there aren't any such things as vampires," she finally blurted out, "but there are. As crazy as it sounds, they really exist."

"I'm not questioning that," the doctor pointed out calmly. "You needn't convince me of anything, Neely—you're not on trial for a crime, you know. You needn't justify what you believe. Just talk."

Tears welled in Neely's eyes, blurring her vision, and she snatched a tissue from a box on the edge of Dr. Fredricks's desk to dry them. "I met my first vampire on Halloween night," she began, sniffling. "Isn't that fitting? Of course, I didn't *know* Aidan was a vampire then—I just thought he was, well, a little different—"

Dr. Fredricks nodded encouragingly.

Neely spilled the whole story, over the next forty-five minutes, and even though nothing was resolved at the end, she felt better for having told another human being what had happened to her.

"Are you going to lock me up in a rubber room?" she asked, toying with the pile of crumpled tissues in her lap.

The doctor laughed. "No, of course not."

Neely leaned forward in her chair. "Surely you don't believe there really are vampires?" she marveled.

"It doesn't matter what I believe," reasoned Dr. Fredricks. "We're here to talk about you. Can you come back next Tuesday?"

Chapter 19

——•❀❁•——

Neely was just reaching for the handle of the front door at the Steak-and-Saddle when, through the glass, she saw chaos erupt. The fire alarm and the inside sprinkler system went off simultaneously, and patrons and staff alike shrieked and scurried in all directions. Water roared from the ceiling and spattered on the floor, the counter, the people, everything.

Neely stepped back from the entrance just in time to avoid being trampled, and even then she was nearly knocked into the flowerbed.

Duke Fuller, the owner of the restaurant, came out laughing, soaked from the top of his balding head to the soles of his expensive cowboy boots. Duke had a way of taking things in his stride, a trait that made most people like him right away.

"Go on, take the night off," he said, waving a huge hand at Neely as she stepped over the bricks bordering the petunia patch. "I got an idea Coach Riley's boys were behind this—they're feelin' their oats because of that basketball game they won—and I'm damn well gonna make 'em clean up the mess."

Some of the customers stayed to help, but Neely had been feeling drained since her session with Dr. Fredricks that afternoon, and she had cramps in the bargain. So she turned around, got back into the used Mustang she'd bought after arriving in Denver by plane, and drove home.

1320 Tamarack Road was a humble place, a one-bedroom cottage with linoleum floors and plumbing noisy enough to disturb the dead, but it was solid and real, and Neely liked it. Besides, she spent very little time there, since she worked all night and, having developed chronic insomnia, sat reading in the library most of every day.

She hoped she'd be able to sleep, now that she'd told Dr. Fredricks the secret she hadn't been able to give voice to before. The effects of her problem were beginning to show; she had bruise-like shadows under her eyes, she was too thin, and she cried so easily that it was embarrassing.

Every day, every night, she told herself that Aidan would come back to her, and still there was no sign of him, and no word. Had he perished in the attempt to become mortal again? Or had he simply lost interest in her?

Neely hung her coat in the tiny closet just inside her front door and kicked off her crepe-soled waitress shoes as she moved across the living room. She flipped on the television set as she passed to the kitchen, which was really just three cabinets and a sink shoved into an alcove, and the frenzied cacophony of some commercial tumbled into the quiet.

The refrigerator yielded the remains of a carton of cottage cheese; Neely got a spoon and went back to the living room. There, she curled up in the ancient easy chair, still in her polyester uniform and her pantyhose, to eat and watch the news channel.

Neely kept expecting to miss politics, all of a sudden, to yearn for the excitement, the prestige, and the intrigue of being in the center of things. All she missed, however, all she ever yearned for, was the sight of Aidan Tremayne, and the sound of his voice. She could adjust to the rest, even the outlandish truth of what he was.

She sighed, spooning a small heap of cottage cheese onto her tongue even though, as usual, she had no appetite. It was downright crazy to be this miserable, she thought, chewing and then forcing herself to swallow—and over a missing monster, no less—but she couldn't seem to lift herself out of the doldrums.

Neely took another bite, then could bear no more and set the thin plastic carton aside, atop last week's issue of *TV Guide*. She got out of her chair, crossed the cool, smooth floor to the television set, and switched channels until she found one showing classic movies.

When a forties-style Count Dracula appeared on the screen, resplendent in his high-colored black silk cape, Neely made a soft, abrupt sound that might have been either a chuckle or a sob. The Count had very white skin, and his hair came to a dramatic widow's peak on his forehead, but of course it was his overlong and extremely pointed incisors that marked him as the dreaded vampire.

Neely reached out for the old-fashioned channel knob— the TV, like the rest of the furniture, had come with the house—but she couldn't quite complete the move. She stepped backward, away from the set, filled with a strange tangle of emotions—panic, joy, fascination, a fierce desire to deny that any such creature could ever have existed.

She went into the bedroom and exchanged her uniform and pantyhose for warm flannel pajamas, figuring that, by the time she returned, either the movie would be over or she would have found the fortitude to turn to something else.

Instead Neely moved like a sleepwalker, sank numbly to the floor in front of her chair, and sat watching as if she'd been hypnotized. She knew she should get up, go to bed, read a book, take a bath, do anything besides just sitting there obsessed, but she couldn't gather the strength to move. Her gaze slid to the telephone on the other side of the room; she wondered if she was finally going to collapse under the strain. Maybe she should call Dr. Fredricks, right now. . . .

And say what? *I'm so sorry to bother you, Doctor, but it seems I'm watching an old vampire movie—a hokey one, at that—and I can't bring myself to miss a moment.*

Neely caught her right thumbnail between her teeth and bit. The movie went on, darkness gathered at the windows, and still she sat there, mesmerized.

A sudden burst of light, barely glimpsed out of the corner of her right eye, made Neely jump and cry out.

Valerian himself was standing in front of the couch, gaunt and even somewhat scarred, but for all of that, just as magnificent as ever. Instead of his usual dashing evening garb, he wore medieval garments, leggings, soft leather shoes, and a tunic of rough brown wool. A mean-looking sword dangled from a scabbard on his belt.

Watching the screen image of Count Dracula, the vampire laughed aloud.

Neely's inertia finally left her; she scrambled to her feet and looked around for a weapon, but all she found was the cottage cheese.

Valerian's gaze sliced to hers. "What will you do," he drawled, "stab me through the heart with a teaspoon?"

Neely's own heart seemed to bounce spasmodically between her breastbone and her spine. Valerian had been cordial enough in the past, but she had never deluded herself, for so much as a moment, that he was her friend.

"What do you want?" she asked.

Valerian sighed, one hand fiddling with the fancy molded steel handle of his sword. "It would take more time than I have to tell you that, my lady," he said sadly.

Neely collapsed into the easy chair, since she couldn't stand any longer. Now that the first rush of fear had subsided a little, she wanted to ask about Aidan. At the same time she was afraid—what if Valerian answered that the experiment had failed and Aidan was dead? What if he said his friend was alive and well but had decided not to go to all the trouble of loving a mortal woman after all?

"He loves you still," Valerian said; clearly, he found her thoughts as easy to read as one of those big billboards out by the freeway. His voice seemed to echo the combined sorrows of the ages, deep and profound and eternal.

Neely raised one hand to her throat. "He survived, then."

Valerian's great shoulders seemed to sag beneath his tunic; he was the very image of weary despair. "After a fashion, yes. He's a mere man—good-looking, but really quite ordinary, when you consider what he once was. All eternity would not be time enough to work out the puzzle of why Aidan, or anyone, would make such a sacrifice."

A shout of joy rose in Neely, but she stopped it in the middle of her chest. She wasn't about to put her most private feelings on display for the likes of Valerian, but there was another reason for her reticence as well. Aidan had become a man again, as he'd dreamed of doing, but he'd apparently made no attempt to find her.

Even without his supernatural powers, it shouldn't have been that hard to track her down, she thought, heartbroken. True, she hadn't left a forwarding address on file at the Bright River post office or anything so obvious as that, but Aidan could have reached her through Ben if he'd half tried.

Neely's older brother was a stubborn man, and he probably wouldn't have told Aidan where to find her, but he would surely have acted as an intermediary and passed on any messages.

"Aidan doesn't remember you," Valerian said, mind reading again. "Not completely, at least. He clings to a few scattered images, as I understand it, but in time even those will fade. The Brotherhood thought it better if he could not recall too much of his old life."

Fury and relief warred in Neely's soul, fury because someone had come between her and Aidan, relief because he'd *wanted* to remember her.

She sat up a little straighter. "Is that why you came here? To tell me everything is over between Aidan and me? I won't accept that, Valerian—I won't believe it unless I hear it from him personally."

He looked miserable to her, though that could have been an act. Valerian had loved Aidan—he probably loved him still—and it was unlikely that he had Neely's best interests at heart. Or those of any human, for that matter.

"Be that as it may," he responded in a deep voice. "It must be ended. No mortal can be allowed to go about with knowledge of the sacred things. It is dangerous."

"Sacred?" Neely snapped, driven by impulse, as usual, rather than good sense. "What an odd word to use, in reference to creatures who drink blood to sustain themselves!"

Valerian's countenance seemed to darken, and he towered like some mountain thrust suddenly up from level ground; he was a black cloud, roiling and huge, ready to erupt with lightning and thunder. "I will not debate semantics with a mortal!" he roared.

"No problem," Neely assured him hastily.

The vampire took a few moments to compose himself, visibly smoothing his ruffled dignity. Then, imperiously, he announced, "For the sake of all who walk the night and take the communion of blood, this foolishness must be ended at once." He paused, rubbing his chin with one hand and regarding Neely thoughtfully. "I would be well within my rights to feed upon you. However, I have decided that sparing you shall be my last tribute to Aidan."

Neely let out her breath in a rush, only then discovering that she'd been holding it in her lungs and sinuses. In the next instant Valerian was standing close to her, though she hadn't seen him move.

He raised one hand, laid it to her forehead, like a clergyman offering a blessing.

"No vampires," he whispered. "There are no vampires, and there never were. You will forget, and any mortals who knew of your love for Aidan will give up all memory of it as well. . . ."

Neely fought the barrage of thoughts as long as she could, but Valerian's mind was much stronger than her own; soon her consciousness was swamped in inky darkness.

The following Tuesday, Neely arrived at Dr. Fredricks's office right on time, settled into the big chair, and waited expectantly.

"I believe we were discussing vampires last week," the psychologist said, closing Neely's chart and settling back to regard her patient.

Neely laughed. "Vampires? You're joking, right?"

The doctor frowned. "Joking?"

Neely thought back and remembered telling Dr. Fredricks about her job in Senator Hargrove's office and the subsequent adventures with the mob, in detail, but that was all. "I—I talked about vampires?" she asked in a small voice. She felt the color drain from her face.

Dr. Fredricks smiled reassuringly, opened the folder on her desk, and read back the outlandish story Neely had evidently told her the week before.

Neely shook her head, frantic to deny what she did not remember. She blurted out the short version of her adventures with Senator Dallas Hargrove and his criminal associates, in a flash food of wild, eager words.

The psychologist digested the account in respectful silence, then said gently, "Neely, you've obviously undergone quite a series of traumas in the past year. Is it any wonder that you invented a flock of vampires—a sort of theater company of the mind—to help you sort through it all?"

The reasoning seemed sound, but Neely still had absolutely no recollection of talking about vampires. She hadn't even thought of the creatures since last Halloween, in fact, when her nephew, Danny, had worn wax fangs and a plastic cape to go out trick-or-treating.

"I guess that could be it," she said tremulously.

Dr. Fredricks seemed to be on some private roll. "Often," she said confidently, "the human mind will create personal myths in order to cope with some struggle in the unconscious. Generally these little dramas are played out in our dreams, but in some cases we feel called upon to produce something more flamboyant."

From what the doctor had read from her chart, Neely thought uneasily, her own presentation had boasted a cast of thousands. She'd actually mentioned names, if the psychologist's account was to be believed—*Maeve. Valerian. Tobias.*

She sank back in her chair, shaking. "Could I have a glass of water, please?"

After a week of driving west, thinking all the while that he must have lost his mind as well as large parts of his memory, Aidan crossed the Colorado border. He stopped at a motel that night, wolfed down a bagful of fast food while watching the Comedy Channel on cable TV, showered, and slept like a mastodon entombed in a glacier.

The next morning he bought a road map of the state,

located Pine Hill, and pointed himself and his Spitfire in that direction. He had no idea what he was going to do when he arrived in the small mountain town, beyond finding the elusive Neely. Maybe when he looked into those big, luminous eyes of hers, he would remember whatever it was that had happened between them and understand the fascination that tormented him so much.

He arrived in Pine Hill in the middle of a sunny, late-winter afternoon. It was an ordinary place in itself, like a hundred other small towns all over the West, but the scenery was spectacular. The mountains were capped with snow, the landscape densely carpeted in blue-green trees that marched on and on, as far as he could see.

Aidan drove into a filling station parking lot, took the folded sketch from the inside pocket of his jacket, and spread it over the steering wheel to study it for what must have been the hundredth time.

With one index finger he traced the outline of her cheek, the lips that almost smiled—but not quite—the hair he somehow knew was soft and glossy.

For a time Aidan just sat there, engaged in a peculiar mixture of mourning and celebration. Then he folded the sketch and tucked it back into his pocket, as carefully as if it were a map that would lead him to some incomparable treasure.

He frowned as he drove back onto the slushy gray asphalt of the highway. It was just as likely that this was some sort of fool's errand. After all, if whatever had passed between him and this woman had been right and good and real, why weren't they together? Why had he blocked every detail besides her face and her first name from his mind?

Aidan passed a construction sign announcing the building of a condominium complex, shifted into reverse, and backed up to read it again. There was the usual builder's hype, but someone had tacked on a HELP WANTED notice, and that was what had captured Aidan's true interest.

He had a wallet full of money, and much more stashed away in various trust funds and bank accounts, so it wasn't the prospect of a paycheck that attracted him. He felt a craving, in the very depths of his muscles, to work at hard, physical labor, to sweat and pound and carry things under the bright light of the sun.

To put off driving to 1320 Tamarack Road, wanting to savor the prospect a while longer, Aidan located the construction company's temporary office instead. Within an hour he had been hired as a day laborer—he was to start in the morning and arrive with his own tools—and he felt as though he'd just found a part of himself that had long been missing.

He rented a motel room, hastened to the hardware store for a hammer, a tool belt, a handsaw, and a measuring tape, along with a few things the salesman recommended, then bought work clothes and boots at the mercantile. That done, Aidan consumed another of the fast-food lunches he seemed to love—just where he'd acquired the taste was one of many things he didn't quite remember—and continued his search for the woman of mystery.

Neely was waiting tables at the Steak-and-Saddle that night when, through the restaurant's wide front windows, she saw the small white sports car swing into the parking lot and come to a flourishing stop near the door.

She tightened her grasp on the handle of the coffeepot she carried, wondering why the sight of a simple automobile should shake her so. First, she'd babbled out some crazy story about vampires to her doctor, and promptly forgotten the whole thing, and now she was freaking out over traffic.

She'd better get a hold of herself.

Neely poured coffee for her customers and took the pot back to the burner without glancing at the door, even though she felt the rush of cool air when it opened. She was on her way to table 4, carrying two pieces of lemon meringue pie, when she saw the dark-haired man.

He was a stranger, and yet Neely felt a deep connection with him, an almost savage wrenching. It was nothing new; no, this was something ancient, something predating the moon and stars.

He smiled, inclined his head slightly, and said, "Hello, Neely."

The pie plates clattered to the floor. Neely didn't know this man, and yet she did. She knew everything about him, and nothing at all. She had a vague recollection of thrashing on a bed while he loved her, though that was impossible, of course, since they had never met.

She bolted back to the kitchen for a wet cloth, and when she returned, the newcomer was crouched on the floor, gathering up the plates and broken pieces of pie. He took the cloth from her and wiped the tiles.

"Do I know you?" Neely whispered, blushing and painfully conscious of the fact that practically everyone in the restaurant was staring at them with amused interest. His face seemed as familiar to her as her own, so maybe she'd just conveniently forgotten him, the way she'd forgotten telling Dr. Fredricks about those damn vampires.

He shrugged as he rose gracefully to his full height. "Maybe. My name is Aidan Tremayne."

Again Neely felt an inner earthquake; again she had no idea why. "Neely Wallace," she answered. She was flustered all over again. "How did you know my first name?" she demanded.

Tremayne regarded her in wry silence for a moment, then nodded toward the shamble of plates and pies and cleaning cloth in her hands. "Perhaps you'd better tend to business,

Miss Wallace. I wouldn't want to be the cause of your getting the sack."

Neely bustled away in a quiet panic, gallantly pretending that all was well. She disposed of the spilled food and dirty dishes, washed and dried her hands, and made a second attempt to carry pie to the people at table 4. She succeeded that time, and everyone in the restaurant cheered.

Neely's cheeks were crimson when she rounded the counter and made herself wait on Aidan Tremayne, who sat at the far end, watching her with laughter in his indigo-colored eyes. "What will you have?" she said, tapping her pencil against the top of her order pad.

He smiled. "I'll take the special," he said, closing the menu. "For now."

Neely narrowed her gaze. She wasn't angry, exactly—as a waitress, she met more than her share of smart guys, and most of them didn't mean any harm. No, it was her own overwhelming attraction to this stranger, the way he'd made her pulse flutter erotically, that troubled her.

"Before I get you the liver and onions," she said in a low voice, "I want you to tell me how you knew my name."

He leaned toward her. "I'm psychic," he whispered.

After that a tour bus arrived, and a crowd poured into the restaurant, and Neely was too busy to pay any more attention to Aidan Whoever.

Tremayne, supplied a voice in her harried heart.

The next day Neely worked the afternoon and early evening shift again, and Aidan came into the restaurant for supper, in the company of half a dozen workers from the construction site just up the mountainside. He was freshly showered and wearing clean but casual clothes, and Neely felt a sting of annoyance because he didn't seem to notice her, even when she asked for his order.

"Who's that?" Angie, another waitress, inquired with

interest, her warm-syrup eyes bright with speculation as she looked at Aidan.

Neely glared at the other woman. "He's just some construction worker," she snapped, reaching for a steak platter and a cheeseburger in a basket.

Angie popped her gum in good-natured defiance. "Yum," she growled under her breath. "I think I need some remodeling."

Neely stormed away to deliver her order.

She didn't see Aidan again until Sunday, her day off. She'd been to the supermarket and was carrying in groceries when the expensive sports car purred to a stop behind her dented Mustang.

Neely let the wooden screen door slam behind her when she went into the living room, but she felt a contradictory little lurch of pleasure in her middle when she came outside for another bag of groceries. Aidan was still there, leaning against his Triumph, his arms folded across his chest.

"I've come a long way to find you, Neely," he said quietly. "And I won't be easy to put off."

She felt as though she'd been riding a roller coaster and had stepped off before the thing came alongside the platform. She would have dropped the second shopping bag, but Aidan reached out and caught it just as it slipped from her arms.

"How did you know my name?" This time she wasn't going to let him sidestep the question.

"I own a house in Bright River, Connecticut," he said. "I think I must have seen you there."

Neely saw the confusion and bewilderment in those ink-blue eyes, and it stopped her, put a cap on her rising temper. "My brother, Ben, manages a café and motel outside Bright River," she said lamely. "I worked for him for a while, waiting tables and cleaning rooms."

The relief she saw in Aidan's face was too sincere to be

false. Something very weird was going on here.

"That must have been where we met," he said. Then he carried the groceries up the walk, onto the porch, and past the green-painted screen door. "Nice place."

Neely felt herself flush again. Suddenly she was embarrassed by the chipped linoleum floors, the television set with foil flags on its antenna, and the cheap, ugly curtains made of dime-store fabric.

Aidan set the bag on the counter, beside the one Neely had brought in a minute earlier, looked back at her over one well-made shoulder, and grinned.

"You're not thinking I'm some kind of lecher, I hope," he said. "I'm a gentleman, Neely, and you've nothing to fear from me. Why don't you stop looking like a deer that wants to bolt into the nearest thicket?"

She smiled and relaxed a little. "Where are you from originally?" she asked, still keeping her distance as she took off her peacoat and hung it up. "You sound English."

"Perish the thought!" he said with drama and yet another nuclear-powered grin. "I'm Irish, though I've spent most of my adult life in the United States."

Neely wanted to know everything there was to know about Aidan Tremayne. She also wanted never to have met him, because he did things to her senses that made her deliciously uncomfortable.

He stayed for dinner.

Neely guessed she still would have had a chance if she'd just let things go at that, but Aidan asked her to go for a ride in his fancy car, with the top down and the moonlight playing over them both like liquid silver, and she couldn't resist.

On a high point overlooking all of Pine Hill, he parked the car, leaned over, and kissed her. His lips moved lightly against hers at first, almost mischievously, and yet Neely felt as if someone had just threaded her onto a live wire, like a bead onto a necklace. Things awakened inside her and collided in a mad rush to find their right places.

"I've never known you," Aidan said huskily, when the kiss finally ended. "And yet I've *always* known you. Can you explain that to me, Neely?"

She thought—as best she could, that is, given the helter-skelter state of her emotions. "Maybe we were together in a past life," she offered.

Aidan smiled. "Maybe," he agreed without real conviction, and then he kissed her once more.

"I want to see you again," he said a few moments later.

Neely could only nod.

After that she and Aidan were together for at least a part of every day. He rented an apartment on the other side of town, and she helped him furnish it. He chose gracious things, antiques and folk art and one very good painting, and Neely wondered what kind of work he'd done before taking up construction.

"I was a painter," he said when she finally worked up the nerve to ask him. They'd eaten roast chicken, corn on the cob, and salad at her place, and he was helping her take down the horrible living room curtains so she could replace them with the snappy white eyelet ones she'd just bought.

Neely felt afraid, as if she were trying to cross an expanse of wafer-thin ice spanning a deep and frigid river. Caring too much would be the equivalent of falling through; she couldn't afford to love this good-looking, bewildering man because he was just passing by, like the other men who'd come to Pine Hill to build condominiums.

"Did something happen?"

Aidan looked at her curiously, raising one dark eyebrow in that ponderous way he had. "What do you mean, 'did something happen'?"

Neely shrugged, crumpling the new curtains because she was holding them too tightly. "Last time I looked, you were working on a construction site," she said, and though she tried to offer the statement lightly, it came out sounding momentous.

He grinned. "Nothing dramatic. I just got tired of painting. I'm a sensualist, I guess," he said. "I enjoy the feeling of sunlight on my skin, and the way my muscles move underneath." His blue gaze seemed to caress her for a moment, making her flesh tingle beneath her clothes. "I like everything about being a man."

Neely turned quickly away. Ever since that first time Aidan had kissed her, she'd been sizzling like so much water spilled onto a hot griddle. Some primitive sense warned that he had the power to hurt her as no other man ever could, and Neely's emotions were fragile as it was.

If she waited long enough, maybe he'd go away, and she wouldn't have to take the dangerous chance of loving him.

Chapter 20

※⋇※

Twilight gathered behind the mountaintops, then spilled down over the throngs of evergreen trees, shrouding them in pale apricot, and after that lavender, and finally a velvety purple. Neely and Aidan watched the spectacle from the window in the dining room of his apartment, where they sat at the round oak table, each gripping the other's hand.

Neely's emotions were very close to the surface, and the glorious sunset brought tears to her eyes. She moved to rise from her chair, but Aidan held her in place by gentle force.

"Neely," he said quietly. "Don't run away. It's time we talked."

She wanted to look anywhere but at Aidan, but she couldn't; his gaze seemed to hold hers fast. "About what?"

"You know 'about what,' " Aidan sighed with a touch of exasperation.

Neely bit her lower lip for a moment. "You're leaving," she blurted out. "You've been in Pine Hill for six weeks, the construction job is about to end, and—"

"Yes," Aidan said. His dark blue eyes reflected the faint smile that touched his mouth. "I'm leaving."

She sniffled and straightened her shoulders. "Okay, good," she said. "So long." She tried again to stand, intending to bolt, but Aidan wouldn't release her hand. She sat trembling for a few moments, refusing to look at him, but then the compulsion grew too strong. "What do you want?" she snapped.

He said nothing, sensing somehow that there was more she needed to say, silently insisting that she come out with it.

Neely shoved her fingers through her hair. "I know we— we haven't made love or anything, but—well—I thought something was happening between us. There's a lot of electricity, or so it seemed to me. Now you're just going to leave."

"There's a great deal you don't know about me, Neely," Aidan said sadly, staring not at her but through the window, glazed with light on the inside now, dark beyond. "And a great deal I don't know about myself."

She narrowed her eyes and sniffled again, then dashed the back of her free hand—Aidan still held the other— across her wet cheek. "I know you're an artist, that you have a house in Connecticut, that you were born in Ireland but raised in the United States—"

He silenced her with an infinitely tender glance. "All those things are true," he said, running his finger lightly over her knuckles. "At least, they *seem* true. But there are some serious gaps in my memory. You know about my adventures in England, for instance—how I woke up in the hospital, only to be told that I'd been found naked as a flounder in that old pile of stones. What the devil was I up to before that, Neely? How did I get there? Am I some kind of madman? What *else* have I done that I've conveniently forgotten?"

Neely slipped out of her chair, still holding Aidan's hand, and settled on his lap. From the moment she'd met him, she'd wanted him, with every breath she drew and every beat of her heart, but there had been a certain courtly, old-fashioned restraint in his manner. "I don't know," she assured him softly. "I've got a few ghosts of my own, remember—all that babble to my doctor about vampires, for one thing." He smiled at that but didn't interrupt, and Neely went on earnestly. "There are a lot of mysteries in this life, Aidan Tremayne, but there are also a few things I'm absolutely certain of, and here they are: You are a fine, sweet, gentle man, good to the core of your soul, and I love you."

Aidan touched her trembling lower lip with the tip of an index finger. "Suppose you're wrong?" The pain of his own uncertainty was clearly audible in his voice. "Oh, Neely, what if I'm some sort of maniac?"

She rested her forehead against his. "I'll take my chances." She pulled in a deep breath, let it out in a rush, and sat back to look into his eyes. "Is that why you haven't made love to me, Aidan? Because you're afraid you're really a modern-day Jack the Ripper and the fact has simply slipped your mind?"

He chuckled, but there was anguish in the sound. "No, it isn't that—I know I could never hurt you, under any circumstances." Aidan actually looked shy, and she would have sworn there was a blush under that spring suntan of his. "The truth is, I seem to be rather behind the times when it comes to sex. I feel as if I've been searching for you for a thousand years, and when we make love, it's going to be a sacred event."

Neely's tough, scarred heart softened, then melted entirely. "Well, then," she said with sniffly briskness and a pinch of sarcasm, "it makes perfect sense that you're planning to leave, doesn't it?"

Aidan gave her a brief, nibbling kiss, the kind that always drove her crazy and left her aching for hours afterward.

"It does," he affirmed, a few sweetly torturous moments later, "when you consider that I'm asking you to go with me, as my wife."

It seemed that the floor buckled a little just then, and Neely tightened her arm around Aidan's neck, afraid she would tumble from his lap. "You want to marry me?"

Aidan grinned, looking damnably Irish and outrageously handsome. "Do I ever," he replied.

Neely was in a state of blessed shock. All her life she'd been waiting for a man like Aidan, one who could make her heart sing, and help her to be her best self, and she'd been disappointed more than once. In short, Aidan Tremayne seemed too good to be true. "You haven't even said you love me," she pointed out.

He took her chin in his hand and then kissed her, with slow, deliberate heat and a skill that incited a riot of sensation inside her, then drew back. "Haven't I?" he whispered. "Funny, that's what I thought I was saying when I told you I've been searching for you for a thousand years. I do love you, Neely. Very, very much."

She buried her face in his neck and held him tightly for a long time, overwhelmed with happiness, struggling to assimilate it somehow.

At long last he stood, holding Neely close and looking down into her eyes. "Here, now," he said gruffly. "I'd best take you home, Miss Wallace, before I break my own rule and carry you straight off to bed."

There was nowhere Neely would rather be that night than in Aidan Tremayne's bed, for her senses had been humming with anticipation since the first time he'd kissed her, weeks before. "You know what they say about rules," she ventured tentatively.

Aidan ran the pad of his thumb over her moist lower lip. "This is one I don't mean to break," he said. He held her a little closer, though, and went on. "It's a gypsy's life I'm offering you, Neely. You'll never want for anything, but I've no idea when or where we'll settle. I want to see everything, be everywhere—to dance on mountaintops and make love to you on star-washed beaches—"

She stood on tiptoe to kiss him. "Such a romantic," she said with a happy sigh. "Tell me, though—what about that big fancy house of yours, back in Connecticut?"

He sighed again, resting his strong, work-calloused hands on her shoulders. "There's nothing there that I want, Neely— it's as if the place belonged in some other man's life, not my own. I'm thinking of signing it over to one of the universities or perhaps some charitable organization." He frowned pensively. "Would that bother you?"

Neely shook her head. "I think it's a wonderful idea," she said. For now, Aidan was all she needed or wanted; she would take all future days and moments one by one. "Let's get ourselves married, Mr. Tremayne."

He laughed, hooked his thumbs through the loops at the back of Neely's jeans, and hoisted her against him for one deliciously frustrating moment. "The sooner, the better," he answered.

Aidan found Neely's jacket and politely escorted her outside to his car. "Time you were tucked up in your own bed, fast asleep," he said when she was settled in the passenger seat and he was behind the wheel.

Neely blushed and kept her attention focused on the windshield, which had become a star-spangled mural. "Kindly stop reminding me that I'm going to be all by myself."

Aidan grinned, starting the Spitfire's powerful engine and deftly working the gearshift. "We'll be together soon enough," he assured her. "Be patient."

Neely was anything but patient.

That night she tossed and turned, catching only fleeting minutes of sleep. She felt like a complicated clock, wound so tightly that her inner springs were about to burst out in every direction.

The following day Neely gave notice at the Steak-and-Saddle, and Duke jokingly told her to go ahead and clear out, because he didn't want her underfoot for another two weeks.

She was so grateful that she flung her arms around the older man's neck and gave him a resounding kiss on the cheek.

She and Aidan applied for their marriage license later that morning at the courthouse, and then they went shopping for their new home.

Neely referred to their house on wheels as a recreational vehicle, while Aidan called it a "caravan." It was a sleek, shiny marvel, complete with its own bathroom, a queen-size bed, and a small kitchen. There were so many options that Neely expected to spend at least a week immersed in the owner's manual.

Of course, it would be some week far in the future, when the novelty of being a gypsy bride had worn off.

Aidan didn't seem to mind trading in the sports car; he took an object from the glove box, dropped it into his jacket pocket, patted the vehicle's gleaming hood, and walked away. He and Neely were rambling down the road in their RV when he took one hand off the wheel and extended a small box to Neely.

"There were only two things in the Connecticut house that I wanted," he said. "Here they are."

Neely's hands trembled as she accepted an exquisite old music box, surely an antique. When she opened it, a few slow, poignant notes drifted out, then there was silence. She started to rewind the key, hungry to hear more, and that was when she saw the ring glimmering in the worn velvet lining of the lid.

Aidan had pulled the large vehicle off to the side of the road and sat watching her with his heart in his eyes. "According to these strange memories of mine, that ring has been in the Tremayne family for almost a century."

It was a simple piece of jewelry, a wide gold band with a large marquis diamond set at an angle. Inside that magnificent, multifaceted stone glimmered the sunlight of a hundred summers and the sparkle of as many stars.

"It's so beautiful," Neely whispered, slipping the ring onto her finger. It was only slightly too big.

"It can't begin to compete with you," Aidan replied.

That evening Neely found it even more difficult than usual to say good night to Aidan. Yes, she wanted him to make love to her, but even more than that, she longed to sleep in his arms, naked and trusting.

Neely spent the next day cleaning her rented house and packing up the few personal belongings she'd brought with her when she left Connecticut. She found a store selling antique clothing and jewelry in the next town and bought a lovely old dress of ivory and silk, made sometime in the twenties, along with an ornate sterling silver broach, studded with marcasite.

She hung the dress on her tiny back porch to air through the afternoon and evening, then mended a few tiny tears in the fabric while watching television. Even with everything she had to do, it seemed to Neely that time was passing with all the speed of a snail stuck in neutral.

She was lying on the lumpy sofa in her living room, legs sticking straight up in the air and waving her feet back and forth to dry the polish on her toenails, when the jingling of the telephone made her start. She grappled for the receiver and nearly fell off the sofa in the process.

"Hello?"

Her brother Ben's voice echoed warmly in her ear. "Hello, Sis. So, how does it feel to be almost married?"

"You tell me," Neely responded with a grin. The relationship between Ben and Doris had developed into a grand passion, and the two of them were planning a summer wedding.

Ben laughed. "Sweetheart, if you're as happy as I am, then you're doing just fine."

Joyous tears blurred Neely's vision. "How's Danny? Is he glad about having Doris in the family?"

"He's crazy about her." Ben was quiet for a moment. "Neely, you're really sure this is what you want to do, aren't you? I mean, getting married is a pretty big step."

Neely lifted the hem of her T-shirt to dry her cheeks. "I know it sounds strange, but I've never been more certain of anything in my life. I was born to love this man, Ben, and he was born to love me."

"All the same," Ben said grudgingly, "if he mistreats you, I'll take out his teeth. You tell him that for me."

Neely smiled. "Okay, big brother," she said obediently. "I'll tell him, but you don't need to worry your bushy-bearded head, because Aidan Tremayne is a gentleman."

After that, Neely talked to Danny for a few minutes, and then to Doris. When the phone call was over, and everyone had congratulated everyone else, she went into her room to admire her wedding dress, which hung on the outside of her closet door.

The moonlight lent the gown a special sort of magic, catching in the pearl buttons rimmed with tiny crystals, making the exquisite, hand-worked lace seem almost new again.

Neely fell asleep admiring it.

Aidan slept with the peaceful abandon only a mortal is capable of, dark hair rumpled, one arm flung up over his head.

Valerian watched him in silence, knowing he shouldn't linger, but not quite able to tear himself away. A thousand times the dark angel had wanted to reach out his hand and restore Aidan's memory of all he had been before, and he wanted that now, as keenly as ever. He even went so far as to brush his fingers lightly over Aidan's forehead, causing him to stir in his sleep, but in the end Valerian drew back.

Rare vampire tears glittered in his eyes. *We could have owned the stars,* he told the sleeping one.

Aidan rolled onto his side, still deeply asleep, and murmured a single word. And with that one word he broke Valerian's heart.

"Neely," he said.

Suddenly a burst of strangely dark light filled the room. Valerian raised his eyes and felt the most abject horror he had ever known, for Lisette stood on the opposite side of the bed, majestic and evil, plainly restored to all her former powers. Her once-scarred skin was unmarked, her auburn hair was as lush and gleaming as ever, her blue-green eyes bright with triumph, fury, and madness.

She looked upon the sleeping Aidan for a long moment, as if to devour every line and fiber of him, and then raised her eyes to Valerian's face again.

Lisette laughed softly, musically, and Aidan stirred on the mattress, unaware that his soul was about to be stolen for a second time.

"Did you think, Valerian, that I would let him go so easily as all that?" Her face became hard and horrible for a moment; no doubt, she was considering the events of recent months. "Aidan is mine—my creation, my treasure. I will not give him up."

At last Valerian found his voice. "You must," he said hoarsely. "If you have any mercy in you, any decency—"

She laughed again, but it was a silent laughter, much like the unspoken language vampires and other immortals use to communicate with each other, and Aidan did not seem to hear it.

'Mercy,' is it? 'Decency'! Oh, but that's amusing! What good are such fatuous concepts to me, Lisette, the Queen of all vampyres?

Valerian closed his eyes briefly, searching his mind and his soul for a solution, finding none except to plead Aidan's case and, if necessary, to fight Lisette to the death. He held little hope of success either way, however, for the queen was not one to listen to reason, and she had plainly regained her powers, perhaps even garnered new ones through the peculiar graces of suffering.

Think what Aidan has been through, he reasoned, touching the forehead of the sleeping vampire-turned-mortal. *Imagine what he risked, what he endured, to be a man again, to find his way in the mortal world. How can you— even you—take that from him? Great Zeus, Lisette—if you must have a plaything, take me.*

Lisette glared, plainly displeased, and folded her white arms over the even whiter, flowing fabric of her Grecian gown. *You?* she scoffed. *Do you think me a fool, Valerian? You are as elusive as quicksilver—the moment I turned my back, you would be off dallying with some fledgling. No, I don't want you—you're far too troublesome as it is.*

Slowly Valerian rounded the bed, forced himself between Lisette and the still oblivious Aidan. He loomed above the older and more powerful vampire, the first female blood-drinker ever made, and called upon all the showmanship and bravado he possessed.

Go from here, he commanded. *This one you shall not have.*

Lisette was clearly undaunted. The sorceress drew herself up, and Valerian felt her powers focus on his midsection just before she sent him hurtling backward over Aidan's bed to crash silently against the opposite wall.

Valerian recovered quickly and moved to stand and resist her further, but she struck him again with another of her purely mental blows, and he felt himself paralyzed, not just physically but spiritually as well. He watched helplessly as Lisette stepped close to the bed again, knelt, and reverently smoothed Aidan's dark hair.

Valerian struggled to shout a warning to the sleeping mortal, but he could not force a sound past his throat. He had, he realized, vastly underestimated Lisette's powers.

I will make you love me, the vampire queen told Aidan. *I will show you the stars, and we will not be parted again. No power on earth, or in heaven, shall ever separate us.*

Inwardly Valerian shrieked in protest, and his helplessness was in those moments the greatest burden he had ever been made to bear, either as a vampire or as a human man.

No power . . . Lisette vowed again as she bent, fangs plainly in view, to give Aidan the fatal kiss, the one that would damn him for the second time, and for always.

Aidan made a soft, sleepy sound, innocent as a child as he wandered in his dreams, and Valerian could make no move to save him. The only response he could manage, in fact, was the sheen of tears that blurred his vision.

Please! he cried out silently to any benevolent being who might be nearby. *In the name of justice—this cannot happen!*

It appeared there was no hope, for Lisette moistened a patch of skin on Aidan's neck, using her tongue, her eyes raised to meet Valerian's. She was enjoying his torment, the damnable, whoring witch, and he swore that even if it cost him his own existence, if it took a hundred years or a thousand, he would avenge the events of this night.

Lisette's long vampire teeth glimmered, pearly in the dim moonlight, and she moved to lunge, to bury her fangs in Aidan's sleep-warmed flesh.

Valerian managed an anguished groan, but he still could not move. Still, the fog in his mind began to clear at last, and he was able to send a single name, in itself a plea for help, echoing into the universe.

Maeve.

In the next instant, just when Lisette's fangs would have broken Aidan's skin and begun to draw upon the healthy blood flowing through the veins and arteries beneath, the chamber seemed to burst with blinding, silvery light.

Valerian's heart surged with hope, though he knew this was not Maeve, or Tobias, or any of the vampires of his acquaintance. No, this was a holy being, sanctioned by Heaven itself, and as such it would surely destroy Valerian.

If Aidan could be saved, he didn't care.

The being of light seemed to push the walls out with its power; Valerian was sure the room, indeed the building itself, would explode into splinters. He soon realized, however, that the temporal world was not affected by this phenomenon—even if Aidan had been awake, he would not have seen or heard anything out of the ordinary.

Humans.

Slowly the entity took on shape and splendor, and Valerian realized that the newcomer was an angel. It was male and dressed, oddly enough, in the garb of a Spartan warrior.

Lisette had raised herself from Aidan's bedside, abandoning her prospective feast, staring in horror. *Nemesis,* she whispered fearfully.

The spirit laughed. *No one so important, Vampyre. I am Jafar, and I am an ordinary enough creature—what mortals call a guardian angel.* He looked fondly upon Aidan, who had begun to toss and turn upon his modern pallet. *This one is my particular charge, and I am sworn to protect his soul with all the powers of Heaven.*

Jafar had not yet spared a glance for Valerian, who was recovering now that Lisette's powers had slackened so dramatically, but Valerian watched the angel in stricken fascination. In all his existence he had never seen a being so magnificently beautiful.

What must Nemesis, one of the greatest angels in creation, be like?

Lisette had backed herself against the wall of Aidan's very ordinary bedroom, her eyes wide with terror.

Go from this place, Jafar told her. *And do not come near my ward again, for if you do such a foolish thing, I will be permitted to destroy you.*

Lisette made a mewling sound, one that could be heard only in the spirit, like all that had transpired that night, and vanished.

The angel bent over Aidan with a tenderness that was heartbreaking to see and carefully straightened his blankets, the way a mortal father might do for an exhausted child.

With the return of Valerian's physical powers came a serious fear that Jafar would turn his angel-strength upon him.

The splendid creature knew he was there—there had never been any question of that—but his regard, when he finally looked at Valerian, was remarkably gentle. *You did an uncommonly generous thing by summoning me back to the mortal's side with your cry of despair, but now you must keep away from him.*

Valerian nodded, though he wasn't at all certain he could comply with such an order, even if it came from the most wonderfully frightening being he had ever encountered. He found that he could move, and rose slowly to his feet.

He looked at Aidan, memorizing his features and frame, and then met the angel's gaze once more.

I hope you'll be more efficient in the future, he said, and as he vanished, he heard the seraphim laugh.

Come the morning, Valerian knew, Aidan would awaken and marvel over the strange dreams he'd had.

Vampires and angels, indeed, he would think, perhaps with a chuckle.

On Saturday morning Neely and Aidan were married in the big gazebo in the center of the town park, with a justice of the peace officiating. Neely's friends from the restaurant came to share their joy, as did Aidan's buddies from the construction job.

Neely felt beautiful in her antique dress, and the whole ceremony passed in a glorious haze. When the judge reached the I now pronounce you husband and wife part, and Aidan kissed her, she almost fainted with the joy of it.

Duke held a reception for the bride and groom at the restaurant, complete with wedding cake, supermarket champagne, and lots of rice and birdseed.

"I'll look after that car of yours," Duke said when Neely went to him to thank him and say good-bye. He was an old-timer, and it was hard for him to express emotion.

Neely stretched to kiss Duke's freshly shaven cheek. "When somebody comes through who looks like he needs a dented Mustang," she said with a misty smile, "you just hand him the keys and tell him to drive it in good health."

Duke smiled. "You've got a generous heart, little lady. I always knew that. I know somethin' else, too."

Neely had never been happier, but she felt sad, too, saying good-bye to such a good friend. "What?" she sniffled, still smiling brightly.

The big man planted a shy kiss on her forehead. "That joy will follow you everywhere you go, from now on," he answered. "You stop in and say howdy to old Duke i you're in this neck of the woods again, you hear?"

"You can count on it," Neely answered softly.

A few minutes later she and Aidan left the reception and drove away in their brand-new "caravan," a couple of very proper gypsies.

Aidan, who had bought a suit and tie for the occasion, looked comfortable behind the wheel of the RV—perhaps too comfortable. He pulled off his tie and tossed it over one shoulder, then quickly unfastened the top three buttons of his shirt.

"Forgive me if I sound like a bumper sticker, Mrs. Tremayne," he said cheerfully, keeping his eyes on the open road ahead, "but today is the first day of the rest of our lives."

Neely scrambled into the back of the RV to exchange her wedding dress for a pair of jeans, a lavender T-shirt, and sneakers. "That's very profound," she responded, trying to keep her voice light. The truth was, she was thinking about the patch of strong masculine chest she'd glimpsed when Aidan opened his shirt, and wondering when the honeymoon would begin.

"What are you doing back there?"

Neely rejoined her husband in the front of the RV, plopping into the passenger seat and giving him a sultry look as she fastened her seat belt in place. "What do you think I was doing?" she teased. "Sipping champagne from my shoe? Sprinkling the bed with perfume?"

A slow blush moved up Aidan's neck and glowed along his jawline. He gave her a sidelong glance and a high-voltage grin. "I wouldn't put it past you, you hot-blooded little vixen. You've been after my virtue from the first."

Neely felt her own cheeks glow, and she sagged deeper into the seat with a soft but long-suffering sigh. "Now what are we going to wait for? Our golden anniversary?"

Aidan laughed, and the sound was rich and masculine, causing Neely to want her husband that much more. "That or the first wide spot in the road," he teased. "Whichever turns up soonest. Great Scot, woman, did you think I was going to fling you into the sheets the moment we stepped over the threshold and have my way with you, right there in the steak-house parking lot?"

This time Neely laughed, too; but her blush deepened, and she reached across to give her husband a playful slap on the arm. Then she squirmed in her seat and said, "Are we there yet?"

An hour later Aidan brought the RV to a stop at the edge of a sun-splashed meadow. Then he came around to open Neely's door and help her out.

She had looked forward to being alone with her husband, yearned for it, in fact, but now that the time had arrived, Neely suddenly felt shy. "Here?" she whispered.

Aidan laid a hand to either side of her face and kissed her lightly, and much too briefly. "Here," he confirmed. "Look at the way the sun slants between those trees over there. There's something cathedral-like about the place."

He was right, but Neely suspected the reverence they both felt came from their own hearts, rather than from the landscape around them.

"It's beautiful," Neely agreed.

Aidan eased past her, into the RV, and returned in a few moments carrying blankets, a chilled bottle of very good champagne, and two fluted glasses. Slipping one arm around Neely's waist, he escorted her toward the trees where the light fell so gracefully onto the fragrant grass.

He put the champagne and glasses aside to spread the blankets over the soft ground, then beckoned to Neely. "Come over here, Mrs. Tremayne."

She went to him happily, and he took her into his arms and held her close. He kissed her thoroughly, as he had so many times before, but this time he would not be leaving her to merely imagine his lovemaking.

After a while, when Neely was half-dazed with wanting her husband, Aidan began stripping away her clothes. He worked very slowly, tossing aside her T-shirt first, caressing and admiring her for a long time before unclasping her bra and disposing of that, too.

Her breasts stood bare and proud, their tips hardening in the spring breeze, and when Aidan bent with a groan to touch one morsel with his tongue, Neely cried out in hoarse joy and pressed him close.

They sank to the ground one limb at a time, like some graceful four-legged creature, and Aidan continued to enjoy Neely's full breasts. She kicked off her sneakers and tore at the zipper of her jeans, and Aidan chuckled against her nipple and stilled her frantic hand with his own. He made her wait.

Finally, though, each was bared to the other.

Aidan stroked Neely's thighs lightly and made teasing circles on her belly with his fingers.

"No longer, Aidan," she whispered franticly, slipping both arms around his neck. "I've waited too long, and I want you so much—"

"And I want you," he said, his mouth falling to hers. Their tongues battled, then mated. With a groan Aidan mounted Neely, easing her legs apart with one knee.

She cried out and arched her back as he glided inside her and settled deep for a moment, claiming her, letting her body get used to his.

He chuckled as he nibbled at her lips. "Little vixen," he teased. She struggled beneath him, wanting to thrash and writhe, but he held her firmly in place.

Neely made a sound that was half passion and half frustration. "Aidan," she pleaded, "make love to me—please— or I swear it's going to happen on its own!"

Aidan raised himself onto his elbows, withdrew from her, then made a steady, smooth lunge into her warmth again.

That was all it took. Neely's body was so primed for Aidan's conquering that one stroke brought on a raging, cataclysmic climax. Eyes unfocused, she jerked helplessly beneath him while a low, lingering wail of pleasure poured from her throat.

Aidan held Neely while she responded, lodged far within her, and murmured gentle, senseless words against her ear. She'd been still, dazed and sated, for some time before he moaned and stiffened and spilled his warm seed inside her.

For a long time they lay there, arms and legs entwined, bodies joined, and their breaths might have been one breath, their heartbeats a single steady meter.

"I'm sorry," Neely said when she could finally speak.

Aidan raised his head and looked at her with incredulous, ink-blue eyes. "What did you say?"

"I was so eager. It happened so fast." Tears started in her lashes because she wanted Aidan to be pleased, the way she was, and she thought she'd failed.

He kissed the moisture away, aroused her all over again simply by caressing her eyelids with the tip of his tongue. "No, darling," he whispered tenderly, "this day has been an eternity in the making." He slid lower, brushed his lips over her collarbone and the soft rounding of her breasts. "And the best part is," he added presently, "that this is only the beginning."

Neely spread her hands over Aidan's muscled back then, and a sob escaped her, a hoarse, splendid sound born of jubilation, not sorrow. Their souls spoke a silent, private language, and their bodies needed no words at all.

When they had spent still more of their passion, they drank champagne from their wedding glasses and, with laughing reluctance, began to dress each other. When it became a game, however, and the players started kissing places before they covered them, the clothes came off again.

"We're going to catch pneumonia, lying out here in the breeze in the altogether," Aidan said some time later.

"You're right." Neely sat up and started reaching for scattered garments and pulling them on. She was ridiculously happy, and she couldn't help humming a little under her breath. "I'm glad we didn't wait for our golden anniversary."

Aidan, who had dressed more quickly, pulled Neely to her feet and kissed her as they collided. "I could never have lasted past the silver one," he teased.

Once they'd put away the blankets and glasses and the champagne, Aidan got behind the wheel and started the engine.

"Well, Mrs. Tremayne, where do we go now? South to Mexico, or north to Canada?"

Neely considered, smoothing her hopelessly crumpled T-shirt and straightening her seat belt. "Surprise me," she said.

Late that night Aidan and Neely stopped in a moonlit RV park, at the edge of a southbound highway. There they grilled hamburgers on their tiny stove, crowded into their minuscule shower stall together, and finally made feverish love on the fold-out bed.

Aidan slept when it was over, but Neely lay curled against his side, watching the stars through the skylight in the roof of the motor home as they did their intricate, shining dance around the moon. If anybody had ever told her she was going to be this happy, she reflected, she would have thought the notion was insane.

After the sky patterns had shifted several times, Neely rose, pulled an oversized T-shirt over her head, and crept to the drawer where she kept her most treasured belongings. Inside were school pictures of Danny, a necklace that had belonged to her mother, and the antique music box that

Aidan had given her the night he proposed.

Holding the box close to her heart, Neely made her way to the door, opened it quietly, and stepped out into the silver-spangled night. She needed to be in the open spaces, at least for a few minutes, because the RV was simply too small to contain all the love and gratitude she felt.

Standing on the metal step, Neely wound the key on the bottom of the rosewood box, then lifted the lid. Sweet, oddly familiar music flowed into the night, and Neely danced in the damp and scented grass, turning round and round, like the stars overhead.

When she had spent her energy, she stopped the music and went back inside to crawl into bed next to her husband.

Aidan slept without reservation, sprawled every which way, with one arm flung back over his head. "Hmmm?" he said.

Neely smiled, kissed the pulsepoint at the base of his throat, and thought briefly of a wondrously handsome, elegant vampire who had once visited her dreams.

How odd, she thought as she toppled into sweet sleep, that she should think of him now.